PROXY

by GARETH OTTON

Cover design by Gareth Otton

ISBN-13:
978-1983979842

ISBN-10:
1983979848

www.gareth-otton.com

Prologue

Wednesday, 16th June 2004
02:14

Tyres screeched and Dinah winced.

Police cars waiting at her destination while she transported an unconscious body was too much even for her. Survival instinct forced her to brake hard. Tyre screeching was the natural result. It was a rookie mistake and a good way to get caught, but she hadn't done this sort of thing in a while and was rusty.

She swore in her native Hebrew and took a second to calm herself. She was better than this.

Closed eyes. A deep breath. In through the nose. Out through the mouth. Calm.

She assessed the situation.

Three police cars parked outside the old, red-brick office. The parking was neat, so it hadn't been a hasty arrival. Maybe they weren't waiting for her. Maybe she had time to act.

She threw the van into reverse and backed onto the main road. The midnight traffic in that part of Cardiff was non-existent, so she didn't cause a scene as she drove away.

A scattering of cars littered the carpark of a nearby industrial estate, enough that she risked being seen, but her van would attract less attention amongst other vehicles. Just to be safe she parked in the shadow of the large sign at the entrance.

She glanced at the unconscious shape in the back. The drugs should keep him out for another hour, but she didn't like to leave him. What other choice was there? She stepped from the van and locked it behind her.

It was an old, white Transit. No automatic lock to beep and flash the indicators. Just the way she liked it.

Satisfied it was secure, she walked back the way she had come.

This was her first job for her new employer and she was nervous. That was not like Dinah. Twelve years in the Israeli Institute for Intelligence and Special Operations, the Mossad, had long since removed the butterflies from her stomach. She thought herself unfazed by anything life had to offer. That was until she met her new employer.

He made the consequences of getting on his bad side all too clear and she had no intention of failing. More than her life was riding on it. If it was just her life, she could handle it. She had long since lost count of the times she risked her life for a job. Her life was cheap.

But Moshe, Adam and Gabriella. Her husband, son and daughter. Their lives were everything.

She approached the building from the rear, keeping to the shadows and remaining vigilant. The brightness of a mild summer night did nothing to aid her efforts, but she was good at this, born for it. She was confident she hadn't been spotted when she reached the old, cheap fire door. It took a full five minutes of fighting against rust and disuse before she managed to pick the lock.

The hallway beyond smelled of fake lemon and furniture polish, a remnant of its recent occupants. The building had been in use as little as a week before, famously so. Her employer's forced purchase of this building made national headlines. The original owners didn't want to sell, the tenants didn't want to leave, yet the sale went through regardless. There were talks of political scandals and back room deals. Dinah didn't care other than for what it said about her employer.

She'd researched him after his threats. He proved himself on their initial contact and she knew his threats weren't idle, but she wanted to know more. Her standard searches turned up no results, but when she looked deeper she found a different story.

He had done a fine job of hiding himself, but his name carried weight. Some contacts Dinah spoke with were too terrified to talk beyond saying she should stop looking. Strange, because they were not the sort of people who scared easy.

By the time she gave up on her research she was terrified. That a man like him could exist was beyond understanding. There should be an international task force with the dedicated purpose of wiping him out.

The sound of voices, muffled by the fire door at the end of the corridor, called her from her thoughts. Dinah could see shapes moving through the squares of glass in the door, their silhouettes outlined against the glow from the streetlights washing in from the carpark.

She crept closer, keeping herself in the deep black of the corridor and daring to crack the door open, letting in the voices.

"…good men. We'll all come through for you, sir."

Dinah recognised the sound of thinly veiled fear in the rushed words. She'd heard it enough over the years.

"Of course you will. I never thought any different, sergeant."

This second voice made her nerves tingle. It was surprisingly deep to come from such a small frame and it always had that mocking, amused tone. She placed the accent as East London, but it was muddied enough to show he no longer called the English capital home.

He was a short man, thin to the point of malnourishment. His sharp cheek bones, bald head and sunken eyes leant him a sickly appearance. That deep voice told a different story.

As with the first time she had seen him, he held the ruin of his left arm to his side. Withered and twisted, it ended in fingers that resembled gnarled twigs entangled in a complicated knot.

He looked unhealthy, but he didn't seem to care.

Even outlined against the dim light she could see his wicked smile.

His skeletal body hid under a tailored suit that helped improve his appearance. But, the true attention grabber was his voice.

That damned, deep, hypnotic voice that so terrified her and was talking again.

"Is she now?"

"What was that, sir?" the sergeant asked after a slight hesitation, glancing at the five, uniformed men behind him.

"I wasn't talking to you, sergeant."

The sergeant clearly wanted to ask who he was talking to. He wisely remained silent.

Her employer spoke again.

"Eavesdropping is she? How rude. But, if she has good news then I suppose I can forgive her."

He turned his head and looked directly at Dinah. There was no way he could see her. Surely.

"Come out, Mrs Mizrahi. We're all friends here."

Shit. How the hell did he know?

Again she felt the grip of fear, a foreign feeling for so long she didn't know how to handle it. She pushed it down, swallowed and then pressed harder against the door.

"What the...?" one policeman asked, surprised by her entrance. He was younger than the rest, not so seasoned.

Dinah ignored him and looked at her employer. "I didn't know if it was safe to show myself."

He laughed, not unkindly, but neither was it a comforting sound.

"You don't need to worry about these men. They're here to discuss a new working arrangement. Isn't that right gentlemen?" Ignoring their nodded agreement, he asked, "Did you bring him?"

She hesitated one final time, glancing to the police before nodding.

"Good. Did he give you any trouble?" She shook her head. "Really? I thought he might have been... difficult."

She knew what he referred to but couldn't bring herself to acknowledge it. "I took him by surprise. He... *they*... weren't ready for me."

Her employer looked impressed.

"Wonderful. You're every bit as talented as I hoped. I'd heard you were the best at what you…" His words trailed off and he waved his good hand dismissively. "Never mind. Where is he? Have you got him stored away back there?"

Dinah shook her head. "Half a mile down the road. I didn't want to bring him here with police parked outside."

Her employer was nodding. "Of course. Wise. It would do me no good to lose my prize before I've had chance to see him." He turned to the young policeman who had jumped so hard when Dinah appeared. "You… what was your name?"

"Mark… Uh… Mark Patterson."

"Why don't you go with Dinah to collect my delivery?"

The young man looked to his sergeant for approval, to which he received only a sharp, almost panicked nod.

Mark's feet dragged as he followed Dinah out of the building and they were on the street before he dared to speak.

"Uh… What are we going to get?"

"My van."

"Right." Another few seconds of silence before, "Um… Sorry to ask. But… what's in the van?"

Dinah sighed. She didn't like bringing unknowns to a crime scene, especially when those unknowns were policemen and the crime in question was one she had committed. Not for the first time, she was without a choice.

"A man." She'd travelled two steps before she realised he'd stopped walking. "Come on. I don't want to keep *him* waiting."

Mark didn't speak again until he was in the van. He opened the door as though it were a viper that would bite if he wasn't quick. He took a deep breath, snatched the handle and jumped in before his nerve could fail him. Said nerve lasted only until he looked at their cargo.

"Oh shit. What the fuck? I thought… Jesus."

Dinah thought he might cry. Poor kid. Clearly didn't know what he was getting in to.

"Mark." He didn't respond. "Mark!" Still nothing other than staring and cursing.

She slapped him.

Hard.

She finally had his attention. He turned back to her with wide eyes and she met that gaze levelly.

"We good here?" she asked.

He swallowed and nodded. Dinah started the engine. She wanted tonight over with.

They drove back to the building in silence and this time she pulled into the carpark. No other buildings looked into that carpark so they were safe to move the body.

It took more coaxing and the threat of another slap to make Mark touch the unconscious man. It had been a hell of a struggle getting the body in the van, Mark's six foot three rugby player build made it much easer getting the body out.

The other police held the door open for them as her employer cackled gleefully.

"Just there will be fine," he said and they let the unconscious man down. "So, where were you when all this went down?"

It took a few seconds to realise that he was talking to himself again. His eyes focused on something above the unconscious man.

"That's not much of an excuse. There are three of you and you couldn't keep him safe from one little woman. I would offer you the chance to join my menagerie, but... well, you're pathetic, aren't you? What talents do you have?"

He listened for a few seconds, then laughed. "Pathetic. They mean nothing to me. Still, I'm in a generous mood. Join me and I'll let you live... or whatever you call your kind of existence. Otherwise..." he left the threat hanging.

Though Dinah couldn't see who he was talking to, she knew he wasn't mad. He had proved himself before and she would never forget it.

"Really? That's a shame. Never mind. Easy come, easy go."

He moved so fast he was a blur. Her employer's good hand stretched out and suddenly he was holding a woman by the throat, her feet not touching the floor. She struggled against his choking hand and lashed out. She did no damage, and he just laughed.

Suddenly the woman stopped thrashing and stiffened, her arms and legs going straight and every muscle tensing up. She started to glow from within, an eerie red and orange glow that grew ever brighter until the orange turned to white and Dinah had to cover her eyes. A second later there were spots in her vision and blackness beyond that. When her eyes returned to normal, the woman was gone, her employer had another shape by the throat, a man this time, and the whole thing started again.

A few seconds later he did it a third time and then he was done.

Dinah was stunned. She had seen evidence of his gifts before, but she had never seen the figures. What were those people? Ghosts as he claimed?

"Oh shit. Mother of god. What the fuck?"

It was Mark again, babbling to himself as he struggled to make sense of what he'd seen.

"Get him out of here," her employer ordered. "In fact, all of you go. I'll talk to you later."

No one needed convincing. They turned and rushed for the door, Dinah being no exception. She stopped when he called her name though.

"The money will be in your account by the time you wake up. There'll even be a bonus for you. This was good work."

"Thank you," she said woodenly, eager to be away and not mollified by the huge payday waiting for her. The threat may be what forced her to work, but the compensation was immense.

"No problems. Keep up the good work and I see you being a rich woman soon."

He casually reached for the unconscious figure. The man must have weighed at least fifteen stone but her employer lifted him as easily as if he were filled with straw.

"You can leave me now. I have things to do and you won't want to see them."

He couldn't have been more right.

She was too proud to run, but she power walked to her van. She got in, fired up the engine and nearly cried out when her lights illuminated her employer standing over the body that was laid over a table in the reception. He had a knife in his hand and he was talking to himself again… or to ghosts, maybe.

Dinah had seen enough. She pulled out of the carpark and drove, soon going seventy in a thirty mile per hour zone and not caring. She needed to be away from that place, from that man.

But where to go?

She felt dirty and knew she couldn't go home. She needed time alone and a scalding shower.

As she drove she couldn't help hating herself for what she'd done. She hated herself more for the knowledge of what she still had to do. There were more nights like this to come. A lot more. She would lose a little of her soul with every one.

Dinah drove into the night and the tears finally started. They wouldn't stop until morning. They would be her last for a long time.

1

Sunday, 15th November 2015
22:06

The typical patriotic pride of a Welshman can be hard to maintain. This night's *horizontal* rain was making it harder than ever. The heavy drops flew directly at Tad, bouncing off stinging, cold skin, soaking him in spite of the hood drawn tight about his pale face.

Keeping his eyes open was struggle enough, but navigation was impossible. All Tad could see through the wet blurriness was the vague glow of the illuminated, ancient walls of Cardiff Castle.

His supposedly waterproof coat kept out the rain about as well as a string vest. Wet and clingy, it looked about as good on him as that same string vest. Tall and skinny, Tad had never been one for close fitting clothes. He looked enough like a stick already.

His real irritation was that he alone of the four in his group was affected by the rain. His companions had come to an understanding with the weather, agreeing not to bother the rain if it in return wouldn't bother them.

He hated them for that.

"I never appreciated rain when I was alive. It's rather beautiful now

I think on it. The way it dances with the wind… magnificent."

The voice belonged to Charles Dickens.

Not *the* Charles Dickens, but a ten year older model who was often put out that the other Charles Dickens hogged all the glory. As one of his oldest friends, Tad normally got on well with Charles. Right then, Tad was prepared to bring about his second death.

"You have a point," said a second voice, equally unbothered by the weather. Tony appeared to be a fourteen-year-old boy of Chinese ancestry. However, appearances are deceiving when dealing with a ghost. He was fourteen when he died, but was now two years older than Tad's twenty-seven. "I never thought about it before."

"Of course you didn't," said Tad's third ghostly companion. "You only have your mind on one thing. You should be locked up."

Miriam, a short blonde in her early forties, had joined Tad three years earlier and had been on Tony's case ever since. A detective inspector for Cardiff Police in life, she did her utmost to continue her calling from beyond the grave.

Give any teenage boy invisibility and let him walk through walls and you won't win any prizes for guessing what he'd do next. Tony had been dead for fifteen years and he'd put his ghostly powers to what he considered good use ever since.

"You're just jealous because you haven't learned to have fun. One of these days you should come with me. Some new college-girls have moved in down the street and they look great in the shower. You know you'll like it."

Like any good parent, not that he was their parent, Tad knew the perfect moment to intercede and stop an argument escalating. Miriam had been in a civil partnership before her tragic demise, and Tony never failed to impose his perverted brand of lesbianism on her relationship. Nothing annoyed her more. Tad had to act fast.

"Everyone, knock it off. Don't forget why we're here. You're supposed to be keeping an eye out because I can't see a damn thing."

"Everyone? What did I do?" Charles demanded, his moustache twitching.

"You're trying to annoy me with talk of the rain. Congratulations, it worked."

"Well I never," Charles huffed. "I would never intentionally annoy you, Thaddeus."

Had Tad not been shivering, fighting a headache, and still nervous about what they might be heading into, he may have felt guilty at the tone of hurt behind Charles' words. As it was, he ignored the ghost and kept walking. That was a mistake.

A ghost's biggest frustration is boredom. Charles had been a ghost for a very long time and was not one to let silences, no matter how awkward, linger. Within seconds of his last words he was dredging up information from his centuries of knowledge to fill the silence.

"You want to know something interesting about Cardiff Castle?" he asked.

"No," Tad, Miriam and Tony answered, but not quick enough.

"The castle was built on top of the ruins of an old roman fort. In fact, part of the ruins still visible today are the ruins of—"

The words sparked an alien tidbit of knowledge in Tad's mind and he finished the sentence. "The ruins of the fourth fort, built in the 3rd century to deal with a pirate threat along the coast. Yes, I know this—"

"Pirates?" Tony interrupted, interested in spite of knowing that showing Charles attention was like showing an alcoholic whiskey. Let him get his hands on the stuff and there'd be no stopping him until every last drop was gone.

"Tony, don't encourage him. Charles, be quiet."

"Well if that's not of interest, maybe hearing that the old motte-and-bailey castle was either built by William the Conqueror after returning from a pilgrimage to St Davids, or Robert Fitzhamon, who used it as—"

"Oh my God! Why must we do this every time? You've been using Proxies for how many centuries now? You know I share every scrap of knowledge in your big head. The second I saw the castle all these useless facts filled my mind. So why, for the love of God, are you telling me them again... in the rain... and the cold... while we're on our way to potential danger? Why must you always do this?"

"Maybe some facts slipped past your recollection. For example, did you know—"

"Yes, I already knew that."

"You didn't even wait to hear what I had to say."

"That's because I already knew it."

"Well, what about—"

"I know that too. Now shut up. Tonight is bad enough without you prattling on."

"Tad, be nice," Miriam said.

Ganging up on him. Great.

Tad took a breath, forced back an angry response, and struggled for calm.

"Okay, you're right. I shouldn't have snapped. But Charles, you know that annoys me, and this weather isn't making things better. Now please, scout ahead. I haven't heard from Tommy so who knows what might be waiting for us."

Even Tony sobered at the mention of Tommy. Like Tad, Tommy had a family of ghosts who lived through him by proxy. Tad wondered if they were as much trouble as his ghosts were. He worried he might not get the chance to ask. He hadn't seen nor heard from Tommy in three days. That in itself was not unusual. Spending so much time with the dead made Proxies solitary by nature. However, it was good to keep in touch, especially recently.

Nancy warned Tad first. Three of her contacts, all Proxies, had disappeared. She'd gone looking, but hadn't even caught sign of their ghosts. That was three years ago. Nancy herself had been missing for half that time and Tad knew of four others who'd vanished. The worrying thing was that Tad only knew six Proxies, and one of them was Tommy.

"Why do you think he'll be here?" Miriam asked as they walked up the steps toward the castle.

"One of his ghosts told me she lived here when she was alive."

"Really? How old was she?"

"Older than Charles," Tony teased.

On cue Charles snorted. Of the few ghosts who remain after death, most move on after a few decades at the longest. At two-hundred-and-nine, Charles was proud of his age. Thankfully he didn't take Tony's bait.

"That's a thin theory," Miriam said. "Just because she lived here doesn't mean she'd come back."

"I have to hope she might. I know it's a long shot, but I'm out of options."

The rain was becoming less of an issue. It was less to do with it slowing than it was with it being blocked by the walls of the castle. Whatever the reason, Tad was grateful for the reprieve.

"A little help here would be good," Tad said as he approached the barred entrance. No further prompting was needed before Tony, Charles and Miriam stepped into his head. It was less of a step and more of a merging. Their physical forms faded and he breathed in their essence.

The feeling was hard to describe. When they were with him he felt... full... stronger... *powerful.*

He normally only joined with his ghosts when he slept. Until recently merging when awake only increased his strength a little and boosted his senses. However, within the last few years he and his ghosts had been getting stronger. He got that boost by merging with only one now.

Drawing in their strength, he willed himself to be like them. The cold and wet vanished, not to be replaced with warmth but instead with nothingness, just as he was now nothing. The rain passed through him as he became as spectral as any of his ghosts.

He stepped through the solid, locked gate as though it wasn't there.

He came back to the real world feeling drained as he always did when using that ability. Stepping away from the living was a tiring experience, and he needed time to catch his breath. Through their connection the ghosts sensed this and one by one they stepped from his head

"You wait here," Miriam suggested. "We'll search the place. You too, Charles."

The old ghost hesitated.

"I thought I'd stay with Thaddeus. He's not looking so well and—"

"And you're being a wimp again," Tony teased. "You're a ghost. What do you think might be waiting here that could hurt you?"

"A great many things," Charles snapped, anger masking his fear. "There are malicious spirits, cruel Proxies who only want to destroy ghosts… and… and there are… well… a great many other things, I can assure you."

Tony and Miriam looked to each other, sharing a rare moment of unity as they rolled their eyes.

"Whatever. Charles, partner with Tony and he'll keep you safe—"

"I don't need a boy to keep me safe. I'm thinking of what's best for Thaddeus. We need someone to stay here and keep an eye on him."

"Whatever. If you're comfortable knowing you're not as brave as a fourteen-year-old boy then—"

"What? Fine. If you want to be like that, I'll lead the way." Charles rushed past them, taking two steps into the darkness before stopping and nervously glancing back. "Aren't you coming?"

Tony's mocking laughter cut off abruptly as Miriam smacked the back of his head.

"Of course we are," she said, before doing just that and leading them on a tour of the castle.

Light headed and happy to see them go, Tad told them to be careful before falling against the gate and closing his eyes.

He didn't like to go insubstantial often. It was mentally draining for a ghost to remain in the living world. The longer a ghost remained, the harder it was to hold themselves together. Only spending the night in a Proxy's mind grounded them in reality and gave them a limited reprieve from the madness that approached if they lost the fight. When Tad became like them he got a sense for that feeling, like being pulled apart.

He was slowly recovering when he felt *them*.

Tad was accompanied by death daily. He knew it intimately and could sense when it was near. He could feel his ghosts searching the castle, but there was another flavour of death present. As much as he might wish otherwise, he didn't think it was Tommy's ghosts.

There was a bitterness to this presence, a foul taste that spiked Tad's heart rate. He'd encountered it before and as with all aspects of his peculiar world, it was a phenomenon that was increasing every year.

Something was wrong with the world. He knew it in his soul. The trouble was that he was one of the few left who could clean up the mess.

He pushed himself away from the gate and walked into the large, round courtyard. The rain came at him again, though the high walls kept out the worst of the wind. He could live with that.

Three figures materialised from the shadows at the other side of the courtyard. They had been human once. Unlike most ghosts they had neither moved on nor found a Proxy to keep the madness away.

They were twisted. Humanoid only in the vaguest sense. They stepped from the darkness, pale where they tried to imitate human features and billowing tendrils of shadow everywhere else.

The biggest downside to being a Proxy was that just as he could interact with the dead, they could interact with him. Ghosts this crazy troubled normal people, messing with him was that much easier.

It was an element of danger most people didn't face. He'd dealt with it before but had never been good with it. He was that kid who was bullied at school and had to live with it because he wasn't built for fighting. Other than arguing with friends, confrontation was alien to him. Situations like this rarely ended well. He was lucky to have escaped with his life in previous encounters.

It left only one thought that he couldn't keep from verbalising.

"Oh, shit."

As if that were the starter pistol in a race, all three spectres left their marks.

The central one was fastest. It flew across the ground as pale shadows of hair whipped back from a face more skeleton than skin. Its jaw opened inhumanly wide as it wailed and reached for him.

Tad moved at the last second, an act as much luck as timing. He turned, the outstretched hand passing by his face, nearly clawing his eyes.

He fled. There was nowhere to go and he would tire long before the ghosts, but what choice did he have?

He didn't get far.

Only a few steps away and already the ghost caught up. Its fingers sank into the meat of his left shoulder and numbness spread as the ghost pulled his life through their contact. Tad grunted in pain, but as much as he wanted to, he didn't pull away. To survive, he needed to do the opposite.

He clasped the ghost's hand and held it in place, forcing contact. Now he was touching it with naked skin he could feel it in his mind. It was a writhing mass of chaotic emotions, completely alien and almost overwhelming.

Tad fought his panic and searched for his spiritual centre. When he touched it, a calm washed over him. He took that calm and projected it outward, forcing it through his link to the crazed spirit and soothing the madness.

Lucidity spread fast, changing the ghost from a spectral nightmare to a frightened, young woman.

"It won't last long," Tad said before she had a chance to speak. "You need to choose. Move on or be destroyed."

Lucid for the first time in years, she realised what she had become and a ghostly tear spilled from her eye. She whispered a single thank you before she grew hazy and lost her shape. Her form collapsed until there was a sphere of glowing light that was ever shrinking until suddenly it was gone.

She vanished from this world and Tad was pleased to feel a supernatural, warm satisfaction from her departure. Sometimes a spirit departed and he felt the icy dread of nightmare, it was a feeling he was happy not to experience again.

The incident took only seconds, but it was long enough. Distracted by the warmth of that other place, he failed to notice the next ghost on a collision course with him. When he finally saw it, there was nothing to do but cringe.

The impact never came. At least, not the one he expected.

Another shape collided with the ghost, knocking it aside with an almighty roar that was part anger and a larger part terror. The shape rolled with the impact before breaking apart from the mad ghost.

Charles scrambled to his feet, his round face flushed with blood he no longer had and his eyes wild. He shook as he faced down the ghost, with fear not anger.

That he interceded in spite of such fear was one of the reasons Tad loved him like family. What kind of friend would Tad be without repaying the favour? For the first time he pushed back his distaste for conflict and hurried to Charles' aid.

He arrived just in time to push Charles aside as the ghost re-launched its attack. They narrowly avoided clawing hands and snapping teeth, but never made up any ground. It was advancing quicker than they could retreat and even without contact, Tad felt the cold of death. This ghost was strong, able to pull the life from an area without touching anything.

Its skeletal mouth was snapping as it came closer, opening wide enough to bite off his head. The third time it did this Tad felt icy teeth brush at the skin on his nose. In panic he reached up to push the spirit away, catching the spectral figure in his bare, outstretched right hand. As soon as he touched it, he was ready and this time he was quicker in forcing lucidity on it.

Another woman. Older, wider, more haggard and meaner even in her lucid state. But she was no more hesitant. She didn't need to hear the deal. She took advantage of her sanity and moved on. The warmth was not as strong with this passing.

"Are you alright?" Tad asked his friend as he sought the last spirit. He found it pinned between Miriam and Tony. The normally bickering pair worked together and were more than a match for it.

Charles blinked slowly, checking himself for injuries and shaking his head. "Your adventures are getting too dangerous, my boy. I'm suited to the classroom, not this."

Tad clasped him on the shoulder and nodded. "Well, tonight I'm glad you came."

Tad didn't wait for the small twitch of a smile from Charles before he moved to the other fight. After dealing with two crazed spirits a strange state of confidence slipped over him. He quite liked the feeling. Something told him it wouldn't last long.

Even in madness the ghost recognised its fate. Suddenly it was fighting to get away rather than to attack. It lunged for a gap by Tony only to be caught by Miriam. The spectre turned to face her, hissing and biting only to have Tony strike it from behind.

It turned again and this time it was Tad who interceded.

A simple touch. Calm thoughts. The ghost stilled.

The man under his fingers was enormous. His shaggy hair and beard were dark enough to make Tad think he had not changed from his shadow form. Deepest eyes of midnight black stared hard at Tad and the ghost grinned in defiance.

"Do your worst," he dared. Then, even lucid, he swung to attack.

He was ancient, Tad could feel that much. Broad of the shoulder, well muscled and almost as tall as Tad himself, he had been a warrior in life where Tad was certainly not. But no matter how quick or strong, he was not as fast as thought.

Tad hated to do this, but he was left no choice. He reached into the ghost with his mind, seeking its core. Once he found it, Tad sent his energy into it until the ghost's energy reached critical mass.

The man stiffened, his arms going rigid and his eyes widening as he started to glow from within. Red and orange at first, slowly turning to white. Soon the light was blinding to all but Tad, his gifts giving him protection against it.

Then it was gone.

The energy exploded outward and vanished into the world. The spirit had not moved on, but had been destroyed. Tad felt empty for having to do it.

He closed his eyes and fought back the tears that always came. It pained his soul to complete that task, and it was all he could do to keep from sobbing. His strength came from a simple touch, Miriam's hand on his shoulder.

"I've never seen three together before," she said.

"Neither have I," Charles noted; a much bolder statement considering his vast age.

"What does it mean?" Tony asked.

Tad shook his head. "Nothing good. None of this is good. The disappearances. The boost in my powers. Your strength increases. None of it feels natural. It's all just…"

He let his words fade into a sigh. He was exhausted, right to his core.

"This is getting us nowhere," Miriam said, echoing his thoughts. "We keep searching for these Proxies, but we're not finding answers. It's getting dangerous. I saw how close that first one came to grabbing you, and I doubt the second one was easier."

Actually, both were easier than he remembered. Now the fear had passed, he recognised that, but didn't verbalise the thought.

"I know, but what am I supposed to do? I can't give up. Tommy's the last Proxy I know other than Jen. I need to make sure he's okay. We need to know what's happening to them or you all know what'll be next."

"They'll be coming for you," Tony said.

Tad shook his head. "I don't care about that… Well, actually I do. But that's not important."

"Jen," Miriam said, her voice suddenly hard. "You're right. You need to figure this out and stop it. That means you need to get better at this sort of thing. This isn't the first time we've run into trouble. You need to up your game, fast. If you die out here, Jen will be on her own and whatever is happening to Proxies will come for her next."

"I know," Tad snapped. He'd reached the realisation himself and didn't need reminding. His sharp tone was short lived as he remembered his ghosts risking themselves to save him. More softly he added,

"I know. I have to get better. I will, I promise. Just not tonight. Right now, I need my bed and rest. We can figure out what's next tomorrow."

At his weakest and most vulnerable he was suddenly bathed in bright, artificial light, and the chance to rest was taken from him.

"You there, stay where you are. This is the police."

What choice did he have? Tad raised his hands over his head and waited.

2

Monday, 16th November 2015
00:08

Sitting in wet clothes for two hours was unbearable. As midnight came and went, Tad was considering escaping. A moment before his patience snapped the door opened.

The woman standing in the door looked like she'd stepped out of a movie. With silky black locks straight from a shampoo commercial and eyes bluer than a summer sky, this woman knew exactly how good she looked. Her tanned calves were bare beneath her knee-length skirt, and her tight, white blouse had enough buttons undone to make Tad blush. She had perfected the sexy executive look.

It wasn't right that someone could look that good so late at night. It was worse when she stared at Tad with that predatory gaze she always wore when she saw him.

"Yes! It's D.I. Slut. Please don't screw it up this time, Tad. Tell her that as she's a detective inspector, you've got something for her to inspect... Ow! Don't hit me."

Typical. Tony couldn't wait one second before breaking Tad's long-standing rule about not distracting him around people... especially those with the power to get him committed. Thankfully Miriam was there to smack him while Tad tried to ignore Tony's outburst. He forced a smile.

"D.I. Martin. You're here late."

To say she sat in the chair wouldn't do the motion justice. It was more like she slid into place and the chair was just happy to be of service. She offered Tad a quirky half smile and shook a manicured finger at him, drawing his attention to her black, painted nails.

"Now, now. We're long past titles and last names. Or would you rather be called Mr Holcroft?" Tad's wince transformed her half smile into an earth shattering grin filled with straight, pearly-white teeth. "Or maybe Thaddeus?"

"Dear God no. Just Tad will do fine."

Her throaty chuckle came from somewhere deep in her chest and stirred up awkward feelings in Tad. Not used to beautiful women at the best of times, ones who flirted with him made him decidedly uncomfortable.

"Alright then… *Tad.*" She stretched the name and gave him a look that made him forget how tired he was. Thank God for Miriam's snort of disgust or he might have started drooling. "Why don't you call me Stella? We're friends now, right?"

Of course her name was Stella. She couldn't exactly have a normal name, could she?

If Stella wasn't distraction enough, his ghosts were at it again. He was forced to ignore Miriam's disgust and Tony's attempts to break free of Miriam's grip so he could look down Stella's top. At least Charles was a gentleman… almost. The chubby ghost was doing his utmost to not look directly at Stella. However, what he thought were sly glances were not at all subtle.

"Well?" Stella asked again and Tad realised he hadn't responded.

"What? Friends… Right… Of course… Yes… No problem."

Tony laughed. "Smooth."

Refraining from shooting Tony a hateful glare was the hardest thing he'd ever done. He managed it, just, but his eyes twitched and his frustration slipped through enough for Stella to notice.

Tad had access to the talents and knowledge of his ghosts. As he considered Stella's insistence that they were friends, Miriam's police background and talent as a detective told him that Stella was trying to build a connection to put him off guard.

That knowledge was slow coming. It had been over eighteen hours since he last slept with his ghosts, so their link was fading. He couldn't rely on Miriam's skills much longer.

Tad wasn't actually friends with Stella. He'd met her through Kate, Miriam's life partner. Kate was also a detective and wasn't exactly friendly with Stella, but whenever their paths crossed when Tad was present, Stella made a point of saying hello.

Tad never really liked her, though he knew he should. You didn't need Tony's perversions to recognise she belonged in every man's fantasies. But she'd made one crucial mistake when she met him.

She'd hit on him.

Women did not hit on Tad. They never had, and never would. A woman as beautiful as Stella making a genuine pass at him would signal the apocalypse.

Tad had always had the tall and dark part down, he was just missing the handsome. His was a face that he needed personality to pull off, and he'd spent too much time with ghosts to develop one amongst the living. Stella wasn't after him because of attraction, she wanted something else. But what?

"So, why don't you tell me what you were doing in the castle tonight?" Stella leaned closer and whispered in an excited tone, "Maybe start with how you got in. We're all baffled at that."

Tad didn't think she'd buy the truth, so ignored her amendment. "I was looking for a friend."

Stella leaned back, a touch of her smile fading as she made a motion for him to continue.

"I've been trying to get hold of him for a few days, but no luck. I feared the worst, so I tried the castle… uh… he hangs out there sometimes. He's a history buff."

"Ah. No wonder you get on so well. You teach history at the University, right? People tell me they're surprised you're still in Cardiff. I hear you've had offers from Cambridge and Oxford."

It was Charles who had the interest in history. Channeling his interest and extensive knowledge had built Tad's career. Charles' one stipulation was that they stay in Cardiff, a place to which he had a strong attachment, so Tad had to turn down even the most lucrative offers.

"I suppose Tommy and I had that in common."

She arched a perfect eyebrow and sat forward again. "Tommy? That wouldn't be Thomas Butcher, would it?"

Tad blinked. She knew Tommy? Suddenly on uncomfortable ground, he hesitated before nodding.

"I thought so. We'll get back to that shortly. Tell me, did he often go to the castle at night after the doors were locked and there should be no one inside? Or did something else draw you there tonight? Maybe the same thing that took you to Brighton two months back. You were looking for Carys Brett then, right? Maybe it the same thing that had you asking after Michael Crocker in Newport last month? I've got a few other names here you might have heard of."

She drew a sheet of paper from a bag he hadn't noticed her carrying and she started reading off a list. "Nancy Fisher. Dan Brooks. Marian Salvatore. Cheryl James. Any of those ring a bell? You've been looking for all of them over the last two years."

Tad was speechless.

He hadn't met all of them, but knew the names. They were Proxies. How did Stella know them? Worse, how did she know where he'd been and what he'd been doing? Was this why she had been so friendly?

The smile was gone from her pretty face. She wasn't scary or hostile yet, but she wasn't flirting either.

"You need to say something, Tad," Miriam hissed, keeping her voice low as though somehow Stella might hear. "You don't want her looking into you more than she already has."

He wanted to ask her what to say because he was drawing a blank, but couldn't without looking crazy. It didn't stop him shooting Miriam a pleading look. It was just a glance, but it was enough for Stella to follow his gaze and frown.

Stella waited only a few more seconds before speaking again. "Let me level with you. I don't care that you broke into the castle. I also don't work the late shift. I came here just for you."

She leaned close enough that he was overcome with the smell of her perfume. It was sweet, flowery and intoxicating. Yet another tool at her disposal.

"I don't want you to worry, I'm not accusing you of anything. I just want answers." She tapped a black nail against the sheet in front of her. "I think you know that all of these people are missing. There are more names, a lot more. The thing is, I can't see what they have in common.

"We have a group of people that include all ages, sizes, genders and races. There's no commonality. Not religion. Not even a Facebook group. Other than living in the UK, they couldn't be more different. But I know their disappearances are connected, and I think you know why.

"You need to tell me. If I can find a connection, then I have a place to start. I can find these people and stop anyone else being taken. But I need help."

This time she waited for him to speak. Still struggling for words, he finally found his voice.

"I knew a few of these people, but I don't know what they had in common." Other than all being Proxies. He doubted she would buy that.

Stella sighed and sat back.

"Here's the thing. It's strange that a group of people as random as this would have you in common. This puts you in one of two camps. Either you're a potential victim in which case you need to tell me what you know so I can protect you. Or—"

"I didn't fucking do this," he blurted. "You have to believe me. I don't know what's going on, but it wasn't me. I knew a few of these people. They were acquaintances, nothing more. I just wanted to find them. I haven't been doing anything to them. I promise."

Miriam hissed at him to be quiet and he listened, though maybe a little too late. Tony whistled in a way that told him he had just messed up. Again Tad tried to ignore them, but was only partially successful.

"I believe you" Stella said. "The trouble is, you're not giving me anything to work with. That doesn't look good—"

"Ask Kate," Tad interrupted. "I spoke to her about these. I told her I was worried and asked where I should start—"

His words cut off when Miriam hit the back of his head and told him to leave Kate out of it.

Too late. Stella's eyes lit up.

She ignored his wince and how he couldn't resist rubbing the spot where Miriam hit him, instead focusing on his words.

"Have you now? Funny, I haven't heard anything from her about it."

"It was only in passing," Tad backtracked. "I mentioned that some-one I knew had disappeared and asked if she had any advice."

Stella didn't look convinced.

"Alright. Say I believe you. That puts you in the first category… a potential victim. You need to tell me what connects these people. You clearly knew them, so what did you have in common?"

"I don't know. We weren't that close."

"That's not going to cut it. You were close enough to look for them. You must know something."

"But I don't."

Stella said no more. She leaned back and tapped her nails against the paper again, waiting him out. It shouldn't have scared him as much as it did. He had just faced down three angry ghosts, what was one annoyed police woman against that?

But he had been dealing with ghosts since he was nine. Being in trouble with the law was new.

"We need to get you out of here," Miriam said.

"No shit," Tad answered before he could stop himself.

"What was that?" Stella asked.

"Nothing."

She didn't look convinced.

"Say you want to leave" Miriam advised. "I don't think she's supposed to be working this case. Like she said earlier, there's no solid connection and I know how the system works. Without a clear connection there's no way this is a single case. She has a hunch, and she's grasping at straws, but she's not got official backing. The only way to make it official is to follow her one lead, and that's you. She can't do that if you're stuck in jail. Just ask to leave. She'll let you go."

He wasn't so sure, but he wanted to leave so he did as she said.

"It's getting late. If you're not charging me for the castle thing, can I go?"

"I have more questions."

"But I don't have answers. Like I said. It's late, my daughter's babysitter is probably pissed off with me by now. I need to go."

It was the daughter comment that swayed her, he could see that. He wasn't sure how the fact that he had a daughter had escaped her notice.

"Are you charging me?" he asked, playing a line he'd seen on every police procedural show ever made. She shook her head and he stood. "Then I'm leaving."

It worked.

Stella sat motionless, staring at him with an unreadable expression as he walked by. Just as he got to the door she asked the most shocking question of the night.

"Does this have something to do with ghosts?"

He froze, not daring to look back less she read his face.

"What?"

She laughed. "I know. It sounds stupid, but here's the thing. Over the last few years we've seen a rise in nine-nine-nine calls that have been related to ghost sightings. It was a joke at first, a few stories here and there. But then we got video evidence. Since then they've become more common and... I know this sounds crazy... but it'll soon be official policy to acknowledge the existence of ghosts and treat calls about them seriously."

Tad was stunned.

He knew the number of sightings had gone up, it was one reason he'd been so busy of late. It wasn't officially his job to deal with hauntings, but he was uniquely qualified. With no other Proxies around, he couldn't live with himself if someone got hurt because he didn't act. This side job had been non stop recently and the supernatural issue was becoming a media darling again.

But for police policy to change, that really surprised him.

"The reason I'm bringing this up is that it's the only link I know of with these disappearances. Not all, but a few, have had friends or family that we've questioned who've mentioned ghosts. We haven't got much more than that and normally we would just put it aside as crazy talk, but…"

She paused as she stood from her chair, her heeled boots clicking on the linoleum as she covered the distance to stand by Tad's side.

"As I said, it's the only possible connection." She took his hand and he turned in surprise, finding himself face to face with her and staring into her beautiful eyes. "If it is something like that, you can trust me. I promise. Say what you want and I'll take it seriously."

He blinked like an idiot before losing the battle to keep from looking at his ghosts. It wasn't often he found himself in this situation, and even Miriam who had been in a room like this countless times, was stunned.

Stella looked triumphant, alternating her gaze from him to the empty spaces he had been looking at. That more than anything snapped Tad from his stunned state and he said, "I need to go."

Stella sighed again and nodded. She kept hold of his hand and lifted it to chest height before turning it palm up. Her other hand was suddenly holding a pen, and she wrote on his palm.

"This is my personal number. If you change your mind, give me a call." Her smile and that predatory look returned. "Hey, even if you just want to chat." She leaned in close so she could whisper directly into his ear. "Call me."

Then she was gone, stepping away so suddenly that he stepped back in surprise. Stella walked from the room and it was only when he couldn't hear her clicking heels anymore when he came back to himself.

"Holy shit that woman's hot," Tony said, breaking the silence. "Don't get me wrong. She's scary as hell, but... well, that's kind of hot, right?"

Miriam snorted yet again. "You're sick," she said almost absently, then looked at Tad's hand in disgust. "The slut could just have given you her card."

Tad looked at his palm, noting the neat handwriting and the message below the number. *Call me.* This was followed by a little heart.

Tad shook his head and curled his hand into a fist. It was too flirty. He couldn't trust that woman. She already knew too much.

"Come on," he said. "Let's go home."

He got no complaints.

They got a taxi to his car and it was more than an hour before he pulled up outside his house. The entire time he couldn't help thinking over Stella's words. Were the police really going to take ghosts seriously? Was that what the world was coming to?

In theory it should be good news. Maybe he could now talk about his life without people wanting to lock him in a padded cell. But he couldn't help but feel it was further evidence that things were not right with the world.

He was so lost in thought that he wasn't paying attention to the atmosphere of his end-terrace house as he opened the door. He apologised to Letty, his neighbour, who had been watching his daughter. She was angry, but when he described his night she calmed.

He had dealt with a haunting for her in the past and she was always happy to return the favour. The seventy-year-old widow was ever eager to watch Jen, and Tad enjoyed not having to hide his activities around her.

Still, he was glad to see the back of her. He watched her cross the street before he closed the door. He was ready for bed, but when he stepped into the living room he realised his night wasn't over.

His three ghosts stared at a fourth with varying expressions. Charles looked scandalised and Miriam was frowning. Tony however, stood with a huge grin on his face. When Tad walked in, Tony turned his attention to him briefly enough to say, "This has to be the best night ever."

At his words the fourth and newest ghost in the room turned. She was in her late twenties, pretty and naked. Her blonde hair was cut to her jawline, so it was no use for strategic modesty. Not that she seemed to even notice her nudity.

She was completely unashamed as she turned around and met Tad's eyes. Of all his shocks of the night, this was the biggest.

"Maggie?" he asked in a stunned whisper.

She smiled a smile he had not seen in five years and said, "Hello Tad. It's been a while."

3

Monday, 16th November 2015
01:39

Tad struggled to get his over-taxed brain working.

Maggie was here.

In his house.

Naked.

And she was a ghost.

He got caught up with the *naked* part. Tad always thought Maggie had the girl-next-door look perfected. Blonde hair framed her round face complete with green eyes, button nose and cute dimples. She wasn't overweight, but was curvy in what Tad had always considered to be the *right* places.

He caught himself staring, blushed and looked away. It didn't help that he'd wanted to see this woman naked since he was a teenager. He'd loved Maggie since he was old enough to know what love was.

"Shit, sorry Maggie."

She giggled nervously and the sound closed a five-year gap. Memories he thought long buried flooded his mind, reawakening the pain and bitterness of their parting. From said bitterness he drew the strength to collect his thoughts.

"Do you think maybe you should get the young lady some clothes, Thaddeus?" Charles asked. Tad nodded and silently walked into the hall, still trying to recover from the shock. That was Maggie… *his* *Maggie*. She was dead.

How did that happened?

Tad's end terrace had once been two houses that were combined to create one large house with three spacious bedrooms. Rather than heading to one of those bedrooms, Tad waited in the hall outside the living room, listening at the door.

"So, you're Charles," Maggie said. "You're exactly what I imagined. It's amazing, I've known you all these years and this is the first time I've seen you."

"Yes, I don't think I've been friends with someone I haven't spoken to, either. It's good to see you again, Maggie," Charles answered.

Tad easily predicted the startled look on Charles' face. His wide eyes pushed those bushy eyebrows up his head, and his double chin shook as he struggled to find the words to correct himself. Tad smiled even without seeing it.

"Not that I'm glad you're dead, of course. I would never… I mean it would have been better to… I mean…"

"It's okay. I understood what you meant." After a slight pause, Maggie said, "Tony. You haven't changed."

"But you have, Mags. I approve. How about a twirl so I can look at— Ow. Will you stop hitting me?"

Tad took his cue to return and entered as though he had something draped over his left arm. Maggie looked up and suddenly he felt a weight on that arm. He looked down to find a pair of worn jeans and an over sized black t-shirt with a skeletal design on the front, his clothes from when he was growing out of his teens. He had long since tossed them, but Maggie didn't know that.

Like most ghosts, Maggie didn't yet to realise how much her reality relied on perception. Tad could see and interact with ghosts, but they weren't part of the living world. Their reality was what they made it.

Ghosts appeared as they expected to appear. Some assumed this would be without clothing or any material possessions. In her new state, if Maggie believed herself clothed she would be. However, a lifetime of thinking you know how the world works takes a while to overcome. She'd get it eventually, but until then Tad had a few tricks up his sleeve.

Telling her he had gone to get clothes left her with the impression he would do so. When he returned, her belief in his word made the clothes real. It would do until he could show her how her new world worked.

"I never thought I'd be this happy to see these again," Maggie said as she pulled the t-shirt over her head. "Thanks."

Tad nodded and motioned to three large sofas arranged in a U around his TV. So many sofas were overkill for just he and Jen, but with the ghosts the extra seating was useful.

Tad grabbed the acoustic guitar that was resting in the corner of the room before taking his seat on the central sofa. As he got himself comfortable, his fingers moved along the strings, picking a few quiet notes that wouldn't intrude on their conversation.

He never considered whether it was the right time for music. When he was nervous he needed to be doing something with his hands. The habit wasn't even his own, it was Tony's, one played out through Tad by proxy. The longer Tad spent with his ghosts, the more he became like them. Even with his bond to Tony fading, the habit and enough of Tony's talent remained that the guitar made the beautiful noises that can only be produced by a master musician.

Maggie smiled at the familiar sight of Tad with a guitar and took the seat at the far left on his same sofa.

After a few minutes listening to Tad play, Maggie took charge of the conversation. She turned to Miriam and said, "I'm sorry, you weren't about when I last spoke with Tad."

Miriam shook her head and offered a smile filled with sympathy, but was neither overly pleasant nor condescending. Tad guessed she had perfected it as a detective talking to grieving families.

"I've only been around a few years. My name's Miriam Winslow."

"Maggie Patterson."

"I know all about you, dear. Part of the Proxy thing. What he knows—"

"You know. Of course. I'd forgotten." Maggie laughed nervously and brushed her hair over her ear as she turned to look at Tad. "It's weird. I always believed what you could do. But there's believing and there's being a part of it. I never expected to be here."

"Why are you here? After everything I told you when we were friends, I assumed that if you died you'd move on."

She winced at his use of the past tense and looked away. Tad knew what was going through her mind and struggled past the memory their parting. He started into a faster song, trying to lose himself in manipulating the strings, using the music to leave his awkwardness behind.

"I would have, but..." Her words trailed off as she composed her thoughts. "I couldn't move on. Not yet. You were right. About everything... About Mark. I can't move on until... well..."

"Maggie. What happened?" Tad asked, mimicking Miriam's polite, police tone.

There was a momentary pause in his playing as he surprised himself. That tone was something he shouldn't have access to now his bond with his ghosts was almost gone.

"He killed me. A few hours ago."

The bitterness in her voice was sharp and understandable, but Maggie looked ashamed. She took a deep breath to calm herself before her story poured from her.

"He started drinking a while back. There's something about his work that's bothering him, but he'd never tell me what. I knew it was eating at him so I kept asking. It got in the way of our marriage. He would walk around as though haunted by ghosts—" She looked at the three ghosts in the room and said, "No offence."

Charles waved her off, Tony grinned and Miriam offered another tame smile.

"I kept asking, he kept telling me to mind my own business. We argued, and with each argument we grew further apart. Then he became violent." She wasn't looking at Tad, no doubt expecting an *I told you so* expression. She wouldn't find one, he had more compassion than that.

"He was so distraught the first time he slapped me that things got good again. He treated me like a queen for months. We didn't argue, we laughed, we… well, lets just say we were properly man and wife again."

Tony sniggered and received another slap from Miriam. Tad was glad for their distraction, it hid the hitch in the music as he struggled with is own feelings.

"But then it started again. This time it progressed quicker. The next time he hit me he wasn't so upset about it. Rather than trying to make amends, he drank instead.

"That was our pattern for a year. We'd fight, he'd get angry, hit me, and then hit the bottle harder. This evening he came home pissed off his head and angry about something. I guess I asked the wrong question."

She took another deep breath and Tad saw tears streaming down her cheeks. Whatever *I told you so* speech he'd been composing vanished and he moved on instinct, dropping the guitar and sliding to the end of the sofa. He put an arm around her shoulders as he had a million times before.

At first she stiffened, shocked. Then she smiled and melted into him, resting her head against his chest.

Tad ignored the judging looks from his ghosts. They knew how he felt for Maggie and he knew how this must look. They could think what they wanted. This wasn't about them, it was about Maggie.

"When he hit me tonight I was in the kitchen. I tripped and fell, and I remember banging my head against something. When I landed the world felt wrong, like it was moving too slowly. He stood over me with a guilty look on his face. But then his look changed and he got angrier than ever.

"He started kicking me. I lost consciousness after the first three.

When I woke up I was naked and standing in the park near my gallery. There was this bloody mess in the bushes at my feet. I think it was me."

The tension of the night, the pain of her death and the shock of her new life overcame her all at once. The new tears were accompanied by heaving sobs that weren't going to stop anytime soon. It was understandable. Most ghosts were emotional at first. Death was a big thing to adjust to.

When Tad looked up, he saw Miriam mouthing the words, *Call Kate.*

If Maggie had been killed only a few hours ago, then she might not have been found. If he could tip off Kate, then he could get Kate on the investigation. Kate knew he was a Proxy, so he might be in on the investigation as well.

He nodded to Miriam and waved her over. Handing Maggie over was less than graceful, but Maggie was too distraught to notice. He left them and walked toward the kitchen, fishing his phone out of his pocket.

He was half way through dialling when he stepped into the hallway and cried out in shock.

In spite of knowing she was busted, the girl sat on the bottom step couldn't help but giggle at his reaction. Her humour didn't last long. At twelve years old, Jen was getting the feel for teenage mood swings a year early. She didn't take well to being told what to do and Tad's glare sparked her innate defiance.

She straightened her back and stood proud at her full five-foot-two, her hazel eyes hardening as she stared Tad down. Her coppery curls were tied back and lent a sharp look to her narrow face. Even her freckles did nothing to soften her menacing appearance. Tad felt a pang of sympathy for her future husband before he remembered that was years off and for now she was his headache to deal with.

"Why aren't you in bed?"

Jen ignored his question, instead answering the question she thought he should have asked.

"You can't have another ghost when I haven't got one of my own."

He sighed and shook his head.

"You need to be in bed. You've got school in the morning." She wouldn't go to bed no matter what he said, so he continued into the kitchen. Jen followed him.

The case that had brought Miriam and Kate into Tad's life had also brought him Jen. Her parents had never been responsible, and by the time Jen was nine they were heavily in debt and there were people looking to make an example of them.

After they died, they realised that when their daughter said she talked to invisible people she wasn't lying. Feeling guilty, they stuck around using Jen as their Proxy until they could get her to safety.

Even now Jen didn't realise how easy her parents had made the experience. Sharing your mind is beyond intimate. Without a strong will it can be all consuming, and if a Proxy isn't alert a ghost could overpower them.

Jen's parents didn't do this, but what little time they spent in her head was damage enough. She was exposed to memories not meant for a nine-year-old and it took Tad a long time to unravel that particular knot.

With her parents on board, Jen had gone to the police. She had trouble being taken seriously until Tad, who was in the station looking for answers on the first disappearance, got involved. It took some convincing, but he had fifteen years experience of getting past people's scepticism. Soon enough he and Jen were speaking to Miriam, the lead detective on Jen's parent's case. It was a career move that would claim Miriam's life and see her then uniformed life partner promoted to CID.

Once their killers had been arrested, Tad convinced Jen's parents of the damage they were doing to their daughter. He offered to Proxy for them, but they wanted to move on. However, they had no family and didn't want to leave Jen to foster care. Knowing she would need more guidance than a normal parent could offer, Tad volunteered.

He posed as a distant relative and was armed with just enough knowledge to prove it. With a written recommendation from Kate, a good legal history and the tenuous proof that he was family, it was just enough for her to slip through the gaps in the system and into his guardianship.

She made him pay for that decision every day since. When her parents first moved on, she was understandably distraught. Over the course of the next year Tad came to love her as a daughter whereas Jen came to resent him as a parent. She blamed him for her parents moving on and she rebelled against his every decision since.

By far the largest argument that still hung between them was that Tad wouldn't let her Proxy until she was eighteen. He had seen the damage her parents had done to her and knew it was a talent that could damage the young and innocent.

"I'm serious, Tad. You can't have four ghosts while I don't have any. You should let me have this one."

"No. Go to bed."

Tad picked up his phone again and searched for Kate's number.

"No? You can't just say no. You need to give me a reason." He was fortunate enough to be standing on the other side of the breakfast island, putting a much needed barrier between them. The distance meant he felt safe enough to meet her eye.

"We've been over this. You're too young. Just like you're too young to be up at…" he glanced at his phone and couldn't hold back his despairing sigh. "Nearly two in the morning."

Jen was not yet out of the habit of stamping her foot when frustrated. Dressed in pink, cotton pyjamas and barefoot, her stamp made a slapping sound on the cold stone floor and she looked ridiculous.

"Tad. This isn't fair. You had Charles when you were nine. By the time you were my age you had Tony as well."

"That was different."

"Why?"

"Because there was no one else to have them. You ask any Proxy what their thoughts are on children being Proxies and they'll tell you the same thing."

"That's convenient when all the other Proxies are probably dead."

Which was the other reason he didn't want her using her abilities. The last thing he wanted was for her to draw the attention of whoever was hunting Proxies.

She knew she'd gone too far without Tad having to say anything. Her expression softened. She was a good kid really, and he knew she was only acting out as all children did. But he'd had a long night.

"Go. To. Bed." He said again.

She looked like she might be about to say something else, maybe the sorry he was waiting for. Instead she turned and walked away.

Tad knew by the lack of the footsteps climbing the stairs that she hadn't gone to bed. He sighed again. He'd call Kate and then drag her to bed if he had to.

Kate picked up on the tenth ring and she barked in her thick, Valley's accent, "Holcroft. Do you know what fucking time it is?"

"Yeah. Sorry about that, Kate. I've got a favour to ask."

She snorted. "Figures. What's up?"

"I've got a new ghost with me. She was murdered about midnight and her body was dumped in the park near Jensen Gallery. I figured you might want to take a look."

There was a moment of silence before a more alert voice said, "Give me the details." He retold Maggie's story, explained where he expected her body to be, and when Kate said she'd look into it he thanked her and hung up.

As the phone went dark, he fully felt the lateness of the hour and was determined to put this day to bed. Beyond battling with a pain-in-the-ass pre-teen, he also had to have a conversation with Maggie that he wasn't looking forward to. She was here for reasons beyond getting Tad to look into her murder. The trouble was, he didn't know what his answer would be yet.

He was still thinking as he returned to the other room.

Sure enough, Jen was curled up on the sofa in the farthest spot from the door. It was as though she thought that by putting distance between herself and her bed he would let her transgression slide. He decided it was a battle that could wait for a moment and instead he turned his attention to Maggie.

She wasn't crying anymore. Instead she had a stunned look on her face and she was staring at Jen.

"Tad, who's this little girl? She says she's your daughter—"

"Adopted," Jen interjected before realising it was probably best if she stayed quiet. She went back to looking at her knees.

"She is," Tad said. "It's a long story."

Maggie stared at him as though expecting to hear it, but that was not a conversation he wanted to have. Instead he asked, "What are your plans? Why are you here?"

Some of the sadness returned to her expression.

"I hadn't really thought about it. Mark killed me and my mind went straight to the one person I knew who could talk to ghosts. I thought that maybe you could help me get justice."

Tad read between the lines. He knew Maggie too well and the careful lack of heat to her words made him suspicious. Maggie had always been passionate. When that passion disappeared he knew she was hiding something. This time he expected she was less interested in justice as she was in revenge.

It was because he knew her so well that he knew what she wanted to ask next. He had worked hard to put Maggie and his past behind him, agreeing to her request would awaken those old wounds in the worst way possible. He felt horrible and wished he had the strength to give her what she wanted, but he couldn't help this time.

"I can't be your Proxy, Maggie."

She stiffened. "Why not?"

"Because of our history. Because of how invasive the process is. Because of a lot of reasons. I don't think I'm going to be the right person for you. I can recommend someone—"

"I can do it," Jen said.

"No!"

The word came from four voices at once and made both Jen and Maggie flinch. Charles and Miriam would never allow it, and even Tony knew it was not something suited to a little girl. It was one of the few things they all agreed on, much to Jen's frustration.

"As I was saying. I know another Proxy that—"

"I want you to be my Proxy. I can't believe you'd shut me out like this."

"It's not like that, Mags. From all the things I told you, I thought you'd understand."

"I understand alright. I understand we *were* best friends before Mark, and now five years later you're still holding it against me. I thought I meant more to you than that."

"Of course you mean a lot to me—"

"Then be my Proxy. It's not like we had secrets before. I'm not afraid of you looking into my mind. What are you so afraid of?"

That was just it, the question he'd been dreading. In all the years he had loved Maggie, he knew she never felt the same way. He'd never brought it up knowing what it would do to their friendship. If he was to do as she asked then she'd finally know. Who knew where that would leave them?

"Please, Tad. I'm begging you. What do you want me to say? You want me to admit I was wrong about Mark? Fine. I was. You were one-hundred percent right when you warned me away. Want me to take all the blame for us not speaking in five years? Fine. That was my fault too. I felt like you were making me chose between Mark and you, and I chose Mark. I threw away the best friend I ever had over a man who eventually killed me."

She moved up the sofa, grabbed his hand and squeezed hard. "I know I've fucked up. But please don't hold it against me. I need you more than I've ever needed you in my life. Please. Help me."

He wasn't sure if it was her touch, the tears filling her eyes or Jen waiting to step in if Tad chickened out, but he gave in.

"Fine. I'll do it. But remember, I tried to warn you."

"I know. Thank you. You're a better friend than I've ever deserved."

She kissed him on the cheek to seal the deal. Now the decision had been made he realised it hadn't really been his decision at all. It had been a foregone conclusion the moment he had seen her in his house.

It sapped the last of his strength and he was finally done in. He looked and spoke to Jen, but his words were for everyone.

"Come on. Bed time. We'll talk more in the morning."

4

Monday, 16th November 2015
02:20

Even Jen knew a losing battle when she saw one, and she went to bed. Tad turned off the lights as he followed, intending to accompany her to her room to say goodnight. A slammed door put an end to that idea.

"I'll check on her," Miriam said before Tad could respond. Not for the first time he was glad she was one of his ghosts.

He turned and headed into his own bedroom, too tired to be embarrassed at the state he left it in. It had been a long time since he hosted bedroom guests. His bed was a welcome sight and he stripped down for it. He'd already lost his t-shirt and was undoing his trousers when he thought of Maggie watching. He pushed aside his embarrassment. He was about to do the most intimate thing one person could do with another, near nudity wasn't a big deal.

Tad dropped his trousers in a pile and slid under the covers. He groaned in pleasure at being back in the comfort of his bed.

"How does this work?" Maggie asked, fidgeting in the corner near the window, peeking behind the blinds, looking anywhere but at him.

"In the future, you won't need to come here. For now, just lie down and try to sleep."

"I don't feel tired."

"You never will. But I do. I've been told a sleeping Proxy is like a beacon to spirits. Try to fall asleep and think of me. When I drift off, the rest should happen naturally."

She swallowed and nodded, taking one last look out the window before coming to join him. She slipped off her jeans revealing a lot of bare skin. He looked away. He didn't need arousal making this more awkward for them both.

"A little help?" Maggie asked as she struggled to lift the quilt.

"Of course, sorry."

He lifted a corner and she slipped in, frowning as she settled against the pillow.

"How come I could touch the clothes but not the quilt?"

He smiled and shook his head, not ready for that conversation. "I'll tell you in the morning. For now, I need sleep."

Her frown deepened, but she nodded. He didn't notice as he'd already closed his eyes.

"I appreciate this. Considering everything that's happened between us... well... Thanks."

"No problems," Tad answered, his words slurred by drowsiness.

Just as sleep claimed him, he felt a push against his mind. There were four touches, each a distinct flavour. His ghosts sought entry.

His last act before he slipped into unconsciousness was granting permission.

When Tad was four, he suffered a blow to the head which blinded him. He struggled with this disability until he was nine. Then he met Charles, and from that meeting gained a friend and his sight.

Unlike with their knowledge and talents, physical attributes like increased strength and healing, only lasted so long as the ghost remained merged with him. Therefore, the miracle of his returned sight should only work while a ghost shared his head.

He never discovered why his sight was different, he just feared the day his blindness returned.

Maybe that was why in his dreams he was always blind.

It was not true blindness. While he couldn't see, in his dreams he possessed instinctive knowledge of his environment. He knew the placement of everything, could read facial expressions, and discern colours. If asked, the answers simply appeared in his mind.

Tonight, as ever, when his sight left him he panicked. To get past that panic he reminded himself that Proxies are masters of their dreams, always in control.

Tad released his anxiety with an outward breath and concentrated on where he was.

As ever, his dream began in a circular room that normally held four exits. This night there were five. Behind each door was a mind. Walk through them and he would enter his own memories or the memories of his ghosts.

Normally he could choose which door to walk through, but this night only two doors were unlocked. This was his first merging with Maggie, so he had expected this. In everything else he was in control, but on this first night he had no choice but to walk the pathways of Maggie's memories and she the paths of his.

Their two doors merged into one. The path they walked this night would wind through both of their memories.

He hesitated as he collected his strength. It was his last chance to back out. Maggie would lose the benefit of using a Proxy, but his secrets would remain undiscovered.

He decided to stay the course. Maggie needed him and as always, he would be there for her no matter the cost.

The door opened at his touch and he stepped into the world beyond.

There's no light.

He tries to open his eyes, but they're already open. He has forgotten he's blind. How can life be so cruel as to make him forget every morning for five years?

He goes through his morning routine, built over a long time with a lot of trial and error. Routine is his friend, it helps him cope. When the routine slips, problems form.

Bathroom. Back to bedroom to dress. Breakfast. Morning small talk. Taken to school. Helped to class. Try to ignore the hurtful words of the sighted kids. Wish there was a blind school closer to home. The bell rings. Break time. He is escorted to a bench where he sits and waits while his helper visits the bathroom.

He hears the sound of footsteps. Heavier than a child's and different to those of the woman who helps him. No stones crunch or twigs crack beneath their feet, yet he hears the footsteps clearly.

"Why do you sit alone, boy? Shouldn't you be partaking in frivolities with the other children?"

The voice is strange. The boy is reminded of a book read to him in class, a classic. It's a deep voice and his words are hard to understand, but the boy can sense the friendliness.

"I'm blind. I can't play with the other kids."

"Nonsense. There's plenty you can do. Never mind. Maybe I can keep you company."

The man sits on the bench and the boy is surprised. He can sense the man. He can't see him but he knows he's there. He can almost picture him, a man in his sixties with a receding hairline and bushy, grey eyebrows. His mutton chops, old-fashioned moustache and funny old suit makes him look like someone from a play.

"What's your name, boy?"

"Thaddeus."

Again comes an amused snort. "Your parents mustn't like you very much to call you that. I think I'll call you Tad."

Tad likes that name. He thinks he likes the man.

"What's your name?"

"Charles, my lad. Charles Dickens. Now don't you go confusing me with that other Charles Dickens mind you. I've got nothing to do with that fame stealing—"

"I don't know any other Charles Dickens."

He senses the man blink. "You don't?" The man grins. "Well keep it that way. I'm the only Charles Dickens you need to know. You remember that and we'll get on just fine."

"Thaddeus?"

It's the voice of his helper. He hasn't heard her approach because he's so interested in the conversation.

"Who are you talking to?"

"Charles Dickens. He's a nice man. Do you know any other Charles Dickens, Mrs Hopewell?"

"What? Charles Dickens? What are you talking about, Thaddeus?"

"I was just chatting with Charles and—"

Mrs Hopewell interrupts him and she sounds worried.

"Thaddeus. There's no one here. You're talking to yourself."

They moved through the memories quickly, stopping at random. It had been a long time since Tad thought of the day he met Charles. That day changed his life and he should visit it more often.

Maggie walked his memories beside him and he sensed her interest in that particular memory. It was the first memory that had drawn her interest. Maybe that was why they lingered so long.

They couldn't linger forever, and soon enough they were moving again, glancing at most memories but stopping longer at those that were most revealing.

"You're the boy that used to be blind."

She knows she's not supposed to speak to him. They say he's strange and she should stay clear. Typical. They tell her to stay away from the interesting ones. Everyone else is boring. No one else has been blind and learned to see again.

The boy looks surprised that she's talking to him. He nods and looks back to his book, expecting her to walk away. She feels sorry for him. He must be lonely.

She sits down next to him and waits for him to look up.

"What do you want?" he asks. He sounds nasty. She's only ten, but she knows when people are being mean and she doesn't like it.

"You shouldn't talk to people like that. My mum says if you don't have anything nice to say, don't speak at all."

He looks up from his book. He's angry.

"Then what are you doing here? Going to sit in silence because you don't want to say anything mean?"

She realises he isn't angry, he's upset. He thinks she's teasing him. The other kids do that, but she doesn't like it. They tease her too. They say she's fat.

"I just wanted to talk to you." He doesn't answer. She waits, then asks, "Why do you talk to yourself?"

He sighs and looks back to his book. "I don't know."

He's lying. "Yes you do."

"I'm not talking to myself, okay? I am talking to my friend."

That's strange. But he isn't lying this time. She's sure of it.

"Who's your friend?"

"His name is Charles Dickens."

"Like the writer?"

"No. Not like the writer… Okay Charles. I'm telling her. He says he's nothing like the writer. He says *that* Charles was ten years younger than him and it's a travesty that he's taken all the fame for their name."

"What does travesty mean?"

The boy shakes his head. "I don't know. Charles is always saying stuff like that. He gets mad when I don't understand. He asks me what the world is coming to when I can't even speak English."

"He sounds silly."

The boy smiles for the first time and he nods his head. "He is. But he's nice too. He gave me a new nickname."

"What is it?" she asks.

"Only my friends can know."

"I can be your friend."

He looks over her head and she follows his gaze. There's nothing there.

"Are you sure?" The boy asks, and she turns back to him. He's not looking at her. "But what if she's like the others?" There's a pause. "No. I know that… Why not? You're my friend. That's enough… Why?… Oh, okay. Fine."

Finally he looks at her and says, "He calls me Tad."

She sticks out her hand. "Nice to meet you. My name's Maggie."

Maggie's parents don't like her hanging out with Tad even though he's been her friend for three years. She's snuck out to see him so many times she's an expert, once more is hardly an issue.

Her big news can't wait. She had her first kiss that morning. It was weird and she doesn't know what all the fuss is about, but she needs to tell Tad. She shares everything with him.

She gets to his house and goes around the back. He won't be inside. His mum and dad still think he's talking to himself. He pretends to be normal around them. It's hard. She's the only one he can be himself around. She likes that. It's why they're best friends.

She doesn't call before climbing up to the tree house. She already knows he's there, and she sees him as soon as her head clears the floor level.

"Hey Tad. You'd never guess what I did today…"

She pauses. He's laying on the floor, his skin is pale, and he has dark rings around his eyes. He's always been skinny, but now he looks like he's sunk in on himself.

She gasps and runs over, kneeling beside him and grabbing his hand.

"Oh my God, what happened?"

"Ghost," he whispers. She barely hears him. His fingers are cold and she wonders if he'll die. "Charles says I'll be fine. I just need to catch my breath."

"What happened?"

"A bad ghost. At the school. I nearly… it nearly." He shakes his head and says, "Had to fight… destroy it. It touched me. Charles said it was feeding off my life."

"Oh my God. Are you okay? Should I call—"

"No. I'll be fine." He squeezes her hand and tries to smile. "Just glad you're here. What did you want to tell me?"

"What?"

"When you came in—"

"Oh that. It's nothing."

"It sounded important. What was it?"

He's sounding better already. Maybe she overreacted. Some of her excitement returns.

"You'd never guess what I did today?"

He smiles. "What?"

"I kissed Johnny Walbeck."

He stops smiling. He doesn't say anything. He just looks at her and he's so still he might have died.

"Tad? What is it? What's wrong?"

He turns away and shakes his head. "Nothing. Just tired. I think I want to be alone. I'll see you tomorrow at school, okay?"

She doesn't understand. "Are you sure? Maybe I should get some-one—"

"No. I have Charles. I'll be fine."

Great. He has his imaginary friend. Sometimes she believes Charles is real. Other times…

She shakes her head and tries to not think about it. Tad is her best friend and if he says Charles is real, he's real.

She doesn't like leaving him alone with just a ghost and says as much.

"I don't mind. Honestly. I'll be fine. Why don't you go find Johnny, hang around with him."

"What?"

He shakes his head.

"Never mind. Just go. I'll be fine."

She goes. She doesn't like it and stops on the way out to look back one last time. It looks like he's in pain. He's crying. But he's whispering too. He's talking to Charles.

She leaves. She'll see what he's like in the morning.

Tad paid close attention to Maggie as they moved through the memories. Seeing how she remembered that night left him amazed at how oblivious she was to his feelings.

She was a girl then, now as woman he could tell she'd noticed a pattern. Reliving their time together as children was more revealing as adults. She stole glances at him when not studying the memories. He did his best to ignore it.

They traveled through a thousand other memories, each one further confirming her suspicions. It was every bit as painful as Tad thought it would be.

He dreaded the rest of the night.

"I can't believe you fucking did this," Maggie screams. Tad cringes from her anger but doesn't back down. She needs to know.

"He's a dirty cop. Tony followed him and—"

"The dead teenage pervert followed my boyfriend to… what exactly? No. Fuck it. I don't want to know. You've gone too far."

Maybe he has but he won't apologise. He's been looking out for her since he was nine. That's thirteen years too long to give up now. If she stays with Mark, she'll end up hurt.

Deep down he feels a familiar monster stirring. He ignores it and tells himself he's not jealous. After suffering through Maggie seeing other boys, he's learned to live with it.

No. This time it's serious.

"Maggie. Trust me. This guy is involved in—"

She hits him.

It's the first time she's ever done it and it surprises both of them. She looks at her hand in shock before looking at his face. There are tears in her eyes and her lip trembles.

"Fuck you, Tad. I thought you were better than this. I thought you were my friend. But if you try this hard to make me unhappy, then you really must hate me."

She gets up to leave. He tries to stop her but she's having none of it.

"Mags. Don't go," he shouts after her. "I don't hate you…" Before he can finish the door slams in his face. "I love you."

He sighs and slumps onto the sofa. Has he gone too far? No. She'll get over it like she always does. She'll ring later when she's calmed down.

He knows he's lying to himself. He can see it in Tony and Charles' expressions.

"Shit," he says. "What now?"

The night was a bad one.

They explored countless memories, and neither escaped unscathed.

Maggie had viewed thirteen years of friendship from a new perspective. He could tell how uncomfortable she was and felt justified for keeping his secret.

Of course for him it had been just as bad. He finally had the answer to a question he'd asked a billion times.

Was there ever a time when Maggie was attracted to him?

The answer was no.

She had never loved him as he loved her. It left him numb as they moved into the memories that covered the years they were apart. Maggie watched as he tried to get over her. There were a few failed relationships until eventually he adopted Jen. Suddenly he had an excuse to stop trying for love.

Maggie's memories played as she said they would. There were some sickeningly happy ones that were each a new stab of pain for Tad. Slowly they became darker as Tad's predictions from their last conversation played out.

Finally they were standing over her mangled corpse. He shared her pain. It was the first time she realised what a mess she made of her life. The first time she accepted Tad's words. She hadn't thought about Tad in a long time, had forced herself not to. Now, the prospect of seeing him again was the only thing she could think about.

Her world had turned upside down and she needed her best friend.

Tad suddenly felt guilty. He worried so much that she would discover his secret feelings that he failed to think like the friend he should have been. She may not have loved him how he wanted, but he meant more to her than he expected. They were closer than family and he broke her heart the day she thought he turned on her.

Tad promised himself he'd be a better friend now she was dead. He would stop pining after something that couldn't be and would help catch her killer.

The last memory faded, and he stepped back into the round entry room of his mind. This was normally where he willed himself awake.

For some reason tonight, he couldn't bring himself to do so.

5

Monday, 16th November 2015
14:56

Stella couldn't believe her eyes.

She only found the right address because of the two men talking in the open doorway. The one outside wore a heavier raincoat than when last she saw him and it was his presence that made her curse. He was the reason for her late night and foul mood.

"You've got to be kidding me," she muttered.

Tad looked over his shoulder and stared into space for a second before turning again and looking directly at her. It was spooky. Surely he couldn't have heard her.

She was reluctant, but knew she had to slip into her *friendly* persona. There was something important about Tad that she had to uncover. Whether he was a big part of this case or it was just that Kate found him fascinating, he had something Stella wanted. She learned long ago that to get what she wanted from men, it was best to be her *friendly* self.

She was still thinking of Kate as she checked her reflection in her rain-spattered car window. To this day she had no idea how Kate had done it. Stella worked with Miriam before she was killed and back then Kate was just the uniform who dated their gay boss. Then she solves Miriam's murder out of the blue and was promoted to CID. Since then she hadn't put a foot wrong.

In three years she had landed and solved more homicides than anyone else in Cardiff, enough to make Stella think she was committing them herself. She had gone from a know-nothing street constable to a detective with a higher arrest rate than Stella.

Unheard of.

Stella didn't like being second best. When some nobody comes along and shows her up, you bet she's going to take interest.

It didn't take much detective work to see how much time Kate spent with this Tad guy. Stella considered Kate to be an Adam's apple short of manhood, so it couldn't be romantic. Something fishy was going on.

Now Thaddeus, what a stupid name, was part of her investigation and her chance for answers had fallen into her lap.

She finished checking her reflection with clinical detachment. Even surprised, wrapped in a heavy coat and her hair tied back to protect it from the November wind, she was still better looking than anyone Tad was likely to meet. An arrogant thought, but she didn't care. Her beauty was often more of a hinderance than a help.

She turned from the car just in time to see the door close and Tad walking down the drive.

Show time.

"D.I. Martin," Tad greeted as he stepped around the corner. She had forgotten how tall he was. He towered over her even though she had her boots on.

"Now now, Tad. We wen't over this last night—"

"Stella. Of course. I'll remember one day."

She was momentarily flustered. She hadn't expected him to talk over her like that. Had he grown more confident since last night? Was there something in the way they left things?

Taking another look, she realised it wasn't confidence, it was exhaustion. His dark hair was a birds nest at the best of times, now it stuck out all over. He hadn't shaved, there were rings around his eyes and he'd missed a button on his shirt.

He was a mess and obviously too tired to worry about pretty women. She took it as a challenge.

"Good God. Look at you. I didn't think I kept you up *that* late last night. I hope you were thinking of me at least."

He smiled half heartedly and looked away, his eyes settling on nothing as a frown formed. It looked like he wanted to say something but decided against it, turning back to Stella.

"Sorry, but this…" he motioned to his whole body in acknowledgement of the mess he was in. "Is the result of an unexpected guest and an ongoing battle with my daughter. Apparently I'm not as cool as the other dads."

Stella understood he was joking but couldn't bring herself to smile. She had looked into his so-called daughter last night and smelled something fishy. Stella would only play the friendly card so far. If he was a danger to that little girl then she would be on him so fast he wouldn't know what hit him.

"Ah yes, your daughter. I looked into her last night. It was certainly… unusual, how that adoption came about."

All signs of Tad's weariness vanished in an instant. Stella took a step back.

"What's that supposed to mean?"

Stella suddenly felt cold, and though she hated to admit it, a touch apprehensive. In a fraction of a second his whole persona changed, and she found herself re-evaluating her opinions. She thought back over her words and could see how he might have taken it as a threat.

"Nothing. Just conversation. I was surprised you had a daughter. It's good of you to take in a little girl like that when you were only twenty-four."

He continued to stare, weighing her with eyes that looked darker than she remembered. It was bizarre, and she wondered if she imagined it a moment later when she looked again and they were back to normal. He had reverted to the familiar, weary geek.

What the hell?

"Sorry. I'm jumping to conclusions. Like I said, it was a late night."

"Speaking of jumping to conclusions, what should I think of meeting you here? I was just on my way to that house to interview the man who lives there."

"Marcus? I thought so." He fidgeted, rubbing at the back of his neck and looking away. "He's a friend of Tommy's. I wanted to check in with him."

Damn. She believed him. No matter how much he might be her only lead, she didn't like him for this. She wasn't stupid enough to let her hunch override the evidence, but she didn't have any evidence.

"Tad. I know we spoke about this last night, but I need you tell me what you know. If you're not careful, next week I might be interviewing people looking for you."

He opened his mouth to answer, but then shook his head. "I told you last night. I don't know anything. Now, do you mind if I go? I've got to pick Jen up from school?"

She sighed, unable to even summon the strength to tease him a little more. "Go. Just be careful. And remember, call me if you need anything."

"I will. See you around, Stella."

He wasted no time stepping past her and walking to his black BMW. It was a nice car. Cardiff uni must be paying good money to keep him.

She was about to turn away but stopped. Tad was pulling the car out, and it was hard to make out for sure but… yes. He was talking to someone. A headset? Hands-free? She didn't think so. It looked like he was looking at something too.

Before she could confirm her suspicion, he turned at the end of the street. She shook her head. Maybe it was her who had been up too late last night.

Ah well. Stella was on her way home, anyway. She wasn't even supposed to be here. If her boss knew she was here, and alone, he wouldn't be pleased. Just working the investigation he had been clear should be dropped could get her suspended.

She didn't care. She had to solve a big case. She couldn't have Kate continue to sit on her pedestal of solved cases, nice and high where everyone could kiss her arse. That was Stella's seat, and she wanted it back.

She walked up the gravelled driveway toward the house and knocked on the door. She was still thinking about Tad talking to himself and how much this case meant to her so was unprepared for the response that awaited.

The man who opened the door was overweight and three inches shorter than her. His round head was bald on top with thinning brown hair in a band around the sides and back. His beady little eyes widened when he saw her. That look of sudden terror was enough to break her from her thoughts, but not quick enough to stop him pushing past her and running.

"Shit."

For a little fat man, he sure could shift. Stella sighed once, told herself she shouldn't be doing this and then started the chase.

"Stop! Police. I just want to ask a few questions," she shouted as she came to the end of the drive. He wasn't listening. He was running for all he was worth.

Stella swore again. She wasn't wearing the right shoes for running. The heels weren't too large, but they were heels so they would always be in the way. It turned out not to matter. He had the drop on her, but he was overweight where Stella had been a runner since secondary school. Eventually her conditioning payed off.

"Stop," she called again.

He looked over his shoulder which was when his foot caught an uplifted paving stone and he went rolling. Stella didn't have chance to wince in sympathy before she was upon him and had to act.

He ended up face down in a puddle of freezing water, Stella knelt with her knee in the small of his back and her hand on the back of his head. The moment she had the cuffs in place, he stopped fighting and surprised her again.

He started crying.

"Oh God. Please don't hurt me. I don't want to die. Please don't kill me."

It was an effort, but she rolled him over so she could look him in the eye. Marcus wasn't having any of that. He stared anywhere but at her, tears streaming down his cheeks. There was a nasty cut over his eye from his fall.

Stella groaned. Things were just getting better and better.

"I won't hurt you, idiot. I just wanted to talk. Didn't you hear me shouting *police*?"

The blubbering finally stopped, and he faced her nervously. "You mean, you're actually the police?"

She fished her warrant card out of her coat. "Yes I am. Who the hell did you think I was?"

He shook his head nervously. "I thought you were her."

"Her who?"

"The woman Tommy told me about. That's why you're here, right? About Tommy."

Suddenly she was excited. "Yes. About Tommy. What woman?"

He groaned again and tried to sit up. It was difficult with his hands behind his back. "A little help?" he asked.

"You won't run?"

"Not now I know who you are. Besides, you already got me once."

She fished her key out of her pocket. "The pavement did most the work."

The man laughed. When his hands were free, he scrambled back to his feet.

"This is embarrassing. If I knew you were a cop then—"

"Don't worry about it. All I'm interested in is whatever you know about this woman and what you told Tad."

"Tad? You mean that guy who was here a few moments ago?" He chuckled again. "I didn't tell him anything. Didn't know if I could trust him. He seemed odd, not on the level. Maybe he's working for them?"

She was starting to think that this guy wasn't on the level. "Them who?"

He looked at her as though she were slow. "Whoever took Tommy and the others. It's got to be something to do with the ghosts, you know. I always told Tommy that stuff wasn't natural."

Damn. There it was again. Ghosts. Why did people keep talking like that? She couldn't believe she had to take it seriously. Word had come down from on high, but could she really write that in her reports?

"Slow down. Go back to the beginning. What do you know?"

He took a deep breath and nodded. "I knew Tommy from way back. He's always been weird, talking to himself and all that. He used to say he could see ghosts. We thought he was nuts."

He leaned in closer and looked around as though he were about to divulge a massive secret.

"But then I saw one last year. Started as cold spots in the house, you know, the usual stuff you see in movies. Then I saw it. It was a scary fucking thing. All shadows and the like. It came right at me like it wanted to eat me, but all it did was touch me and I went cold."

"Cold?"

"Yeah. Cold and numb. It was strange. But then my mind started working and I got the hell out of there. I mean, come on. Big scary ghost, right? I wasn't sticking around. That was when I remembered Tommy. I gave him a ring, and he told me he'd take a look. I never went in with him so I don't know what he did, but the ghost never came back."

He chuckled again. "I know this sounds crazy, but it's the truth. It's just like all them news stories. Ghosts are real, I promise—"

"I believe you. Please. Keep going."

"Right. Well, I was grateful to Tommy and I felt kinda bad. I'd given him stick in the past. I started hanging out with him to make up for it. Then about two weeks ago he acts all strange. Keeps telling me he's being followed. I asked him how he knows and he says his ghosts told him."

"His ghosts?"

"Yeah. He used to have a few of them. Nice ones. They followed him around." He started snapping his fingers over and over as he tried to remember something. "What was it he called himself? Ah yeah, that's right. He said he was a Roxy."

"Roxy?"

He laughed. "Yeah. That's what I thought. A girls name, right? You know, I saw the ghost, but I still think he was a little touched. Anyway, he says his ghosts saw a woman following him. Gave a description that pretty much matches you. They didn't mention how pretty she was, so they probably weren't talking about you. They would have said something otherwise, right? I mean, you're really hot."

She smiled indulgently but it was all she could do not to look away in disgust. Honestly. Some guys.

"I thought he was just being paranoid. Then he disappears and people start looking for him, weirdos like Tad."

"You get names and contact info for these people?"

"Yeah, I've got something back at the house."

"That's good. Really good. So what happened next?"

"That's it. Tommy went missing, weird people come looking and you turn up looking like her. I figured you were here to kill me."

"That's it. Nothing else about this woman?"

He shook his head but then clicked his fingers again.

"Wait, there was one thing. Tommy said she was foreign. He wasn't sure where from, but definitely not the UK. That's all I know though."

Not much. But it was more than she had before.

"That's great. What do you say we head back to your house and get those numbers?"

"You going to leave yours in return?" he asked. It was a testament to Stella's professionalism that she didn't lose character for a second.

"Of course." She reached into her pocket for a business card. He looked crestfallen when she didn't give him something more personal, but took it anyway and stepped away from the wall. He took one wobbly step and would have fallen had Stella not been there to catch him.

"Whoa. You feel that? I didn't think we got earthquakes like that in Wales."

"We don't." She glanced at the cut over his eye and winced. She should have done something about it sooner. "Let's hurry and get those details. Then we'll take a trip to the emergency room."

By the time Stella left the hospital the sun was long gone, it was pouring down again, and she was ready for bed. She wouldn't sleep though. She was too wired. Finally she had something to work from.

The woman. The constant references to ghosts. This Tommy guy being a Roxy, whatever the hell that was.

And then there was Thaddeus Holcroft.

Even though she had something that led her in a direction away from him, she was sure he knew more than he was letting on. The more she thought about it, the more certain she was that he was talking to himself earlier.

A weird bloke. She'd find out what he was hiding before this was over.

For now she needed pyjamas, a glass of wine and some trashy TV.

As good as her intentions were however, she was back at the station by nine. She was sure that there must be mention of a woman that matched her own description somewhere in the statements she collected. She just needed to find it.

6

Monday, 16th November 2015
18:00

Kate lived in the valleys, more than an hour from Cardiff. Whenever Tad drove there he questioned how she managed the commute. She was waiting at the door when they arrived, making him think she had his car tracked. It was more likely that she was eager to see Miriam. Not for the first time his heart broke for her.

Her ex-council house, built in the forties, had been extended recently. Sadly, as nice as it looked, it remained in the valleys so it was up a massive hill. It was even higher than the road with a steep grassy incline separating the front of the house from the street.

The moment Tad parked, Jen, who still hadn't forgiven him for last night, opened her door, letting the freezing cold into the toasty BMW interior.

"Jen wait," Tad said. "Give Miriam and Kate some time alone."

She glared at him long enough for Miriam to slip through the door and run up the hill. She stopped just short of Kate and they talked briefly before leaning in close as though to kiss. They couldn't touch though, and again Tad's sympathies went out to the pair.

"There, they've had some alone time."

"Jen, no—"

He was too late. She sprinted up the hill, pushed past Kate, and turned right after entering the house. Had she turned left to the kitchen where Kate entertained, he'd have given into his frustration and chased her. Right was the living room and, more importantly, the PlayStation which might keep her quiet, so he decided to let her be.

He leaned back, sighed and decided to wait five minutes before going inside. This left him alone with Maggie for the first time all day.

"You're doing a good thing with Jen," Maggie said.

"I don't know. I love her, but I don't think I made the right choice. It's hard. We argue all the time."

"That's just families."

"No, it's more than that. She blames me for her parents moving on. After this whole mess with Proxies disappearing is sorted, I'll think again on whether it's working. It'd kill me to give her up, but I've got to do what's best for her."

"Don't second guess yourself. You're better together than you think. Trust me. I was her age once. You should know after last night. Remember how often I had to sneak out to see you? It's the same with Jen. You'll sort it in a few years."

"Years?" He almost choked and she laughed.

Before the awkward silence could return, Maggie asked, "How come Kate can see Miriam?"

He looked at her and tapped his head. "You could find out yourself if you look for it. You have access to everything I know now we've merged. It'll fade in a few hours, it only lasts about a day, but should still be there now."

"I'm new at this. Humour me."

"It's my gift. I can show ghosts to people who aren't Proxies."

"Since when? Have you been holding out on me?"

"I figured out how to do it a few years ago. It's getting stronger as well. Until recently I would've had to be in the same room with them. Now I can manage it so long as they're within a hundred feet."

"Did another Proxy teach you?"

"Most of what I do is instinct, no one has to teach me. The only problem with this is that they can't touch. It makes me wonder if it's a gift or a curse. This way neither of them has chance to move on. Seeing each other but not being able to touch just opens old wounds."

"That's awful," Maggie said. "Maybe Miriam should move on."

"You try suggesting it. She says she has too much to do."

"I thought they'd caught her killer."

"They did. That's why Kate's a detective. No, it's Miriam's personal hangups. She's always been awesome at what she does. She can't do it directly, but through me and Kate, she can still help. At least that's what she says. I think she's just waiting for Kate."

Tad decided enough time had passed. He caught Maggie's attention, nodded to the house, and stepped out of the car. He burrowed deep into his coat and kept his head down against the bitter wind. Winter had been late coming and was trying to make up for lost time. At least it wasn't raining. He didn't want to test out his new coat quite yet.

Tad was half way up the steps when he realised Maggie wasn't with him. He turned to see her mouthing the words, *Open the door.*

He laughed and shook his head. He'd been willing to accommodate her the night before, but wouldn't go so far as opening the door for a ghost on a street as busy as this. She'd have to learn sooner or later.

The first he knew that she made it out of the car was when she hit him on the arm.

"You could've opened the door, you bastard."

"Why? You just needed to step through it."

"That's weird. It makes me feel like I'm—"

"Dead? I hate to break it to you—"

"Shut up. Say one more word and I'll be the one breaking it to you… with my fists."

He laughed and stepped into the house, this time holding the door for her. "You always were crap at threats."

"That's because you catch more flies with honey than vinegar."

"Yes, and you catch even more with shit so—"

She snorted. "I saw that episode of The Big Bang Theory. Don't go ripping off their jokes."

He smiled, closed the door behind her and led her into the kitchen, slipping off his coat as he walked and relishing the warmth of the house.

Kate and Miriam were deep in conversation but hushed upon seeing them. Judging by the look on Kate's face, she already knew everything there was to know about Maggie.

Kate was dressed down for the night. She was tall for a woman, nearly six foot. The trouble was it wasn't all legs and curves like a supermodel, but instead a thickset build that could be quite masculine unless she took pains to emphasise her femininity. Jeans and a t-shirt along with her fair hair being tied back did little to help.

She stood and walked to the fridge, removing a bottle of beer that was tempting. She waved it Tad's way with a grin, and when he refused, she laughed wickedly and kept it for herself.

"I keep telling you. Come over on the weekend and you won't have to worry about driving home," Kate said in her thick, valley's accent.

"Yeah well, things to do and all that. Kate, this is Maggie. Maggie, Kate."

Again Kate laughed. She had a deep but wicked laugh that she wasn't afraid to use.

"Oh, I know who she is, I've been looking at her face all day." She grinned and nodded to Maggie over her beer. "I've got to say love, you're looking better than when I last saw you."

"That bad?" Maggie asked, awkwardly sitting on a chair behind the table without having to manoeuvre it. Tad wondered how she thought she was sitting down without touching it. She'd get it soon enough.

"It was bad," Kate agreed, bringing her beer to the table and taking a seat. To Tad she said, "There's a Coke in the fridge, help yourself."

He did so, grabbing a can before joining them around the table. Kate sat with Miriam on one side so Tad took his place next to Maggie on the other.

"What do you know?" he asked.

"Pretty much what you told me. The body... sorry hun, I meant your body. I'll never get used to this ghost thing." Maggie waved her off. "You were right where you said to look. As we hoped, I landed the case."

She swigged her beer, burped loudly which earned a frown from Miriam but made Maggie laugh, and then continued.

"Like I said, you were a mess, and you were hidden pretty good, so it wasn't a hard sell to get it classified as murder. The trouble is, there wasn't much evidence at the scene."

"What about's Mark's place?" Maggie asked.

"That's what I'm trying to tell you, love. There's no evidence tying your murder to Mark, definitely not enough for a warrant."

"Her word isn't enough?" Tad asked. "Stella said that—"

"Yeah, well Stella doesn't know everything." Her answer was sharp and angry, there was no love lost between those two. "We've been told to take ghost sightings seriously, but there's ghost sightings and there's letting a ghost stand witness to her own murder. On top of that you'd need to make a statement before we could act. That would mean Tad showing the world what he could do. Even then I'm not sure it would stand up."

"Why not?" Maggie asked, her good humour gone and her tone accusatory.

"Because you're not easy to get hold of anymore. It's not like we can call you when we need to ask something. Who knows, you might even move on before the trial."

"I could promise not to, and you can always reach me through Tad."

Kate continued as though Maggie hadn't spoken. "All that's without mentioning that this is new ground. Our laws don't account for ghost testimony and not everyone will believe what we're selling. Tad's gift won't work on video... it won't, right?" Tad shook his head. "That's another reason not to do this. If we can't record your statement, then..."

Look. There's just too many downsides and unknowns at the moment. I can't move on Mark yet."

"This is bullshit. I'm actually telling you who the killer is and you won't do anything about it."

Maggie stood up so fast her legs went through her chair. She was shaking and pulled away when Tad grabbed her hand. Eventually she relented and sat back down, but her anger remained. If Kate was fazed by it, it didn't show.

"I know where you're coming from. It's not fair and it's hard. But that doesn't mean we're out of options, just that *I'm* out of options."

"What does that mean?"

"That you're forgetting what you are," Miriam answered, a sly smile on her face. "Kate can't do any more, but that doesn't mean we can't. We're ghosts. No locked doors can keep us out. You and me can pay Mark's place a visit and see what we can find. If that doesn't work we can follow him." Her grin broadened further. "Ghosts are very good at following people."

Kate gave her ex-girlfriend a quick grin before turning that smile on Maggie. "See. We're not out of this yet. You and Mims should look for something concrete that I can act on. We'll get him. Don't worry."

That mollified Maggie somewhat and she nodded at them. She apologised for her outburst and with typical casualness Kate waved the apology away.

There was a sour mood until Maggie asked, "So. *Mims?* That's cute."

Kate laughed and Miriam blushed, glaring furiously at the woman she loved. Miriam had always been conservative. Public displays of affection and pet names were not her thing. Kate however was a valley girl to the bone. She didn't care what people thought of her and had no problems saying anything that was on her mind.

Her laughter set the tone for the evening from there on out.

"So where's my pal Charles? Not enough room in the car?"

Tad sipped his drink and shook his head. "He's babysitting."

"But the munchkin's here," Kate said before realisation dawned and her face clouded. "Tony."

If Miriam was put out by the teenaged ghost, Kate hated him. She had a short temper at the best of times and didn't have Miriam's understanding of what it was like to be dead. It was easy to think Tony should have grown up, but he had been locked at that mental age since he died. There's no progression for the dead. They make new memories, but otherwise are the exact bundle of emotions and desires they were when they died.

"Yeah, he's keeping an eye on the little perv," Miriam confirmed. "But I think he needed a night off. Last night really got to him."

"Last night?" Kate asked.

Miriam and Tad filled her in on their adventure at Cardiff castle. When they were done Kate shook her head and whistled in appreciation.

"Wow. Who knew Charles had it in him? I always said he was one of the good ones. I see why he's shaken up though."

"Am I missing something?" Maggie asked.

"It's not normal for ghosts to stick around as long as Charles. Most only hang around for a few years, even with a Proxy, maybe a few decades at most. Charles has been a ghost for a hundred-and-fifty," Tad said.

"So why has he stayed so long?"

"He'll tell you its because he loves to watch human progression. The truth is he's terrified of moving on. He's also terrified of becoming mad like the ghosts we saw last night. The longer he sticks around the closer he gets to being like that. A Proxy keeps him grounded, but if I wasn't around, then it wouldn't be long before he lost his sanity. You might last a year or two, but Charles has been here too long."

"And last night he had to face a few of those fears," Maggie said as understanding dawned.

"Not just last night," Kate said. "Tad's been getting himself into all kind of shit recently. Since the Proxies have been disappearing Tad's been picking up their slack, dealing with hauntings and stuff. Tad's often in danger and with fewer Proxies around, Charles has less chance of finding a new one before he goes mad. Personally, I think the big idiot needs to bite the bullet and move on. He's got nothing to worry about. We all know he's going to a good place."

Tad smiled and shook his head. "He wasn't a model of human goodness in life. It's not nearly enough to warrant punishment, but it's enough to frighten him about where he might end up."

"He's done enough good since he died," Miriam pointed out. "Last night wasn't normal, but it's not the first time he risked himself for someone else. He's a good man."

"You don't have to tell me," Tad said. "I agree. It's convincing him that's the problem."

"It might not be a problem after tonight," Kate said. "After a night with Tony, he'll probably move on just to get away from the little freak."

"Talking of the little freak," Miriam said. "You'd never guess what he did the other day."

Her story started out as complaints, but soon had everyone laughing. As annoying as he was in person, Tony never failed to make people laugh when they remembered his antics. It lead to more shared stories about him, and even Maggie had some from when she couldn't even see Tony.

The good natured complaints turned into general chatter, and for the next few hours they spoke about more mundane matters. The evening turned into a pleasant affair that brought Jen out of hiding. She still wasn't talking to Tad, but she liked everyone else well enough.

However, as pleasant as the evening was, there was the matter of an hour long drive to get home. When Tad called it a night, it wasn't just Miriam and Kate who were reluctant. He suspected Jen's motives had more to do with extending her bedtime than anything else. He was about to tell her to get herself ready to go when Kate came to her rescue.

"Leave the munchkin here. I haven't seen her in ages and we could do with a little girl time."

Jen suddenly had that hopeful gleam in her eye. Kate and Miriam had come into her life at the same time as Tad. He may be her guardian, but Kate was a close second in her affections for the child. The annoying thing to Tad was that she never had to put up with the version of Jen he lived with.

"She's got school in the morning."

"And I've got to be at the station by eight. If she can handle getting up early, it's not going to be a problem."

"What about her uniform and books?"

"I'll swing by on my way in."

Tad still wasn't convinced. It was a long way out of her way.

"Please?" Jen begged, addressing Tad directly for the first time that day. "I'll be good. I promise."

He snorted. "I know. It's not you I'm worried about this time."

Kate cackled gleefully.

"You worried about me corrupting her? You should be. I'll make a valley girl out of her yet."

He winced but couldn't help but smile. "Fine. But don't let her stay up too late."

Kate waved her hand dismissively. "As if I would." She winked at Jen without subtlety which made Jen giggle. It was a good sound, one he hadn't heard much of recently. That more than anything swayed him.

"Fine. You can stay. But—"

"Yay. Thank you. Thank you. Thank you." In her excitement Jen forgot her hang ups and hugged him, each *thank you* being punctuated with a kiss on the cheek. In spite of everything he grinned. Why couldn't he see this Jen more often?

"You won't regret this," she promised.

Now she said it, he knew he probably would, but was prepared to take her at her word.

Five minutes later he was at the door hugging Kate goodbye, then he and Maggie walked to the car alone to give Miriam time for her own goodbye.

Again, he refused to open the door for Maggie, so she stuck her tongue out at him, scrunched up her eyes and jumped at the door. She went through but landed in an awkward position.

Tad burst out laughing which earned him a glare from Maggie that slowly turned into a laugh of her own.

"That was the most ridiculous thing I've ever seen."

She again stuck her tongue out, but was still smiling.

They settled in to wait for Miriam and slowly the good mood evaporated. Tad realised that as soon as Miriam came down that hill they would head home and eventually to bed. That meant merging with Maggie again. They didn't need to share any more memories, but the awkwardness remained.

"Why didn't you tell me?"

He knew what she was talking about. Evidently he wasn't the only one not looking forward to the coming night.

"It wouldn't have made a difference."

"It might have."

His laugh was a touch bitter. "Really? I saw your memories, Mags. I know you didn't feel the same way. It's fine. This is why I never said anything. I knew it would come between us."

"Well I suppose it did in the end anyway."

She had a point, but he shook his head. "I was only looking out for you."

She didn't answer for a while. "I get it now."

"What?"

"Why you're the way you are. You've had experiences like last night with all your ghosts, haven't you?" He nodded. "Then that's why you can't see that you did anything wrong by following Mark."

"Mags, he was a bad dude."

"That's not the point. He was my boyfriend and I loved him. You decided you didn't like him and had him followed. Don't you see what a violation that is?" Again the bitter laugh. "Of course you don't. You haven't had a moment's privacy since you were nine. It's probably not a big deal to you, but it massively violated my trust in you."

"I had to protect you, Mags. Just like I always have."

"You could do that by being there for me when I needed you, not sneaking around my back. Mark was a dick and his true colours would've shone through eventually. Who knows how things would have turned out if you'd been there for me to talk to about it."

"So it's my fault you're dead?"

"What? No. That's not what I meant. I just… Fuck. I don't know. I suppose I wanted you to know how I felt. It's only fair after… well, you know."

Again there was a pregnant pause before she added, "You could have told me. I didn't feel that way about you, but if you'd told me it might have been different. You were the most important person in my life. If you said something I'm sure I could have learned to—"

"That's just it. I didn't want you to *learn* to do anything. Having to learn to like me isn't the start of a good relationship. I'd rather we kept things the way they were."

Just as Miriam was coming out of the house, Maggie asked, "Do you want me to find another Proxy? I know how hard this is for you and I will if you—"

"No. Don't. I'm past the worst of it. You know now and we can move on. I can get past this, I promise. Besides, you were right last night. I was letting our last argument get in the way of helping a friend. It's not right."

"So long as you're sure."

Just then Miriam slipped into the back seat of the car. "Come on, lets go." She was always eager to leave after a visit with Kate. It was almost as though she thought a hasty exit could save her from the inevitable heartache.

For once, Tad was happy to comply.

7

Tuesday, 17th November 2015
02:39

As always Tad was blind within the entry room to his dreams. Yet there was no way he could miss it.

There was a new door in his mind.

Strangely, it felt familiar. It wasn't a door into memories, but somewhere else.

For four years Tad's strength as a Proxy had increased. The benefits gained from merging with his ghosts were lasting longer, as was his impact on them. Beyond that he could do new things like making the dead visible and walking through walls. The rate at which these strengths developed increased with every passing year.

It should be a comfort. Surely it was never a bad sign to get better at what you do. But, as he examined this new door, Tad couldn't help but think yet again that things were not right with the world.

Considering curiosity had always been his downfall, he reached out and turned the handle.

He stepped into an all consuming grey space that stretched on forever. It was the epitome of the word empty and was easily the most terrifying thing he had ever encountered. His mind recoiled in horror and only instinct protected him as he turned his mind inward to escape this reality. He thought of home.

Just imagining his home made it real. He both recognised and didn't recognise the room he stood in. It was an odd sensation. He knew in his heart that it was his bedroom but it looked nothing like his bedroom. It was too big and he had never had a large glass wall that overlooked a tropical beach.

Yet, it was his bedroom. He was sure of it.

It took a while to recognise the sensation. When he figured it out, he had to fight back tears.

He was dreaming.

He hadn't dreamt since he first joined with Charles. Tad's nights were spent either in his memories or his ghost's. He never came to this place where anything within imagination was possible.

The few dreams he remembered as a child were like this. Fantastic places that were familiar while he slept, but when he woke he wondered how he ever thought they were like anywhere he had ever been.

Unlike when he dreamed as a child, he was aware he was dreaming. Being aware you're asleep was much like being a ghost, you became the master of your reality.

Tad was suddenly grinning and eager to explore this dream. He didn't know what to expect and didn't care so long as he was somewhere new.

He opened the door to his bedroom and looked out. The corridor beyond was endless with thousands of doors lining each side. The idea of walking it was uncomfortable, but when he turned back his bedroom was no longer there. Instead there was just the other end of the hallway stretching off to nowhere.

A sense of unease gripped him but he forced a laugh. "Freaky," he said out loud.

"What?"

He turned and was surprised to find Jen stood in an open doorway, dressed for bed and rubbing her eyes. The rubbing stopped when she saw Tad.

"You're not supposed to be here."

He laughed. "I think it's the other way around. This is my head."

She frowned and took another step out the door. "What do you mean it's your head? This is my dream. The one with the endless corridor and…" Her words trailed off and her eyes widened. "I know I'm dreaming."

"What?"

"I know I'm dreaming," she repeated, amazed. "It's like when mum and dad were still with me. I know I'm dreaming. I mean, I know I'm asleep but I feel awake."

A suspicion formed in Tad's mind.

"Jen. I want you to tell me something about what you've done with Kate since we left. Something I couldn't know."

Surprisingly quick on the uptake, Jen understood instantly and looked even more amazed. Tad enjoyed seeing the expression of childish wonder on her face, it had been too long.

"You think you're not part of my dream. You think you're actually Tad and our minds have merged, just like with the ghosts."

"Not like with the ghosts," he disagreed. "But yes, that's close enough. I don't know how this happened, but I think the new door lead me to—"

"New door?"

"The one in my mind that normally leads to my ghost's memories."

She frowned. "I don't remember that. Maybe it was different for me. I was in a sweet shop, but there were only three jars on the shelf. When I opened one and tasted a sweet, I would see a memory of either my mum, my dad or me."

He blinked. "You never told me that."

Her good humour slipped. "You never let me talk about Proxy stuff. I like my way better. A load of doors sound boring. Kind of like this."

She nodded to the long corridor. He had to agree and wished he was somewhere more open. Instantly the walls sank into the floor, the ceiling vanished, and they were left standing in a carpeted corridor that ran down the centre of an open field. He sensed nothing but rolling hills covered in lush, green grass and daisies for miles around. The sun that beat down on him felt all too real.

When he turned his attention back to Jen, he found her wearing a pale blue summer dress and sandals. Her hair, which she normally tied back for bed, was loose and curled about her shoulders.

"Wow. How'd you do that?" she asked.

"I don't know. I wished I was somewhere more open, a field was the first thing that came to mind and then… this."

She laughed, tugging her new clothes as if testing how real they were. "That. Is. Awesome."

For once they were in agreement.

"What else can we do?" she asked. "You think we can fly?"

No sooner had she said it when suddenly her feet left the floor. She wobbled and let out a startled yelp, but then she was laughing and she floated up higher.

"This is awesome!"

With a thought, Tad rose beside her. "You already said that."

She glanced at him out of the corner of her eye and he didn't trust her crooked grin. "Race you back to the city."

She didn't wait for his response before she zipped away. It was like watching a Road Runner cartoon. One minute she was there and next there was only a cloud shaped like her and a blur leading off to the distance.

"Awesome," Tad agreed before suddenly there was his own Tad shaped cloud and another blur chasing after Jen.

He didn't catch sight of her right away, but the sound of her giggling came back over the vast distance between them. Again he thought of the Road Runner cartoons and he had a plan to close the distance.

No sooner had he thought it when suddenly the giggling stopped and he heard a startled grunt.

He zipped by Jen who was now tangled in a large net that appeared from nowhere and it was his turn to laugh as he flew by.

"Not fair," Jen said, and the words were audible even though she was already miles behind. "Two can play that game."

The impact was staggering.

He saw the shadow first, but not in time to react. It was the size of a mountain and came down on him with such force that he had no choice but to let it crush him against the ground.

Just a thought made that ground marshmallow, and he sank into it. Another thought and he was standing beside the object that had crushed him. He was covered in pink marshmallow gunk and standing beside the world's largest, wooden mallet. It was taken right from a cartoon.

Jen was only a few feet away, and she was crying with laughter.

"A mallet, Jen. You could have killed me?"

She just laughed harder. He tried to remain stern but there was no way he was keeping his frown with her laughing like that.

"It's like that, is it?"

It took her a moment to understand his meaning, but she wasn't quick enough to react to the steam train that came from nowhere to wipe her out.

A giant fly swatter was her retaliation. He dropped a squid on her head. That got him a hive of bees dropped on him from a height which in turn got her blown up with Wile E. Coyote's famous Acme dynamite.

It was a constant game of escalation that continued to be fun until she sent the shadows after him.

Everything to that point had been the brightly coloured fun of a cartoon. Just dreams that weren't harming anyone. The shadow creatures were not bright, and he had felt that kind of cold before.

With their appearance the sky turned black as night, while the grass at his feet withered and died. For once he was glad he didn't have eyesight. He had a feeling that with sight alone he would have thought Jen was channelling the darker parts of her imagination. With that other sense, an instinctive knowledge of the world, he knew she had gone to a much more terrifying place.

"Enough Jen," he called as the shadow creature came closer. It was a long billowing cloud of smokey shadow that coalesced in places into the vision of a skeletal hand that reached for him. He flashed back to the ghost of the other night and at once the shadowy creature twisted into the same scary visage.

"It's not me," Jen cried, and he turned in time to see a second shadow approaching her.

Panic and fury gripped him at once. He was overcome with the need to fight them, to save himself and, more importantly, Jen.

He imagined the destruction he had dealt to the final ghost the other night and applied it to these spectres. In his panic he made it much more powerful and the ghost in front of him burst into radiant light that washed away the shadows and brought back the warmth, before being quickly overcome again.

Tad ran toward where Jen was backing away from another ghost. This one had twin heads that were shaped like her dead parents. He didn't hesitate before destroying it as well. He scooped Jen into his arms and she clung tight, burying her face against his chest and crying hard.

"What's happening?" Jen asked between sobs. "Why did they come for me like that?"

The answer, like everything in that place, came by instinct.

"They're nightmares," he said. "They're taking your deepest fears and turning them against us." Even as he said it he saw another shadow descend. He destroyed it as quick as he could.

"I want them to go," she said. "Why won't they go?"

That he had no answer for.

He instinctively knew the rules of the place. It was a dream, they were its masters. They should be in charge here and they should be able to banish the nightmares by thinking more pleasant thoughts. But it wasn't working.

As easy as Tad was finding it to destroy the creatures, he could feel the true power of nightmare sinking into him. Despair.

"Come on. Let's try to leave. Maybe they won't follow."

"Oh, they always follow." The voice that answered was every bit as despairing as Tad felt.

Tad sensed the appearance of a new figure behind him and suddenly knew why the nightmares were here. They had come for this man.

"Who are you?" Tad asked.

"It doesn't matter. It'll be over soon enough."

He was old, maybe seventy, and wore a cardigan with corduroy trousers, the hems of which were baggy over his slippers. Everything about him said retiree, comfortable in his own home save for the knife that protruded from his chest.

Blood poured from the wound far too freely to be real or he would already be dead. Who knew, in this place maybe he was dead.

"Tad? I want to go home," Jen whispered from her position against his chest. He wanted nothing more than to take her home, but he needed answers first. He had the sense that whatever was happening was important and he couldn't go yet.

"Who are you?" Tad repeated.

The man sighed and said, "James Tanner."

"You're a Proxy?"

The man looked surprised to be recognised, but nodded.

"I'm Tad. This is my daughter, Jen. We're Proxies too. What's happening here?"

"She got me. Took me too him. There was nothing I could do."

"What are you talking about? You're not making sense."

The world was growing colder and darker with every passing second. Anything living had long since died away and all that was left was an empty wasteland of blackened dirt and clouds of dust. Overhead thousands of shadows spiralled like some great tornado of circling vultures.

"My ghosts kept spotting a dark haired woman following me. They said she had the Cleopatra look, whatever that means. We were all keeping an eye out for her, but it didn't help. Last night I was getting ready for bed, turned around and there she is. Came from nowhere without any of my ghosts seeing.

"Next thing I know I'm waking up in a place that's looking a lot like this. Only there was a great, stone table and… *him*." He must have been catholic as his hand made the sign of the cross. "He's the devil. You'll understand if you ever see him."

"I still don't understand what you mean," Tad said in frustration. It was in vain. He had lost the old man's attention. James was looking into the distance and all his strength had left him.

"He's coming," he said. "I can feel it." Turning back to Tad and Jen he said, "Go. Wake yourselves and run. Don't stop until you have half the planet between you and this nightmare. Who knows, maybe that will keep you safe. I doubt it. But maybe."

Tad was shaking his head. "What are you—"

He didn't finish his sentence. Suddenly there was another presence pressing against his senses, another Proxy. The power he felt from this Proxy was like nothing he had felt before and suddenly he was terrified.

"Go," the man whispered, a look of resignation on his face. "Get out of here before he comes."

"Come with us."

He shook his head and smiled sadly. "It's too late for me. Go."

With his final word the last of Tad's resolve left. That thing was coming closer, and he knew that above all else he did not want to be here when it arrived.

He took one last look at the man and then willed himself to safety. It was as simple as anything else in the dream. One minute he was in a deserted wasteland and the next he was in his round room with the six doors. It felt as though they hadn't even moved, that the walls had grown around them. Even so Tad knew they were far from that place. Whatever nightmare came for James would not find them.

"I want to wake up," Jen said. He could sense the panic radiating off her in waves.

"I know. I'll show you how in a second. First, say that man's name for me."

"What?"

"Humour me. Please."

She pulled away and looked up at him with tear filled eyes. "James Tanner," she said. "I'll never forget it."

"Nor I," Tad agreed. "Tomorrow, when we see each other, I'll ask you for that name. If you can tell me—"

Her eyes widened in understanding and she finished his sentence. "Then we'll know this wasn't just a dream."

He smiled at her. "Exactly. Now, time to wake up. All you have to do is say, *Excitare*. It means awaken in Latin. It's like a magic word. When you say it, imagine waking up and you'll wake up."

She stared at him, her hazel eyes round and filled with tears. In a stage whisper she said, "Excitare."

She vanished.

It was all rubbish. Another of his tricks like giving clothes to Maggie. All he had to do to wake up was imagine himself awake. He knew other Proxies who had trouble with it though, so he made up that nonsense for them to try. The truth was much like it was for ghosts. All they had to do was realise they were in charge and they could wake up. He just gave them a way to do that.

Knowing that Jen was safely gone, he too opened his eyes.

Twenty-five past seven found Tad in the kitchen with a steaming coffee and a racing mind.

His ghosts woke with him, confused by the lack of his presence in their memories. Tad decided not to tell them what happened. He needed proof before he bothered them with another worry.

It was no good. They knew him well enough to see through his deception, but had the grace to leave him be.

He was lost in thought when the silhouette grew against the window of the back door. When he heard the handle turn he was out of his seat in a second. Jen was just as fast, rushing through the door into his arms.

"There he is. Happy now?" asked an irritated Kate. "If you two can't spend one night apart then you've got problems."

Tad ignored her. Instead, he pushed Jen away and asked, "What was his name?"

"James Tanner."

It had been real.

After a morning of consideration, he was certain they had witnessed the end of a Proxy last night.

"Don't worry," he said in response to her rising panic. "We don't know it was real yet."

"We just proved it."

"No. We proved that you and I shared a dream. We won't know for sure until I find out if he's missing… or if he even exists."

She took a step back and wiped a tear from her eye. "I want to help."

"No. You've got school."

Her typical anger returned and she said. "You need my help. That thing is too dangerous."

"You have school," he repeated. "That's final."

She glared at him, her mouth open as though she were about to shout, but finally accepted her fate and stormed toward her room. Whatever bonding they had done in the dreamworld was lost to him already.

Easy come, easy go.

Kate stepped into the kitchen. "I think I've missed something here?"

He nodded, but waited until his ghosts arrived before explaining his shared dream.

"What are you going to do?" Charles asked. Of them all, he knew Tad best and knew he wouldn't sit around waiting for this danger to find them. It was why his voice shook and he looked on the verge of fleeing. Things had been bad enough already, no doubt all Charles saw in this latest complication was an escalation of their troubles.

"I'll find out if James Tanner exists, then figure out where to go next." He looked at the clock and said, "But we've got a lecture first,

Charles. We'll head to work, then after that you'll have to come with me if you don't mind."

"Of course not. We have a responsibility to those students so we must attend the lecture. But I'm not sure you're making the right play here, Thaddeus. If what happened in your dream was true, then going after it is the last thing we should be doing."

"Alright. You don't have to come with me," Tad said, not looking for the argument he could feel coming. "I'll go to the lecture with you and then I'll look into James Tanner on my own."

Charles' nostrils flared, his eyebrows shot up and his chin quivered. Tad took a step back as Charles turned purple, looking like he would explode.

"Now see here, don't think to call me a coward, Thaddeus."

"I never said—"

"I just recommended staying clear of this because it would be the safer course of events. I am thinking of Jen's safety, and your own. Don't think to—"

Tad didn't want to argue, but he was operating on very little sleep and a rough few days. The implication that he wasn't putting Jen first struck him the wrong way and suddenly he was every bit as angry as his oldest friend.

"For God's sake Charles. It's not a competition. I'm not calling you a coward or passing judgement. Don't get so defensive. Never suggest that I'm not doing what's best for Jen or use her as an excuse to get your own way.

"Yes, investigating what happened last night could be dangerous, but ignorance is worse. If I took James Tanner's advice and moved, how would I know which part of the world is the furthest away from a threat I've never even heard of? I need more information if I'm going to protect Jen, so don't fucking lecture me about keeping her safe."

It wasn't just Charles who stared at him in shock, but it was Kate who broke the silence.

"Holy shit guys. That got out of hand quickly. I've never seen you two go at it like that before."

"Me neither," Miriam was quick to add.

"Nor me," Tony whispered. Maggie just nodded, otherwise staying out of it.

Seeing all of their eyes on him, Tad fought back a wave of embarrassment, sighed and tried to shake off the adrenaline tremors in his fingers.

"You're right. I'm sorry… I shouldn't have—"

"No Thaddeus, that was on me. I… I'll admit, I could have handled it better. Things have been getting dicey around here and… well… I will confess to feeling a little more anxiety than normal. I think that maybe it got to me. You're right, I should never have doubted that you would do anything for that little girl. We all know it. Please, forgive me."

"Of course. And Charles, never think I believe you're a coward. We've all seen you face your fears to save others. But you're right that things are getting more serious and we need to be cautious. That's why I need you with me this afternoon. I need to find out what's happening before whatever it is that came after the others comes after me and Jen. I've got this feeling that if we don't act soon, we'll be too late to do anything."

"Of course I'll be there, Thaddeus."

Tad smiled and clapped his friend on the shoulder. He turned to Miriam. "Why don't you stick with Maggie today. You two should go see what you can find about Mark."

"Are you sure? This thing with the Proxies sounds serious and maybe we should concentrate on that for now."

"It is serious," Tad agreed. "But, we only have the one lead. Charles and I are more than capable of handling it. However, Mark could be destroying evidence on Maggie's case as we speak and you'd be most helpful there."

Miriam hesitated only a moment longer before nodding at Maggie.

"What about me?" Tony asked.

"What about you?" Kate snapped. "You've probably got a busy

day of peering into the girl's changing room or watching uni-students showering."

Tony grinned. "No, I just hang out at the locker rooms at the police station and see what's going on there."

"You're lucky you're dead you little perv. If you weren't—"

"Then you still wouldn't do anything because you're a cop and can't do things like that."

Kate's grin was filled with menace. "There's lots of places to hide bodies in the valleys. Being police has just taught me how to better get away with it."

"It's a good thing I'm dead then. You can't get me here."

"But I can," Miriam said. Tony blew her a kiss in response and when Miriam's face darkened, he made his first smart move of the day. He backed off.

"You know," he said as he was walking out the door. "I think I'll hang around with Jen today. She appreciates me at least. Besides, it'll be good to watch her back."

"When she's clothed, Tony!" Tad warned and for the first time Tony looked uncomfortable. A pissed off Proxy was not something any ghost wanted to worry about.

"Of course. She's twelve, dude. That's—"

"Nothing to you. You're still fourteen in your head. It won't be long until she looks your age. I'm saying this now to get it out the way. Steer clear. Be her friend, watch over her, but that's it."

Tony held up his hand in surrender and backed out of the room. "Of course. Sheesh. What's with the Tony hating this morning? It only happens whenever there's a dyke reunion—"

"So help me God, Tony," Kate snarled.

Tony fled. He was a good kid at heart, but Tony always could rub people the wrong way. Tad turned his attention back to the day ahead. He had things to do and people to find.

He hoped that James didn't exist, but he knew deep down that would not be the case. Someone was hunting Proxies, and if he didn't find out who soon, then he or Jen might be next.

8

Tuesday, 17th November 2015
20:12

Jen wasn't in the mood for Tony, so Tad got stuck with him after all. After dropping her at school, they headed into work with a grumbling Tony along for the ride.

This didn't bother Charles who cheered up as they approached the lecture hall. He was in his element when teaching, but had grown to love it more than ever in recent years. Tad used to utilise Charle's knowledge and talent for teaching, but Charles had little actual input. Today, just as he had for the past year, Charles was going to run the show.

There was a time when the number one rule of being a Proxy was to never let your guard down. Even the benevolent ghosts had days where they couldn't resist trying to take charge of their host and live again. A Proxy's will is normally much too strong for this to happen, but the more ghosts they have, the harder they have to concentrate. Wrestling control back from a ghost in charge was even harder again.

Once, Tad wouldn't have dreamed of surrendering control to Charles for any reason. That changed when he realised it was getting easier to protect his mind. He didn't like to think of it too much less his ghosts find out, but he was finding it easier to impose his will on them.

The benefit was that he didn't have to worry about lectures. He could sit back, let Charles take charge and he would be free to think of other things until the lecture was over.

Today he thought on his dream, and by the time Charles had finished the lecture he was raring to go. They grabbed Tony and hit up as many contacts as Tad had left, seeking a lead on James Tanner.

When the time to pick Jen up approached, he got a call from one of her friend's parents saying she would take Jen home for dinner. Tad was glad not to have to go home and see his daughter. In the back of his mind he hated himself for that, but she had been stressing him out and he had enough of that already.

Another four hours, another ten conversations and he was still getting nowhere with his leads. It didn't help that he was having trouble even tracking down his old contacts. Those that weren't already missing had gone into hiding. It left Tad with few places to turn.

By the time eight o'clock rolled around, he had a second call saying that Jen would be dropped off shortly. There was no way Tad would get there in time so he asked to speak to Jen.

"What?" came her harsh greeting.

"I won't be there when you get home. I'm busy." She sighed theatrically, no doubt showing off for her friends, and it was a good job he wasn't there. In the mood he was in he might have strangled her. "When you get back, you might have to show your friends Miriam or Maggie. They should both be home by now. I'll try to get hold of Letty and see if she can—"

"You don't need to. Miriam and Maggie are enough. I like hanging out with them."

There was no use arguing. He would just agree then call Letty anyway. He was about to go through with this plan when he realised she had already hung up.

"Mother of God. One of these days I'll kill that girl," he snapped.

"I hate to add to your burdens," Tony told him. "But there's a rather sexy problem coming our way."

"What?" Tad asked, following Tony's gaze. "Oh please. Not again. Why does this keep happening?"

"Probably because you're working the same case."

"I haven't got time for this," Tad complained.

"You've got to be kidding me." Stella sounded just as annoyed as he felt. After hearing her tone, he wondered what happened to her plan to seduce him. When he turned and saw the thundercloud of her expression, he almost wished for the succubus back.

Tad stood outside a modern pub that sat on a corner overlooking an alley in the city centre and was appropriately named Hidden. He had hoped to find an old drunk who had been a Proxy once upon a time and hadn't enjoyed the experience. The man had been trying to drown his memories ever since. The Proxy gift never left him though, and he sometimes heard things that Tad didn't know.

"What are you doing here, Tad? I'm getting fed up of this."

"Nice to see you too," he deadpanned. "I'm looking for a guy called Michael Midas. He drinks here—"

"Every day of the week," Stella finished. "I've heard. And just why are you looking for him? You still chasing Tommy?"

He nodded, preferring the lie to explaining the truth. However, Stella was better at detecting lies than he gave her credit for.

"I'll ask again, and this time I want the truth. I'm this close to arresting you, I swear. What are you doing here?"

"Fine. I'm looking for news of a man named James Tanner."

Stella stared at him, her eyes narrow and wearing an expression that promised violence. When she reached for him he thought she was acting on that promise, but instead she gripped his arm.

"Stella. What are you doing?"

"Going into this pub for a drink. You're coming to."

"Actually, I need to be going."

She stopped in the entrance and gripped his arm tighter. She looked like a woman about to snap.

"That wasn't a request. I don't care what you've got waiting. You're coming with me and we're going to lay our cards on the table."

Before he had chance to respond, she dragged him inside.

The interior of the bar was all straight lines and clean edges, black tables and tall chairs, all lit up by LED lights everywhere. It was like every other soulless bar that popped up recently and were taking over the Welsh capital.

Stella marched him to the sofas in the far corner and pushed him hard so he had no choice but to fall onto one.

"What are you drinking?" she asked as she shrugged out of her coat and laid it over the back of her sofa opposite his.

"I'm not—"

"What. Are. You. Drinking?"

He hesitated before saying, "Lemonade please."

"I'll be right back. If you so much as move a muscle in that time, I swear to God, it'll be the end of you."

She stormed off and Tad was so stunned by her attitude he didn't even take the time to appreciate the view of her walking away. Her charcoal-grey trousers were tight across her rear which of course caught Tony's eye.

"She's really something, right Tad?" he asked. "I think I'm in love."

"You say that about every girl you meet."

"This time I mean it. I think that she's the one for me. That is, hands down, the best arse in Cardiff."

Tad closed his eyes and sank deeper into the chair. Where was Miriam when he needed her?

"Eyes open old chap," Charles whispered. "Here she comes."

He opened his eyes as she approached and was just in time to miss a thorough splashing as his drink was slammed down hard on a coaster in front of him.

"Right. I want answers. I've seen you three times in three days, always in relation to this case which gets weirder every day. Now you have knowledge of someone who's been missing less than a day. I'm not even supposed to be investigating it yet. How the hell do you know about James Tanner?"

So, he was real then. There was no question anymore. Worse, it sounded like he actually lived in Cardiff.

"He's a friend of a friend. I heard of his disappearance through the same friend."

"Names, Tad. I need names."

Tad hesitated. "I don't have any."

She choked on her cola and those blue eyes of hers frosted over.

"Not good enough. I've got enough to arrest you right now, Tad."

He still had access to Miriam's knowledge and was certain that wasn't the case, but wasn't ready to push the issue. She would probably be within her rights to demand he accompany her to the police station at least.

"Look. I heard it from a friend, probably the same one that reported the crime to you."

He hoped she would provide a name, but was disappointed.

"Who's Maggie Patterson?"

He blinked. He hadn't expected that question.

"What?"

"Who is Maggie Patterson? You were friends once, right?"

"Yes. A long time ago. Why? What is this?"

"Did you know that she's dead?"

"What?" He tried to sound shocked. It didn't fly and her eyes narrowed further.

"You not only know she's dead, you told Kate about it. That's how she's got herself assigned yet another murder."

Tad panicked. How had Stella put that together?

"You listen. I've been good to you so far. I've been friendly. If I find out you're investigating these disappearances with Kate behind my back, trying to cut me out of the credit, then you'll see my bad side."

"That's not what's happening. Kate has nothing to do with this."

"She has something to do with Maggie Patterson though. What happened there? Did you kill her? Is that how Kate keeps landing these cases? You kill them and then Kate cleans up the mess, claiming the rewards?"

"Dear God. You're mad." Tad stood up abruptly and Stella stood with him, the black nail of her index finger pointing at his face.

"I'm not done with you. Sit down."

"No. I'm done with you. I'm not listening to any more of this. If you're going to arrest me, do it. If not, I'm leaving."

For the first time she seemed uneasy. Tad called her bluff and had guessed correctly. He didn't wait to act on his advantage, he left the pub as quick as he could and tried to put as much distance between himself and Stella as possible.

He barely got around the corner into the narrow alley when he heard the sounds of her boots clacking on the pavement as she ran after him.

"Does she have her cuffs out?" he whispered.

"I wish," was Tony's answer. Tad ignored him.

"Tad, wait."

"No," he called over his shoulder. "I don't have to listen to this."

"Sorry. I didn't mean to scare you. I'm just frustrated."

Frustrated? She didn't know the meaning of the word. He was more intimately involved in this case than her and he was getting nowhere. His daughter's life might very well be in the balance and he knew little more about how to save her than he had months earlier.

He was suddenly angry and rather than escaping, he turned to face her. Something in his gaze forced her to skid to a stop.

In her rush to chase him she had grabbed her coat, but not put it on. With the rain growing heavier, her charcoal jacket was growing darker and already her hair had a glossy sheen. That, combined with her tone and expression, made her look a touch pathetic and desperate. It was a look he hadn't seen on her before and he had to fight down a bout of compassion to keep hold of his anger.

"I don't care. I'm not the bad guy and I don't have time for this nonsense every time I see you."

"Then let me help you," she begged. "I know that you know more than you're letting on. You're not a good liar whereas I'm great at spotting lies. So please don't insult me again by lying. Can't you see that I am trying to help you?"

I don't need your help, was what he meant to say. Instead it came out as, "You can't help me. Don't you get that?"

She looked triumphant. In that one statement she almost got him to admit he had a problem and was trying to deal with it on his own. Stella recognised her emotions had given her away when a moment later he turned and walked away again.

She called his name but he didn't look back. She called a second time and a startled sound replaced the end of his name.

Nice try, he thought. Yet in spite of himself he turned to see what happened.

Stella was no longer following him. Instead she was struggling against a giant who had grabbed her from behind.

His broad face was cast in the shadow of a hood. He had one heavily muscled arm around her neck and he had her left arm gripped in his free hand. The awkward positioning forced her to arch her back and bend her knees, so she couldn't get the leverage to fight back.

At first Tad couldn't believe what he was seeing. Was this really happening? Had someone just snuck up on Stella to… what? Mug her? Rape her?

Tad was stunned.

His wheelhouse was firmly in dealing with the dead, the living were a whole other bundle of problems he kept away from for most of his life. In spite of dealing with the odd ghost here and there, Tad's history of physical conflict usually involved someone hitting him while he curled into a ball.

Tad was ashamed to admit that he felt a moment of paralysing fear while watching Stella and her attacker. His first instinct was to run. Stella wasn't even a friend. At best she was a pain in his arse. This would solve one of his problems, wouldn't it?

It's surprising what will go through a mind at a time like this. Tad was every bit as shocked by his train of thought as he was with the situation. Who the hell was he to be so dismissive just because he didn't like the victim? Stella may be a pain, but she didn't deserve this kind of treatment. His shame allowed him to push past his paralysis and reach a new emotion that was much more freeing, anger.

Why did this sort of thing keep happening? First the missing Proxies, then the rise in ghost sightings, then Stella's investigation, and then his dream the night before that brought a whole new level of danger. Now, when he could have done with a break, he got this.

That made him angry.

As his anger built, his logical mind went to sleep and instinct took over. He didn't even notice his fingers ball into fists, and was not conscious of his first steps down the alley toward Stella and her attacker.

After he closed half the distance, the big man looked up. He grinned when he caught sight of Tad, thinking nothing of the scrawny guy coming to her rescue. For Stella's part her eyes widened, but Tad couldn't tell whether that was fear or her begging for help.

He payed neither of them any notice, he was too caught up in anger and instinct.

He mentally called to Tony a moment before he reached the giant, and felt the familiar rush of power that flowed through him when he and Tony merged.

He reached for the large man who released Stella's arm to knock Tad's reaching hand aside. He was just as surprised as Tad when instead of being knocked away, Tad's hand grabbed his and gripped it hard.

Years of pent up aggression at always being the helpless victim flowed through him and Tad squeezed with strength he didn't know he had. Tony powered his muscles from within, giving him a grip ten times stronger than natural. Were Tad not so angry he might have let go in surprise. Instead he grinned and squeezed.

The giant gasped as his hand twisted at an unnatural angle and he was pulled forward. He released his grip on Stella's neck so he could reach Tad with his other hand. Stella used that moment to find her feet again, turn and knee him squarely between the legs.

Tad let go as the giant man crumpled into a heap. Stella coughed hard and Tad turned to see if he could help her.

She wasn't looking at him though, she was looking at the end of the narrow alley where dark shapes were stepping into view.

There were five of them and when Tad turned he saw another five coming from behind. His anger still ran high, making his heart beat hard and his limbs tingle. There was a rush to what he had just done to a man so much bigger than himself. Rather than experience more fear at the sight of so many men, he had a different thought.

Eleven men just to mug one lady? He didn't like it. Something felt off. He was sure they were here for him.

Was this what the other Proxies had seen before they were taken? If so, he was not about to go down easy. If he went down here, who would protect Jen?

That thought only added to his anger.

Fresh from his victory over the thug and still buried deep within the realms of instinct, he suddenly came down on the opposite side of *fight or flight* than he normally chose. If he were in a more analytical state, he would have noticed that this new, amazing, alien feeling that replaced his fear was confidence.

Mentally calling Charles to his side, he got himself ready to show these men why it was not a good idea to corner this particular Proxy.

9

Tuesday, 17th November 2015
20:27

The men near the pub approached as Tad stepped in front of Stella to make her less of a target.

"I don't know what you've been told," he shouted. "But this is a mistake you'll regret."

Both Stella and Charles looked at him as though he were mad, but he ignored them, still caught up in this strange new confidence. He was ready for this fight, maybe even eager for it.

"The mistake was your girl sticking her nose where it doesn't belong." It was a dark alley and Tad struggled to make out who spoke. It could have been any of the men as they all looked big enough to own such a gravelly voice.

He took a second to absorb what they'd said before the first seeds of surprise filtered through his confidence. He asked, "You're here for Stella?"

Stella nudged Tad aside with her left hand and flipped open her warrant card with her right.

"I'm a police officer. You don't want to do this."

They didn't reply, just kept coming closer.

"Tad, run. They don't want you." Stella tried to step in front of him, but he stopped her and shook his head. He wasn't about to let her face this alone.

"Cheers for the offer, but there's no getting out of this for either of us." He nodded toward the pub "Getting to the street is our best option. It's busier than here and there'll be CCTV. If we can get there, we might just get out of this."

She looked like she would argue, but eventually nodded.

"Sorry for bringing this on you," she whispered.

He didn't have chance to answer as the first attacker was within reach.

The alley was narrow so they couldn't come all at once. Normally they wouldn't need to. Any of these men had twice the bulk of Tad, even if he was a little taller. However, Tad was not just a normal man, and he still had Tony in him and Charles at his back.

The first attacker swung a crowbar at Stella. Tony's strength made Tad not just stronger and faster, but improved his senses and reactions. His hand moved quicker than the attacker was prepared for and he caught the descending bar. He twisted, pulling the bar from the man's grip. His forward momentum drove his shoulder into the man, knocking him into two other attackers at his back. They landed in a tangled heap.

"What the fuck?" said one of the surprised men left standing, echoing Tad's own thoughts. He could scarce credit that he wasn't dreaming. His instincts kept him moving.

The thug didn't have time to say anything else before Tad put the bar he had confiscated to good use. He struck the man's arm with his ghost-aided strength and speed. There was a sickening crack, and a startled gasp as a bone snapped and the thug's arm bent backwards. One more step and Tad has his foot against the man's chest and he kicked hard, knocking him to the other side of the alley where he bounced off a wall.

Where the hell did I learn that? Tad's logical brain asked. There was no answer.

He had just taken out four thugs in a matter of seconds. It left him with only one thought.

This is fucking awesome.

The attackers approaching paused to re-evaluate their opponent. The man who bounced off the wall wasn't moving while the man Tad shouldered aside climbed to his feet with the two men he had taken down. The one who'd lost his crowbar didn't look eager to continue the fight as he gingerly held his twisted wrist.

They weren't the only ones in shock.

Stella stared at Tad, dumbfounded. He met her eyes, smiled and shrugged.

"Run," he said to her, and that word started everything moving again.

It turns out that there was a reason Tad had not drawn Charles into him and received a level 2 power-up. It was not a decision he had consciously made, but it turned out it was the right one. There was another use for a ghost who could not be seen but could interact with Tad.

Charles kept his place at Tad's back, watching the men coming from behind. Unlike his time in the castle, Charles was not scared. There was no danger here. These men were not Proxies and were no threat.

An attacker swung a bat at Tad's head from behind, but Charles was there, pushing Tad's head down and manipulating his body to guide him out the way.

Tad identified Charles' touch and flowed with it, letting himself be manipulated without resisting. He struck back with his crowbar, and as it crunched against the side of the attacker's head, Tad was confident that this was one more person out of the fight.

He caught sight of Stella who hadn't run. Instead she rushed to the first fallen man and retrieved the blade he had dropped. It was twice as wide as her wrist and as long as her forearm. To say she looked menacing as she approached a man at the rear of the pack was an understatement.

Suddenly Tad felt Charles' touch again, and he turned with it, side-stepping one blow and then a next until his back was against a wall and there were two men in close. He only just dodged a knife that struck at his face, and a fist sheathed in polished steel knuckles bounced off the wall beside his head a half second later.

He dodged and blocked furiously, trying to use his speed and strength to his advantage. Though he had speed, strength and reach, he wasn't a kung fu master, far from it. That lack of skill and experience was showing. Eventually that knife came in before he could avoid it and it slipped into his side.

His sideways step stopped it from going too deep, but he felt a sharp fire against his ribs and he had to fight back a scream. He focused on grabbing the hand holding the knife inside him and twisted. The thug grimaced and stepped in closer, directly into the path of the knuckle dusters that were on a collision course with Tad's face.

The blow struck the knifeman in the back of the head and he dropped in a heap. Tad used the moment of shock to punch the other man in the face. He was rewarded with solid crunch and a shower of blood as cartilage broke.

A broken nose was enough to distract any man. He staggered back, his hands cupping his nose, and he was blind to the next punch that took him in the throat. Tad wanted to hit him again, make sure he was out of it, but already he felt himself being manipulated.

He turned again and this time he wasn't quick enough. An elbow glanced off the side of his head and he cringed away from it, already hating how thick his face felt as he registered the blow. That would leave a bruise. The attacker followed it up by stamping at the back of Tad's knee.

Suddenly the world was falling up around him and he couldn't see a way out of this. By his count he had only incapacitated three men. There were seven more where they came from and now he was on his knees.

This time it was not so much gentle guiding as it was an almighty shove. Charles hammered into Tad so hard he knocked him over. Tad fell to the ground and a moment later he felt a pain in his leg as an over balancing attacker tripped over him and crashed to the floor.

Tad wrestled with him, seeking a way to cause as much damage as possible. He gouged and poked until eventually he got a hand to the back of the man's head which he took great pleasure in slamming into the ground. On the third repetition he was sure that his work was done.

Four. Still not enough.

He struggled to his knees, wincing at the pain from the cut in his side. As he got one foot under him he looked up to see Stella struggling with an attacker who stayed back to deal with her. She had lost her knife and there was a dead or unconscious man in her wake. Good for her. But it wasn't enough.

The man she wrestled with had both of her wrists in his hands and he was forcing them apart. Tad could see him lean back, building up momentum so that he could bring his head into her face. It would be game over for Stella. No way she would walk away from such a vicious blow.

Again Tad didn't think, he just acted. He pointed to Stella and with a mental shout he ordered Charles forward. Charles moved like a man possessed, crossing the distance between Tad and Stella in a second and screaming as he did so.

The man holding Stella froze, his head turning towards Charles and his eyes going wide. Stella took advantage of his shock. She kicked his knee, hitting him hard enough to make him wince and relax his pressure on her hands. She slipped one free and stepped away while Charles did the impossible.

He collided with the man, a living man, and with the weight that Charles had on him the collision drove the man from his feet and into the wall.

One of the nearby men swung for Charles, but he had become insubstantial again, the weapon passing through him as though he wasn't even there. Charles was every bit as shocked as his attacker.

Stella stared at him with a stunned look in her eyes and was completely ignoring the man approaching from behind with a bat in his hands.

Tad was in no position to help so he gave up his last remaining advantage. With another mental shout he urged Tony forward. The ghost sprang from him without hesitation and Tad felt his world fall apart.

He didn't realise how much he was relying on Tony's strength. The wound in his side was deeper than he thought. The blow to his knee had done serious damage and the side of his face felt like it might cave in. On top of this he felt sluggish and weak. He was in no position to fight.

Tony however, was.

He repeated Charles' success in interacting with the living and took great delight in knocking the startled attacker away from a stunned Stella. He was not as heavy as Charles so he inflicted little damage, but most of the work had been done.

These men had been expecting an easy victory. They had not expected that half their number would be incapacitated. They didn't expect Charles to appear from nowhere. Tony's appearance was the last straw. Those that could stand were suddenly running. They'd had enough.

Of course it was in that moment when Tad thought it was all over when one of the fleeing men paused long enough to swing a club at his head. Without Charles to guide him he couldn't dodge it. Without Tony's strength he couldn't fight it.

All he could do was take it in the face and know that it was game over.

10

Tuesday, 17th November 2015
21:00

Jen couldn't believe Tad hadn't called Letty. Instead of the old woman waiting when Hannah's mum dropped her off, there was no one home and the lights were off.

"It doesn't look like anyone's here," Hannah's mum said with a frown.

"There will be. Tad sometimes works in the spare room. You can't see the light from here," Jen lied. "Thanks for having me, Mrs Thompson."

She didn't wait for an answer before climbing out the car and rushing to the house, fishing her keys out on the way.

"Hello," she called when she got inside.

"Jen?"

Great. It was Miriam.

"Come here a second." Miriam did as asked and Jen exerted her will, just as Tad had taught her... the only thing he taught her. She made Miriam visible.

Miriam looked confused, but waved automatically when Mrs

Thompson waved at her. A moment later they drove off leaving Jen alone. Miriam finally caught on.

"I hope Tad told you to do that. If not, then you're in serious trouble when he gets home."

"Yes, he did."

"Why isn't Letty here?"

"Because Tad knows I'm old enough to look after myself."

Miriam didn't look convinced. "I don't think so. Let's talk to her."

"No."

"Now, young lady."

Jen flashed her a disgusted look. "Kate wouldn't make me do that." Kate was always on her side. She used to think the same about Miriam, but she had changed. It was all that time she spent in Tad's head.

"You don't know Kate as well as you think. Come on, let's go."

"No."

"No? I'm telling you, Jen. Let's go."

"No. And you can't make me. If you want to see Letty, why don't you go see her yourself."

Miriam got that same look on her face as when Tony was speaking. It made Jen hesitate, but then she remembered that Miriam couldn't do anything about it. She was just a ghost.

"This is your last chance, Jen. Either come to see Letty with me or when Tad gets home, I'll have to tell him."

"Where is Tad?" Maggie asked as she stepped into the kitchen. She gave Jen a friendly grin which Jen was happy to return. She liked Maggie. She hadn't spent enough time with Tad to stop being interesting yet.

Jen shrugged. "He only said one of you would have to show yourselves to Hannah's mum so she could drop me off. I don't think he'll be long."

"Oh," Maggie said. Then to Miriam she added, "We can watch her. No point disturbing the old lady."

"Jen shouldn't be home alone."

"She won't be. We're here."

"We're ghosts. It's not the same."

Maggie rolled her eyes in a way that made Jen giggle. "So everyone keeps telling me. Don't worry about it so much. If the worst happens, Jen can show us to any intruders and we can scare them to death. Besides, Tad won't be much longer."

Miriam wasn't happy, but she was outnumbered. Caught between Maggie and Jen, she finally gave in.

"Thirty minutes," she said. "Any longer and we'll get Letty. Okay?"

Jen wanted to say it wasn't okay. She didn't need Letty at all, not just in thirty minutes. Maggie gave her a look which told her not to push it so she smiled at Miriam and nodded. As a bonus, she kissed her on the cheek and hugged her. Miriam was a sucker for a hug. Jen knew she missed human contact, and she always gave in when Jen hugged her.

When she stepped back Miriam was still scowling, but Jen could see she was fighting to keep it in place. She didn't say anything, just walked from the kitchen leaving Jen and Maggie alone.

"Thank's Mags," Jen said, adopting Tad's nickname for the woman.

Maggie smiled and offered her hand for a high five. Jen grinned and eagerly slapped Maggie's hand. Maggie accepted the high five and strolled to the kitchen counter, not making a big deal of the gesture or their bonding moment. Jen hated herself for trying too hard. Maggie was so cool. She needed to be more like that.

She took a seat on the other side of Maggie.

"How did today go?"

Maggie shook her head. "Like shit." Jen had to fight back a grin. Tad never let people swear around her. He always treated her like a baby.

"That bad?"

"Yeah. We could go inside and follow Mark, but we couldn't touch anything. Makes breaking an entering pointless when you can't rifle through people's stuff or kick your murdering scum of an ex-husband between the legs."

"You'd do that?" Jen asked in awe.

"In a heartbeat."

"It would be hilarious. He would just be walking around one minute and then the next he would be on the floor crying for his mummy without knowing what happened."

Maggie grinned. She had a pretty grin, and such big dimples. Jen hoped she looked as pretty as Maggie when she was older.

"I never thought of that. That would be fun." She sighed. "I could use some fun. It's been all drama here the last few days."

Jen snorted. "That's because Tad's moody recently. He doesn't have any fun."

For once Maggie didn't side with her.

"You should take it easy on him. I know dads can be hard to get on with sometimes, but they mean well. Besides, he's got a lot going on. He's worried—"

"Yeah. Well he'd be less worried if he let me help out. If he let me Proxy, I could stop him getting so stressed out and keep him safe."

Maggie smiled in a way that made Jen think she must have said something she shouldn't have. She looked away, blushing furiously.

"You don't think he trusts you?" Maggie asked.

"Well, he doesn't. He never lets me do anything."

"You know, Tad was three years younger than you when Charles came to him."

"I know. It's disgusting. He was nine and I'm twelve, but I'm still not allowed any ghosts."

Maggie laughed. "You don't understand. I'm not saying it was a good thing. I'm trying to tell you how hard it was. He was nine and had no other Proxies to help him learn. Charles has been around for a long time, but he only sees things from the eyes of a ghost. Tad needed to learn how to do everything by himself. Being that different is a lot to cope with, especially when you're young. Tad got bullied a lot back then. He also struggled to cope with the stress of Charles in his mind."

"It's not as bad as Tad says it is," Jen argued. "I've had two ghosts before and it wasn't that bad."

Maggie arched an eyebrow and Jen blushed. Okay. It had been

bad. That first night she had been exposed to memories that no child should ever know of her parents. She knew all their thoughts and their secrets. Some were worse than others. The ones about her were worst of all.

She had been an accident. Her parents had been happy before she came along and didn't know how to deal with a baby they didn't want. They kept her because they felt it was the right thing to do, not because they loved her. They loved her by the end, but she hadn't realised how much of a burden she was. Especially when they thought she was crazy.

She couldn't remember the ghosts she talked to as a child. They just seemed like people to her. They'd always been there and were easily forgotten. For her parents, every time they caught her talking to one it was like a stab in the heart.

After that first night it wasn't as hard having them around. She didn't have to look in their memories and she could try not to remember what she had seen. But the damage was done. She would never admit it, but she was glad when Tad advised them to move on.

"Okay, it was a little overwhelming, but it got better. After a couple of days it was almost as though they weren't even there. Besides, I'm older now. I can handle it. I'll be thirteen in seven months."

Maggie's smile showed just how little she was impressed by that fact. Jen slumped.

"I'm not saying you're wrong. I'm saying that Tad has his reasons. It was hard, he had to learn by trial and error and sometimes it didn't go well. I think it might be time to cut him some slack. He's trying his hardest."

Jen wasn't listening. She tuned out as she thought of Tad learning on his own. He didn't need an adopted father to teach him. He got himself a ghost and learned what he needed. That was what she should to do.

She was so caught up in the thought that she missed Maggie asking her a question. She was saved from having to answer when Tony burst through the wall.

Jen took one look at his usually smirking face and knew something was wrong. She wasn't the only one. Maggie was off her chair in an instant and called for Miriam.

Miriam appeared a moment later, her expression hard. She took one look at Tony before arriving at the same conclusion. Something was wrong.

"Jen," Tony said. "You need to come with me."

"What's wrong?" Miriam asked.

"Tad's hurt. It's bad. Stella called an ambulance, but he needs to be with us. We can do a better job than those doctors."

Tony usually acted as though everything was a joke. He got on Jen's nerves from time to time, but she usually liked that about him. None of that humour was there now, and that worried her.

"What do you mean he's hurt?" Maggie asked. "And who's Stella?"

"The cop working the disappearances," Tony said before turning back to Jen. "Come on. I need you quick. Stella's called for backup and there'll be ambulances soon. You need to let Stella see us so that we can convince her to get Tad out of there."

"Why can't you take him out of there?" Maggie asked. It was Miriam who answered.

"Ghosts can't touch a Proxy when they're sleeping or unconscious. Unless we have their permission, we can't get anywhere near them. It's like a natural defence or something. I don't know." She was already moving towards a stunned Jen who was still sitting on the stool, frozen in place.

Tad was hurt? She always knew this would happen. He kept hunting ghosts and trying to find missing people when he was just a teacher. Of course he would get hurt.

She jumped when Miriam touched her shoulder.

"Jen. I need you to concentrate. You need to call a taxi." She turned to Tony. "Where are we going?"

"A pub called Hidden in the city centre."

Miriam nodded and turned back to Jen. "I would do it, but I can't. You can make us visible when the taxi gets here so I can do the talking, but you need to get us that far. Can you do that?"

Jen hesitated, fighting down panic. Tad was hurt and needed her help. She only calmed down when she felt Miriam grip her a little harder.

"Jen, Tad needs us. Can you do it?"

Jen nodded.

"That's my girl."

Tuesday night in November wasn't busy, so they had no trouble getting a taxi. Getting to the city centre took ages though, and Jen was sure they would see flashing lights by the time they arrived.

Amazingly, the only flashing lights were TVs flickering in the pubs. They had somehow beat both the police and the ambulance to the scene.

Jen paid the driver with Tad's emergency cash before he asked for it. It had taken her a long time to get over her shock that something had happened to Tad. Now all she could do was worry and try to get there as quick as possible. She was out of the taxi before the ghosts and as soon as she saw the backlit sign for the bar called *Hidden,* she ran for the alley beside it.

She skidded to a stop when she reached it, her eyes going wide. There were four big men sleeping in the alley. One was sprawled against a wall, another curled in a ball on the floor, and two more were laying on top of each other.

The sight of them were shocking enough. What terrified her was the pretty woman. She was soaking wet and knelt low over a shape that Jen recognised all too well.

Tad looked smaller laying down. The woman had his head cradled in her lap and she was sheltering his face from the rain.

The first Jen realised that she had stepped into the alley was when that woman looked up. She stared at Jen with wide, unseeing eyes that slowly focused as she came back to herself.

"Don't come any closer, sweetheart. This is a crime scene. The police will be here soon."

Jen ignored her, coming closer and staring at Tad.

"Didn't you hear m—"

"What happened to my dad?" Jen asked. It was the first time she ever called him that. She didn't notice. All she saw was Tad's face and blood... lots of it.

He had a big bruise on the side of his face and his hair was wet and sticky. She looked down and saw more blood coming from a tear in his coat.

This was worse than what she imagined. It looked like he would die. Jen felt tears in her eyes and that made her angry. She was nearly a woman. She couldn't cry like a little girl. She wiped them away with the back of her hand and turned her anger on the woman.

"What did you do to him? What happened?"

The woman was momentarily speechless.

"You're Jennifer?" she asked. "Why are you here?"

The question stoked Jen's anger, and she took another step closer.

"I asked first. What did you do to him—"

"Jen, calm down. It'll be okay."

They both turned in surprise to the new voice. In her anger she had not seen him and had lost control of her powers, unintentionally making Charles visible. Stella jumped, her mouth dropping open but unable to speak.

"This isn't Stella's fault. These men attacked them. Stella got hurt as well."

He tried to hug Jen, but she pushed him away. "Why were they after him? What did they want?" Charles didn't answer quick enough and Jen put the clues together fast. Miriam may not be her ghost, but Jen had learned a thing or two about putting together clues from her.

"They weren't here for Tad. They were here for you." She turned back on Stella who flinched away from her accusation.

"I didn't know this would happen," she said. "I tried to—"

Jen wasn't listening. All she could think of was that Tad was hurt, and it was this woman's fault. She took another step closer, ready to hurt her.

A hand on her arm stopped her. Not Charles this time, but Miriam. The other ghosts had caught up.

"Jen. This isn't her fault," Miriam said. Her voice was so calm. How could she be so calm when Tad was laying there and there was so much blood? "Remember what we're here for. We need to help Tad?"

"Oh my God. Inspector Winslow... No... No, it can't be. You're dead. You're—"

"Hello Stella," Miriam interrupted, her voice still annoyingly calm. "Never mind me. I need to know if you've called this in."

The woman blinked and straightened, growing more confident.

"I called it in, but there's been an incident on the other side of the city. The ambulances are tied up and the uniforms on route will take a while."

Miriam smiled. "That's good. It mean's we've still got time. Now, what I'm about to say will sound strange."

"Stranger than my dead boss standing in an alley with two guys who appeared from nowhere in the middle of a fight and disappeared the minute Tad was knocked unconscious? Weirder than Tad's daughter somehow being here within minutes of this all going down?" She looked to the final figure and her eyes widened further. "Holy shit. Is that Maggie Patterson, the murder Kate's working? What the hell is happening?"

"I'll explain later," Miriam said. "I promise. But for now, you need to trust me. Can you do that?"

Stella hesitated, frowned, but finally nodded. Again Miriam smiled. How was she so calm?

"Right. The first thing you need to know is that we can help Tad better than any doctor. You need to trust us."

Stella shook her head.

"No. He needs to go to the hospital. He's so cold and—"

"It's raining, Stella. He's bound to be cold. But he's not dead. Trust me. I'd know. But if we don't act he might be soon. Is your car close?"

"What? My car?"

"Yes. Is it close?" Stella nodded. "First, we need to get Tad to your car. Then you need to wake him up, just for a second, but he needs to be conscious. He has to give us permission to help him."

Stella looked confused. "I don't think I... No. We need to wait for—"

"For fuck sake," Maggie said, interrupting Stella and Miriam. "Look lady. This is a messed up situation and we're clearly not getting through to you. Maybe this will help." She took a step to her right and pushed her hand through a wall. Stella yelped. "See that. We're not alive... well, except for Jen. We're ghosts. Tad here is like a medium on steroids. We need you to trust that we can use our ghostly mojo and can make him better."

Stella looked overwhelmed and not at all convinced. She was about to say something when Jen spoke up first. She only said one word, but it was enough.

"Please."

Whether it was her tone, that she was the only living person there, or if Stella had just given up, she finally nodded.

Stella slid out from underneath Tad and moved to help lift him. Jen went to his legs. Even between the two of them they didn't make much headway. He was a dead weight and far too awkward to carry.

That was when a thought struck Jen. It was instinct. She concentrated on touching Tad and thought about their shared dream. Was he dreaming now? Could she reach him?

She closed her eyes, searching within the core of herself for her Proxy abilities. She sent out a questing thought for Tad's mind.

She found it instantly. It was as though his mind was waiting for her this whole time. She delved into that thought and found herself once more in that round room where Tad had taken them the night before. He was laying on the floor looking dazed. Just like last night, she could tell that though his eyes were open, he saw nothing.

He turned towards her the second she materialised. It was freaky. "Tad?"

"You shouldn't be here, Jen." He sounded tired and turned away again. "You should be in school."

Jen almost laughed. He was delirious.

"Tad, you need to listen. You need to let Miriam, Tony, Charles and Maggie touch you."

"Don't change the subject—"

"For God's sake, Tad! Listen. I need you to please, let them touch you and give them permission to come into you."

"I don't know. It's been so long since I was here alone," he laughed. It was high pitched, and he sounded drunk. "I like being alone. It's… quiet."

"Please, Tad. For me. I really need you to do this."

He sighed. For the longest time he said nothing, and she thought he had forgotten she was there. Finally he said, "Fine. If it's that important to you."

Suddenly Jen felt the world shift, and she knew it had worked. Four shadows appeared on the walls. They were tall and rectangular, the places where the doors to the ghost's memories would go.

"Can I get some peace now? I'm so tired."

Jen didn't answer, she just whispered the word *excitare* and came back to herself.

"What did you do?" Charles asked the second she was back in the freezing, dark alley. He stared at Tad in amazement, as did Miriam, Maggie and Tony. Only Stella looked confused.

"I just spoke with Tad and got him to lower his defences. He's also given you permission to join with him when we get him somewhere safe."

"I didn't know you could do that," Tony said. "Well done, Jen."

She felt immensely proud of herself and couldn't help but standing a little straighter.

"What are you talking about?" Stella demanded.

They just waved her off and got back to work. With the ghosts able to touch Tad it was much easier. Thanks to the rain there weren't many people on the streets so they weren't spotted as they carried him the short distance to Stella's car.

It was more of an effort to manoeuvre him into the back seat of the

Mini, but they managed.

"Right. That's great, Stella. Now I need you to do me one last favour," Miriam said. "I need you to look after Jen while we get to work. Once you're finished here, take her to Tad's house and stay with her until Tad wakes up. Can you do that?"

Stella was done questioning things and just nodded.

"I don't need a babysitter, Miriam," Jen protested.

Miriam ignored her. "Thanks Stella. I really appreciate this. I promise, come the morning you'll have your answers. But for now we need to work." Turning to Jen she added, "Be good for Stella. Do it for Tad."

Her final words took the remaining fight from Jen and she nodded. Miriam smiled one last time before turning her attention to Tad. Each ghost faded, their forms became little more than light mist that Tad breathed in.

"Oh my God," Stella said in what sounded like a groan. It was the sound of an exhausted woman at the edge of breaking.

At that same moment sirens wailed in the distance. Hearing them, Stella perked up.

"I need to deal with that," she said. "Are you going to be alright waiting in the car?"

Jen nodded. Stella told her she would be back soon and then returned to the alley to wait for the police.

Jen was left alone with Tad. Looking at him, so damaged and close to death, all her frustrations about him vanished. All she wanted was for him to be well again. She climbed into the front passenger seat and turned so she could keep an eye on him. She reached for his hand and held it in hers.

Then, the true waiting began.

11

Wednesday, 18ᵗʰ November 2015
08:32

Stella snorted and woke up.

She was confused to find she wasn't in her own bed, then horrified that someone might have heard her snort. She wiped her mouth, was disgusted at finding drool, and looked around the room.

This was not her room.

The walls had been painted white and left that way with no pictures or decoration. That amount of blank space made her fingers itch to fill it. There weren't even curtains, just venetian blinds. It didn't matter that they blocked out light; the room needed something to frame those windows.

What really drew her eye was the mess. Clothes were tossed casually on a chair in the far corner and left in piles on the floor. Drawers were ajar in the dresser next to the chair, and the wardrobe in the opposite corner was open. She had to look away. From shirts hanging half off their hangers to jackets that had fallen and not been picked up, it was Stella's personal nightmare.

She had no idea how he could sleep in such mess.

She sat up straighter in her chair, a twin to the one on the other side of the room. Her back ached from her uncomfortable position and she cringed at the other pains that tugged at memories from last night. Her full recollection crashed into focus when she saw the face of the man in the bed.

To say Tad looked better was an understatement. The bruise on his cheek had faded and his skin was a much healthier pink than the dull grey it had been. His hair was still in that God awful tangle that made her want to brush it, but at least it wasn't wet with blood. Some dried blood remained, but she remembered washing off the worst of it after she and Jen had wrestled him upstairs.

Jen. Of course. Was she okay?

Stella struggled to wake her mind. She was never at her best in the mornings, and this morning was especially hard. Shock could do that to a person. Last night had definitely been shocking… world changing.

Her mind cringed from that thought and she shivered, but forced herself to remember everything she had done last night.

She had returned to the scene to deal with the first responders. In the time it took to wrestle Tad to the car, another man had woken and left. That left only three of the injured six for the paramedics and police to work with. As much as she was annoyed that they would get away with their attack, it made explaining the situation easier.

In her statement she dialled down her own actions and included a lie about a good Samaritan that helped her out. No, she never got a good look at him, and she was in no position to stop him leaving.

It was not her best lie, but better than those Tad had been feeding her.

The paramedics gave her a once over and declared her healthy enough to avoid a trip to the hospital. She finished giving her statement and went through the usual after action reports. By the time she was free to go it was eleven and Jen was asleep in the car, curled up so she could keep Tad's hand clutched tightly in her own.

Stella smiled as she remembered the scene. It was cute how worried Jen had been for him.

Stella woke her up for directions to Tad's house and from there they undertook the arduous task of getting Tad to bed. With no ghosts to help it was much more difficult.

After getting him to bed, Stella hustled Jen from the room. Cleaning Tad up was not something his daughter should see. Jen put up a token protest, but was exhausted. She mumbled something about shared dreams keeping her up the night before and agreed to get some sleep.

Stella stripped away Tad's dirty clothes, wincing when she saw the wound in his side. It was nasty, and would need cleaning and stitching. She debated the wisdom of not taking him to a hospital and wondered how she would forgive herself if he died.

It was too late for second guesses, so she got to work. She made no attempt to stitch the wound, she knew her limitations, but she made sure it was clean and dressed at least.

Stella cleaned the worst of the blood and tucked him into bed. Exhausted, she debated going downstairs to sleep on one of those huge sofas, but decided against it. She would stay in his room and keep an eye on him. If he took a turn for the worse, then Miriam be damned, she was calling an ambulance.

With the light of the morning seeping through the gaps in the blinds, she wondered how she had been so stupid to have gone along with this. Tad could have died, she would have lost her job, and Jen would have lost her father. She wasn't confident she had been in her right mind.

Ghosts? Really?

Even with the official word from the bosses, the constant turns her case had taken, and her own assurances that she would take Tad seriously, she couldn't believe they existed. Yet how could she deny what she saw with her own eyes?

She willed Tad to wake up. He had answers, and she was determined to get them.

However, answers weren't the only reason she wanted him to wake up. He saved her life last night. She didn't know how he did it with those guys being so much larger than him, but if he hadn't been there she wouldn't be alive today.

For some reason he risked his own life to save hers. She wasn't sure of what happened, but she was smart enough to recognise what he had done for her. He sent his ghosts to save her, and she guessed that was why he went from being able to take down four guys on his own to getting himself knocked unconscious by a cheap shot Stella saw coming a mile away.

To make matters worse, she knew he didn't like her. She had never had a guy ignore her advances as long as him. She could tell he found her attractive from the way he looked at her and, almost more telling, the times he tried not to look at her. But, for some reason he held himself back.

Over the last few days she questioned him, threatened to take away his daughter, and accused him of murdering people. They had even been arguing when the attack started.

Even after all that, he risked himself to save her. She didn't think that behaviour existed outside of a Hollywood studio.

Overnight he moved from interesting to fascinating. He definitely had to wake up. Not only did she have questions, she had apologies and a big thank you to bestow.

She froze when he sucked in air like it was his last breath. Stella watched in fascination as mist flowed from him, not just from his outward breath but from every pore.

That mist broke into shapes that solidified into the four people she met the night before. Stella couldn't close her wide open mouth. Thankfully, they weren't looking at her to witness her weakness. They stared at Tad as he opened his eyes.

He blinked, focused on the faces, then groaned.

"What the hell? You know I can't stand being watched when I wake up."

"Well this morning's special, Thaddeus," the fat ghost said. "We need to check our work."

"Your work. What are you talking ab—"

He paused mid sentence when he spotted Stella. He didn't speak for a few seconds and she wondered what kind of a mess she must look. She hadn't seen a mirror since the incident and knew she was filthy. She panicked that she was looking frightful.

"Uh. Guys. Did I hit my head last night, or is that really Stella in my room?"

"Finally, hey Tad?" the young Asian kid said, nudging the big ghost suggestively. Miriam huffed, the big ghost rolled his eyes, and Tad had a look that said he had long since given up reacting to such comments. Only Maggie, the murder victim in Kate's latest case, commented.

"Before you get mouthy, Tony. I think she can hear you."

The boy turned and looked at Stella who stared right back. He waved a hand, and she waved back. He yelped and turned away.

"Not cool, Tad. You're supposed to warn a guy before you show him to the living."

Miriam burst out laughing and it was Stella's biggest surprise of the morning. She didn't remember her boss ever laughing.

"It's about time you got caught, you little perv."

The boy shot Stella a nervous glance and looked back to Tad imploringly. Tad struggled to sit up and shrug at the same time.

"It must be Jen. I'm not doing it. She's upset, and you know how she gets."

"How do you know she's upset?" the fat ghost asked.

"Well I…" his words trailed off, and he frowned. "I don't know. I can feel it. She's dreaming and I think she's projecting… Huh. Weird." He stretched and winced as pain pulled at his ribs. Turning to Stella, he said, "So, I guess I did get hit in the head last night, but you're real nonetheless."

"Pretty much," she answered.

He looked from her to his open wardrobe and the dirty clothes on the chair, most of which were underwear. He sighed.

"That's about right," he muttered. Turning back to Stella, he said, "I expect you've got questions."

"You could say that."

"Give me five minutes to pull myself together and you can ask away."

She was about to do as asked when she thought better of it.

"Hang on a second. You're injured. You're not going anywhere."

"I feel fine," he said. He really was a terrible liar, and she made that clear with a glare. "Well, maybe not fine, but I'm on the mend. Here, look at this."

He peeled the padding, stained red with his blood, from his side. There was wincing and a curse or two, but eventually it came free and Stella could see the wound had closed.

She gasped. It was pretty much healed.

An angry red line showed where he had been cut and judging by his expression it was still painful. However, it was a remarkable improvement.

Tad wasn't so happy.

"Did you guys feel like half-assing it?" he teased. "This thing still hurts."

"The fact that you have your fine motor skills and your cranium is no longer cracked should give you more than enough reason for thanks, Thaddeus," the larger ghost said with an indignant sniff and a twitch of his moustache.

Tad grinned. "I know, Charles. Just kidding. Thanks." Turning back to Stella he added, "See. I'm fine. Now why don't you give me five minutes and we'll talk."

She just nodded and stood. This was just too much. Suddenly feeling awkward, she headed out the door.

When Tad re-emerged, Stella sat at the breakfast counter with a mug of coffee. She was pleased that Tad stocked her favourite brand. It was expensive and hard to find. Maybe there was hope for him yet.

"I poured you a mug," she said in way of greeting. "Miriam said you take three sugars. That's blasphemous with coffee this good."

He grinned and sat on the opposite side of the island. "I know. But I have a sweet tooth. Can't be apologised for. It's my only vice."

The ghost of Maggie Patterson guffawed and Tad grinned even wider. He was in better spirits now he had a few moments to tidy himself up. Stella guessed that surviving an injury that should have killed him with only a scratch to show for it was reason enough to be happy.

Stella looked at Maggie, but her eye travelled back to Miriam. It was Miriam that she *knew* was dead. The rest of them could be in a magic show and were good at pulling tricks. But she had seen Miriam's body. Yet there she was, perched on another breakfast stool, frowning at Tony on Tad's side of the island.

Tony stared at Stella. She had learnt long ago to ignore the unwanted attentions of men, but it was hard to ignore him. Tad must have noticed.

"Tony. Go for a walk. I need to talk with Stella."

"But I—"

"I'll take him," Maggie offered, cutting off Tony's protest.

"But..." Maggie grabbed his arm and pulled him off the stool. "I didn't do anything." From the way everyone ignored him, Stella assumed it was a common occurrence.

Maggie hesitated at the door, then stepped through it without opening it. Stella choked on her coffee. Once she caught her breath, she put the mug down and pushed it away. She needed answers, and she would not have her beloved coffee tainted with the memory of this conversation.

"I want to say this before we start so you know that no matter how I react to anything you might say later, I really appreciate it. Thanks for saving my life."

Tad was torn between looking uncomfortable at the compliment and laughing at how it was phrased.

"You're welcome. Though, I think you saved me in the end. If you hadn't trusted Jen and my ghosts, then I would be dying in a hospital somewhere."

"We would never let you die, Thaddeus." The fat ghost that leaned against a counter looked appalled.

Tad smiled over his shoulder at him and changed his story. "Maybe I would just be stuck doing a lot of explaining. Either way, thanks."

She shook her head. "It's not the same. You risked your life for me last night. I won't ever forget it."

"Does that mean you won't be bothering me about me showing up places I shouldn't be?"

His smile was mischievous and Stella struggled to keep her frown. She didn't know what was wrong with her, but she wanted to grin right back at him.

"No. You'll still get stick over it. I just won't go accusing you of murder again."

"You did what?" Miriam asked, appalled.

Tad laughed. "She thought I killed Mags so Kate could solve the murder."

Information clicked together in Stella's mind and she had a eureka moment.

"You've been leading Kate to murder scenes," she accused. "Only you weren't the ones killing them, their ghosts were telling you what happened."

Tad had the grace to blush. "Well, I suppose that's the way of it. Not many police listen when I tell them a ghost told me who killed them. Kate does."

"I knew there was a reason she kept getting those murders. It's been bugging me for months."

"Has it now?" Miriam asked, and it was Stella's turn to blush. She forgot about their history. It didn't curb her curiosity though. One solved mystery ignited a hundred other questions. She needed answers or she thought she might burst.

"I need to know everything, Tad. What's going on? What are you?"

Tad winced. "That wasn't the nicest question. I'm a man, just like any other." The fat ghost, Charles, coughed suggestively and Tad grinned again. "Okay. Maybe not quite like any other. I am what those in the know call a Proxy."

She'd heard that somewhere before. Where had she heard it? It was on the tip of her tongue...

"Wait. Proxy or Roxy?"

"Proxy."

"That idiot Marcus heard it wrong."

"Marcus? Tommy's friend?"

She nodded and told him what happened after he left. Tad thought about as much of Marcus as Marcus had of Tad. She had a fascinated audience, and he laughed when she recapped a few choice parts of the incident. She smiled as well. It wasn't often that people outside work enjoyed her stories from the office.

"What an idiot. No, we're definitely Proxies."

"So what does that mean?"

"It means ghosts use us to interact with the world, they live through us by proxy."

Stella nodded as though she understood, but didn't in the slightest. "And what you could do last night? The way you fought?"

"To be honest, that surprised me. You might not believe this, but that was my first fight… or at least the first fight where I fought back."

He was right, Stella didn't believe it. However, she had learnt his tells, and she sensed only honesty from him.

"Maybe you should have tried fighting back sooner, you seem to have a knack for it."

"So it seems. But that was because I had Tony inside me… uh… look. I'm getting ahead of myself. It works like this. When a ghost dies and decides not to move on, they need to find a Proxy. The pull of the next life is so strong that it drives ghosts mad soon after death. By spending the night with a Proxy they get grounded in the real world for a day and can keep the madness away.

"When we merge, a part of me is with them for a day and a part of them with me. The part of me with them gives them access to my knowledge and keeps them grounded. The part of them in me gives me access to their knowledge and also imbues me with their talents. Recently I've learned how to show the ghosts to people, hence how they're talking to you now. You with me so far?"

Stella blinked and shook her head. "No. But keep going, I'll store my questions for later."

He smiled again and once more she found herself grinning right back. What was wrong with her?

"If I merge with a ghost while awake, I add their strength to my own. Last night I was fighting with Tony's strength added to mine… uh, or maybe more… But that's complicated for right now. I also got a boost in speed, stamina, a touch of healing… oh and my senses got a boost as well. Mr Dickens over here was watching my back."

"Dickens? As in Charles Dickens? *The* Charles Dickens?"

"Yes I am," Charles said proudly.

"No he's not," Tad said with a sigh.

"Well if she means the true Charles Dickens, the one who was here first and was a damn sight more talented than that scribbling idiot, then I sure am."

Stella looked at the odd ghost in amazement. She only now noticed his fashion sense was not from the modern world. His suit, though neat, was centuries out of date. His mutton chops were something she never saw other than on the stereotypical farmers on certain soap operas she had long since given up on.

"Don't listen to him, Stella. He's just sore about the Charles Dickens that history forgot."

"What does that mean?" Stella asked.

"It means I was robbed," Charles shouted. "Ten years older than that upstart and it's his works that everyone remembers. I might be one of the most brilliant historical minds in Britain, but I still get showed up by a bloke who writes about thieving little orphans."

"So did you know the other Charles Dickens?" she asked. His face reddened, and he pushed himself away from the counter.

"You bet I did. I gave him the idea for a Tale of Two cities."

"You did not," Miriam and Tad said together and Charles looked even angrier.

"Did so."

Tad just laughed. "I've been your Proxy too long for you to pull that one."

"I've been on this world for two hundred and nine years, Thaddeus. Don't think you know me better than I know myself."

Tad just laughed and shook his head. "Whatever, Charles." He turned back to Stella and rolled his eyes as though she should somehow understand what it was like to argue with a two century year old ghost over the inspiration for a Dickens' classic.

"Uh... Are you sure it wasn't A Christmas Carol you inspired?" Stella asked. "I mean, with you being a ghost and all—"

Tad burst out laughing and Charles nearly exploded with rage.

"Well I never. I have never been so insulted... I... Listen here..." Flummoxed over what to say next, he shook his head and stormed from the room.

Stella felt awful.

"Sorry. I didn't mean to upset him."

Tad wiped the tears from his eyes and shook his head. "Don't worry about it. He's always like that when people talk about Dickens. I'll give you one of his papers to read and you can mention it to him. He'll be your best friend for life."

"Oh. Okay." She hesitated another moment before saying. "You know this is weird, right? This isn't a normal way to start a morning."

"It is for me. Been this way since I was nine. Charles was the first. A couple years later Tony died. He was one of those child prodigies you hear about. He lived that stereotype where his parents made him play musical instruments for five to six hours a day when he wasn't at school. He got to be a hell of a musician but never lived his life. When he died, he decided to do all the things he missed out on. Of course he needs me to do it."

"He's been doing his impression of Casper the perverted teenage ghost ever since," Miriam said.

"What does that mean?"

"It means he spends most of his time looking at naked women. All those things that people joke about doing if they could be invisible, Tony does on a daily basis. I wouldn't be surprised if he's even seen you—"

"Miriam. Let it rest," Tad warned.

"But she—"

"Leave it."

Stella put the clues together and was horrified.

"He's spied on me in the shower?"

Tad winced and shook his head. "I'd like to say no but… with Tony you never know."

"That little bastard. How do you stop him doing it?"

"If I knew, I would," Miriam and Tad said at the same time.

Stella shuddered and tucked herself deeper into her jacket.

"This is all too much," she whispered. "First people talking about ghosts on the case, then last night, now this. I don't know if I can take it."

Tad touched her hand. "It get's easier, I promise."

"Does this means you can finally tell me what you know about the case?"

The smile slipped from his face and his hand left hers.

"I suppose so. But I wasn't holding much back. You've probably already guessed most of it."

"They were all Proxies?" He nodded. "Someone is targeting your kind?" Again he nodded. "Then I was right. You're in danger. We have to get you protection."

"I wouldn't know where to begin. For starters we don't know who's coming after us or how they're finding us. If we don't know that, how can you protect me?"

"I could relocate you."

"And how would you keep my location a secret when a ghost could be standing over your shoulder trying to find out where we've gone?"

"What? Oh my God. I never thought about that. Maybe we could just get you police protection."

Again Tad shook his head.

"From everything I've heard it doesn't matter what kind of protection you have. James told me that the woman who grabbed him did it while his ghosts were watching for her. That should be impossible."

"Wait. James told you this? James Tanner? How did you speak to him?"

Tad told her of his dream, another story that was hard to swallow. Considering how bad a lier he was, she had no choice but to believe him.

"This is just too crazy," she said. "I don't know what to do with it."

"Join the club."

She was about to speak again when suddenly there was a shout from behind her.

"Tad!"

A blur shot by her and Tad grunted as a little shape almost knocked him off his stool. Stella was treated to the sight of Jen hugging an astonished Tad so hard that Stella thought he must be in pain. If he was, he didn't show it, he just hugged her back.

"Hey munchkin. What's this for?"

"I thought you were dead," she said into his chest.

He laughed. "Hardly. Takes more than eleven armed men to see me off." Jen didn't laugh at his poor attempt at humour. "Seriously, I'm fine. I hear you had an interesting night."

She leaned away and looked excited. "Tad. I went into your dreams when I was awake."

He frowned. "What?"

"We needed the guys to carry you and you were doing your sleep mojo thing. So I visited you in your round room and asked you to—"

"I remember," Tad said. "I thought it a dream but... well I suppose it was. You were awake?"

She nodded. "Isn't it awesome?"

He nodded as well, also grinning. "You want to hear something else cool?"

"What?"

"Last night, I somehow made Tony and Charles able to touch living people."

Jen's jaw dropped. Most of the conversation was flying over Stella's head but she could sense their excitement and it made her inexplicably happy.

"Oh my God. Could you do it again?" She looked to Miriam who wore a stunned expression. There were tears in her eyes.

"I don't know yet. Don't get your hopes up, Miriam. If it's like it was with the seeing ghosts thing, then I might have to be in the same room. That would be awkward."

"I'm sure Kate wouldn't mind," Jen said with a cheeky grin.

Tad laughed, Stella finally got what they were talking about, and Miriam blushed.

"Jen, shut up," she protested, but there was a smile on her face.

In spite of the teasing, Stella felt the strength of feelings between these three. In fact, even with Tony and Charles those feelings were evident. It took her until then to realise what those feelings represented.

They were family, complete to all the little dysfunctions that made life interesting. As soon as she realised that she felt like the one person in that kitchen who didn't belong.

Suddenly awkward, she looked at the clock and swore. It was ten. Her shift started in two hours and she wanted to go home and shower first. There would be a long day of questions waiting for her, and she needed to be fresh for that.

However, she was reluctant to leave. Tad had answers she wanted, and though she wouldn't admit it out loud, she enjoyed the company of these strange people… ghosts… whatever.

She pushed herself away from her stool and stood.

"I need to get going." To Tad she added, "Thanks again. For everything."

"Anytime."

"You mean that? I have more questions and—"

He laughed. "Anytime. Seriously, Stella. Now you're in the know it might be handy having another set of eyes on this. Just do me a favour, keep me in the loop."

"I will. You've got my number just in case, right?"

He nodded.

She was already at the door by this point, eager to leave before something else crazy happened.

"Alright. Well… see you later I guess."

With that rather awkward goodbye she walked out the door and headed to her car. She was exhausted. After last night and the weird revelations of the morning, she wanted to go to bed rather than work. But she knew that as soon as her mind had chance to calm down that would change. No doubt soon she would kick herself for not asking more questions.

She climbed in the car and started the engine. Just as she was about to pull away she looked over her shoulder and saw Tad standing in the doorway. He grinned at her and waved once before closing the door. She caught herself grinning happily and waving back like an idiot.

Seriously. What the hell was wrong with her?

12

Friday, 20th November 2015
08:45

Tad rubbed his eyes. It was no different. When he looked back, he saw the same thing. Jen was surrounded by a pulsing nimbus of red light. Every time she looked at him it grew more intense. Had she slipped something into his coffee?

"You don't have to take me all the way to the door," Jen said bitterly from five paces ahead. "I don't want to get known as the girl whose dad walks her to school."

"Better than being known as the girl who once came to this school and then disappeared one day."

Jen snorted and upped her pace. When you're only five foot two and the man following you is six foot four, an increased pace isn't going to cut it. Tad already walked at half speed to keep from tripping over her.

She was close to the school gates when she looked over her shoulder and saw he was right behind her. That strange, red glow flickered, a hint of purple seeping into it before it turned crimson again.

What the hell was wrong with him?

"You wouldn't have to walk me to school if you would just—"

"We're not having this argument again."

She stopped so abruptly he nearly knocked her over. She turned on her heel and with one pointy finger, jabbed him in the gut.

"I don't care. You don't get to decide that about someone's life. If you let me get my own ghost, then I can get stronger and watch your back. I'd like to see those guys knock you out when there are two Proxies fighting them."

"Or maybe by learning to be a Proxy you'll attract the kind of attention that's making people disappear. I won't risk it."

"Have you ever thought that the reason people are disappearing was because they were alone? Your friends are lonely losers. At least with me you'll have a chance."

He forced a grin that he knew would infuriate her and said, "So that's what this is about. You want to spend more time with me. Why didn't you say?" Before she could stop him he pulled her into a hug and said, "That's so sweet."

Jen was making retching noises, and struggling to get free. When she did, he saw that the light surrounding her had changed to a deep purple. She looked at him with disgust and was about to tell him off when sudden laughter brought her up short.

She turned in horror to find her friend Hannah and another girl giggling behind their hands. That purple glow blinked out of existence and a second later there was a deep pink that was so bright Tad had to look away.

He glanced up again to the two girls and saw a similar nimbus around both. Hannah was a mixture of blue and orange. The other girl was a bold, vibrant blue.

A quick look around told him it wasn't just limited to the girls. The lights were everywhere. It was both distracting and wondrous. Something about the lights felt right, like they had been there his whole life and he was only now noticing them.

"You are such a dick," Jen grumbled.

"Watch your language."

"Maggie says it all the time."

"Well she's talking about Mark and he is a dick."

"Can I call him a dick then?"

Tad pretended to think about it and then said, "No."

The pink vanished and purple flickered to life once more. "You ass." She turned and walked away, keeping her head down and not looking at her friends as though she could avoid them.

Tad knew he shouldn't, but couldn't resist. Jen's relief at him being alive had vanished over the previous few days and she was back to being flippant all the time. He wanted pay back.

"See you after school sweetie," he called in his most sickeningly sweet voice. "Remember don't talk to strangers and if you go anywhere, hold the teacher's hand if you have to cross the street."

Jen tucked deeper into her coat with every word and the light around her went pink again. There were shades of red coming through from deep down and he wondered how long before the red won through. He suspected that red had something to do with anger. Jen had plenty of that.

"That was mean, Thaddeus," Charles said. "I would have thought that all the times you were bullied at school would have made you more sensitive to such things."

Tad fell into step beside Charles as he walked away from the school. "Please. Can you imagine anyone stupid enough to bully Jen? She'd knock their teeth out before they got out the second word in the insult."

Charles thought this over and smiled. "She does have fire in her."

"You don't know the half of it." He was suddenly glad it was just Charles with him today. The excitement of the past few weeks had died off since the fight, and things had returned to normal. Now that panic stations were over, Tad was comfortable walking to school with just one ghost for company. It was just like old times. He had missed his heart to hearts with his oldest friend.

"I think I'm getting a new power," Tad admitted.

"Another one? You do like to keep it interesting. What is it?"

Tad thought of a way to explain it and struggled for words. "It's like someone's slipped me something, to be honest. Everywhere I look I see these weird glowing lights around people. They're all different colours and—"

"You're aura reading."

"What?"

"You're reading peoples auras. I've heard tell of it over the years, but always put it off as a myth. Like all good myths there must be a grounding in truth somewhere, so I imagine that's what you've stumbled on. Can you describe these auras?"

Tad was grateful yet again that Charles had been the one to find him all those years ago. When he thought of all the ghosts that would have taken advantage of such a young Proxy, he was lucky it had been Charles. His near encyclopaedic knowledge of the past two hundred years was the icing on the cake.

"Think Northern Lights but surrounding a person. Also the colours are fairly distinct."

"Hmm. Interesting. You know, I've always wondered if your gifts might have less to do with death and more to do with souls. It would explain how, as you get stronger, you're able to affect the living. First you and Jen share dreams, then Jen going into your head the other night, and now this. It's almost as though you're reading souls." He paused to think, then asked, "Have you any idea what the colours mean?"

"I'm thinking emotions. Jen kept flicking back and forth between anger, irritation and embarrassment, and the colours seemed to change in time. It's hard to tell for sure without being inside her head."

"Well I wouldn't try that at the moment. The mood she's in she'd eat you alive if you go anywhere near her head."

"You probably right." He sighed, and after a short silence asked, "Am I doing the right thing with her? She's so stubborn about having a ghost of her own—"

"You need to be strong, Thaddeus. We both know that if I had another choice, I would never have inflicted the kind of stress on you that you had to deal with at such a young age. Jen doesn't know how easy she has it. As strong as she seems, she is still fragile on the inside. You see it in the moments she lets her guard down."

"What can I do about it? We can't keep living like this. She's unhappy."

"You know it's times like this when I remember how much the world has changed. When I was born, happiness was a luxury not a right. The most important thing in life was security. Having a parent who loved her as much as you do, provided for her, educated her, kept her safe… well, that was the jackpot. Today… you're all spoilt. The lot of you."

Tad laughed. "So your advice would be?"

"Stick it out. She'll either move on or she won't. The important thing is that you're doing what's best for her. If she hates you for it, then that's a price you must pay. It's better to be hated and see her grow into a better person for it, than to be loved and see her suffer in the long term."

"I thought you might say that. I guess time will tell."

"As with all things my friend, it always does."

They had no sooner walked through the door when Maggie pounced on them. She grabbed Tad's hand and lead him to the sofas where Miriam sat.

"What's going on?" he asked as she pulled him down to a seat beside her.

"We've got news," she exclaimed.

He looked from Maggie to Miriam. "You do?"

Miriam nodded but didn't speak, not that she had a chance.

"We were following Mark, and he's finally slipped up."

"You've got something to nail him with?" Tad asked, excited for her. Maggie had put on a brave face over the previous week. She was anything but patient most of the time, and he could tell how angry she was that so long had passed without Mark paying for her murder.

"Not quite. But we have information that's just as important," Miriam said. After a flicker of irritation crossed Maggie's face, she added, "Okay, not as important, but it's still big news."

"Alright. What is it?"

"They're going to move the evidence soon. Mark's got something that ties him to my death and wants to get rid of it, but he needs help. We'll be able to catch them in the act."

Tad frowned. "Have I missed something. Them? Who are we talking about?"

"His friends. They're going to help him clean the house up and get rid of the evidence."

"Okay." Tad still felt as though he was missing something, "When are they doing this?"

"I don't know."

"What's the evidence we need to look out for?"

"I don't know." Maggie frowned. He didn't need their history or that strange red glow surrounding her to know she was getting mad. "Why aren't you more excited for me? This is big."

"It doesn't sound like we have much to go off. All we know is that they're moving evidence soon. To be honest, I'm not sure why you're so excited."

Tad spoke to Maggie, but he kept looking at Miriam.

"I know," she said before Maggie could speak. "It's not much, but it's something. However, that's not the only reason we're back. Tad, his friends are all police, like him. We followed him to a place near Cardiff Bay. It was way too nice for anyone on a copper's salary. Mark met with five people and he got angry the minute he walked inside. He had a go at one of the older ones, said he'd been there time and again for them, yet when he needed help none of them were there for him.

"This was where it got interesting. He mentioned that they were always more than happy when hiding the evidence of a murder for their employer, but now it was him they were dragging their feet. It was obvious that if they didn't help him and he went down for it, he wouldn't go down alone."

Suddenly Tad knew why Miriam found this interesting. This was huge. A group of corrupt police covering up murders was newspaper headline big.

"Yeah. Sure, they're doing that too. But the important thing is that we can catch Mark red handed," Maggie said. She was seconds away from a meltdown and he knew just how to mollify her.

"Mags. You don't understand. This is huge for your case. If we give this news to Kate and she can find something to support it, then she has something real to take to her bosses. Corruption in the police is always a big deal and they'll want to get on this. The support Kate will have to solve your case will become unlimited at that point.

"If what you heard this morning is correct, then if they can solve your murder, Mark will take everyone down with him. That means that the entire Cardiff police force will have a strong incentive to get your murder solved fast."

Maggie stared at him, the red nimbus surrounding her fading to a blue so pale it was almost white. He could only hope that meant she was happy.

"What are you waiting for then? Call Kate."

He pulled up a note taking app and wrote some names that Miriam had memorised.

"What about the employer?" Tad asked. "You get his name?"

"Joshua King."

The name felt familiar, but he wasn't sure why. "I don't think I know it. The only thing that comes to mind when I hear King is that God awful tower that was put up about five years ago. You know the one near the M4—"

"King Tower," Miriam agreed. "I remember you saying how much you hate it."

"What's wrong with the place?" Maggie asked. "I always liked what they did there. It's much better than that old office block."

"There's something wrong with the place," Tad said. "It makes me shiver every time I pass it."

"I've said it before and I'll say it again. You're weird. Now go call Kate."

Maggie practically pushed him off the sofa.

Kate answered on the second ring and by the sound of her voice she was not happy about him calling her at work. By the end of the conversation that had changed. In an excited whisper she told him that this was every bit as huge as he suspected. If she could find something to support it, it would do huge things for her career. She hung up so fast she forgot to say goodbye.

"What did she say?" Maggie asked.

"She's on it."

Maggie jumped up and shouted happily before wrapping Tad up in a hug. "I knew there was a reason I stuck around. It's about time we got something going."

Tad just laughed and hugged her back.

When she was calm enough to sit, she asked, "What are you doing today? Any lectures?"

Tad shook his head. "Nah, got the day free. I was thinking of—"

"Good. Then why don't you come to Mark's place and you can do some lifting for us. Maybe we can find the evidence they're talking about and get the ball rolling."

"I don't think that's a good idea, Mags," Tad said, looking to Miriam for support.

"No, definitely not," she agreed. "If you want a conviction to stick, then you don't want to interfere with the evidence. It's best to let the police handle it."

Maggie shot her an annoyed glance and looked back to Tad. "Come on. What could it hurt? Just come and take a look around. He's at work so you won't be caught. You can even wear gloves so you don't—"

"Mags, no. It's asking for trouble. You've waited this long for justice, what's a few more days?"

"I just want this over with." She grabbed his hand. "Tad, once this is over, I can put it behind me. I can move on with my life… afterlife… whatever."

She took another step closer and in a whisper so quiet that only he could hear she said, "Who knows, maybe I could even think about moving on to new things. New… *relationships."*

Tad pulled back and stared at her. There was no mistaking the implications, and his mind short circuited. How long had he wanted to hear words like that? How much did the younger version of himself yearn for it?

But she was dead. Could they have a relationship even if she wanted one?

He had wanted this since he was a teenager and thought he'd do anything to make that dream come true. On the other hand, there was something about the whole situation that gave him pause.

Once more he caught himself studying that strange light. If it represented emotions as he suspected, he didn't think the ugly, dark grey that was almost black was the colour he wanted to see when she looked at him so hopefully.

He was saved from having to speak when the phone rang. He stepped away and answered it.

"Hello."

"Hello. Is… uh… is this… Mr Holcroft?"

"That depends. If you're a telemarketer then definitely not—"

"A man named Jordan Collins gave me your number."

Jordan Collins. That name meant something to him. He could picture a sharp angular face set in an expression of worry. Where had he seen that face?

Suddenly it came back to him.

"Jordan. I solved a… problem for him last year. It was one that only I could fix. Is it something of the same nature you're calling about?"

There was silence for a few seconds before, "Um… I don't know how else to say it, but I think I've got a ghost."

The way the woman said it made him think she was waiting for him to laugh.

"Is it there now?"

"Yes. I think so. It's freezing upstairs and—"

"What's your name ma'am?"

"Mary. Uh… Mary Adams."

"Right Mary. I want you to stay downstairs for now. Don't go up there until I arrive. Where do you live?"

She gave him an address just inside the city. He knew the place, he passed it on his way to work.

"Are you saying you can help me, Mr Holcroft—"

"Tad. Please call me Tad. And yes, I can help. I'm leaving now and should be there in ten minutes. Stay downstairs."

"Oh… thank God. I was so worried and I—"

"I understand. I have to go. I'll see you in ten minutes."

"Okay. Bye."

She hung up and he put the phone back. Maggie stared at him surrounded in a purplish light that he was beginning to think was irritation.

"Where are you going?" she asked.

"Gotta go, sorry Mags. Got a ghost to deal with."

"Another one?" Charles asked. He sounded worried. If these lights were emotions, then worry and fear was a light grey colour. Surrounded by that light, Charles looked more ghostly than ever.

"You don't have to come—"

"No. What kind of man would I be if I let a friend walk into danger alone?"

"I don't mind—"

"Let's talk no more on it, Thaddeus. The matter is closed."

Tad smiled, nodded and headed for the door. He held it open for Charles and Miriam, then waited for Maggie. She stood still, looking at him with a glare of disbelief.

"Please tell me you're not going to deal with this problem over helping me. I thought you were supposed to be a friend."

"I am a friend. But I can't help with what you want. The best thing you can do—"

"Fine. Go. But I'll watch Mark. Someone needs to keep an eye on him at least."

He wanted to tell her it would be good for her to come. Crazy ghosts were more dangerous to other ghosts than they were to people.

It would be good for her to see one up close.

One look at her face made him think again. He turned and walked out the door. His inner teenager who had loved her forever was screaming at him as he did so.

13

Friday, 20th November 2015
09:34

Tony was on his way back from one of his outings as they got to the car. After Tad filled him in, he decided to accompany them. That was fine by Tad, when it came to ghosts, all the help he could get was appreciated.

Less than ten minutes later, they pulled onto a street filled with red-brick homes finished with Victorian styling. Large windows, pointed roofs and tall chimneys helped to make these houses desirable property, though their luxurious sizing was the real selling point.

Some of the houses were large enough to turn into offices and Mary Adams had called from such an office. The first thing Tad noticed as he approached the address was a small group of men and women dressed in business attire. They clustered around the front of a building and were broken into groups that chatted amongst themselves.

"What the hell is this?" Tony asked. Tad shook his head. He had no answer for him, but he was getting a bad feeling about it.

He was spotted a moment before he found a place to park and by the time he got out of the car there was a woman waiting for him.

She was in her late forties. Her hair was cut short, her glasses were large and not the latest fashion, and her dress was conservative. All combined, she looked much older than Tad thought she actually was.

Even after only a morning of seeing them, he was getting used to seeing auras. Hers was an off white colour that touched on being light grey. Combining it with the way she hugged herself and looked back to her colleagues nervously, he was confident this was the colour of fear.

"Mr Holcroft?" she asked.

"Mary?"

She nodded and offered a skeletal hand to shake. "Is this your team?"

He blinked in surprise. She was looking at his ghosts. The thing was, Tad wasn't using his power to reveal them.

"She can see us?" Tony whispered to Miriam. As always he wasn't subtle and his voice carried.

The woman's aura flickered, then intensified. Her eyes grew round as they passed over each of them and settled on Charles, no doubt taking in his outdated fashion and unusual facial hair.

"Oh my God. You're ghosts, aren't you?"

"Is she a Proxy?" Miriam asked instead of answering. Tad stared at the woman and shook his head. He wasn't sure how he knew, but he could identify other Proxies. This woman was not one.

She was normal and yet somehow she could see ghosts.

"Sorry Mary. I didn't mean to go silent on you. Yes, these are ghosts. I'm just a little surprised you could see them. Most people can't."

She looked flustered and had to struggle to get her eyes back on Tad.

"I couldn't see the one inside," she said. "I could only feel it... we all could."

Tad looked past her to the group of nervous looking people. "They could all feel it?" he asked. She nodded. "That's... well... it's unusual. Normally ghosts don't like crowds."

He looked up at the first blue sky he had seen in a month and was further troubled. They didn't like daylight either. In his experience the crazier the ghost became, the less they acted like the living. They liked to stay away from other people and enjoyed darkness. Tad guessed it had something to do with not wanting to be reminded of what they lost.

For a ghost to be there on such a bright day with so many people present was worrying.

"This one doesn't seem to mind. He… She… It has been bothering us for the last week. It started out as a cold chill here or there and a feeling of being watched. Then this morning it got worse. Whenever it was near, our screens would flicker. Sometimes our computers would crash or reboot. Then it started throwing things, staplers and the like. It progressed to keyboards and phones when I called you."

Tad tried to look professional and give the impression he knew what he was doing, but he was stunned. He had known some strong ghosts in his time, but none that were like what she described.

Ghosts that were mad enough could leave cold spots and make it feel as though you were being watched. However, that's it. The only other way they could interact with the living was by touching people and feeding on their life. This caused the worst of the cold spots.

Only prolonged exposure to such feeding could cause permanent harm. However, that was changing of late. He had heard a few rumours here and there of ghosts knocking people unconscious from their touch. But he had never heard of them interacting with objects before.

For it to happen this morning in correspondence with the emergence of his new power was troubling.

"Do you think you can help?" Mary asked, snapping Tad from his thoughts.

He nodded. "I should be able to."

"Do I need to come in with you?" He could hear the reluctance in her tone and knew that no matter what he said, she would do no such thing. He shook his head, and she sighed in relief. "Right. How much do you charge?"

"Charge?" Tad asked. He'd never considered it. "I don't charge—"

"Hang on a second, Tad. We could make some—"

"I don't charge," Tad interrupted Tony. "The ghosts need to be removed and I can do that. You don't need to worry about it."

"But Tad. This is becoming common," Tony protested again. "We should charge something."

"Not this time," Tad answered. Then to Mary he asked, "That building there?"

He pointed to the only house on the street that had a bronze plaque outside with a business name etched into it. Mary nodded. He smiled at her, then walked towards it, doing his best to ignore how the other employees backed away from him as though he had a disease.

Unlike Mary, they couldn't see his ghosts. He filed that information away to consider later. He had more important thoughts on his mind, not the least of which was curiosity about what waited within that building.

They entered through the front door into a narrow corridor with stairs running up the right-hand wall. Though the building looked like a house on the outside, the inside was a different matter.

The walls were bare and painted white. A faux wooden floor had been laid in the corridor and white plastic trunking for cables was running above the skirting. The stairs were lined with a black, non-slip linoleum. The hand rails were polished steel and there were glass panels underneath the outside hand rail that ran right to the top.

It was a place of business and again it was not the kind of place Tad expected to find a ghost.

"You need to think about charging," Tony said the moment the door swung shut behind them. "You've been doing this more and more and it's not as though this job is danger free."

Tad opened his mouth to shoot him down again, but hesitated. For once Tony had a point. This was his twelfth call in six months, not including the incident at Cardiff castle. It might be something to look into. Extra cash wouldn't go amiss.

He didn't answer Tony and instead climbed the stairs. As ever with

Tony, his attention didn't last long, and he switched to another topic.

"How could that woman see us?"

That was a troubling question, and Miriam spoke up before Tad could. "I'd like to know that. If we become visible, then it'll make following people and searching for evidence difficult."

"Among other things," Tony grumbled. Tad forced himself not to laugh. Most of Tony's reason for living would vanish if he could no longer be invisible.

"I don't know," Tad said as he stepped off the stairway into a large, open plan office that spanned the entire building's first floor. "If I had to guess I would say that normal people seeing ghosts is like anything else. People have different aptitudes for different things. Some people might just be sensitive to paranormal things."

"It's never happened before," Charles stated. If anyone should know, it would be him.

"A lot of things seem to be happening recently that have never happened before. I guess it's just another change we're going to have to roll with. Just be careful from here on—"

His words cut off as he sensed another presence. He couldn't see it yet, but that was sometimes the way with crazy ghosts. They were more spectral than Tad's entourage and it took them a while to build up their physical form.

As ever, it started as shadows coalescing into a featureless cloud. It was building on the other side of the room close to a window. As it did so, the monitor next to it flickered wildly.

"That's new," Tony said. He may not be as old as Charles, but he had been with Tad almost every time he dealt with a ghost like this. He had experience enough to be shocked.

"And worrying," Charles said. "If it can affect the living world like that, then what else can it do?"

"I guess we're about to find out," Tad said as the cloud solidified in places and turned pale. Soon enough Tad could make out a skeletal face with eyes that were pools of darkness. It was looking at him.

"Prooxxyyy."

The word was a quiet hiss. Tad shivered and Charles yelped. The firsts just kept coming. He had never heard a ghost that was so far gone talk before.

"Hello," Tad said, thinking to reason with it. "Do you understand me?"

He took a step forward only to be stopped by Charles' hand. "Are you mad? Let it come to you."

Tad saw no reason why he should and knew it was only Charles' fear that caused him to speak. He took another step.

"Can you understand me?" he repeated.

The malformed, white head tilted as though considering him.

"Proooxxxyyy."

This was louder and more like a wail than a hiss. No sooner had the word finished when suddenly it came for him. The explosion of speed was staggering and by the time Tad recognised that it moved it was almost upon him.

It cut a shadowy path across the room, claw like hands outstretched and a trail of smoky shadows left in its wake. It passed through desks, computers and other office staples without hesitating. Every time it moved through electronics the device would overload and spit sparks.

Tad didn't have time to dive aside, it was moving far too fast. He lifted his hand on instinct and willed it to stop.

A shield sprang into existence in front of him, invisible but solid. The ghost struck it as though it were a brick wall. The impact of the ghost against the shield was enough to knock Tad back into Tony.

The ghost ricocheted from the shield towards Charles who shrieked in a tone not meant for a man his size. The ghost didn't waste a second and took advantage of this new target. The moment its skeletal fingers sank into Charles' soft flesh, Charles screamed.

Tad righted his balance and stared in horror as Charles' form broke apart. Much like when he merged with Tad, the edges of his figure blurred and he was fading.

It was feeding off Charles. Mad ghosts had always been a danger to other ghosts in the same way one man was dangerous to another. It could fight and damage, but Tad had never seen this before.

He was so shocked that a full second passed before he did anything about it. He was ashamed that it was Miriam who had to break him from his stupor. She yelled at the ghost, catching its attention which caused Charles to flicker as the feeding ceased. It was only a moment before the ghost ignored her and turned back to its lunch, but it was long enough.

Snapped from his shock, Tad grabbed the ghost from behind, and the moment he made contact it was over.

In an instant he forced sanity on the tortured soul. He also pushed the alien energy that was Charles away from the creature and back into his old friend. The creature shrieked once as its shadow twisted and solidified, taking the shape of an old lady with steel grey hair.

She was dressed in a long, white night gown and was the closest thing to a stereotypical ghost as anything Tad had seen.

"This place is mine," she hissed in a voice that was too similar to her mad state for comfort. Tad knew from that single sentence that she had no intention of moving on. He was about to destroy her when he sensed a new option.

As he mentally reached for her core, he caught attention of a thread stretching off to nowhere. It was connection to some place beyond Tad's understanding, a pathway that was invisible but immovable at the same time.

With the same instinctive knowledge he had in his dreams, he knew what this was. It was the force that pulled a soul into the next life.

Rather than adding his own energy to that of the ghost's core, overloading it and destroying the ghost, he instead added his energy to that unbreakable thread. It was still not visible, but he felt it intensify and grow as he pushed his energy into it.

As if from some great distance he heard the ghost's terrified wail, and he felt the fingers that clawed at him, but it was already too late. With his power added to that of the one already tugging at her, the pull from the next life became too strong to ignore.

He felt an icy cold, a great unease that every soul in the room could feel as somewhere a door opened to accept this soul. Once the door closed Tad shivered and took a step back. He knew deep down where that soul had moved on to and hoped never to have to go to that place. When he died, he wanted the warmth of the other destination.

No longer looking inward he turned his attention to Charles. His old friend was leaning against a wall, breathing hard, though it was a redundant action, and muttering to himself.

"Charles," Tad said as he took a step closer. His ghost ignored him, still talking to himself and closing his eyes against the rest of the world. His arms wrapped around himself and he rocked back and forth.

"Charles," Tad said a second time. Still no response.

On the third time Tad accompanied his words with a gentle touch upon his ghost's shoulder. He sensed the onset of chaos that he often found within the mad ghosts. Icy dread fell over him. In his panic he slammed lucidity on Charles with much more force than he ever had before and it hit his ghost like a blow.

Charles' whole body rocked back, pressing against the wall and causing him to grunt in shock. Even when his eyes cleared, the aura of fear remained.

"Thank you," Charles whispered.

Tad didn't need to hear more. He knew what his ghost was thanking him for. If he hadn't forced lucidity on him, Charles might not have come back from whichever place he had gone to. The madness of his existence had come while he was too weak to protect himself.

Tad felt tears form when he realised just how close he had come to losing his friend. Charles saw those tears and nodded once to say he understood. Without another word he stepped backward through the wall and out of sight.

"Where's he going?" Tony asked in surprise, trying to follow him.

Tad didn't even think, he simply acted. He extended his will into the wall, solidifying it with a barrier like the one he used against the mad ghost. Tony bounced from the wall so hard he fell over.

"What the hell?" he asked from the floor.

"Tad?" Miriam asked. When he turned he found stunned expressions on both of their faces. "What's going on?"

She was asking about his powers, about what happened to Charles and where Charles had gone. All Tad could think of was the bigger picture.

What was going on with the world?

"Charles needs time alone. He'll be fine, but… that was close."

"Is he going to be okay?" Tony asked.

"He will be. He just needs space."

"What about the rest of it? How did you stop that ghost? How did you make the wall go solid?" Tony's questions were fast and excited, but his final question was far more hesitant. "Did you force that ghost to move on?"

Tad was saved from having to answer when his phone rang. It was an automatic reaction to slide it out of his pocket and press the answer button.

"Hello."

"Tad Holcroft?"

"Speaking."

"Hello Mr Holcroft. This is Norah Parker, head teacher at—"

"Of course," Tad interrupted, suddenly more interested in his call than the events he just lived through. "Mrs Parker. Are you calling about Jen? Is she okay?"

There was a moment of silence followed by an awkward answer.

"Actually Mr Holcroft, that was what we were calling to ask you. We wondered if you came and collected Jen for any reason?"

"What? No of course not. What's going on?"

His tone became more intense with every word and he could almost sense her cringing at the other end.

"Well the best thing to do is not panic, Mr—"

"I'm not panicking, I assure you. Just tell me what's happened."

"Jen signed into registration and her first lesson of the day. However, she didn't turn up for her second lesson and there's still no sign of her after the morning break—"

"Mrs Parker," Tad interrupted. He had to force himself to whisper less his sudden dread overcome him. "Are you telling me that Jen has gone missing?"

He saw Tony and Miriam flinch and he turned away from the distraction.

There was another awkward pause on the other end of the line and then his worst fears were realised.

"Uh… Mr Holcroft. I think it might be best if you came over here."

Tad didn't even say goodbye. The phone was off in a heartbeat and he was running down the stairs two steps at a time. Mary tried to stop him on his way out but he ignored her and ran straight to his car.

Miriam and Tony barely got in before the engine roared to life and he sped away from that house to the sound of an angrily revving engine and squealing tyres.

It was a ten minute drive to the school, Tad aimed to get it done in under five. If that meant doing double the speed limit, then so be it.

Jen was missing. Nothing else mattered.

He pressed his foot onto the accelerator ever harder and the speedometer continued to climb.

14

Friday, 20th November 2015
12:42

Jen poked her head around the corner of the street, made sure no one was there, then hurried along the path. She wasn't sure who might watch for her, but it was best to be careful. She hadn't skipped school before and her heart had been beating like crazy ever since she'd left.

After her unproductive talk with Tad on the way to school, she knew she had to take matters into her own hands. Since her talk with Maggie, she had been working out how to get a ghost of her own and teach herself what Tad refused to teach her.

She couldn't concentrate in class. Her mind was stuck going over how helpless she felt seeing Tad injured and knowing she could get stronger if Tad would just let her Proxy.

When the bell for the end of the first lesson rang, she was ready to go.

Slipping out of school was easier than expected. They locked the gates, but the doors were still open and there was lots of cover around the edges of the school grounds where she could hide. Exploring the perimeter, moving from hedge to hedge and tree to tree had eventually turned up a broken part in the fence, and she was free.

It had taken her a few days to figure out where to find a ghost. Being a Proxy would make it easier, but ghosts weren't common. Outside of Tad's ghosts, she didn't encounter more than two or three a year. That was unacceptable. She needed one now.

She set her target location as the one place she expected ghosts to congregate. If she couldn't find any ghosts there, then she doubted she would find them anywhere.

A quick look both ways before crossing the street and then another quick dash through a gate and finally she was standing in the shadow of an old church.

It was a spooky, old gothic construction that had been built when churches were supposed to be grand affairs. Stained glass windows, huge spires, ancient stones, and an arched doorway made it an impressive building.

Jen ignored it. Her interest was in the grounds surrounding it.

The church hadn't been used in a while and though someone cut the grass and kept the place tidy, the graves looked forlorn.

The oldest ones were closest to the church. Jen glanced at a few cracked and faded stones as she passed, and couldn't even read the names. She wondered how long they had to be there for the names to rub off like that.

She stepped deeper into the graveyard and tried to tell herself that the shiver that ran down her spine was because of the cold rather than fear. It was just an abandoned church in the middle of the day. What was there to be scared of?

There was something creepy about graveyards. Maybe it was the reminder of her mortality that made them frightening. But she was a Proxy. If there was anyone who didn't need to fear death it was her. She tried to walk tall as she moved deeper into the graveyard.

Considering there were houses on all sides, it was well sheltered. The trees had kept their leaves longer than usual this year, and though there were a lot of them on the ground, there was still enough shelter to leave Jen confident she wouldn't be spotted.

There wasn't another living soul in the place. The trouble was that she couldn't see a dead one either.

She didn't give up hope. It was a big graveyard. She kept her head up and continued through the stones.

The ancient grey tablets and statues were replaced with clean, marble graves that were much easier to read. She liked these less than the older graves. There was a touch of character to the older ones that was fitting with the church. These new ones were ugly and mass produced.

She stopped by one that was carved to look like an open book. There was a teddy-bear etched into one page and a name on the other. A child's grave for a boy who had been a few years younger than her. Jen wondered if someone would have got her a grave like that had she been killed with her parents.

She hoped not. It was tacky and horrible. Jen would much rather one of the big ones with the statues of angels on them. She liked their sense of drama.

She was so caught up in her thoughts that she missed it at first. The sound was soft and barely carried. However, Jen slowly noticed it and looked up. Someone was crying.

Finally.

Standing over one of the newer graves closer to the perimeter of the graveyard was a ghost.

Jen couldn't make out much about him from the back. He was tall, not too old, and fat. She was disappointed. Jen wanted a younger ghost, maybe one about her age, and preferably a girl. She didn't want an obese ghost. This ghost made Charles look thin.

But he was the only one there and he would have to do. A surge of excitement rose in her, and she had to fight down her grin. She was about to get her first ghost, not counting her parents.

The ghost didn't hear her approach and didn't even turn when she was right behind him and close enough that she could read the grave stone.

WILLIAM THACKER. 1982-2014. BELOVED SON, FATHER AND BROTHER. WE'LL MISS THE JOKES.

We'll miss the jokes? She wondered what that meant. Was he a comedian? Was this even his grave? She figured there was only one way to find out.

"Hello."

It was as though she hadn't spoke. The fat man continued to look at the grave, crying so hard that his shoulders shook. He seemed to get louder and more dramatic. Jen thought it was overdone. She debated leaving him and waiting for the next ghost to come along. She didn't want a cry baby.

She doubted there would be another ghost though, so she tried again.

"Hello."

The crying slowed.

"Hello, mister. Is everything okay?"

The shakes ceased as did the sobs, but he still didn't look her way.

"Are you okay, mister? I didn't mean to interrupt, but I thought I could help. I am a Proxy, and I—"

"Proooxxxyyy."

Jen shivered. She couldn't help it. There was something not right about that voice. It was a hiss and wasn't natural. She took a step back.

"Yeah. That's right. I'm a Proxy and I can—"

"Prooxxyy."

It was quicker this time, sounding more excited. It frightened her even more.

That edge of fear she had been fighting since entering the graveyard got a stronger grip. Suddenly her heart was beating fast for another reason. There was something wrong with this ghost.

This had been a mistake.

She was about to walk away when the ghost turned. It was all she could do not to scream.

His face was wrong.

Rather than eyes there were deep pits of endless black. His nose was missing and his mouth was too high up his face, far too large and inhumanly crooked.

As he turned her way, trails of shadow spilled from his eyes. Jen choked back another scream as his crooked mouth split into a too wide grin and she saw the broken, jagged teeth inside. They weren't human teeth, they were the teeth of an animal, a predator. They were teeth of nightmare.

"Prooxxxyy," it hissed one final time. As it talked shadow spilled from its mouth, pouring like liquid at first until it caught the breeze and billowed like smoke.

Jen stared in stupefied horror as it lunged for her. Finally she screamed.

For such a big ghost it moved quicker than it had any right to. It's reaching hands seemed to appear by her face and she shrieked as she tried to avoid them. The ghost hands flinched from her shriek, wavering as though the sound was rippling through them. The effect didn't last long, and then it was reaching for her again.

This time Jen didn't wait around to scream at it, she was running. It was an awkward backward shuffle as she dare not turn her back on this thing, but when her leg bumped up against a gravestone, she knew she couldn't keep going backwards.

She turned and ran, sprinting as hard as she had ever run and knowing deep down she wasn't quick enough. The grave stones past by her in a blur as she danced and dodged between them. With every sidestep she knew the ghost was gaining ground, and when she reached the line of ancient graves, she felt something grab her shoulder. Instantly her left arm went numb.

That cold was like nothing she had ever felt. It was ice growing within her, slowly spreading like a disease, and she knew if she didn't stop it soon, it would take everything from her.

She looked at the hand on her shoulder, then followed that hand to a face that grinned and came closer. Its massive mouth opened so wide she could fit her whole head in it. Within that mouth was nothing but blackness.

It descended as though he intended to eat her.

It was no simple shriek or yelp this time. When she screamed, it was from the core of her being and held within it was every ounce of terror and regret she felt in that moment.

The sound ripped through the creature like a blast from a shotgun. Its gaping shadowy maw blew apart, and the creature disintegrated into clouds of shadow that shrank back from her. The moment the hand released her, her shoulder tingled. Pins and needles ran through it as it tried to come back to life.

Her scream faded as the ghost retreated. As the sound died, the ghost came together again. Gone was the form of the fat man and in its place was a shadow figure curled in on itself, pale hands clutched over a bald, round head as though protecting itself from the sound.

She realised that she had injured it somehow. It had no protection against her scream. She was sure of it and at the same time didn't want to wait around to test it further. She took advantage of its disorientation and she ran again.

She didn't look back until she was out of the graveyard and in the shadow of the church once more. Her reprieve was over and the ghost was coming for her again. It had abandoned its human form and was flying, a wraith of trailing shadow and true ghostly appearance. It was the most terrifying thing she had ever seen.

She could have stopped and screamed, tried anything to defend herself, but she wasn't interested in trying something new. She just wanted it to be over. She kept running as fast as she could, out past the end of the church, down the path and finally reaching the gate.

Just as she was about to get her fingers on the iron latch it reached for her again and the cold spread through her other shoulder. She thought it had her, but there was a thump and it was gone, the cold leaving before it had chance to truly take hold.

She didn't bother looking back, just ran through the gate as fast as she could. Jen never thought of direction or even cared. She simply had to escape.

She ran until she could barely breathe and there were stars in her eyes. She drew attention this time, and by the time she had five streets between her and the church she was bumping into people as they went about their business.

Finally, panting hard and sweating, she stopped and dared to look back.

There was nothing behind her but rows of cars and startled faces. The ghost was gone, lost at the church, and she was safe.

Tears of relief filled her eyes, and she started to shake. What had she been thinking? This wasn't her. Skipping school was a bad idea. Going after a ghost on her own was even worse. Even Tad took the others with him when he went to deal with mad ghosts. It didn't matter that she hadn't known the ghost had been mad. She should have expected it.

Her tears flowed freely, and most of them were from self loathing. How could she be so stupid? And why was she so useless? One ghost attacks her, and she loses her head. She should have fought it, proved that she was strong like Tad. Prove to him once and for all that she was ready.

Just the thought of fighting that thing was enough to make her panic rise again.

She needed to get back to school. Better yet, she needed to go home. She would never admit it, but all she wanted was to see Tad again. She would be safe with Tad.

Decided, she tried to figure out which direction home was, then walked toward it. Three hours later she was lost. In that time she had been turned around so badly that she couldn't even find the graveyard yet alone her house.

Her fear was constant and she knew things had gone too far. It was time to call for help and let the chips fall where they may. Tad would be furious, but she could deal with that. She just didn't want to be lost anymore.

She reached for her bag and her phone. After turning it on she was alarmed to find that there were a huge number of missed calls from Tad, Kate and a few of her friends.

She rethought her actions yet again. She hadn't expected that kind of response. Suddenly the prospect of calling Tad seemed worse than ever and she hesitated.

That, when she was most absorbed in her inner turmoil, was when the hands grabbed her. These were not the cold hands of a ghost. They were strong, and they were warm. They were human.

This time when she screamed, they didn't let go.

15

Friday, 20th November 2015
13:00

As Dinah climbed to her feet, she struggled to identify this strange emotion. She hadn't experienced it in so long. At least eleven years.

It was pride.

Strange that the first time she felt it for her own actions was the one time she was so stupid. She was there to capture the girl, not save her. Now this long-forgotten emotion made everything worse.

She had grown numb to the evils she perpetrated to keep her family safe. She had even grown used to not being able to face her family and having lost contact with them. She was used to it all, but now her carefully crafted walls were crumbling.

Faced with this one good feeling in eleven years, her deeds felt darker than ever. And to think, she started the day intending to kidnap a twelve-year-old girl.

On her feet again, she shivered to fight off the unnatural cold and looked around the graveyard. It was once more a reflection of the peacefulness of death, not the more violent aspect she had grown familiar with thanks to her employer.

The girl was the latest in a long list of jobs. There had been so many faces over the last decade, she had long since lost count.

Not the kids though.

Those faces would haunt her until she died. Thirty-three. Thirty-four when she took Jennifer Larson.

She had been putting it off as she always did when she went after kids. Adults she was not so picky about, and would take them at the first sign of their talent. For kids she wanted definitive proof. She was enough of a monster handing over children anyway, but ones who didn't have the power would be that final step into madness.

She was close to losing it after she took her first child. Her depression following that was the last straw for her family and she had not seen them since. She was glad. Even though they knew nothing of what she did, she always imagined judgement in their eyes.

She was not the same woman she had been a decade ago. Only one thing remained of the old Dinah Mizrahi, her love for them. It was why she had not ended it years before. She dreamed for so long about killing her employer. She had no illusions that she was capable of it; she doubted anyone was. But she would happily die trying.

Save that the attempt would cost her family their lives. That price was too high. So she kept taking his calls, accepting his contracts and committing acts of evil.

Three nights earlier she travelled to Cardiff at his request. Her employer sent a local gang after a woman investigating Proxy disappearances. The woman was not close to solving them, but she was looking in the right directions and Dinah's employer was nothing if not careful.

However, someone had intervened. In doing so they revealed that there was another Proxy in Cardiff. He sent Dinah in response.

She arrived as the police were finishing up. She had a picture of the woman her employer wanted dead and followed her to her car. There was only one other person waiting, a young girl.

There had been a time when she would never have considered the girl was the one her employer wanted. That a girl so young could be so decisive in a fight was ludicrous. But that had been before she was exposed to Proxies, before she had seen the impossible so many times that nothing surprised her anymore.

She had been following the girl for a few days, looking for proof she was a Proxy and hoping for proof she was not. When she followed her to the graveyard, there was no longer much doubt.

She watched the girl walk through the graveyard as though searching for someone. The girl was excited when she spotted something Dinah couldn't see. Dinah watched the girl talk to herself and saw the moment the girl realised something was wrong. The girl's panic invoked her gift which showed Dinah the ghost she was trying to engage. It was the most terrifying thing she had ever seen, and she was standing hundreds of feet from it, outside the graveyard. The girl stood directly in front of it.

In that instant her professional mind vanished and all she could think was how unjust the world was. No child should have to deal with such things. That it happened in the shadow of a church was further proof that if God existed, He had no interest in their world.

Dinah watched in fascination as the girl ran from the spectre. She was quite a little runner, but Dinah knew it would be no good. She had to dodge the gravestones, but the ghost went through them.

When it grabbed her shoulder Dinah was sure it was over. She wondered which end was worse for the girl. No one should die at the hands of her employer, but to be killed by that thing…

She was debating the point when the girl screamed and Dinah got another surprise, this one not so shocking. The girl's scream blew through the creature like an explosion, tearing it apart and freeing the girl to run again. It was the first time Dinah had seen a Proxy do that. However, Dinah was used to Proxies doing the unexpected.

The child was running again, heading for the edge of the graveyard. It was a mistake. When you find a weapon that can hurt your enemy, you keep pulling the trigger until they're dead.

The ghost was reforming, coming for the girl again, and it looked worse than ever. The girl sprinted for the gate as though somehow that was a barrier the ghost couldn't cross. Dinah knew different.

The ghost would not be the reason for this girl's death, it was her innocence. She hadn't been in enough danger to know how to keep her head clear.

Dinah was half way across the street before she realised she had moved. She was acting on instinct, never stopping to think about the logicality of her actions. All she cared about was that no one should die at the hands of something so evil.

It was almost on top of the girl as she reached the gate. Dinah was almost there as well.

The spectral hand landed on the girl's shoulder, but in that instant Dinah reached the edge of the cemetery. She launched herself over the wall, onto the shape behind the girl.

In hindsight it was stupid. She wasn't a Proxy. She should have gone right through the ghost and made no impact. But she didn't.

She collided with it as though it was made of flesh and bone and the impact forced the ghost from the girl.

An incredible cold spread through her before they hit the ground and rolled. She had felt it before, but only briefly. She had been warned of it and knew it came from contact with a deranged spirit. Her employer said that to touch it too long was death.

She continued to roll, forcing herself away from the ghost and rising into a crouch. She was on her feet just in time for the ghost to strike again. It hadn't rolled like her. It had dissolved into shadow and reformed facing her. The girl was forgotten by both of them as they faced off. The ghost was enraged that it had been forced from its prey. Dinah was sure this was the end for her. She was debating whether to welcome it with open arms or fight as always.

Either way, she wasn't paying attention to the girl as she escaped.

The ghost came right at her with speed she could never match even if she wanted to. She didn't want to. She was ready for death no matter how it came. She stood tall and opened her arms, welcoming it.

It never came.

An instant before it hit, the girl moved out of range and her influence over the ghost ended. It disappeared just before striking, no longer able to do more than make her shiver.

The realisation that she would be denied the release of death she so desperately wanted drove Dinah to her knees. The pain, bitterness and self loathing of the past eleven years washed through her in a flood and she sobbed.

It was too much. A moment of weakness after so long being hard.

Now, ten minutes later, cried out and feeling herself again, she debated her sanity. What made her act like that? She knew the cost of failure and risked it all for a girl she didn't even know.

There were two kids, one of them not much older than that girl, who she knew intimately. Their lives were the cost of failure. That could not happen.

She turned in the direction the girl had run and got hold of herself. The girl could be anywhere by now, but Dinah didn't let that put her off. She would do what was needed.

Pulling herself together, Dinah once more hunted her prey. She hadn't failed to deliver yet, she was not about to this time.

She'd have the girl to her employer by nightfall.

16

Friday, 20th November 2015
13:12

Tad left the poor head teacher in tears. He put the blame of Jen's disappearance on the school, even though they didn't deserve it. If Jen wanted to play hooky, she'd have found a way sooner or later. He also knew that if she had been taken like the other Proxies, the school couldn't have protected her.

By the time he got back to his car he was in a foul mood.

He had sent Tony and Charles out looking whilst he dealt with the head teacher. He had sent Miriam to find Maggie and enlist her aid. As he arrived at his car, he found Miriam waiting. He knew by the look on her face and the way her aura flickered between red and purple, anger and irritation, that something was wrong.

"What is it?"

"She's not coming."

He took a few seconds to register what she said. Slowly the words sunk in and he felt his anger rising.

"She said what?"

Miriam looked equally annoyed. "She said she wasn't coming, that she doesn't know Jen very well, has no idea where she'd go and wouldn't be of much help. In the meantime, she won't give up following Mark."

Tad swore and had to stop himself from hitting the roof of his car. He couldn't believe it. He knew Maggie was annoyed that he hadn't gone with her to Mark's, but to not help find Jen…

The old Maggie from five years ago wouldn't have hesitated. At the mention of Jen being missing, she would have been the one organising the search.

"Fuck her," he said out loud. "I haven't got time to worry about this. Any news from Charles and Tony?"

Ghosts could move much quicker than humans. It was another of those perception things. The laws of physics meant little to them. They were as quick as they had the imagination to be, and a motivated ghost could be quick indeed.

Tad expected Tony or Charles to be back by now. At Miriam's shake of the head he felt something snap. He was waiting for someone to tell him they had found her, that he didn't need to worry. Every missed opportunity for that to happen was causing him pain.

"Never mind. Let's get looking. You coming with me or—"

"I'll head out on my own," Miriam interrupted. "Divide and conquer."

Tad hesitated before nodding. Miriam going alone would leave Tad on his own. Since he met Charles, he had barely spent a moment of his life alone.

As uncomfortable as it made him, Jen came first. If he had to be vulnerable while they found her, then that is what he would be. At his nod Miriam turned and ran toward the tree line. She moved quicker than a normal person and by the time Tad was in the car, she was long gone.

"Bloody hell, Jen. Where are you?"

He shook his head to clear it and pressed the button on the dash to start the engine.

Three hours later, after he had driven down what felt like every street in Cardiff, his phone rang. He thumbed the answer button on the steering wheel.

"Jen?"

"Uh… No. Stella."

Stella. He didn't have time for her right now and was about to tell her so, but she beat him to the punch.

"Tad. Jen's with me."

"What?"

"I found her—"

"Hang on a second, Stella," Tad pulled the car to the side of the road and parked up. He wanted to listen to this, and he didn't want the distraction of driving while he did so.

"Right, I'm parked now. What did you say?"

"I was on my way out of town and I caught sight of Jen."

"Oh. Thank God. Is she there with you now? Is she okay?"

"Yes, she's fine. She's shaken up and hasn't told me much. I thought I should call you to let you know I have her."

Tad breathed a huge sigh of relief. He closed his eyes and leaned his head back against the headrest, suddenly exhausted.

"Thanks Stella. God, I was so worried. Where are you now? I'm in my car anyway so—"

"Actually, I'm in a serious rush. I've got a lead to chase up in Llanelli and I need to be there by five or I'll miss it." He looked at the dash, it was quarter past four. If she wanted to get to Llanelli in that time then she would need wings. "I haven't got time to wait. Any chance I could keep her while I go see about this and drop her off with you later?"

Tad hesitated and looked at the clock again. He desperately wanted to see Jen. It was one thing knowing she was safe and another to see it with his own eyes. On the other hand, Stella had done him a huge favour just by finding her.

"Are you sure she won't be in your way? I can follow you to Llanelli if you want. Just give me the address and—"

"No. She'll be fine, I promise. So long as you're okay with it I'll keep her with me and drop her off at your place later tonight, maybe eight-ish."

Again Tad hesitated, but finally he let out another sigh. Jen was safe, that was the important thing.

"Okay. So long as she won't be in the way. If you wan't I'll put you up some dinner for when you get back."

"You really don't need to—"

"I insist. I owe you big time for this. You eat lasagne? I make a mean lasagne."

There was a slight hesitation on her end and finally she said, "Okay. You've twisted my arm."

"Right. I'll see you then. Any chance I could speak to Jen before you go?"

"Of course. Hold on." Tad heard that muffled silence that was the sound of a phone been pulled away from someone's ear, and in a much more muted tone he heard, "Jen. Your dad's on the phone. He wants to talk to you."

"I don't want to talk to him. He'll just shout at me."

"He wants to know you're okay."

"No. Please. I don't want to speak to him."

The argument went on for a few minutes and became harder to hear as Stella must have covered the phone with her hand. Tad got the gist of it. It was typical of Jen to put up a fuss. He had been worried sick about her and no doubt she had been off having the time of her life.

A moment later he heard the popping and crackling as the phone was picked up again.

"Tad. It's still Stella. Jen doesn't want to talk right now—"

"I know. I heard. I'm so sorry about her, Stella. She's normally better behaved than that. Just let me know if she's too much and I'll—"

"No. Honestly, she'll be fine. I'll have her back to you in a few hours. I've really got to go now, Tad."

"Of course. Sorry. Thanks again. You're a lifesaver. I'll see you later."

She said goodbye and hung up. The car went silent.

Tad closed his eyes and banged his head against the headrest. His anger returned. He had been frustrated with Jen a lot over the past year, but this was the first time he really felt like strangling her.

Then there was Maggie. He couldn't believe she wouldn't help him.

It was all too much. The disappearance of his friends, his increasing power, and his growing certainty that there was something wrong with the world. Now this.

He fumed as he tried to get a grip on himself and finally he pushed it aside He knew dwelling on it would get him nowhere. He just had to be happy that at least he had one crisis solved.

He started the car and pulled into traffic, intending to leave his negative thoughts behind.

Sadly, life doesn't work that way.

Tad opened the door and was greeted with apple pie.

It was a supermarket bakery model, in a plastic box but no less delicious looking for it. Attached to that box was a big red sticker that said one pound, along with two hands that were attached to a smiling Stella.

"I hope this is okay?"

Tad was a little too stunned to speak. He had never seen Stella dressed down before. She seemed to fit those blouses and business suits so well that he presumed she always wore them. He was not prepared for this version of Stella.

Rather than trousers and boots, she had skinny jeans that hugged her athletic legs and trainers. In place of her blouse and business jacket was an over sized hoodie. Even the way she tied back her hair was more casual and less considered than usual.

Everything about her had been dialled down a notch. Not that she didn't look great. In fact, she looked better than ever. Before she always appeared like some picture perfect cutout from a magazine. It made her untouchable and therefore not real. This was no longer the case and the awkwardness Tad thought he had lost around her crept back in.

"You really didn't have to," he said. He stepped aside so she could enter and he finally caught sight of Jen.

She was dressed in the same getup as Stella. She even had her hair tied back the same way. Her head was down and she stared at the floor, only glancing up when she thought Tad wasn't watching. He wondered where she got the outfit. By the size of the clothes he expected they might belong to Stella.

"It was no trouble. It was just staring at me on one of those stands as I waited at the checkout, and I thought, why the hell not?" Stella made a point of looking to the kitchen and said, "It smells amazing. Jen tells me your lasagne is the best."

Tad had not taken his eyes off Jen so he caught the moment that the beige, almost brown aura he didn't recognise, turned a shade of pink.

"Did she now?"

Stella give them a quick glance before turning back to the kitchen. "Shall I put this in here?"

"Thanks Stella. Miriam's in there if you want to say hello. I'll catch up in a second."

Stella hesitated, catching Jen's eye and giving her a look that Tad didn't understand, before she walked into the kitchen.

"Well?" Tad asked, drawing Jen's attention.

"I'm so sorry. I didn't mean to cause this much trouble."

He had been practicing what he would say all day. It was typical that when confronted with the tears building in her eyes, all of it went out of his head. Before he realised he had moved, he had her in his arms and she was hugging him just as tight as he hugged her.

"God Jen, I was so worried. Never do that again."

"I won't. I promise."

"What were you thinking?" Jen hesitated and before she could speak Tad thought better of it. "Forget it. We'll talk about it later."

He stepped away, and he caught her look of surprise.

"We will? You're not going to shout at me?"

He laughed. "Oh, there'll probably be a few words. But right now dinner's nearly ready. We'll talk more tonight. Why don't you go drop your things upstairs then come down for dinner?"

She didn't move, she just looked at him with a puzzled expression. "You don't sound mad. It's weird."

He laughed again. He had been mad all day. He had raged to himself while he tidied the house, raged with the others when they had come back from their searches and continued to rage silently until he opened that door to Stella and Jen. Seeing her home and safe sapped that rage from him. Suddenly he was just glad to have her back.

"I've been mad. We'll definitely be having words. But for now I'm just glad you're okay. Now hurry up." He turned to walk into the kitchen, then remembered something and turned back. "And don't think you've got off lightly. Tony and Miriam will probably give you an ear full as soon as they see you. You know what they're like. You've had them worried too."

Jen winced. "And Charles?"

"Please. You know what he's like. He's a big softie. Wait to see him last. You'll need one of his hugs after Miriam gets through with you."

In spite of everything she smiled. Seeing that smile, Tad felt a lot of his worries slip away.

"I'll never get used to seeing her," Stella said as Miriam left the room. Stella was curled up in the right corner of the centre sofa, her bare feet tucked under her and a mug of coffee steaming in her hands. She stared at the door Miriam left through and shook her head.

"I saw her body. She was definitely gone. Now look at her. Walking around as though it's the most normal thing in the world."

"Give it time," Tad answered. "It gets easier."

He leaned back into his own corner, stifling a groan from a bloated feeling as he ran his fingers over the guitar. Between Stella, Jen and himself they had polished off a whole lasagne, two sticks of garlic bread and the apple pie. Now he struggled to move. Even his fingers felt fat as he plucked at the strings.

"Easy for you to say. You were born for this. It's second nature to you."

"You could say that. Of course, it took a bit of getting use to when I could suddenly see again. That was a shocker."

"What?"

He told Stella of how he had been blinded as a child, how he was still blind if he didn't have his ghosts with him. She listened with an excited smile and surrounded by an aura that was as blue as her eyes. She hung on his every word.

"You keep getting weirder and weirder," she said when he finished. He laughed. Who was he to disagree?

She was about to say something else when she paused and stared at him. Her smile faded and he couldn't read the expression that replaced it. The blue glow remained, but it was muted, so that was no help either.

"What's wrong?" he asked.

"That's beautiful," Stella said in what sounded like awe.

As they had talked, Tad had worked out the tension in his hands and had moved onto a more complicated song. It was Tony's talent at work, so it was no effort to play while he carried on a conversation with her.

"Thanks. I'll pass your praise onto Tony. It's his talent I'm channelling right now."

"What?"

He continued to play the song as he reminded her of the benefits of being a Proxy. He also told her of how the longer his ghosts were with him, the more he became like them. It was why he was getting better at thinking like a detective, a talent he got from Miriam, and why he had a genuine interest in history, though he would swear otherwise to Charles.

"What did you get from Maggie?" Stella asked.

He fought back a frown as he thought of the one ghost who had not returned yet.

"She was an artist. She owned the Jensen Gallery and did well for herself. I haven't tried it yet, but I'm sure I'll have her artistic talents if I ever want to use them. If she was with me for a few more years, then

I wouldn't be able to stop myself. Like I said, the longer they're with me the more I become like them. The things they want becomes the things I want. It's how they continue to make their mark on the world."

"By doing what they did in life through you by proxy," Stella said. "I think I'm starting to get why you're called that now."

"It's fitting," Tad agreed.

A comfortable silence settled over them as he continued to play. After dinner, first Jen and then his ghosts had excused themselves one by one, until Tad sat alone with Stella in the living room. Eleven o'clock approached, but she was making no move to go home.

"I can't thank you enough for looking after Jen."

"You have to stop thanking me. Seriously. It was no bother."

He sighed and shook his head. "It shouldn't have happened. I can't believe she did it. She's been acting up recently, but to leave school like that... I don't know where she got the idea."

"She had her reasons," Stella assured him. "You should talk with her."

Tad tried to hide his wince, but failed. He'd been putting it off all evening and now she was in bed he wouldn't bring it up until the morning. He wasn't ready to confirm his suspicions, to hear she had left because she finally had enough of him.

"I'm serious, Tad. She has her reasons and they might not be what you think."

The tone made Tad suspicious, and he looked at Stella who was patiently watching him and sipping her coffee.

"You know something?"

She nodded. "We talked in the car."

"And?"

"And you should talk with her. It's not my place to get in the middle of this."

"You're right. Sorry. It's just... Forget it. It doesn't matter."

She surprised him by leaning across the sofa and laying a hand on his arm.

"No. Tell me. What were you going to say?"

He hesitated, then gave in.

"It's just getting to be too much for me. I didn't know what I was agreeing too when I took her in. I love her, I just don't think I'm good for her right now. She doesn't seem happy here."

Stella squeezed his arm and her smile never wavered.

"You're too hard on yourself. You're doing a better job than you think."

"She wouldn't be acting out the way she does if I was doing such a good job. I'm sure deep down she still blames me."

"Blames you for what?"

"For making her parents move on."

Stella shook her head. "No, she doesn't. Trust me, that girl doesn't blame you for anything. Quite the opposite."

"What does that mean?"

"Just talk to her. And stop being so hard on yourself. Trust me, I wish I had a dad like you when I was Jen's age."

Her tone didn't change when she spoke, but he saw the flicker of shadow pass over her aura. He was still not used to what the colours meant, but he doubted that shadow was anything good.

"You not close with your dad?" he asked.

This time the shadow spread through her aura like poison and she couldn't keep the flicker of distaste from her face. A moment later her expression was neutral again even if her aura remained dark. She waved the question away.

"I'm not saying that." For the first time he sensed the lie in her words. He felt the potential for an awkward silence so he changed the subject.

"So, Llanelli. Did your lead pan out? Is the case solved?"

Stella laughed and a flicker of blue and purple pushed back the shadow.

"Hardly. It was a waste of time. Yet another dead end." Suddenly the blue sparked to life and pushed the other colours away as it turned paler and brighter. She turned back to Tad and her eyes were almost sparkling as she looked so excited. "I almost forgot, I was going to call you this evening anyway?"

Her excitement was infectious. "A break in the case?"

"No, but I have news. You know I said that the official word is to take ghost sightings seriously these days? Well, it turns out that there's been a lot more going on than I thought. There's been sightings and strange happenings all over the country. The powers that be aren't just looking to take these stories seriously, they're looking for help.

"They've been approaching mediums, psychics... anyone they can think of to get their head around this stuff. So far they've not found anyone who is anything more than a fake."

She reached over again and poked him in the arm. "That's where you come in. I told my bosses I might know someone who can help. Don't worry, I didn't give them your name. But I told them what I had seen you do. They said that if you're interested and can prove yourself, they'd be happy to hire you as a consultant."

Tad was about to tell her he didn't think it was a good idea. He didn't have a good track record of telling people what he could do, even if he could prove it. A lifetime of keeping his abilities secret was a hard habit to break. However, Stella spoke again before he could answer.

"If you come on board, you'd officially be part of the investigation. I can bring you to the station, show you everything we've got so far and work together from here on out. No more sneaking around and keeping secrets. We'd be in this together. What do you say?"

He didn't know what to say. A few seconds earlier it would have been a guaranteed no, but now he wasn't so sure. Stella had access to different resources than he did. It might give him the opportunity to get some answers for a change.

After thinking it over he said, "You know. That sounds like a good idea."

Stella grinned. "I thought you'd say that. You've got an appointment for Monday at ten."

He blinked. "I do?" She nodded. "What if I was busy?"

"You're not. You haven't got a lecture until one, and I'm sure you'll be done by then."

He blinked again. "Have you been stalking me?"

A hint of pink crept into her aura, but she just smiled. "You wish. No. I got your timetable from the university when I thought you might be a person of interest."

Tad winced. "You really thought I might have something to do with this enough to get my schedule?"

Stella shook her head. "No. Of course not. But I had to cover my bases."

She was too good at keeping her expression cool and he couldn't tell if she was lying. Had she really been that interested in him for these disappearances? Was she still? Was that why she was here?

Just a few days earlier she had been doing everything she could to seduce him. He knew then that something wasn't right. Was she trying a new angle?

He suddenly felt uncomfortable and Stella sensed it. Her smile slipped, and she stared at him with a serious expression.

"Tad. You saved my life. I'll never forget that. I never liked you for these murders and now I know you, I don't even remotely suspect anything. Please, you have to trust me."

For once Miriam wasn't in his ear to tell him what to think. Tony wasn't there to say something inappropriate that would break him from whatever woman-voodoo-magic Stella cast whenever she spoke. He had to rely on his instincts. Those instincts were telling him that she was being serious. He could trust her.

"I think I do. Especially now I've seen the real Stella."

She arched a perfect eyebrow. "The real Stella?"

He gestured to her sitting curled up at the other end of his sofa. "This relaxed version of you that's not wearing the kind of clothes that make me sweat, or making me feel like a gazelle talking to a hungry lioness. That Stella scared me. I like this Stella more. I think I could be friends with this Stella."

Pink flushed through her aura, and he wasn't sure if it was the glow he was seeing or if she really was blushing. Her grin was impossible to miss though.

"I think I'd like that," she said. "Did I really scare you?"

"I was more scared around you than I would be around a real lioness."

She laughed again. "I wasn't trying to be scary. I just wanted to get your attention."

"I know. That was the problem. Beautiful women don't normally want my attention."

"I wanted to know why Kate was so interested in you. When you got involved with this case and were holding things from me, I might have gone overboard."

"Overboard? You're the only thing Tony has talked about for weeks."

Stella looked worried. "He hasn't really watched me shower has he?"

"Probably not. You never know with Tony, but I don't think so. I don't think he's half as bad as Miriam says. He spends most his time at strip clubs. He won't really spy on people against their will."

"That's still weird for a boy his age."

"His age? He's older than either of us. Tony was fourteen when he died, but he's been dead for over fifteen years."

"And he still acts like that?"

"Ghosts don't change. There might be a few personality shifts here or there, but they're the same person they were when they died."

She shook her head, her smile fading. "This is still so weird for me. A few days ago I thought it was a joke that I had to take ghost talk seriously. Now here I am sitting here with a Roxy talking about a thirty-year-old teenage ghost."

"Proxy," Tad corrected and got a cheeky grin in return.

"I know. Just teasing." She glanced past him as caught sight of the clock. "Shit, is that the time? I need to go."

Tad looked over his shoulder. Half eleven. He was surprised how quick the evening had gone considering how long his day had been.

Stella stood up and Tad stood with her, putting the guitar back in its corner and walking her to the door.

"Thanks for dinner. Jen was right. You do make the best lasagne."

"It's me that should thank you. I owe you after today."

"Like I said, it was nothing." She opened the door and hesitated. "So I'll see you at work Monday, ten o'clock?"

He nodded. He was suddenly excited about it. He'd never been part of a police investigation before. He had seen a few through Miriam's memories, but he suspected that it wasn't the same.

"Yeah, I guess I will."

She grinned at him, then leaned in and kissed him on the cheek. It was soft, quick and surprised both of them.

"Thanks for tonight. See you Monday." Her words came out in a rush and before he had chance to respond she was jogging to her car. The rain had blessedly held off for one day, but it was still cold.

The indicators on her Mini blinked as she unlocked the car and climbed in. He waited while she started the engine and pulled away. She gave him a brief wave before she left and he waved back, his eyes following her tail lights down the street until they disappeared around the corner.

"I see you had a good night."

Tad jumped and turned toward the sarcastic voice.

Maggie stared at him with an odd expression on her face. Her aura was purple flecked with green and he was too tired to work out what that meant. He was also too tired to have it out with her as he meant to when she got home.

Now that Jen was back, he just wanted to put the day behind him. He didn't have the energy for anything else.

He nodded to Maggie and closed the door. He didn't ask her about Mark, she didn't offer anything. Other than that initial comment they ignored each other as Tad went about the house doing some last minute cleaning and turning out the lights.

He was ready for bed. He had to talk to Jen in the morning and he might as well talk to Maggie then. The annoying thing was that he had been in a good mood until Maggie showed up. As he climbed the stairs he was determined to capture that good mood again.

He thought of the evening, the relief at seeing Jen again and the pleasant conversation with Stella. It was a surprisingly pleasant end to a crappy day.

The moment that stood out to him as he climbed into bed and closed his eyes was the goodbye kiss at the door. It had been a chaste, friendly kiss, but he could still feel her lips against his cheek.

It was an interesting thought that occupied his mind until sleep claimed him.

17

Saturday, 21st November 2015
10:00

It was tense in the Holcroft household the next morning.

Tad woke at nine, heard Jen moving and decided to stay in bed until ten. He needed time to get his mind working.

After showering and changing, he made his way downstairs and found Jen at the breakfast counter talking with Maggie. Their conversation ended as he walked in and he got the impression he wouldn't have liked what they were talking about. He stifled a groan. He was barely awake and was already exhausted. He needed a holiday.

Tad said good morning and made himself a coffee before joining them. He sat on the stool next to Jen and turned his attention on her.

"Come on then. What happened yesterday?"

She sighed, glanced at Maggie, then went into her tale. Tad was stunned by the time she got to the ghost. As fascinated as he was with its reaction to Jen's scream, the emotion that won out was his returning terror for her safety.

"Damn it, Jen. This is exactly what I'm talking about. You need to wait until you're older to do this sort of thing. You could've been killed."

Jen's aura was muted until he spoke, but a hint of red woke it up again and she turned on him.

"Maybe if I was prepared for yesterday then I would've been better able to handle myself?"

"No, you shouldn't have been in that position. You can't go out looking for trouble and blame me when it finds you."

"Please. Trouble is never far away you're around."

The comment had physical weight and Tad flinched. His expression took the fire out of Jen, but it was too late to take it back.

"I think I've done a good job of making sure whatever trouble I get involved in doesn't find its way back to you. Frankly, I'm fed up of having this argument… of arguing with you full stop. All you ever do is go against what I ask. What even gave you the idea to do that yesterday?"

Jen's anger flared, and she wasn't thinking when she answered. "I was talking with Maggie about how you learnt to be a Proxy. I figured that if you couldn't be bothered to teach me, then I would teach myself like you did."

Tad looked at Maggie who seemed every bit as surprised as he was.

"This was your idea?"

Her shock quickly turned to stubbornness.

"I'm not your daughter, don't think to talk to me the way you talk to her. No, I didn't give her the idea. But that doesn't matter. You're not listening. What she did yesterday was because you don't trust her enough to teach her what she needs to learn."

Her voice grew louder and drew attention. Faces appeared in the doorway.

"She's told you again and again since I've been here that she wants to learn to protect herself. You keep ignoring her and then blaming her when—"

Tad lost control. He slammed his hand on the counter, making Maggie jump and stop speaking. He pointed at her.

"You have no idea what you're talking about. I suggest you stop before I lose my patience. I'm already pissed that you refused to help look for Jen yesterday. Don't make me angrier by sticking your nose into business that doesn't concern you."

She wasn't intimidated. "What the hell do you mean I don't know what I'm talking about? I think I'm pretty well qualified to comment on this. I had a front row seat to your childhood and being a ghost gives me some authority on the subject."

"You think being a ghost for a week gives you an understanding on a subject Tad has been dealing with for eighteen years?" Charles spoke in an uncharacteristically harsh tone. "You think it makes you an expert in something I have been living for over one-hundred-and-fifty years? Trust me. You have no idea what you're talking about."

He turned to Jen. "What this young know-it-all ghost has failed to tell you was how hard Tad had to work growing up. We were forced together by necessity, not because he wanted this. It was hard for both of us, not to mention dangerous. No child should suffer through it."

"I'm old enough to decide for myself," Jen answered.

Charles laughed and nodded at Maggie. "Yes, you are just like her. Old enough to think you know everything, but too young to realise just how little you actually know. Tell me, you decided for yourself yesterday, how did that go?"

Jen opened her mouth to speak, but no words came out. Maggie had no such problem.

"You're using the outcome of one incident as proof that Jen shouldn't get to decide her own fate? Shut up old man. Your way of thinking was over before we got electricity. You have nothing to add—"

"Enough!"

All eyes in the room turned to Tad in surprise. He'd had as much as he could take of this. His recent existence was nothing but stress and he reached his limit.

"This is getting us nowhere. Yes Jen, you're getting older, but you need to trust that I know what I'm doing. I'm not trying to be cruel, I'm trying to keep you safe. Whether you agree with that decision or not is irrelevant. You need to trust that I'm acting in your best interest or this will never work."

He turned to Maggie. "And you. I understand you're having a hard time and have issues to iron out with me. But you're not a parent, you're not a Proxy, and as Charles pointed out, you're new at being a ghost. You haven't seen a fraction of what Proxies and ghosts deal with, so no, you don't know what you're talking about."

Maggie shook her head.

"I think you were right when I first came to you. This isn't going to work. You being my Proxy was never going to be a good situation. I should've listened." Turning to Jen she asked, "Is your offer to be my Proxy still open? If it is then we both get what we want and he—"

"No!"

The impact of the word was four times as strong as it came from four sources at once. Tony, Miriam, Charles and Tad were of a like mind on this. In spite of herself Maggie flinched.

"That will not happen," Tad said in a deadly tone. "You want another Proxy? Fine. I'll give you a list. But you will not force yourself on Jen. I forbid it."

Jen had been quiet, just listening and not daring to speak. At Tad's words her stubbornness returned.

"You can't stop me if I want to be Maggie's Proxy and she wants to be my ghost."

Tad glared at her. "You go on thinking that. I promise, you'll be disappointed."

Jen just glared right back. "What are you going to do? Watch me every second of the day? Even you can't do that. Sooner or later a chance will come when you aren't looking and I'll let Maggie in. You can't stop me."

Tad knew that wasn't the case. He could force Maggie to move on. Either that or destroy her. Either way she would no longer be around.

But he couldn't do that.

This argument and her recent actions aside, she had been one of his closest friends. He would also lose any hope of gaining Jen's trust. It would be an act of betrayal that went beyond what anyone could forgive.

He was still struggling with an answer when there was a knock on the back door and a second later it opened.

Kate entered, dressed for work with a happy smile on her face that faded as she realised she was interrupting something. She looked from face to face, lingering on her ex-lover as though she could read something from Miriam's expression.

"It looks like I've interrupted something juicy. What's going on?"

"Nothing," Jen snapped. "Just Tad trying to control everyone's life as usual." She didn't wait for a response, she just hopped from her stool and stormed from the room. No one spoke as she stamped her way up the stairs and slammed her bedroom door behind her.

"Hmm. It sounds interesting," Kate said. She still sounded happy and as she no doubt planned, her tone cut through the tension. "But whatever is happening, it'll have to wait. I've got big news."

"You can arrest Mark?" Maggie asked, forgetting the preceding conversation and glowing in excitement. Her aura was a blue so pale it was almost white.

Kate snorted and stepped further into a kitchen, taking the stool Jen had vacated. "Hardly. We've still got nothing on him. But, like I said, I do have news. I checked out what you told me about yesterday. I looked into those names and as you can probably tell," she motioned to her clothes that were creased and had obviously been lived in for a day and night at least. "I've been working on it all night."

She leaned on the counter and made eye contact with each person in the room. Kate had always known how to get the interest of a crowd.

"I looked into the cases they've worked, searching for anything unusual. At first I didn't see anything, but then I noticed they've all been involved in unsolved murders. None of them are detectives so they weren't in charge, but they were all first on scene.

"Again this wasn't too much of an issue, unsolved murders aren't the most uncommon thing in the world, sadly. However, there was something of interest."

She paused just long enough to make sure she had their attention, and just when it looked like Maggie was about to burst, she finally spoke.

"All the victims worked for Joshua King."

She leaned back looking pleased with herself. It was Maggie who took the bait.

"So?"

"So I've been looking all night and have so far found over twenty deaths that were either murders that weren't solved or looked like natural deaths, but were related to both these policemen and Joshua King. No one has put the connection together before. Either these people worked for different companies that were only related by their parent companies, or they worked directly for King and there wasn't enough of a pattern to draw attention to it. Whatever the case, no one has put together the fact that there are a series of deaths over a short period that are all related by employment to one man and have your boys as the first officers on scene.

"It was enough for me to take it to my bosses first thing this morning and lay it out for them. It was enough for them to open an investigation and put me in charge. I'm officially the head of one of the biggest investigations in the UK right now."

She allowed another moment of silence for that information to sink in. Again it was Maggie who broke the silence.

"So? How does that help us nail Mark?"

"The police won't like corruption on this level within the department," Tad guessed as his borrowed talents from Miriam's analytical mind put the pieces together. "This is a big deal and will look bad for a lot of people if it gets leaked before it's dealt with. They've given you serious backing for this, haven't they?"

Kate nodded proudly. "The word unlimited wouldn't be true, but it might as well be. All my other cases have been given to other detectives and I have the full resources of the Cardiff police available should I need them."

"I don't care about any of that," Maggie said irritably. "I just want Mark to pay."

Miriam's laughter was mocking. She was growing less impressed with Maggie every day. "You should care. Kate is saying that the number one priority for Cardiff police is dealing with this issue. We know that if Mark goes down for your murder he will bring the rest of his crew with him. That means the new highest priority in the entire police department is solving your murder. Kate has been given unlimited resources and backing to do exactly what you want. Do you care now?"

Maggie's irritation turned to excitement and her eyes grew round. Suddenly she was grinning.

"You need to be careful," Tad told Kate. "We have no idea how far this King guy's reach is. If the wrong person finds out what you're looking into, then you'll be a target."

Kate waved away his concerns.

"I know what I'm doing." She pushed herself away from the counter and stood. "Anyway, that's all I came to tell you guys. I need to go home and get some sleep. Probably a shower as well. I'm starting to stink."

"You can crash here rather than having to go all the way back home," Tad offered.

Kate smiled and shook her head. "Nah. I need a proper rest. I'd never get that here." She looked pointedly to Miriam and Tad understood. As much as they liked to see each other, they could never be together when they were separated by death. It was uncomfortable for both of them.

"I might take you up on the offer over the coming weeks though. I see a lot of late nights in my future and I don't think going all the way home will be fun then."

Tad nodded. "Anytime, you know that. You're always welcome."

Kate smiled and made her way to the door. Miriam followed her out and Tad saw their silhouettes talking on the other side of the frosted glass once the door was closed.

When he turned back to the kitchen Maggie was getting up to leave. He wanted to call her back and continue their talk, but it would do no good. He would just end up at the same place.

Jen was right. If they had their minds set on this, then short of doing something that would make him lose both of them, there was nothing he could do.

Not for the first time he felt powerless. He could do with a win some time soon.

With a sigh he pushed himself to his feet. Sitting around all day wasn't going to help. He needed to be busy. There were contacts he hadn't been able to track down and it wouldn't hurt to touch base with some of the ones he had already spoken to.

He decided to bury himself in work to take his mind off his troubles. He should have known it would never be that easy.

18

Tuesday, 24th November 2015
11:22

Miriam walked around the small room, touching everything and amazed whenever the thing she touched moved. If Stella didn't know better, she'd have thought her old boss was on drugs.

"What's up with her?" she whispered to Tad.

He turned an amused smile on her and she felt her own smile grow in turn. His good moods were infectious. She wondered if it was one of his gifts or if there was still something wrong with her.

Stella had been weird around Tad since the morning after the attack. It was to be expected. How many guys literally change your perception of the world? No matter the reason, she didn't like it. It had her doing things she wouldn't normally do.

Like that kiss the other night.

She was not a cheek kisser. It wasn't how she was raised, she knew no one who did it, so God only knew why she had done it. Now here she was, grinning like a fool just because he was amused. She needed to get hold of herself.

"She's just enjoying the moment. She's not been able to do this in a while?"

"What? Walk around an evidence room?"

"That too," Tad agreed. "But I was talking about touching things. The other night in the alley was the first time I've seen ghosts physically interact with the living. The other day I was dealing with a rogue ghost at—"

"There are rogue ghosts?"

He nodded. "Yeah. When a ghost isn't with a Proxy—"

Stella stopped him and rubbed her temples, faking a look of frustration. "Wait. One explanation at a time. It's my fault for interrupting."

"Didn't your parents tell you it was rude?" he teased.

"Just get on with it. You know, I'm already regretting getting you this job. You were saying about Miriam?"

"Right. Well, after the attack and making a wall real for Tony the other day, we've been experimenting." He pointed to Miriam. "That's the result."

Miriam had settled and was looking through Stella's files. "So she hasn't touched anything real since she died. That's how long? Three years?"

"Give or take. You think she's bad? You should have seen Charles."

"Why, what's up with him?"

"Miriam's acting like this after three years. Charles has been a ghost for one-hundred-and-fifty. It was overwhelming."

Stella's eyes went wide. "I'd think so. Has anyone ever told you how weird your life is?"

"Yes. You've been telling me that constantly since you found out about this."

"Well it's because your life is weird, Tad. Every time I speak to you, you throw some new concept at me that wants to break my mind."

"I'll try to dial it back." He looked at Miriam again and then up to the clock. "If I know Miriam, and by now I do, she'll be at this for hours. Want to grab a coffee while we wait?"

"Not to be rude, but we've employed you, not Miriam. As much as it was funny to see the Chief Inspector nearly mess himself when you showed her to him, it's your eyes he wants on this case."

"I know. But there's no point us both looking over this. I'll know it all in the morning."

Stella felt a headache coming, and had to resist rubbing her temples for real. "I know I'll regret asking this, but how is it that you'll know it all in the morning?"

Tad tapped his head. "This is where they live during the night. For a day after we merge, though I swear it's getting longer, I get their knowledge and they get mine."

Stella groaned. "You're weird, Tad. You're just so damn weird."

He grinned at her again. "Coffee?"

"Oh God yes. How close do you need to be so she can do her thing?"

Miriam had finished with the files and moved onto Stella's personal notes. Stella would be glad to leave. She never liked it when people looked through her notes. It didn't matter how careful they were, they never left them how they found them.

"A couple hundred feet"

"There's a break-room downstairs. We can get a coffee there."

Tad winced. "I was hoping for a Costa or something?"

"No Costa, only instant."

He rolled his eyes. "I suppose that'll have to do." To Miriam he asked, "You going to be okay on your own?"

She didn't answer, so he repeated the question. Stella recognised Miriam's expression from when she used to work with the woman. It was impatience at being interrupted for no good reason.

Tad held up his hands in surrender and backed out.

Stella led him down the corridor towards the stairs and was unnerved by the looks they received. Being looked at went hand in hand with her appearance, but she was not used to people staring past her to the person she was with, nor the varying expressions.

There's nothing harder to keep down in a police station than gossip, and Tad's performance with the Chief Inspector was certainly gossip worthy. By now he was probably infamous in police circles throughout the city, if not the country.

When she reached the door to the stairs, Tad rushed ahead to hold it for her. He stared at that door, refusing to make eye contact with anyone.

"Are you okay?" she asked as they walked down the empty stairway.

"I will be. Just having flash backs to secondary school. I've seen those kind of looks before."

"What kind of looks?"

"The ones people give someone they catch talking to themselves. It ranges from pity to hatred. I'm not a fan of either extreme or anything in between."

She nudged her shoulder against his which forced him to look at her. "This isn't school. They aren't children who pick on the weird kid and no one will steal your lunch money. You'll be fine."

He held the door for her to exit the stairwell.

"Spoken like the pretty girl at school. Trust me, bullying doesn't stop at the playground."

"A tough Proxy like you? I can't imagine you lost many fights."

"You forget, until the other night I've never been in a proper fight. I'd call those other altercations, uncontested beatings."

They arrived at the break-room. Stella led him inside, insisted on getting him a coffee and then joined him on the table he chose for them.

He accepted the drink, sipped from it, and grimaced. "This is terrible," he said as he put his mug down.

"It's one of those unbranded blends that come in bulk from the wholesalers," Stella said. "I drink it because it makes you appreciate the good stuff. I suppose to a coffee snob like you then—"

"Hey. I'm not a coffee snob. I just know what I like." He pushed the mug further away and said, "This is not it. Is there any more sugar around here? I need to kill that coffee taste."

Stella laughed and nodded to where the kettle was stowed by the plethora of mismatched mugs. Tad excused himself and came back with six sachets which he opened and slipped into his drink one after the other.

"How you're not diabetic I'll never know."

"One of the side effects of Proxying, the ghosts keep me healthy. The more ghosts I have, the stronger I get. When I had Maggie, I was healthier than ever."

"When you had Maggie? She's not with you anymore?"

She regretted asking when the look on his face soured.

"No. She's not."

It didn't look like he would expand on his answer and she was tempted to let him get away with it. However, a mixture of curiosity and police instinct got in the way. She found that one of the best ways to get people to talk is to stay silent. Most people need to fill silences. Tad was no exception.

Reluctantly at first, but with increasing passion, Tad told her about what happened with his strange family on Saturday. At first she didn't understand what was so bad about Jen being Maggie's Proxy, but when he explained the details she was suitably horrified.

"You can't let that continue," she told him. "What happens in childhood affects who you are as an adult. No child should be forced to grow up too quickly."

He laughed bitterly. "Oh, I know that. This is what Jen doesn't understand. I'm talking from experience. Charles had no choice but to use me as a Proxy, and it wasn't a good situation for either of us. But there's nothing I can do and Jen knows it. My only options would be to force Maggie to move on or destroy her. I do either of those and I lose both of them forever. I'm stuck."

He took another sip of his coffee, grimaced again, then put it down with finality. When he looked back, he was forcing a smile.

"You know, everything with me has been doom and gloom recently. Let's talk about something else."

She didn't want to move on. The conversation fascinated her and it was close to a subject she had a serious interest in. The trouble was, it was a subject she didn't like to talk about. It was probably best that they move on.

"Fair enough." She put her next question down to the madness that possessed her of late. "So, how come you're single? I'd have thought girls would line up around the block to snap up an eligible Proxy like you."

He grimaced. "Yeah. I wake up every morning and have to beat them away with a stick. Come on, be serious. I'm not a prize catch anyway, when I come with literal ghosts as a package deal it scares people away."

"You're too harsh on yourself. The right girl could look past that."

He looked at her as though she was mad. "Really? Because except for Maggie, no friendship I've ever had has made it past the *I see dead people* speech, yet alone relationships."

"What about Maggie? She's cute. Why didn't you two hook up?"

His hesitation told her everything she needed to know. She could see by his shifty look that whatever he said next would be a half truth at best.

"She was my best friend, a sister. It wasn't something either of us wanted."

Stella translated that to, *I loved her but she didn't feel the same way.* She wondered if he still felt that way. The thought annoyed her.

"You know, I think we need to change the topic again. I don't like where this one's going either."

Stella shook her head. "No, you can't keep doing that when things get interesting. I'm sure there's more to tell."

"Oh yeah, well lets see how you like it. Why are you single… uh… you are single, right?" She nodded. "See. You have less reason to be single than me. You're a beautiful woman that most guys would give their right arm for a shot with. How come there's no Mr Martin?"

It was the second time he'd called her beautiful, and she was annoyed with herself for keeping count. What really annoyed her was that she liked the compliment. She never liked it before. From anyone else it felt like yet another pickup line from some new asshole who wanted to see her naked. It was shallow and said nothing about her as a person. But from Tad it felt different, and it made her blush.

"I'm not interested in relationships, I'm married to the job."

"You sound like you read that answer from a card. Isn't that a standard line from all bad cop dramas?"

"Maybe. But in my case it's true. I like my job and I don't have much interest in anything outside work."

He didn't look convinced, but he didn't push her on it. "Alright then. Why'd you become a cop in the first place?"

She hesitated, then wondered if that hesitation was as telling to him as his had been to her.

"Pretty much my whole family have been police for generations. It runs in the blood."

"That doesn't sound like the whole story," he guessed. She was surprised at his sombre tone and concerned eyes. Had she been that transparent? She was normally better at hiding her feelings.

"It's not. It's a long story." Her comment made him awkward, and she added. "I don't want to—"

"Stella. It's alright. It's your business. I don't need to know it."

He meant it. He could see how hard this was for her and was giving her an out. It had a surprising effect. It inspired her trust.

She looked around to make sure no one was close enough to overhear, then after another pause, she spoke.

"The thing with a family of police officers is that there's no one to call when you've got a problem with them," she started. She held her mug in both hands, staring at it and not looking up. This story was hard enough without making eye contact.

"Police have a tradition of dealing with things in-house. You don't escalate a problem by taking it up the chain of command if you can help it, and you don't air dirty laundry in public. What happens in-house, stays in-house. My family took that attitude home with them."

She took a breath as memories washed over her and she thought of stopping there, but her mouth betrayed her.

"I was younger than Jen when my father first took notice of me. He told me I was special, said I was prettier than mum ever was and that

I was her gift to him. My mum died when I was young, so it was just me and him. He was never what you would call a good father. Between the pain over losing mum, pressures at work and having to look after me, he turned to drink. After that it's a bit cliched. It escalated, he grew depressed and got abusive.

"At some point he decided I was old enough to earn my right to live in the house. I was too young to work, so he said my beauty was his payment. He said he needed… company. When I refused, he beat me harder."

"Jesus Stella. I'm so sorry."

She could hear his discomfort. He wanted to comfort her but didn't know how. It was for the best. People she spoke to in the past tried to hug her, or hold her hand, or some other empty gesture. Their touch made her cringe when she was lost in these memories.

"When I was fourteen, he came home drunk and was pissed that I wasn't waiting up. He yelled about how I was the woman of the house, how I had duties. I already cooked and cleaned, but he was talking about something else. Again I refused. Even drunk, he never forced himself on me. Instead he made his disappointment clear with his fists.

"This time he forgot to keep the bruising to places I could cover up. It was impossible to hide, and though he kept me home, my uncles found out. When they asked me about it, I told them everything.

"Like I said, my family deal with our problems in-house. They didn't turn him into the police, they took him out back and kicked the living hell out of him. They told him not to touch me again, and it worked for a few weeks. It was just long enough for him to recover and go out on the drink again.

"When he came home, he was just as abusive, but was more careful about it. I'm sure he broke something that night, it was hard to breathe for a while.

"I never went back to my uncles. What would be the point? It only made things worse. So I took another way out."

She pulled her sleeve back and took off her watch, turning her wrist upward so Tad could see the scar. It was thin thanks to the sharpness of the blade. It was also horizontal which had been her mistake. She should have gone up the arm to do the job right.

"I did it when he wasn't home, but as luck would have it he forgot something and came back. He had no choice but to get an ambulance. When I got to the hospital people asked questions.

"That was it. He didn't go away for anything, he was a cop and the scandal would've been too great. His buddies kept him out of jail, and he didn't even get a kick-in this time. My uncles turned on me. They said I should've gone to them if I needed help. My aunties turned on me too. I was too pretty, they said. I tried too hard to look good. I could have stopped it if I stopped dressing like a whore. It didn't matter that he bought my clothes…"

That was about all she could say. She kept those memories locked away for a reason. The pain that accompanied that much rejection welled up again. For everything her father had done, it was her family turning on her when she needed them most that really hurt. Tears filled her eyes, and she turned away, wiping at them angrily. She refused to cry in front of Tad.

"Shit. We were supposed to be changing the topic to something less doom and gloom."

"Jesus Stella. Don't worry about that. I'm sorry you had to go through that."

"Yeah, well it's done now. He got away with it and is off living somewhere scot-free. I joined the police so I could stop anything like that happening to another little kid."

Her words were harsh, and she regretted them. She daren't look up because she would either see pity, or a man looking for an excuse to run away. All of her relationships, even ones she thought were serious, never lasted past that conversation. Men wanted Stella for her looks, not her baggage.

Just like her dad.

"He didn't get away with it."

Tad's words were softly spoken, but strong. She looked up. Tad stared at her and yes, the pity was there, but not like she expected. She saw sympathy, but there was also anger. It wasn't the expression of a man looking for a chance to leave.

"I don't speak of this much, even to my ghosts. It's not a comfortable topic for us, but you might find it interesting."

He paused as though figuring the right words to say.

"I don't know much about religion. It's not that I don't believe, I've seen so much it's hard not to believe in something. The thing is, religions are too neat. Life isn't a series of black and white absolutes, and from what I've seen of death, that's not either.

"But one thing I'm sure of is that what we sow in this life we reap in the next. Whenever a soul moves on in my presence, there's a… feeling. It's hard to describe. Some move on and I feel warm, accepted and comfortable. Other times a soul moves and there's just icy cold and dread.

"I'm not saying there's a heaven and hell. I don't know what it means. But I know some people go to a place of warmth which is somewhere I'd be happy to go. Others are so scared of where they're going that they stay bound to this world without a Proxy and go mad.

"These are the rogue ghosts I spoke of earlier. To deal with them, I force a moment of sanity on them. Making them sane permanently is not within my power, but I can give them a moment to decide whether they want to move on be destroyed.

"Those ghosts that refuse to move on, who choose destruction over making that final step, are always the evil ones. They're the killers, rapists, and abusers of the world. Even faced with madness or destruction, they'd choose either rather than go on to that cold place."

He paused and shook his head. "It won't make you feel better, I just thought you should know. You choose the kind person you'll be in life. Those choices take you to either one place or the other."

She'd heard it before. From priests with their versions of heaven and hell, to those who believed in karmic justice. However, none of them were Tad. None of them had spent most of their life dealing with death. If anyone should know it was him.

He was right. It didn't make her feel better. It wasn't supposed to.

He had just repaid her trust with a story of his own. He had shown her his view on the world and in doing so he revealed a personal fear. She sensed that he was terrified of going to that cold place. He was doing what he could to make sure that when his time came, he went to the warmth.

She was saved from having to think of something to say when the sound of startled screams caught her attention. She spun towards the door in time to see Miriam step through it as though it wasn't there.

The few people in the break room got the fright of their lives. Miriam ignored them and strode right to their table.

"Tad. Come quick. We've got her."

"What?" Tad asked. "Got who?"

"Her. Cleopatra."

"What?" he asked again, looking at Stella as though she might know what Miriam was talking about. Stella didn't have a clue. Cleopatra? Was her old boss becoming one of these mad ghosts Tad just told her about?

Miriam looked at Tad like he was a slow child.

"Cleopatra. Remember. You said James Tanner's ghosts saw a woman that looked like—"

"Cleopatra," He nearly knocked over the table in his excitement to get to his feet. Stella was about to ask what they were on about, but they were already walking away.

The people sitting by the door scrambled away from the ghost and her Proxy. Tad and Miriam ignored them, and were already out the door when Stella thought to follow them. They made it to the stairwell by the time she caught up.

"Anyone fancy filling me in?" she asked.

"Remember I told you about my dream?"

"Dream? Wait. You mean the one with James Tanner, the shared one with Jen?" She frowned and struggled to remember what he had said. He'd told her so many things that blew her mind that it was hard to remember every little detail.

"Yeah, that's the one. Tanner told me he'd been followed by a woman. He said that—"

"A woman? You never said that."

They'd reached the door at the next flight up and Tad held it open for Stella again. "Are you sure? I thought I did."

"No. I would have remembered. The reason Marcus run from me that day was because he thought I looked like a woman that Tommy said was following him."

"I suppose you've got the colouring down, but I wouldn't say you looked like Cleopatra."

"What is it with you two and Cleopatra?"

"That's how James' ghosts described the woman. They said she looked like Cleopatra."

"And she does, doesn't she?" Miriam sounded smug as Stella and Tad arrived at the small evidence room.

Miriam pointed at a monitor that showed a still frame taken from a security camera. Stella had requested the footage from the Millennium Stadium when she had a theory that someone was grabbed there.

"Holy shit. You're right. She does look like Cleopatra. This is her," Tad said.

Stella stepped closer to the screen and looked at the faces. There were a lot of people on screen, but she saw who they were on about.

Her first thought was to be offended. Not only did this woman look nothing like her, she must have been at least ten years older. However, she did have a hint of the media version of Cleopatra about her. From straight black hair cut to shoulder length, to her size and colouring.

"This is her, Stella. I can feel it. This is it."

Tad was doing his usual magic again, passing his excitement onto her. And why not be excited? She had been stuck at a dead end for months. Now she had a face.

"This is her?" she repeated as she took another step closer. "It's not the best shot in the world—"

"But we know what to look for now. We can go through everything and see if she's turned up anywhere else." Tad barely stopped for breath. "I can show this picture to any Proxies I can still get in touch with and maybe we can finally stop this."

"Let's not get ahead of ourselves," Stella cautioned.

Tad was having none of it. "Forget that. This is huge. When I didn't know what she looked like, she was the bogey man. Some mythical monster that could be waiting around any corner, but now…"

He let his words trial off as he took a few steps closer to the screen. "That is just a woman, Stella. A normal woman. We can get her. I know it."

He raised his hand to Miriam which she slapped in a high five. It was a gesture Stella would never have associated with Miriam before.

Tad kept his hand raised and turned to Stella.

"Come on. This is huge, don't leave me hanging."

"I don't know how huge—"

"Stella. We need a win. For the last few months I've been losing friends, putting up with shit from Jen, and I've had to deal with this pain-in-the-ass cop who kept getting suspicious about me talking to witnesses. Add the drama last week to Maggie's murder, and I need this. I think you do too. That's her. Cleopatra's our kidnapper. That's worth a high five, surely."

God damn him but he had her smiling yet again. She should be more professional, this picture didn't mean much. It wasn't even clear.

But he was right. She needed this. It had been an uphill slog for months. She needed to take her wins where she could get them.

Grinning, she finally returned the high five.

"Yes," Tad shouted. "That's better. Feels good right?" She laughed at his antics and turned to Miriam.

"He always like this?"

Miriam rolled her eyes. "You have no idea."

Tad just snorted and slid a desk chair over to Stella before grabbing another for himself. Once he was positioned at the computer he asked, "So, ladies. What's next?"

19

Wednesday, 25th November 2015
21:04

Not for the first time that week, Jen found herself in the difficult position of admitting Tad was right.

After months of fighting his decision that she couldn't have ghosts, she had Maggie. She never imagined this victory would be accompanied with waking nightmares, a constant headache and fear to ever sleep again. Jen thought that if she could survive Proxying for her parents and learning that they never wanted her, then she was strong enough to survive Maggie Patterson.

She was losing faith in that argument. Joining with Maggie was supposed to strengthen her, allow her to protect herself, and be useful to Tad. So far the opposite was true.

"I don't think this is a good idea," she repeated. Maggie ignored her.

For once the heavy rain and early darkness was a blessing. It added a level of protection against discovery as she slipped into the garden of the semi-detached house that had once belonged to Maggie.

Maggie assured her Mark wasn't home, but that didn't mean his neighbours would be happy to see her sneaking about. Not for the first time she thought about abandoning Maggie and going home, but she fought that impulse. Tad telling her off for sneaking out again didn't sit well with her, but an upset Maggie was much less appealing.

The forced merging of their first night together had been tougher than she remembered. There were interesting memories, but there was a lot she never wanted to know either. Maggie's early memories of Tad were fascinating, but they grew more disturbing when Jen discovered what Maggie had so recently learned, that Tad was in love with her.

Looking back on memories with new information can change them. These memories of Tad could have been sweet, but Maggie's recent interpretation had twisted them to be an example of how Tad had spent most of his life lying to her.

The really disturbing thing was the dark feeling Jen got from Maggie. Maggie was searching those memories alongside her, as though she was trying to remember specific details for later use. The way she did it felt wrong.

Jen was forced to endure Maggie's adult years, her marriage and death. There were a lot of experiences she knew deep down she wasn't ready for.

The next morning had been hard for her, but she spent time with Maggie, getting to know her better and listening to her assurances that they wouldn't have such a bad night again.

The next night was worse.

Maggie returned to examine some of Jen's memories that interested her from the night before. They were not memories Jen wanted to relive, especially the death of her parents. But there was nothing she could do about it. Maggie had an adult's will and she overpowered Jen's objections.

She was apologetic the next morning. She said she didn't know what she was doing and how much she was hurting her. Jen suspected the truth was she didn't care. She knew Maggie better by this point and sensed she was a woman with a strong will and an over abundance of curiosity. Those traits combined to create an unwelcome roommate for your mind.

Maggie was not as forceful over the next few nights, but neither was she careful. Each night was unpleasant enough that Jen put off sleep and her health was suffering for it. That only made it easier for Maggie to infect her days as well.

Neither of them had been on speaking terms with Tad since Jen broke his number-one rule. It was a constant source of worry that she might have finally pushed him too far. He annoyed the hell out of her sometimes, but she didn't want him mad forever.

Maggie grew increasingly more dismissive of her old friend. As far as she was concerned, Tad should be over it by now. Every minute he wasn't made her less respectful of him. It also gave her more time to concentrate on Jen.

She visited her at school on Monday. It took all Jen's will power to ignore her during class, but even so she earned the suspicion of her teachers and friends. At lunch she had gone off by herself so they could talk.

Maggie wanted her to skip school and go find evidence in Mark's house. Jen resisted that first day, all day Tuesday, and again at school on Wednesday. That night however, after Tad left her with Letty yet again, Jen finally agreed. If nothing else, she hoped it would make Maggie give her a moment of peace.

She told her babysitter she was turning in early, snuck out, and an hour later she was wet, cold and miserable in the back garden of a murderer's home. Even with Maggie as support she couldn't ignore her fear. The last time she so drastically broke the rules, she had to deal with a crazy ghost. If something like that happened again, she doubted Maggie would be of much use.

Maggie didn't show any such fear. She was focused on the job at hand.

"See," she whispered triumphantly once they had done a full lap of her modest home. It was a new build, a cookie cutter model that was identical to the three bed next door. There were no lights on and no sign of movement within. "I told you no one was here."

"This isn't a good idea," Jen said again.

Maggie turned a murderous glare on her. "For fuck sake, pull yourself together. I thought you wanted to show Tad you were strong enough to make your own decisions?"

"I do."

"Well, you can't do that if you keep chickening out all the time. Help me nail Mark tonight, then later you can rub our success in Tad's face. He won't be able to argue when your decisions get results."

Jen didn't think that statement sounded right, but she only bit her lip and nodded. Maggie's smile was large and reassuring, but it was gone all too quickly. Once again her attention returned to the house.

"Let me get inside then do your thing," she said as she walked up the garden path toward the sliding, French doors. "I'll let you in."

Jen didn't get chance to answer before Maggie stepped through the glass door.

The house Maggie shared with Mark may have been run of the mill to start with, but now it was quite nice. Maggie had been an artist in life and her flourishes were everywhere. There were sculptures on the lawn and a large mural on the wall. It took a plain house and made it interesting. Not for the first time Jen thought Maggie was probably much more interesting alive than she was dead.

As soon as Maggie was inside, Jen exerted her will. She watched Tad experiment with Miriam, Charles and Tony the other night. She would have given anything to join in, to ask how Tad did it and learn from him. She had to make do with trying to get the trick working on her own.

She managed, but it was hard. If she let her mind wander, then Maggie became insubstantial. Her anger was enough that Jen struggled to keep her focus steady even with the headaches the constant effort caused.

On queue there was another stab of pain as she exerted her will and a few seconds later the door opened. She let her grip on her powers go with a relieved sigh. It was yet another thing Tad warned her of. He said her skills were like a muscle, they needed to be trained gradually. Doing too much too fast would damage her.

She ran inside before Maggie could grow impatient.

"Take your shoes off," Maggie said.

"What? I'm not staying the night. I might need to run at a moment's notice. I can't do that without shoes."

"Your feet are wet and you'll leave marks on the floor. Take your shoes off."

It was not a suggestion. Jen felt a flash of annoyance. She didn't like anyone talking to her like that.

"I'll clean up after myself if I need to. The shoes stay on."

Maggie shook her head and threw her arms up in surrender. "For fuck sake. You're such a child. No wonder Tad has to baby you so much."

The comment hurt, but not nearly as much as the resentment.

"Fuck you Maggie," she whispered and quickly turned away when Maggie looked up.

"What was that?"

"Nothing. What are we looking for?"

"If I knew that, I wouldn't need you, would I? Just look around."

Jen stepped into a modest living room and closed the door behind her. When she turned back, Maggie was gone. Jen decided to wait before following. She needed space.

She looked around the room, noting the empty beer cans on the table, the half empty bottle of whiskey under the table and the dirty plates everywhere. Even the air smelt stale. It did nothing to help Jen relax.

Jen pulled her phone from her pocket and turned on the torch app. She shone it around the room, looking for anything out of place. She'd never been in the house so didn't know what to look for. She couldn't do a thorough search without alerting Mark that his home had been broken into.

Suddenly she felt another stabbing pain in her head. A wave of dizziness washed over her and she staggered, catching herself at the last minute by grabbing the back of the couch.

Jen could hear things moving upstairs. Every time Jen heard a bump, she felt an accompanying stab of pain. Maggie only drew on Jen's power when she touched anything. Jen might have been interested in that revelation before, now she just wanted it to stop.

She decided to leave Maggie to her own thing. If it hurt this much, then she would sit and wait for her to be done. She carefully cleared a space on the lone armchair and sat, leaning her head back against the leather and closing her eyes.

How the hell had she come to this? All she wanted was independence, a chance to try her skills and be strong for Tad. Now he wasn't talking to her, she hated her ghost, and she hadn't felt so depressed in a long time.

She got caught up in a loop of thinking such thoughts, so was surprised when the pain stopped and there was someone prodding her shoulder. A hand slipped over her mouth to stop her screaming. However, even though Jen felt that hand, it wasn't real, and the yelp came out just as loud as if Maggie hadn't grabbed her.

"Quiet," she hissed. "He's home."

"What? Who's home?" Jen looked at her phone and saw that half an hour had passed. "Mark? You said he wouldn't be home tonight."

"He shouldn't be. But he's here."

For someone who was about to be caught by her murderer, Maggie sounded excited. Jen's spike of fear drove her to her feet.

"Come on, let's go."

She took a step toward the door but Maggie's hand on her arm stopped her cold. "What are you doing? Let go."

"No. Stay. We can end this now."

"What? Are you crazy? I'm not staying here. He'll catch me."

"So. You're a Proxy remember. That's why you're here. You need to learn to be strong. I've seen what Tad can do with a ghost behind him. You can do the same. Between the two of us—"

"Forget it. I'm out of he—" Her words cut off abruptly when she heard scratching as Mark tried to find the keyhole.

Jen shook herself free from Maggie's grip and turned the door handle. Maggie grabbed her shoulder again and forced Jen around.

"Don't abandon me like this, Jen. I deserve this. Don't chicken out."

"Get away from me. If you don't, you'll regret it."

Maggie sneered as though calling her bluff, but she let go. Jen wasn't sure what she would have done if she hadn't, but she had let go and that gave Jen the confidence to defy her further. She opened the door just as she heard Mark enter the hall.

"Mark! I'm in here, come and get me."

Jen was half way out the door when Maggie shouted. She knew from the pain in her head that Maggie had drawn on her strength to make herself heard. There was no way that Mark hadn't heard.

Jen slammed shut the door to her power, but the damage was done. She heard a deep voice curse and the sound of running feet.

Jen wanted to ask Maggie what she was thinking. She wanted to slap her. Wanted to do a lot of things. She needed to get out of there.

She stepped out of the house and shut the door. She was only just away from the window when the living room light went on, illuminating the lawn. Jen stifled a scream as it nearly caught her. She ran to the side of the house and the safety of the shadow, never once looking back.

Again she was just in time. The moment she stepped into the shadow, the door flew open and she heard the crunch of heavy feet as someone large stepped into the garden.

Jen froze. If she ran he would hear her.

"He's right there," Maggie hissed. She stood in the light of the living room and stared at Jen. "We can end this, an eye for an eye. Just help me."

Jen shook her head.

"Come on. Stop being a pussy. You don't even have to do anything. Just let me become real enough to hurt this arsehole. You can close your eyes and go to your happy place for all I care."

Jen was still shaking her head.

Somewhere beyond Maggie's insistent tone, she heard Mark moving around the garden. If he didn't give up the search soon, he was bound to find her. She couldn't see him, but she could see his shadow. It looked big.

Tears welled in her eyes. Why did she do this to herself? First the graveyard and now this. If she somehow got out of this, she needed to have a hard look at whatever was wrong with her.

"Shit. He's going back inside. Come on, Jen. It's now or never."

Jen just shook her head and closed her eyes tight as if that might make Maggie go away. She heard Mark's footsteps retreat into the house and the door close. She let out a gasp of relief along with a stifled sob.

Jen wanted… no… she *needed* to go home.

She walked away, ignoring Maggie's shouting, and pulled free roughly when Maggie grabbed her hand. She was done. Nothing Maggie could say would make her go back.

"Fine. Be that way," Maggie said. "You go back home, but you're going alone. I won't watch over you."

Jen didn't care. She just wanted to be home, wanted peace.

She was so desperate to be away that she didn't check if the coast was clear as she stepped onto the street. She walked straight into someone and yelped, jumping back in fright.

This person was every bit as startled by their contact as Jen. She was a middle aged woman, probably a neighbour, and seemed at a loss for words.

"Sorry," Jen mumbled. She quickly stepped around the woman and walked away.

Jen was at the end of the street when that feeling of being watched became too much to bear. When she turned, she found the woman walking her way.

It was dark, but the street light gave Jen a good look at her. She was pretty, and there was something exotic about her. She reminded Jen of a picture she had seen in a book, an illustration of an old Egyptian queen.

She was picking up her pace and her stare was creeping Jen out. It was just one more reason to go home, fast.

She gave up any pretence at being strong. Jen turned away from the woman and she ran.

She couldn't be sure without looking back, but it sounded like the woman was running as well.

20

Wednesday, 25th November 2015
22:36

For the second time that week Jen was missing. Once again Tad went through the whole gamut of emotions that went along with that. Foremost this time was anger.

"I can't believe she's done this again. After what happened last time I thought she learnt her lesson."

He spoke fast, not expecting an answer. He got one anyway.

Stella, sat in the passenger seat, laid a hand on his arm. It was like quieting a frightened horse with a touch on the nose.

"Don't blame yourself again. We need to find her first, then—"

"Then I can blame myself?" He laughed bitterly, but Stella shook her head.

"No. Then you can get to the bottom of what's happening. In an emergency, focus is your friend. Worrying about things you can't do anything about is less than useless."

He grunted in acknowledgement. "Smart. They teach you that at police school, or wherever the hell you guys go?"

"Something like that."

Her hand slipped from his arm and she went back to searching the nighttime shadows.

He doubted they would see her on the road. He already checked everywhere he could think of for her, and his ghosts were out looking. The only one he couldn't find was Maggie, and he suspected she was with Jen. If this was her idea, then Tad might destroy her after all.

After his afternoon lectures, Tad organised a sitter for Jen so he could go to the station and work with Stella. They went through old evidence, this time with a focus on Cleopatra. It was work Stella could do alone, but Tad enjoyed being on the inside. It made him feel useful.

That was until Letty called to say Jen was missing again. Now, rather than being useful, he was a distraction who dragged Stella from work to look for Jen. He hadn't expected her to come, but she insisted. He was glad she had. Not only did she keep his mind on track, but she had given him an idea of where to look for Jen. She asked if there was anything from Jen's past she might have spoken about, a place where she felt safe.

The question sparked memories of stories Jen had told him that took place in or around a treehouse at her old home. She never outright said it was a safe place for her, but when Tad thought back, he suspected it might be.

As a long shot, they headed in that direction. All the time he drove, Tad did his best not to think of Cleopatra. He couldn't let himself think that Jen finally having a ghost had drawn the attention of the kidnapper… killer… whatever the hell she was.

"You can't think that way," Stella said. He glanced away from the road to find her staring at him.

"You reading my mind?"

"You're thinking Cleopatra has her."

"You are reading my mind."

"It's only natural. You think that by not doing anything about Jen and Maggie you've somehow left Jen vulnerable. Well stop thinking that. It's the same as dwelling on blame. We don't know anything yet."

Tad shook his head as he turned off the main road onto the estate where Jen used to live.

"It's hard. I keep fucking up where Jen's concerned. Every mistake leads to another. Last week was so bad I thought it would make her behave for a while at least. She had a few scares that I thought shocked her. Now she's gone again. If… when we find her, I need to think about something else to do with her. I don't think she's safe with me anymore."

Stella opened her mouth to say something, but was too late. Tad pulled the car into a space outside a large, detached property. A few seconds later he was out of the car and was walking up the gravelled driveway towards a modern, red-brick house.

A bright, white light flicked on as he approached and the door opened before he had chance to ring the doorbell.

"Can I help you?"

The man was tall, though not quite to Tad's eye height, and was well built. He was in his late fifties and showed signs of softness around the gut, but Tad was sure this was a tough man. His short hair, moustache and style of dress made Tad think of the military.

"Hi. This will sound crazy, but I was wondering if you have seen a young girl come through this way tonight."

Tad told him how his daughter used to live here and had gone missing. He explained how it was a long shot, but he was at his whit's end. Slowly the suspicion faded from the man's expression. By the time Tad finished, he looked ready to head up a search party himself.

"No. Not seen a little girl. But, hang on a second." He stepped back into the house before Tad could stop him and appeared a moment later with a huge torch he must have kept close to the door. "Let's go check the treehouse. It's still there. Don't have kids myself, but never found a reason to tear the thing down."

Tad couldn't hide his relief. "Thanks. I hate to be a bother—"

"No bother. Let's find your little girl and—"

"Tad," Stella interrupted as she rushed up the drive. She had gone snooping in case the man wasn't happy to let them look around. "I can't be sure, but I think I saw movement."

Tad felt his hopes rise along with his anger. If Jen was there and had forced Tad to bother Stella and this man for nothing, then he might lose it. Of course, like last time, he might just be so relieved that he forgot everything else.

The home owner took point, leading them around the side of the house, his torch lighting the way and eventually illuminating a large square patch of grass surrounded by trees. Nestled in the branches of a tall oak tree at the rear of the garden was one of the coolest tree-houses Tad had ever seen.

Complete with balcony, windows and a door that looked sturdy, Tad thought the place was probably weathertight. If that was Jen's tree house growing up, then Tad wouldn't be surprised to find it was her safe place. It looked so secure he was considering making it his safe place as well.

The ex-army guy reached the bottom of the tree and shone his light at the door.

"There's definitely someone up there. Normally the door's shut tight."

"Jen, you up there?" Tad called out.

No answer.

He stepped around the man and climbed the rope ladder.

"Jen," he called again. "If you're in there, I'm coming up."

Still no answer, but he heard a gasp. He wasn't sure if it was Jen, but there was definitely someone in that tree house.

Tad climbed onto the platform and reached for the door. He hesitated for just a second, then opened the door and stared into the darkness. The torchlight had done nothing to help with his night vision and he could see nothing, but he could hear breathing. He stepped into the darkness and stopped breathing, trying to listen harder. The other person stopped breathing as well.

All was still for half a minute until Tad's lungs started to burn. He let out an explosive breath.

"Jen. Please God let that be you."

In answer there was sudden movement, and a shape collided with him. He let out a startled yelp that was cut short when slim arms slipped around his waist and he felt the familiar presence of his daughter.

"Dear God Jen. You scared the shit out of me."

She didn't answer, she just sobbed into his chest.

With a final thank you, Tad and Stella said goodbye to the house owner and walked to the car where Jen waited. She sat behind the driver's seat, head down and refusing to look at either of them. It was clear she had been crying.

Tad shared a look with Stella and tried his hardest to apologise with his expression. He wouldn't be able wait until he was alone to talk to Jen, and the next few minutes would be uncomfortable for Stella.

She gave him one of her reassuring smiles that did wonders for putting him at ease, then climbed into the front passenger seat. Tad took one last deep breath and climbed into the car.

He said nothing as he pulled away, but by the time they reached the end of the street he was looking at Jen in the rearview mirror.

"Explain, Jen."

He couldn't string together anything more coherent without anger getting the better of him. His tone was already sharp enough to make her wince and sink down in her seat.

She didn't answer.

"Come on Jen, give me something. What's the reason this time? You can't have been looking for a ghost because you've got one. So what is it? Do you hate it at home that much that you—"

"No!" There was fire in her response, but it was gone as quick as it came. Another look in the mirror showed him the deep pink aura of either embarrassment or shame. Whatever it was, the fiery red of Jen's anger was nowhere to be seen.

"No. Then why? I need something because I'm reaching the limit of my patience. I can't win with you."

Jen was quiet just long enough to make Tad think she was ignoring him. Finally she spoke. She didn't go into too much detail, just giving him the broad strokes, but it was enough for Tad to fill in the gaps.

Maggie pressured her into going to Mark's. Things went bad, and she had to flee, leaving Maggie behind. There wasn't a single part of the story he liked and by the time she finished he was holding the wheel so hard his knuckles were white and his hands ached.

He wanted to ask one of the thousand questions in his head, but they crowded each other out. He caught Stella looking at him out the corner of his eye, and when he didn't speak she asked a question for him.

"I understand the rest, but why didn't you go home where you'd be safe?"

Tad looked in the mirror and tried to catch Jen's eye, but she had figured out how to avoid meeting his gaze.

"I was going to. But on the way back I got frightened and changed my mind."

Stella nodded, but a frown formed.

"Frightened?"

Her tone was flat and clinical, free of emotion in a way that made Tad look to see what colour she was wearing. Her aura was blank, like she was in a neutral state and waiting to see what emotion she should feel next.

"I see. Tell me, does Tad hit you?"

The question shocked him enough that he nearly lost control of the car. It jerked and there were bumps as his wheels went over the thick white paint in the centre of the road, but otherwise no damage.

Did she really think he would hit Jen?

He remembered the story she shared with him the day before. He could see how she would have a tendency to suspect such things, but to ask Jen that, right there with him in the car... It was more than a little hurtful.

The only thing that stopped him protesting was her tone. There was no anger, no disgust.

"No! Of course not." A glance in the mirror confirmed that Jen's anger had returned in abundance.

"Does he lock you up? Punish you in any way he shouldn't?"

"What the hell is your problem, lady? Of course not."

"I see." That tone was different, and again Tad glanced across. It was not as wild or intense as Jen's, but Stella's aura was turning red. "My problem is your answer. Are you so stupid that you're willing to risk your safety when there's someone out there hunting Proxies because you were scared of… what? A talking to?"

Jen didn't answer, but the red retreated and the pink returned twice as strong.

"You don't know how good you've got it. I thought we talked about this on the way to Llanelli, I thought you understood."

"I did," Jen protested, but Stella wasn't done talking.

"Clearly you didn't. Since that trip you've made some idiotic and hurtful mistakes that have done nothing but cause Tad and the people who love you worry. If that wasn't enough, you've wasted my time.

"I was supposed to be working tonight, trying to catch a killer. Instead I'm here looking for you. I've also called in favours with a lot of people to get them looking for you. As far as we knew, you were the next victim. That means that your actions have wasted Tad's time, my time, and police time. All of that because you didn't want to be shouted at?"

She paused, waiting for an answer. Jen didn't speak. She just shook her head.

In spite of the red of Stella's aura growing bolder, she kept her voice steady, almost conversational. When she turned away from Jen, it was as though it was no big deal.

"That's disappointing, Jen," she said. A look in the mirror confirmed just how hard that comment landed.

Tad couldn't think of anything to say after that and silence reigned until they pulled up outside his house. Stella's car was parked there, but she left her keys in the house when they questioned Letty, so she followed them inside

"Is Letty still here?" Jen asked in a small voice as they approached the door.

"I sent her home," Tad said. "I'll have to go see her in a minute to let her know you're safe. The poor woman was beside herself."

He didn't think the girl could look any more ashamed, but somehow she managed it. He felt his resolve slipping. His anger was almost spent as he opened the door and turned on the light.

The sight the light revealed reignited that anger and this time it burned twice as bright.

"Tad. I've got big—"

Maggie never got to finish her sentence. All she managed was a startled yelp as she flew across the hall and slammed into a wall. She hit with both feet off the floor and that was where she stayed, pressed into the wall by an invisible force.

Her eyes widened with fright as Tad stalked down the hallway toward her. As he had with the mad ghost at the office, he erected this mental barrier on instinct. His manipulation of Maggie was an extension of his will as his anger overtook reason.

"I've been too soft on you since you arrived," Tad said in a low, dangerous tone. "Our history made me more lenient than I'd be with any other ghost. That ends now.

"You've put Jen in danger for the last time. If I get so much as a thought that you're putting ideas in her head that will harm her, it'll be the end for you. I'll force you to move on in a heartbeat and you won't get to see Mark put away."

He was still walking forward and only stopped when he was a foot away from her. The muscles in her jaw tensed as they tried to open her mouth, but it was no more effort than a thought for Tad to keep it shut.

"To make myself doubly clear, I want you to understand. That is what I'll do if you put her in harms way. If she's ever hurt because of you, then that's it. No moving on, no future. I will obliterate your soul and that will be it.

"Is that clear?"

He released his hold on her mouth and she gasped as though she had to suck in a deep breath. It was further proof of just how young a ghost she was.

"Is that clear?" he asked again, tightening his grip on the rest of her when she didn't answer.

She winced and nodded, clearly in pain.

"It's clear. I'm sorry," she gasped. "I didn't mean—"

Tad held up his hand and instantly she was silent. It wasn't his power this time, but a reaction to his sudden movement.

"No excuses. I'm not in the mood. A simple yes or no will suffice."

"Yes. I promise. Yes."

Suddenly the pressure vanished and she collapsed to the floor, landing on her hands and knees and coughing, again as though she were a real person.

Tad ignored her and walked into the kitchen, turning on the lights and ignoring Stella and Jen's startled stares. He had shocked more than Maggie it seemed.

The truth was he shocked himself.

His shock had nothing to do with the power he used, or how easy it had been. His shock was because he meant every word. If he thought Maggie would ever hurt Jen, he would end her.

"So what were you going to say?" Tad asked after he removed his coat and turned on the espresso machine.

Maggie hesitated before answering. The conflicting colours in her aura told him she wanted to be excited by her news, but was scared at how he would react to her excitement.

In a controlled tone she said, "I've got the information we need to bring Mark down."

"What do you mean?" Tad asked as he made coffees for himself and Stella. He didn't bother asking if she wanted one. She called him a coffee snob, but he knew she was every bit as bad.

"We freaked him out tonight. No sooner had Jen left when he was on the phone to his buddies. He told them he's not prepared to wait. If they don't help him, he's going to move the evidence himself. If he gets caught, then so be it."

"Do you know what he needs all this help with?" Stella asked, slipping into detective mode.

"I hit my head on the fridge on my way to the ground. There's blood in all kinds of places in that kitchen that he can't get to in order to clean it up. The truth is, he's just panicking. He wants it all gone. The units, the fridge, the lot."

"Sounds like overkill," Tad said as he slipped a coffee across the counter to Stella. She took it with a brief smile before her attention returned to Maggie.

"Yeah, well that's Mark. When something's too much for him, he panics. He goes overboard and won't rest until he's one-hundred percent sure there's nothing that could cause him future problems. It wouldn't surprise me if he remodels the entire kitchen.

"That's what he needs help for. He wants to take the place apart and get rid of everything. And they've agreed. They're doing it tomorrow night."

Tad nodded and sipped his coffee. The second it touched his lips he felt better. It was far too late for a coffee and no way should he feel that good after one sip. Maybe it was time to admit to his addiction. It was a worry for another day. For now his head cleared, and he allowed himself to be happy for Maggie.

"Alright. I'll call Kate and get her on it."

"Thanks," Maggie said. "I'm sorry, Tad. I guess, I just didn't think."

Tad nodded, but he had said all he had to say on the subject. It was time to move on.

He felt the weight of the following silence though, and was about to change the topic when suddenly Jen spoke up. Her voice was barely more than a whisper, but she sounded more shaken than she had all night. Her aura was the pale grey of strong fear.

"Uh… Who's that?"

She pointed at Stella's bag on the counter. It had come open and papers had spilled out. In pride of place at the top of the pile was a pixelated photo of Cleopatra.

Tad's blood ran cold, and he shared a look with Stella.

"Why? What is it?" Stella asked.

"She was there tonight, outside Mark's house. I bumped into her on my way out."

"You what?" Tad demanded, coffee forgotten and rising to his feet quickly. He had nowhere to go, so he felt foolish. "You've seen this woman?"

Jen let out a panicked little chuckle. "Seen her? I've actually touched her. I walked right into her when I left Mark's. I knew she was weird. At one point I thought she was following me, so I ran."

Tad looked at Stella in astonishment. "What do you think this means?" he asked.

"Can't be anything good. It means she knows who Jen is at least."

"Then why didn't she take her?"

Stella had no answer, but Jen did. "I shocked her. She looked stunned when I bumped into her and couldn't stop staring at me. Tad, what the hell is going on?"

"Was she a Proxy, Jen?" Tad asked, ignoring her question for now along with the rising intensity of her fear.

Jen shook her head. "I don't think so. She didn't seem like one. She was just kind of weird."

Stella searched her bag until she had her phone. "Don't worry about this, guys. We've got this, I promise. I'll get Jen protection. I've just got to make some calls."

She excused herself and walked into the living room with her phone on her ear. Tad turned back to Jen to see her on the verge of tears.

"Tad? What's going on? Who is that woman?"

Tad didn't know how to respond. He had just spent the night fearing Jen would be taken by this woman and now it sounded as though that really could have happened. It was only some lucky accident that startled the woman which kept Jen safe.

He walked to Jen's side and leaned down so he was at her eye level. Whatever she saw in his face was enough to make the tears actually start flowing.

"Tad?" she asked again.

"Jen. I know we've been having our problems recently, but this is serious. I mean forget everything that has happened and start over, serious. You understand?" Jen nodded and yet more tears fell.

Tad took a deep breath and answered her question. "That's the woman we're calling Cleopatra. She's the one who's been taking people."

It killed him to watch the fear overwhelm her. He had never felt so helpless in his life. So many Proxies had been taken by this woman already. Now she was coming for his daughter. He'd lost her twice within a week, how could he keep her safe from Cleopatra?

Helpless, terrified and completely without hope, Tad did the only thing he could do. He took his daughter in his arms and prayed.

21

Thursday, 26th November 2015
21:00

Tad followed a droplet of rain that ran down the glass. He was supposed to be paying attention to the house across the street, but his mind was occupied by his desire to be home watching over Jen.

"Here they come."

The voice that broke the silence in the car was tinny as it came in over the radio. Kate grabbed the handset.

"Alright. Everyone to your places. Wait until they're all out before you move in. Don't give them any chance to escape."

He could tell by her excited tone that she was loving this. Why shouldn't she? This was her moment.

Things moved quickly after last night's shock had worn off. Stella wasted no time in organising protection for Jen, and once that was sorted, Tad called Kate.

From that moment on Tad was lost in the hectic momentum of two investigations. Kate kept him updated by phone, and Stella stayed at Tad's while they made arrangements and combed through evidence. They were too wired to stop, and they worked late into the night, side by side on one of his big sofas with papers spread out over the coffee table.

When the bust was organised, Kate told him that even though he worked for the police, he wasn't allowed to be part of it. However, so long as he promised to keep Maggie restrained and not to interfere, he could come and watch. It would be off the books and he would have to keep his head down, but at least he'd be there.

Tad was reluctant to go at first, not wanting to leave Jen alone, even with her police protection. To his surprise, it was Stella who came to Jen's rescue, offering to babysit while Tad went out.

A little more comforted knowing Stella was there, Tad finally agreed to go. He left Charles, but took Miriam, Tony and Maggie. He had been miserable ever since, sure that he made the wrong decision in leaving Jen.

Now things were starting to happen, a hint of interest and excitement slipped past his worry.

"You lot, stay here," Kate said after she replaced the radio. She looked to an impatient Maggie and said, "I mean it. If you want this arrest to go down right, then you need to steer clear. Got it?"

Maggie nodded then looked eagerly out her window towards the opening door to her old home. Two men stepped out, carrying a freezer between them. Mark was in the lead and walked backward while an older man had the other end.

There were three more inside. Tad recognised all of them from the files Kate provided. They were the men Maggie and Miriam had overheard Mark talking to nearly a week earlier.

"Where's Kate's team?" Tony asked, leaning forward from his place in the middle of the back seat so his head was between the two front seats. "I can't see them."

"That's the point," Tad said. "But there are a few in that car over there, some more in that van, and there are definitely others around somewhere."

"Have they got guns? You reckon there'll be shooting?"

Tad hoped not, but said nothing. Kate's bosses had decided to take no chances and had authorised an armed response team to work with her.

"Why haven't they moved on him yet?" Maggie asked.

Mark and his friend had already loaded the fridge into the back of the van and were on their way back to the house when Maggie asked her question.

"I think they're waiting for that," Miriam said, pointing to the front door that was opening again. On cue three guys exited, each carrying dismantled cabinets.

Tad had been right about where he had seen Kate's team, but he had not expected just how many more people there were. On a signal from Kate who hid behind a parked car opposite Mark's house, everyone started moving.

It was like something from an action movie.

Bright lights blinked into existence, illuminating the front garden of Maggie's old house. The men froze, two of them dropping their cabinets as they stared into the lights trying to see what was going on. The one closest to the door was the first to react, trying to run back inside.

Armed police were already moving around the side of the house with their guns raised telling him to freeze. He didn't freeze, but he rethought his plan.

He turned from the house and ran in another direction only to be tackled a moment later by yet more police.

The rest of the men weren't doing much better. Now that one of their number had been brought down it was every man for himself. They darted away at different angles, and in each case there were police ready to stop them.

Tad's heartbeat accelerated as he saw two more take downs before the fourth of Mark's friends simply surrendered.

It left only Mark who ran for the edge of his property that lead down the street towards where Tad watched. Two police stood in his way, but unlike their colleagues, they couldn't bring him down.

Before Mark had joined the police he had been a decent rugby player. He played ten games for Welsh under 21s and had played once for the main Welsh team before he'd injured his knee. He may not be playing internationally anymore, but he was a big guy and knew how to avoid a tackle.

He side stepped one cop and dipped his shoulder into the second, knocking him aside and stepping past in one easy move. Before anyone could come after him he was sprinting up the street. It was clear by the police reactions that there was no one close enough to catch him.

"No! He can't get away."

Tad turned in time to see Maggie faze through the car door and appear on the street outside. She was sprinting after Mark as fast as she could, and being a ghost, that was pretty fast. She would be on him in seconds but it wouldn't do any good. She was only a ghost after all.

He hesitated, remembering that Kate told him to stay in the car. To hell with that.

He suddenly realised he liked the idea of the run. He had spent too long stressing out and getting nowhere. Some physical activity would do him good, and if he got to hit someone at the end of it, then that would be the icing on the cake.

He looked to Tony and didn't even need to ask. Tony jumped straight into Tad and Tad felt that rush as he grew stronger, more alert, and ready for anything.

Tad looked to Miriam who was caught in a state of indecision and decided not to ask her to join him. He didn't want to put her in a position of choosing between him and Kate. Instead he climbed out of the car and ran after Maggie and Mark.

With Tony's strength added to his own he was shifting much quicker than a normal person. The explosive energy in his muscles along with the cold wind and rain against his face was exhilarating. His fears and worries were washed away by his surge of adrenaline. His world narrowed to a single focus, Mark. Mark was his prey and he the hunter.

It was a wonderful feeling, but one that was short lived.

No matter how fast he moved, he couldn't outpace Maggie. She already closed the distance between herself and her ex-husband and she pounced.

Tad expected her to pass through Mark, but to his amazement she collided with him. She was only a fraction of his size, but she had enough forward momentum to knock him from his feet, and they both went rolling.

Tad missed a step in shock. He wasn't using his powers which meant she had done it on her own. The only other time he had heard of such a thing was the other day with the mad ghost. Mad ghosts were stronger than regular ghosts, it was a byproduct of their madness. That they could interact with the living world was one thing, but for Maggie to do it was something else.

Mark rolled from where he landed, a look of intense anger on his face as he searched for someone to lash out at. He shouldn't have been able to see Maggie, but judging by his widening eyes and slacked jaw, he could. Tad still wasn't using his power, this was all Maggie.

"I knew I heard you last night," Mark said in a frightened whisper. "How? You're dead."

"Exactly. You killed me, you fucker," Maggie spat at him. "Now you're going to pay for it."

Tad didn't know what she would do next, and Mark didn't have chance to respond. Even though he was shocked by what he saw, Tad kept running and got to the scene before either his ghost or her ex-husband could act.

With supernatural strength he collided with the stunned Mark and took him from his feet once again, knocking him to the ground face first. The man was unresisting and Tad didn't have to try hard to get his hands secured behind his back.

It wasn't the most satisfying feeling. Tad wanted a fight.

He heard the sounds of footsteps approaching and he turned, expecting to find Maggie or Miriam. Instead he saw Kate and another cop. It was clear from their faces that whatever power Maggie accessed to become visible had faded.

"I told you to stay in the car," Kate said as she pushed Tad aside and had one of her men take his place. Tony slipped out as Kate read Mark his rights and he looked from Tad to Maggie.

"Holy shit Mags, how'd you do that?"

Maggie looked up from her husband being arrested. There were tears in her eyes and a stunned look on her face. All she could do was shake her head.

Before Tony could ask a follow up question, she turned and walked away. Her moment of justice had arrived. The question was, did that justice live up to her expectations?

The next few days would be telling for Maggie. Most ghosts moved on after their unfinished business was put aside. Would Maggie leave too?

He wasn't sure how he felt about that. On the one hand, she was once his best friend. On the other, he said goodbye to that friendship five years earlier, and the woman who returned was not the Maggie he remembered.

The truth was, her moving on would solve a lot of problems.

Time would tell, and for now there were more interesting things to watch. Tad turned back to where Mark was being hauled to his feet. He eyed Tad with suspicion as he passed, no doubt trying to figure out why Tad looked familiar. He had met Mark, but that had been a long time ago and Mark had never paid him much attention.

By the time Mark was out of sight, Tad knew he hadn't been recognised. The man was too shaken from his ordeal with Maggie to realise who Tad was.

"You had best hope your little stunt doesn't mess up my arrest," Kate said.

Tad thought about apologising, but remained silent. He was fed up of second guessing himself. If he and Maggie hadn't been there, Mark would have gotten away and who knew where that would leave them.

"What happens next?" he asked.

"Now the real fun begins. First, we make sure that what we've picked up from him is evidence of a crime, then we get the crime scene guys here to take apart that house piece by piece. Meanwhile, I get to ask questions."

Kate turned from watching Mark being locked away so she could look at Tad. "If I invite you to the station to watch, are you going to behave?"

Tad smiled. "I'll do my best. I'll stop in to check on Jen on the way. She'll want to know what's going on."

Kate nodded. "Fair enough. Give the munchkin my love." Tad nodded and walked back to the car. He stopped when Kate called his name. "Tad. Do yourself a favour and don't be too long. I won't wait for you to arrive before I start having my fun with these guys. I'd hate for you to miss the show."

Tad smiled again and found himself in a happier mood. The arrest of Mark felt like a win after long months of nothing but painful losses. It was a feeling he had almost given up hope of experiencing again.

The smile remained as he drove away and he felt lighter as a though some weight had been lifted from his shoulders. If only the feeling could last.

22

Friday, 27th November 2015
01:12

Midnight came and went. Tad's high went with it.

Kate had exaggerated when she said the fun was about to start. What she meant was three long hours of tedious questions would be asked and nothing would be answered. Tad wished there was a film crew on hand to edit the interrogations down to a five-minute high-light reel.

The only other person in the observation room was Maggie. She had her eyes glued to the monitor and unlike Tad she seemed riveted. She hadn't said much since the arrest, but she had pulled herself to-gether.

By one o'clock everyone was tired, solicitors had been called, and the day's activities were drawing to a close. Tad and Maggie moved into the hall in time to see Mark marched past them in handcuffs. Again he failed to recognise Tad.

"Prick," Tad muttered under his breath, and for the first time in a while, Maggie giggled.

"He is that."

Her words broke the discomfort that had consumed them since their argument over Jen.

"Is this enough for you?"

She hesitated. "I don't know. It's good to see him in chains, but... I thought there'd be more."

Tad was about to answer when he noticed Kate with two other police officers staring at him. Kate understood who he was talking to, and by now the other two knew of him as well. However, they weren't ready to dismiss what looked like him talking to himself.

Their expressions were familiar and threatened to ruin his good mood. Normally he would have endured it, but this time something was different. Why did he have to endure it? These people knew he was a Proxy. Why must he suffer their condemning looks?

He was so used to doing it by now it took barely a thought. One moment Maggie was invisible and the next the detectives either side of Kate let out startled gasps.

Tad didn't bother hiding his smile as he watched Kate try to suppress her own. She whispered something too them and they nodded eagerly. They all but ran down the hall in the opposite direction while Kate approached casually.

"That was mean," she said. Her words may have been admonishing, but her tone was anything but. Finally her smile won through. "You should do that more often. Those two could do with being brought down a peg or two."

"Not their biggest fans?" Tad asked.

Kate shrugged. "More like they're not mine." She looked to Maggie and her smile slipped. "How're you doing?"

"I'm a bit overwhelmed. It's like that holiday you've been dying to take for a year, and when it finally comes, it's over too fast. I don't know how to process it."

"That's just the shock. Don't worry, it'll wear off soon."

"Just tell me you've got enough to put him away for a long time and I'll be happy."

Kate's smile returned, and she nodded. "No promises, but I can't see why not. There was blood all over that fridge, more than enough to give us reason to enter the property. We found bloody clothes and hastily cleaned up blood in the kitchen. The results matching the samples to you won't come back for a while, but I don't see any problems.

"Combine that with negative character references and the dodgy cases he's been working on, and we should have enough to put him away. It's the others I'm worried about."

"Can't you get them with trying to cover up a murder?" Tad asked.

Kate waved her hand in a fifty-fifty gesture. "Maybe. It's a coin toss. They're all saying they thought they were helping a friend get rid of furniture and had no knowledge about a murder. Other than clothing they never saw, the rest had been cleaned down enough that they can claim they couldn't see any blood."

"So they'll get away with it?" Maggie asked, a little heat returning to her voice.

Kate shook her head. "Don't worry about that. You forget the original plan. We never expected this to be enough to grab them, we only wanted Mark. He made it clear that if he goes down, he's taking everyone with him. We'll keep working on that until he gives us enough to go after them. The bottom line is Mark is going down for this. You don't have to worry about him hurting anyone else."

Maggie forced a smile, but Tad could tell by the lack of vibrancy in her aura that she was not thrilled. He guessed she hadn't even thought of Mark hurting someone else. She just wanted revenge.

"Thanks for this, Kate," Tad said. "You've really come through for us."

Kate grinned. "I should be thanking you. This will do wonders for my career. Any other ghosts come knocking, don't hesitate to send them my way."

Tad agreed with a chuckle and a yawn.

"Right. Time for bed I think. Long day and all. Another one tomorrow I imagine."

"Cleopatra?" Kate asked. Tad nodded. "If there's anything I can do to help, just tell me. If this woman's coming after the munchkin then I want in on stopping her. Keep me in the loop, okay?"

Tad told her he would and said his goodbyes. He gave Kate a hug and Maggie followed suit. Kate returned to the interrogation room as Tad and Maggie walked in silence to his car.

"So that's pretty much it then," Tad said as he pulled out of the car park and onto the main road heading home. "Mark's got what's coming to him. Can you be happy with this?"

When she didn't answer straight away, he didn't think she would. He almost crashed the car when she let out an explosive sigh and her head fell back against the headrest. Suddenly she was giggling.

"It is over, isn't it?" she said as though she was only just realising that fact. "I know it's only been about a week and a half, but it feels so much longer." She turned toward him, wearing the most natural smile he had seen on her since she returned to his life. "I can't thank you enough. I know it hasn't been easy and we've been at each other's throats most of the time. But I came to you needing help and you've come through for me. Now it's over, it feels like this weight has been lifted and I can think clearly again. Everything that's happened over the last week, all that's come between us, it doesn't feel important anymore."

Tad opened his mouth to answer, but she talked over him.

"I know. Jen. That's a big one. I'm sorry about that. I should never have gone against you. I had no right and no idea what I was talking about. I blame the stress. I was angry and desperate. On top of that... well... I'm dead. Surely that's got to give me a little leeway. It's a lot for a girl to get used to."

Tad didn't try to answer this time. He didn't know what to say. It was good to get an apology from her, but he was not so quick to forgive and forget. Maggie crossed some major lines, and no matter the reason, it would haunt him.

If she recognised his mood she didn't let on. She kept talking as though they had pressed a reset button on their friendship. He listened politely as he turned onto his street.

"I'm serious, Tad. I want to see this as a new beginning for us.

We've had a rough patch, but now this is all over we can move past it. I think I'm ready to get on with my life… my death…" She laughed. "Whatever you want to call this."

He pulled into his space outside his house and killed the engine.

"You're a good person, you know that, right?" He had been about to get out of the car, but stopped at the seriousness in her tone. He turned back to face her and found her staring at him with her smile gone and a thoughtful look in her eye.

The shade of pink in her aura was one he had never seen before. It was too close to red for embarrassment but too close to pink for anger. It was some new, intense emotion that Tad couldn't get a grip on.

"I've always known that. I might have taken advantage of it in the past, but I see it now for what it is. You've come through for me… again. You were right when you said you always look out for me. I should have listened when you warned me about Mark."

She leaned forward, her gaze lowering to his lips.

"I should have realised a lot of things sooner. You're the best person in my life and always have been."

She punctuated the sentence with a kiss.

For the first time in his life she kissed him on the lips. It was not a chaste kiss, nor a simple thank you. It was something much firmer and with more passion.

The moment took him by surprise and he froze.

Maggie was kissing him.

How long had he been dreaming about such a thing? Since he was old enough to realise that girls were interesting. Most of his life.

And yet…

He gripped her shoulders and pushed her away. It wasn't harsh, but it was decisive. The pink of Maggie's aura shifted from that deep, intense colour to the paler pink he was more familiar with.

"I don't understand," she said. "I thought this was what you wanted."

"It was."

"Was?"

He nodded, then shook his head, then sighed. "I don't know, Maggie. I wanted this for so long it feels like I never wanted anything else. But a lot has happened over the past few weeks… Hell, a lot has happened over the last five years. Neither of us are who we once were."

"So, what? You don't want this any more?"

"I…" He struggled to find the words. "Maggie, I don't know. I mean… you're dead. And… look I'm still a bit sore over what happened last week. It's not that easy to forget. I just don't know anymore."

"Well find out fast. I may be dead, but I'm won't wait forever. I deserve better than that."

It was her anger talking. The fiery red consumed the pink, and it was burning bright enough to make Tad think he could feel heat from it. Before he could respond Maggie stepped out of the car and went into the house. It was only when she stepped around the person standing in the doorway when Tad noticed her.

Stella watched him with an odd expression on her face. He couldn't get a read on it and her aura wasn't helping. It was a sickly green colour he hadn't encountered before. What good was being able to see people's auras without a manual to tell him how it worked?

As he was trying to figure it out, he wondered just how long she had been standing there. Had she seen Maggie kiss him? He had a sudden sinking feeling that in his state of heightened emotion he might have used his powers subconsciously, showing Maggie to anyone close enough to be affected by his gift.

For some reason he didn't like the idea of Stella catching them kissing, and he really didn't want her getting the wrong idea about it. Before he had chance to ask himself why that was important, he climbed out of the car.

"Stella. That wasn't what it looked like," were his first words.

The strange expression left her face, and what replaced it was an expression he encountered a lot before he got to know her. She looked at him with schooled indifference and was struggling to keep her emotions off her face. It made her look cold and more than a little scary.

She couldn't tame her aura though. A red colour mixed with the green, a touch of anger mixing with that unknown emotion.

Why was she angry?

"I really don't care what it was, Tad. It's your business."

"Seriously, Stella. It was nothing. Maggie was just happy about Mark being arrested and—"

"I said I don't care. What you do with whoever, even if they're dead, is your business."

The words hurt. He didn't know why, but he was starting to have his suspicions. His mind was slow coming to the right conclusions, so he missed his window to rectify the situation.

"It's good you're home because I need to leave. I was just about to call you when I saw your car pull up."

"Are you sure? Is anything wrong?"

"No. I just need to go. Now you're back, I can head out."

"Oh. Alright." She turned and walked away. She stopped when Tad called her name, but he could tell she wouldn't hang around for long.

His feeble mind ran through a hundred things he could say, but he was still trying to make sense of everything. All he managed was, "Thanks for looking after Jen."

Stella hesitated. She had been expecting him to say something else. Was she hoping for him to say something else?

He felt stupid, and he got the sinking feeling he was messing something up. An opportunity was passing him by and he was too slow to catch it.

"No problem," Stella said sharply and then she was gone. Tad watched her walk straight to her car, climb in and then without a backwards glance, drive away leaving Tad standing in the street like an idiot.

He was still struggling to get his mind around what happened when he entered his house to find Jen waiting. She was dressed for bed but not looking at all sleepy.

"Tad? Where's Stella?"

"She said she had to go." He blinked. "Hang on a second. What are you doing up? It's nearly half past one."

"Didn't Stella tell you? I thought that was why she went out to meet you. She's been dying to tell you since Charles got back."

"Charles got back? Where's he been?" Slowly his mind was spinning up to full speed again, and he was back in the moment. "Something's happened hasn't it?"

"I'd say," Jen said with excitement. "We know where she is."

"Where who is?"

"Charles spotted her lurking outside earlier. He followed her back to her hotel. She's in a Holiday Lodge near—"

"Hang on a second. Lurking around? Are we talking about Cleopatra?"

Jen nodded eagerly.

"Yep. We know where she is. Stella's been making calls for the last two hours trying to get permission to go break down her door." She frowned and looked at the closed door behind Tad. "I can't believe she left like that. She was dying to tell you."

Tad couldn't believe it either. He looked back to the door and cursed his luck. Just when he thought he was starting to win for a change, something like this happened and knocked him right back on his arse.

He shook his head. His mind was working now, things were growing clearer, and he needed more information. He turned his attention back to Jen.

"Tell me everything."

23

Friday, 28th November 2015
09:03

Stella had not slept well. To be honest, she hadn't tried. From the moment Jen told her Charles had spotted Cleopatra and followed her back to her hotel, she had been pumped. She refused to miss this opportunity.

She woke up people who didn't like to be woken up, pulled strings where she could, and smooth talked her way into a warrant for that hotel room. The bureaucracy of getting it sorted was a nightmare, but she was excited enough to stick with it.

There was another reason she couldn't sleep, but she wasn't letting herself think about that. Unfortunately, not thinking about it was getting harder the closer she got to his house.

Tad had been calling her since seven. She ignored every call until a text came through.

Charles is my ghost. Of course he told me where Cleopatra is. Either answer my call and let me know what's happening or I'm going there on my own.

She called him right back and told him to do no such thing. He said she made him part of the case, and like it or not, he would be there. She could either let him know what was going on or he would take matters into his own hands.

For the first time she regretted getting him involved. She knew him well enough now to know his threat wasn't idle. It was a miracle he hadn't already acted. Above all else, Tad loved his daughter, and he wouldn't let this woman continue to threaten her.

So Stella made the wise decision and agreed to let him in on the bust. To limit his control, she decided to drive him there and keep him with her at all times. As she approached his house, she wondered how wise the decision was.

He was waiting outside, wearing his black raincoat and carrying two take-away coffee cups. She knew one was for her, a peace offering maybe. The thought made her irrationally angry.

He hadn't done anything wrong, just kissed a woman in his car. It wasn't like she had any reason not to be happy for him.

That thought only got her mad at herself as she finally recognised what she had been too stubborn to admit. She liked Tad. There was something about the skinny weirdo that slipped behind her carefully constructed walls and earned her interest.

It was probably nothing more than a crush. He saved her life, introduced her to the supernatural, and lived a fascinating life himself. On top of that, he saw more in her than just beauty. She knew he was attracted to her, but when she threw herself at him before the alley attack, he resisted every step of the way. He hadn't been interested. She thought that might have changed over the last week.

Again her mind flashed to the image of Maggie kissing him. Maybe he hadn't changed his mind after all.

He rushed to the car and climbed in, letting the cold in with him. Once seated, he smiled at her. It was that same smile she liked so much, but it had lost its magic. She didn't want to smile back. She wanted to cry. She hated herself for that.

"Here, I thought you might want this," he said, offering her the cup.

Stella wanted it. She was parched. She'd been busy all night, was exhausted and hadn't had time to shower yet alone make coffee.

"I've already had one. You should have asked first."

Her words were harsh. She turned away so she didn't have to see his reaction. Instead, she put the car into first and pulled onto the road.

"Oh. Well, I guess I'll just leave it here, in case you change your mind."

He put the coffee in a cup holder and put his next to it so he could free his hands to strap himself in.

"Is anyone else in the car?" she asked, remembering he came with an entourage.

"No, they're keeping an eye on Cleopatra. Save Maggie. She's with Jen."

Maggie. Just the name annoyed her. Before she could get hold of her emotions, her fingers tightened on the steering wheel causing the leather to creak.

Tad looked over and she knew he saw right through her mask. It only made her angrier.

"Stella. I tried to tell you last night. It wasn't what it looked—"

"I said I don't want to know. What part of that don't you understand?"

"The part where since it happened you've been acting strange. You ran off last night when Jen said you had been dying to speak to me. You wouldn't answer my calls this morning, and now you're acting weird. Please. Just let me explain."

She didn't want him to explain, didn't want to hear anything from him, but she didn't protest in time.

"I used to love Maggie, a long time ago," he began and her hand tightened on the wheel again. "She was my only friend growing up, and it was one of those one sided things. Maggie never liked me, so I never pushed for anything. When she came to be my ghost, there were no secrets anymore. I told you about the merging right? About—"

"Yes, you told me." Again her words were sharp. He told her about the merging, of how intimate it was. The thought of Maggie being that intimate with him annoyed her all the more.

"Yeah, well, there was no hiding anymore. She learned of my old feelings and it caused trouble between us. It's one reason she took Jen as her Proxy. The thing is, over these past few weeks I've realised those feelings for Maggie are gone. They probably weren't real in the first place. The Maggie I remember was a work of fiction. She was my only friend, so I overlooked her flaws and idolised the rest.

"Last night was emotional for Maggie and… well, I don't know why she did it. The thing is Stella, I didn't want it. I knew before last night that me and Maggie wouldn't work. Those feelings are gone. But she kissed me. I didn't kiss her. I pushed her away. Surely you saw that."

She had seen that.

She had seen it and ignored it. All that mattered was the kiss itself. But now she thought about it, Tad's words made sense. He had pushed her away. More than that, she had seen how he was around her over the past week. He'd been furious, ready to kill her for what she did to Jen.

She had no problems believing what he said. He was over Maggie. So why was she still so angry?

Because she let him behind the walls she spent a lifetime building. She allowed herself to think he was different. Hell, he might be different. But she couldn't take that risk.

Last night was a reminder of what it would be like when he eventually hurt her, just like everyone she let in always did. It was inevitable. The only way to protect herself was to build the wall again and keep him… everyone at a distance.

"Tad, I don't care who you kiss, and I don't care about your history with Maggie, it's none of my business." She struggled to keep her face straight when she said, "We're just colleagues, that's all. Don't go confusing that with anything else. I needed you to help me catch a criminal, now that's done that's it for us. There wasn't anything more and I'm sorry if anything I did made you think otherwise."

She couldn't resist glancing over to see how the words landed. She wished she hadn't.

He looked like a man who had just been sideswiped. It was a pained expression that looked every bit as bad as she felt the night before. Her words scored a hit, and she had never been more glad when the Holiday Lodge appeared around the next corner.

She pulled into the carpark, slipped into her professional persona, and climbed out of the car.

She had work to do.

If you've seen one Holiday Lodge, you've seen them all. That wasn't a bad thing, Stella liked the uniformity. She knew what to expect.

The manager of the hotel led her, Tad and three plain clothed officers down a hall that was familiar even though she had never been there before. It was long, covered in beige, striped wallpaper with a dark, patterned carpet underfoot. Uninspired and deliberately neutral artwork hung at even intervals between the doors.

They were on the fourth floor headed down to the far end of the corridor toward the fire exit. Cleopatra's room was at the end of the hall. Stella expected that the door would open any moment and a woman would run out, go through that fire door and try to escape. It was why she had two more policemen waiting at the bottom of those stairs. She wasn't taking any chances.

But the door never opened, and they approached without incident.

"Open it," she whispered to the manager who hesitated just as he had when she first showed him the warrant. She wasn't in the mood for hesitation. She snatched the key card and pushed it into the slot on the door. The click of the lock was drowned out by the sound of breaking glass.

"Shit," she swore and barged through the door.

She was just in time to glimpse Cleopatra as she disappeared out the window. She was barely dressed, wearing only a robe and underclothes, and her hair was wet. She calmly met Stella's eyes and dropped out the window.

Stella ran into the room, noting the black chord tied to the leg of the desk beneath the window, the burning papers in the bin, and yet more smoke coming from under the bathroom door. If Stella didn't act quickly, she would lose everything.

She got to the window just in time to see Cleopatra detach herself from a device that held her to the rope. She didn't look up, just ran for the car park.

Stella swore, reaching for the rope to climb out the window and go after her. A strong hand on her arm stopped her.

"Don't be stupid," Tad hissed. "A fall from this height will kill you."

She wanted to argue, but he was right. Instead she shook off his hand and grabbed her radio.

"The suspect is on the ground below her room window and is running for the car park. Don't let her get away."

She looked at the burning papers and smoky room with dismay before sprinting again. The manager could put out the fires, she had a suspect to catch.

She took a right as she exited, crashing through the fire doors and starting down the stairs at a reckless pace. The clanging of feet on metal told her Tad wasn't far behind.

The men she posted at the ground floor were in pursuit, so hopefully when she turned the corner she'd find the suspect in custody. She was disappointed. They had caught up to her, but it hadn't gone well for either of them.

One man was unconscious with blood streaming from his nose and another was rolling around holding his crotch. Stella looked past them to Cleopatra who ran over the grass verge between the building and the car park, her open robe billowing behind her like a cape.

At least the officers had slowed her, but if she had a car ready to go then she was likely to get away.

That couldn't happen.

Stella let her single minded focus give her strength and she picked up as much speed as she could. Those hours of running every day better pay off or she would burn her treadmill the second she got home.

"Tony, Charles, Miriam. I need you."

She tried to ignore Tad, but couldn't. What new way was he going to blow her mind today? She had her answer a half second later.

His tall, skinny shape shot past her right side. He had a hell of a stride, so it made sense he was quicker. What bothered her was how much quicker. She couldn't be sure, but she didn't think race-cars accelerated to that speed in so short a distance.

By the time she had taken three steps he had halved the distance between himself and Cleopatra. Three seconds later he was almost on top of her. It would take Stella half a minute to cover that distance.

Tad reached Cleopatra just as she was about to open her car door. He grabbed her shoulder and Stella thought that was it, even slowing her pace. She had seen Tad fight, and the woman wasn't a match for him.

Only, she was.

She grabbed his hand and before he could counter, she twisted it at an awkward angle, forcing him to his knees in a lock no normal person could break. Tad was no normal person. His strength surprised Cleopatra as he forced his way out of the arm lock.

He reached to incapacitate her again, but Cleopatra adapted quickly. She moved before he could touch her, avoiding his hand and striking at his throat. Tad was too quick, but he couldn't get an advantage.

He was quicker and stronger, but his movements were clumsy. He relied on speed, strength and reach alone to win the day. But, if he couldn't catch her, those advantages meant nothing.

The woman was reading Tad easily, avoiding his clumsy attempts to grab her. But, no matter how well trained she was, she couldn't get the advantage. Skill only gets you so far, that much speed and strength was a lot to overcome.

They fought to a stalemate which gave Stella a chance to close the distance.

Cleopatra's back was to Stella as she struggled with Tad. Something alerted her at the last second and Stella got to see her surprised expression as she turned directly into Stella's outstretched hand.

Stella had only been trying to grab the woman, but when she turned

Stella tightened her fingers into a fist. It was not her best punch, but it was good enough to stun Cleopatra and give Stella chance to land a second.

This one was better. It came from the hip and connected with Cleopatra's jaw hard enough to knock her back a few steps. Tad was waiting. This time he wrapped an arm around her throat and trapped her arms with his second. She wasn't getting free.

Stella shook the pain from the knuckles in her left hand and reached for her cuffs with her right.

"You have the right to remain silent," she began, and all fight left Cleopatra.

Stella continued to speak, all the while looking at Cleopatra's face. There was no fear, no frustration, not even anger. She took it calmly and, dare Stella even think it, she looked relieved.

By the time the other police caught up, Stella had her cuffed and secured.

Cleopatra hadn't said a word.

Stella was breathing hard as her colleagues led Cleopatra away, but she was grinning. Months of following this case, just as long getting nowhere with it, and finally she had her woman.

She looked at Tad before she could think better of it, the huge smile on her face taking him by surprise and drawing a cautious one from him in return.

His reticence dampened her mood, and she remembered her thoughts preceding their arrival. She would not let it bring her down. This feeling when she caught her suspect was the reason she was stupid to ever think she needed someone in her life.

What she told Tad was true, she was married to her job. Right then, riding the high of the moment, she wondered how she'd ever forgotten.

Stella didn't look back as she returned to the hotel. She would go find out what survived the fire and if there was nothing, then she at least had Cleopatra to question.

Maybe this day would turn out alright after all.

24

Friday, 28th November 2015
18:00

Tad returned to the police station by six o'clock.

He picked Jen up from school, told her the good news, then arranged for Letty to sit for her again. He presided over their awkward reunion as Jen apologised for sneaking out. Letty was quicker than expected to forgive her, and by the time Tad left they were on good terms again.

He made the short drive back to the police station feeling more relaxed than he had in months. Maggie's killer was caught and in police custody. Cleopatra had been taken down and was no longer hunting Jen. Everything was falling into place.

His mood must have been good as he barely noticed the uncomfortable looks directed his way as he moved through the station. His smile remained until he entered the monitor room. He should be able to see the interrogation underway, but instead he found Stella in front of a monitor rather than in with Cleopatra.

"Hey Stella, any news?"

He forced his tone to be light-hearted, but didn't get a smile in return. She only looked at him long enough to nod in greeting before turning back to the monitors

"Nothing," she said. Short and efficient. No follow up information.

Tad felt a pang of annoyance. So he misread the situation between them. There was no need for this new coldness. Even her aura wasn't giving anything away. She had it muted as though dampening her emotions.

He did his best to put his annoyance aside and stepped further into the room. He took a free chair and wheeled it to the desk next to Stella.

The monitor in front of her focused on Cleopatra, sat in the interrogation room behind a bare table. Her head was resting on her arms that were crossed over that table and she was sleeping.

"What's this?" he asked. "Why aren't you talking to her?"

Stella flicked an irritated glance at him, then sighed. She didn't answer, just kept filling out paperwork.

"Come on Stella, give me something."

"I already told you. There's nothing to say. She's not talking. Hasn't said a word since we got her. We've run her prints but got no hits. I have no idea who she is and I'm fed up of talking to someone who won't talk back."

"So what are you going to do next?"

She turned her attention from the screen and stared at him.

"You don't need to be here for this. Thanks for your work so far, but our suspect is in custody and your services are no longer required."

Tad said nothing for a few seconds as her words registered. Slowly his anger spiked, and he said goodbye to his good mood.

"What? You can't be serious."

"I am. There's nothing more you can do, Mr Holcroft. I suggest you go home."

"Mr Holcroft? Really? That's how you're playing this?" He laughed and climbed to his feet. "Grow up *D.I. Martin*. You had best keep me informed or I'll go over your head. With all the crazy stuff that's been going on, I have a feeling your bosses want to keep the only Proxy they know happy. I'm sure they'll tell me a thing or two."

He didn't give her chance to answer, and neither did he look back. Instead he walked out and nearly collided with someone.

Maggie jumped in shock when he appeared and put her hand over her heart as though she still had a heart to worry about.

"Jesus Tad, you made me jump."

"Sorry. You looking for me?"

She nodded. "I thought you'd be back by now. Figured you might want an update on how Kate's getting on."

"Good news I hope."

She was about to answer when her eyes focused over his shoulder. Tad turned to find Stella standing in the doorway. Her expression had softened, and it looked as though she wanted to say something to him. Then Tad did something stupid. He had got into the habit of letting people see his ghosts when they were present. He did so again on instinct and whatever Stella had been about to say froze in her throat as her eyes darted to Maggie.

There was a moment of frozen silence, then her mouth closed abruptly. She stepped out of the room, slammed the door, and walked down the corridor away from them both.

"What's her problem?" Maggie asked once they were sure she was out of earshot.

Tad shook his head. "I have no idea." Turning back to her he asked, "You said you had news?"

She nodded. "Not good though. They're not talking and Kate doesn't know how much longer she can hold them."

Tad frowned. "Even Mark?"

"No, he's going down for what he did, thank God. The thing is, he isn't talking. For some reason he's changed his mind since we overheard him. I can't figure it out. It's not like him to be this loyal to anyone."

What could keep Mark quiet with so much on the line? Tad would have thought a man like him would offer all kinds of information if it meant he could make his own life easier.

"He's scared," Tad whispered as the realisation struck.

"He should be. If the rumours are true, they don't like cops in prison. He's going to have a—"

"Not that," Tad interrupted. "Whatever information he has scares him. He's more afraid of talking about what he knows than he is of staying quiet."

"That's it. It explains everything. Mark is too selfish to just sit there and let the rest of them get away with it. This is still all about him. But what could make him so scared?"

"That's the question, isn't it?" Tad agreed. "We find out the answer to that and we'll be getting somewhere."

He swore and shook his head, looking away from Maggie to the door twice removed from the monitor room. Cleopatra was behind that door, sleeping.

"Shit. How did this go all wrong for us, Maggie? Half an hour ago I thought we were nearly done with this. Mark was going down for your thing, he would take down the rest of his crew to make Kate look good, and Cleopatra should be spilling the beans about what's going on with Proxies. Now she isn't talking which screws up Stella's case, and Kate will be left with egg on her face when she doesn't get the result she needs. The only silver lining is that Mark's getting what's coming to him."

"You don't have to sound so bummed about that. It's still a win."

He tried to smile. "I know, Mags. Sorry. It's just been a rough couple of months. I was hoping things would get back to normal soon." He looked back to the closed door and again shook his head. "If only she'd talk."

"Maybe you should kill her."

"What?"

"Well, then she'd be a ghost. If she was a ghost, you could merge with her and get her memories."

"I can't force it, Mags. She's got to want—" A memory surfaced and his eyes opened wide. "Of course. Mags, you're a genius."

He didn't wait for a response before walking to the closed interrogation room. He looked around to make sure no one was watching, then he opened the door and stepped inside.

"Tad. What are you—" The end of Maggie's sentence was cut off by the closing door. Once again she forgot she was a ghost and stayed on the other side of the door rather than walking through it. She was about to make a fuss though, so he cut the thread of power that made her visible to normal people. He needed to make sure Cleopatra didn't wake up.

He turned from the door to face this woman who had been such a big part of his life for months whether he had known it or not. It was strange, she seemed to have shrunk since he fought her that morning. She was unstoppable then, a giant even though she was a fraction of his size.

He shivered in spite of himself. She made him feel useless even though he had the strength of three ghosts added to his own. He assumed that the strength and speed he gained would be enough to win any battle. She proved him wrong. If she'd had a weapon, he would be in a bad state right now. He'd been arrogant, she proved why that was a bad idea. He wouldn't make that mistake again. With that in mind he kept his distance in spite of how small she seemed now she was sleeping.

He walked to the far wall and sank down against it. He wasn't sure if he could do this standing up or not, but he didn't want to find out he couldn't the hard way.

He turned his full attention to the shape, trying to analyse her as best he could with both his mind and his talent. Her aura was flickering through a range of colours that he assumed had something to do with her dreams. He hoped so. It was to her dreams that he needed to go.

He tried to remember how Jen had said she'd done it with him. Somehow she connected with his unconscious mind. He hoped it would work with this woman even though she wasn't a Proxy.

His new ability to see people's auras was evidence that his power extended to more than death. Maybe Charles was right and his power was actually to interact with a person's soul. When he had been weaker, his abilities had been limited to the dead because those souls were without the protection of bodies. Now he was stronger he could interact with the living as well.

That was the theory anyway, and it was time to test it.

He focused on the woman's aura. It was a link to her soul, and he thought he might find a way in through that. He concentrated on the colours, trying to feel what each one meant and match his own emotions accordingly. He hadn't stared this closely at the colours surrounding people before less he be seen as a creep, but now he found them fascinating.

They danced before his eyes, constantly moving and changing. It was easy to lose himself amongst their steady rhythm and it was almost hypnotic. What it wasn't though, was a gateway to her mind.

Tad pulled himself out of his trance and shook his head. He didn't have unlimited time to do this. He shouldn't even be in the room so he had to get this done before anyone saw him.

He had to think.

Jen's explanation of how she did it kept slipping away from him. He had learned while trying to teach her that how they used their gifts were not always alike. Their power was based on thought and no two people's thoughts were the same. He needed to find his own path.

His answer came when he evaluated how he normally entered the minds of his ghosts. He would fall asleep and go to what he thought of as his entry room. That was where Jen had found him. Maybe that was where he would find Cleopatra.

He closed his eyes, blinding himself so he could mimic his dream world. He thought of that room, tried to picture it growing around him until he felt it was real. Slowly the ambient sound of the living world faded and his imaginings grew more real.

The round room materialised, but he sensed only the door that lead to his own memories. He was on the verge of giving up when a thought struck.

He envisioned Cleopatra and focused on the picture of her in his mind. He saw again the woman he fought; her strong, dark eyes, her high cheek bones, and narrow face. The woman who looked very much how he imagined Cleopatra.

He took that image, and he applied it to his reality, thinking what her door might look like. From what little he knew of her he imagined she had a military background so he went for something that was hardy and secure. He couldn't help but put a touch of Egyptian decoration around the frame, still tying her with Cleopatra even though she probably wasn't even Egyptian.

Once it was done, it didn't matter what she actually was. As with his ghosts, in his dreams perception was everything.

His imaginings made the door real. More than this, he knew deep down that it worked. In this place, even without his eyes, he knew everything by instinct. He didn't need to see the door, to touch it or feel it. All he needed was his instinctual knowledge, his belief, that it was the door he wanted.

Behind that door were the answers he craved. When it came to dreams, those who were aware they were dreaming were the masters of their world. Tad was always aware when he was dreaming, so maybe he could manipulate the answers he needed from her sleeping mind.

He reached for her door, opened it, and stepped inside the mind of a woman he suddenly knew was named Dinah Mizrahi.

25

Friday, 28th November 2015
18:23

"You ready for this?" he asks.

She looks out the window at the tarmac and airport. She expects someone to come for her. They always said she was too valuable to let go. Could this be real?

The plane moves, and she gets her answer. There's no one coming. They have finally accepted that she no longer works for them.

Dinah turns away from the window and meets her husband's eyes. He's nervous while waiting for her answer. He knows what she's giving up for him, doesn't think he's worth it. He doesn't know how wrong he is.

She kisses him, and he's surprised. She likes that. It reminds her of when they first met. How nervous he was. He's a good man, far too good for her. She loves him.

Is she ready?

Of course she is. He's the reason she'd been waiting for to leave it all behind. She'd follow him anywhere. He was her life now.

She breaks the kiss and wonders if now is the right time to tell him. He's smiling in that way she loves so much. He's so innocent. Everything she's not.

Yes, now is the perfect time.

She leans in again only this time not to kiss him. She whispers, wanting this moment to be just theirs.

"Yes, I'm ready," she says. "And not just me. I'm pregnant."

He's stunned.

She has never seen that on him before. She's seen him nervous, seen him happy, seen him scared, seen him when he's so upset he can't look her in the eye. She has never seen him so silent.

He's always talking, never shuts up. It drives her mad, but she loves it about him. She knows where she stands with him. It's a novel feeling. She's been around secret keepers so long it's a breath of fresh air.

But now she can't tell. Is he happy? Has she ruined everything?

Her smile is slipping. That contented feeling from leaving Israeli soil is falling away. This is why they let her leave. They knew she couldn't survive outside their world.

They had trained her since she was young. She was the best at what she was, belonged in their world of secrets, violence and death. What was she thinking pursuing this stupid, girlish dream?

She feels a lump in her throat and the possibility of tears when he changes everything yet again.

He laughs.

It isn't a quiet chuckle nor a discreet giggle. It's a roar that makes half of the passengers jump. He laughs again, then whoops and punches the air.

Dinah feels her smile return. A stewardess comes to see what's going on but doesn't speak. He won't let her.

"I'm going to be a father," he tells her happily. "This beautiful woman is carrying my child."

He's shouting now and Dinah feels her cheeks burn. The idiot is causing a scene. She doesn't like attention.

But if that's the case, why is she grinning?

An old couple across the isle look at her and they're smiling. She smiles back. The stewardess is smiling also, chuckling at his actions.

"Congratulations," she hears from behind her and she turns to see a middle aged woman has leaned forward in her seat.

"Thank you," Dinah whispers, still awkward but grinning.

"Sir. I understand you're happy, but I need you to calm down." The stewardess is trying not to laugh. A lot of other people aren't so considerate. He doesn't care. He laughs with them and announces it to the whole plane yet again.

"I'm going to be a dad," he says.

There are more laughs, shouts of congratulations and even a few cheers. Dinah didn't think she could blush this much.

"Calm down you fool," she says fondly, laying a hand on his arm. He turns back and kisses her hard. When he lets up she gasps for breath, but she's still grinning. "Calm down."

He nods and takes a breath. "Sorry," he says. Then he turns to the stewardess and says it again to her. She smiles at him and tells him to at least hold it in until they're in the air. He promises he will.

People are still laughing. He finally notices and his own blush rises. He sinks deeper into his chair and grabs Dinah's hand.

"I think I might have caused a scene," he says.

She laughs at him again. It's a fond laugh, one filled with love. She suddenly doesn't mind the attention. All she cares about is that she's never been happier. She kisses him again, then settles back into her chair for take off.

The plane leaves the tarmac, and she leaves her home behind forever. She's still holding his hand. She won't let it go until they land in their new home of England.

For the first time she misses her gun.

It has been ten years since she used it for anything other than training. Now she yearns for it. She grabs the large torch she keeps in the bedroom instead. It will have to do.

Her husband is snoring, oblivious. She decides not to wake him.

It's best that he stays out of this. He's too soft. He'll want to protect her from herself.

She doesn't need protecting. *They* do.

She thinks her past has caught up with her as she creeps down the hallway. She looks in Adam's room. He's sleeping, not disturbed by the noises that woke her. Next she pops her head in the baby's room. Gabriella is also asleep which is lucky because she usually likes to cry at night. Adam wasn't like that and she didn't realise how lucky she was the first time round.

But she's asleep now, and that's good. If Dinah's past has come back to haunt her, them being asleep could save their lives.

Her bare feet make no sound as she descends the carpeted stairs and creeps down the hall on the ground floor. There's light coming from under the kitchen door. She didn't leave it on so there must be someone there.

She grips the torch tighter and falls back into her training. She has been gone from that world for ten years but has not grown weak. They will regret breaking into her house.

She slips into an old mindset, the warrior, and is disturbed by how quickly it returns. The warrior doesn't care for anything like that though. She only cares about the mission. She is focused.

She takes a deep breath, then bursts into the kitchen.

He's waiting calmly. There's no weapon in his hand nor surprise on his face. He leans against the counter with his arms by his side and a gentle smile curling his lips. She looks around for someone else. There's no one. The arrogant bastard came alone.

He'll regret that.

She advances on him.

He laughs.

"Now now, Mrs Mizrahi. There's no need for violence."

He speaks English like a native, his accent mixed. It surprises her. She knows people in her old industry who could speak like a native, but they always had a regional accent. It was the best way to sound local. However, a mix of accents as though he's moved around, makes her suspect he actually is British.

He isn't from her old life.

Her old employers would send one of their own. It doesn't matter to the warrior. All that matters is that he's in her house while her babies are upstairs. That is unforgivable.

She keeps advancing, confident she can teach him a lesson.

He still laughs, uncaring.

He's a strange looking man, too thin. He's bald, and though he tries to hide it with his well cut suit, he looks sick. Cancer? Maybe leukaemia? He's weak.

But he's so cocky. He shouldn't be. Not only is he sick but there's something wrong with his left arm. It's too small, withered and broken. He's crippled.

Why is he so confident?

It gives her pause, but not for long. It doesn't matter what he is, he's in her home.

She's close enough to attack and swings her torch at him, the heavy metal head arcing for his skull.

He moves faster than she thinks possible. His right hand catches the torch. She feels like she has struck concrete. The torch sticks in place, and when he tries to pull it back, it's set in stone.

She watches in awe as his fingers squeeze. The glass in the torch shatters and the metal groans. Eventually it splits under the pressure and she has no choice but to let go.

She's stunned, but shock has no place in a fight. She strikes his throat... only, he's not there.

Her hand passes through where he once was. He has vanished and she over balances, following through with the punch and colliding with the wall.

There is laughing again.

She spins to find him standing behind her, all too real. She turns and tries to punch him. This time her knuckles brush his skin and then he is gone again, fading into nothingness.

When he comes back, he grabs her by the arm. The strength is like nothing she has ever felt and she has to struggle to keep from crying out. She tries to pull away but there's so little give. She might as well be locked in a vice.

He casually twists his wrist and she gasps in agony as her shoulder pops out of its socket.

"Is that enough?" he asks in a bored tone. "I don't have all night for this."

He lets her go, and she staggers away, colliding against the kitchen table and falling into a chair. She stays where she is. She doesn't attack again. He is still standing, still arrogant. He has every right to be.

"What are you?" she wants to know.

His smile is chilling, and she feels something she can't remember ever feeling before, at least not so strongly. Fear.

"I could tell you I'm a Proxy, but it won't mean anything to you. What we really need to talk about is what you are."

He strolls over to another chair and pulls it out, seating himself almost delicately. "I've looked into you, Dinah. I have to say, you're an impressive woman. To have risen so high in the Mossad is no small thing, especially being a woman. But I'm not surprised. Your record is—"

"Sealed. You haven't seen it."

He laughs, and she doubts her own words. "Allen. Marissa. Berkovich. Lewinski. Need I say more?"

More than anything else that surprises her. He should not know those names. No one should outside of her old employers.

"What do you want?"

He smiles again and leans in close. "Now we're getting somewhere? What I want, Dinah my dear, is what you do best. I want you to find people. There are special people all over the country, people like me. I want you to find them and I want you to bring them too me."

She shakes her head. "I don't do that anymore."

"But you're the best. Your speciality is in finding people and... how do they put it... oh yes. Extraction. That's what you're good at, right? Finding and extracting. Well that's what I want."

The smile slips from his face and she shivers. She doesn't like how strong her fear is. She has been close to death before and it never mattered, but this man is scary. He could have spoken to her at work, while she was out shopping, at any time. He has come to her house for a reason. He is making a point.

"There's one thing you should know about me, Dinah. I get what I want. Do you understand?"

She thinks she's starting to, and she nods.

"That's right. You get it now. You've seen what I can do. You know you couldn't stop me. Do this for me and I'll make you rich. Don't and I'll start with your husband. It won't be quick. I'll send him to you in pieces over a couple of weeks, just to make sure you get my message. If you still don't understand then I guess little Adam is—"

"Don't you touch my kids," she hissed, fear slipping aside for her rage to come through.

He smiles at her again. He is so arrogant, so mocking. Her threats mean nothing to him.

"I won't if you do as you're told." He stands up, politely pushing his chair under the table. "I'll leave now, give you a day to think it over. I know what your answer will be. You're a smart woman. Do the right thing and you'll see the benefits. Trust me."

With that he turns and walks to the door. He doesn't open it, doesn't need to. He fades as he did before, vanishing on this side of the glass only to appear again on the other. He turns while in the yard, waves his good hand, then steps into the darkness.

Dinah waits five minutes to make sure he's gone. Finally she gives in to her fear and the dreadful pain in her shoulder. She does something she has never done in her adult life. She can't help it. She has never felt so useless.

Her head drops to her chest and she sobs.

Even after eleven years, she hates going to the tower.

It's no longer the ugly red-brick office building stained with graffiti she first encountered. Now it's a tower of black stone and tinted glass.

It's a highly reflective monolith that is architecturally appealing, but feels... wrong.

Maybe she's projecting. After all, the memories she associates with this place are bad ones. She has lost count of how many people she has brought to this tower over her years working for her employer.

The security guards at the gate don't need to see her ID. They know her by sight and know the consequences of delaying her.

She drives into the underground car park, not stopping long enough to smile at the men who open the gate for her. The car park has the feel of a multi story, only darker.

She parks in a large spot on the second floor, just outside a set of double doors marked for deliveries. Two men, dressed like private security, are waiting with a gurney and restraints. They're a welcome sight. If they weren't there she would need to take him inside herself. She doesn't like doing that.

She stays in the driver's seat as the rear doors of the van open. Normally they take her employer's prize and leave. Today one of them approaches her door. She sighs and curses her luck. She should know better than to think she would have an easy night.

She winds down the window and waits for him to speak.

"He want's to see you," the man says. He doesn't look her in the eye and he says nothing more. He simply walks away as though expecting her to follow. She doesn't disappoint. No one turns down her employer unless they have a death wish.

She sighs again and steps out of the van.

The tower is just as dark on the inside as the outside, just as evil. The hallways are large and black, made of the same stone as the exterior. Like the outside, they're polished to such a shine that she can see her reflection. There are few doors in the corridor which makes her wonder yet again how big the rooms are deeper into the building.

It isn't long until they come to a small reception area. Her employer is sitting on one of the chairs, playing with his phone with one hand and keeping his crippled hand tucked out of sight.

He looks worse today than when she first met him. Not only is he skeletally thin and still bald, but his skin is looking frail. He has dark rings around his eyes and is covered in shadows and bruising. It must be a trick of the light, but he looks sinister and dark.

He is still arrogant, which is evident in the cocky smile he flashes as she comes closer.

"You keep bringing me these wonderful toys," he jokes. "Anyone would think you like me?"

"You wanted to see me?" she asks, trying to cut through his usual nonsense. He sighs like he's being put upon and shakes his head.

"Never any time for pleasantries with you, is there Dinah? Ah well. Strait to business then. Where's the girl?"

"Girl?"

"The one my ghosts have seen you following for the past few days."

His ghosts. Of course they were following her. She should know better. He leaves nothing outside of his control, not even her.

"I haven't had chance to get her yet. She is…" she lets her words trail off and decides he doesn't need to know her reasons for not taking the girl. He doesn't care. He only wants his prize.

"I will get her soon, I promise."

His smile never waivers and he nods again. "Good. The sooner the better. I'm close to finishing all this now. Soon there'll be no more jobs. Isn't that sad?"

Sad? She has to stop herself jumping for joy. She's never been able to imagine an end date. Now he's telling her the nightmare might soon be over.

"How many more?" she dares to ask.

"Not many. Maybe just one. I'm not sure. Bring me the girl and I'll let you know. Do it quickly. I have one other bit of business I need you to complete for me once it's done. It might be your last job."

"What is it?"

"As you know I keep a close eye on the families of those who work for me. There is one boy in one of those families that has caught my attention. The trouble is, he's disappeared. I need you to find him and bring him here. He should be easier for you than normal. He's not a

Proxy. He's just… talented."

Another young one? She doesn't know if she can take yet another child. She keeps that fact to herself.

"What's his name?"

"Gideon Jordan." He picks up a file from the chair next to him and hands it over. "You'll find everything there is to know about him in here other than his current whereabouts."

She nods and accepts the file. She's eager to open it and get started, to finish this business once and for all.

"Is that all?" she asks.

He sighs and nods. "Eleven years and not one smile from you. What a pity. I bet you have a beautiful smile." He waves his hand dismissively. "Fine. Go. Bring me the girl. And no more procrastinating. I want her here by Saturday."

She thinks to tell him about the girl's new protection. She wants to tell him it will be more difficult this time. She knows he won't care.

Instead she nods and walks away.

As she retraces her steps and climbs back in her van, a smile grows. It's the first one in a long time, but she can't help it.

This is the first time she has been able to imagine this ending. All she has to do is take two more kids, and this nightmare is over. She has no illusions of going back to her old life. She doesn't deserve it after what she has done. But she no longer has to see *him* anymore. She would even be free to kill herself.

That last thought allows her grin to fully form. She had been putting that off for so long in fear of what he would do to her family in recompense. Now she would be free to end it.

With that longing thought of death still playing through her mind and making her smile, she starts the engine and pulls out of her parking spot. It's nearly over and she has work to do.

For the first time in her life she is eager to kidnap a child. She leaves the garage and instead of heading back to her hotel, she heads for Jennifer Larson.

✳✳✳

Tad returned to the waking world the moment the door exploded inward.

"What the hell do you think you're doing?" Stella demanded. She was beyond angry. He didn't get chance to answer as Dinah spoke first.

"Please. You can't say anything," she begged.

He was looking at Stella and saw the sudden change in her expression. She was still angry, but incredulity was winning through. They were the first words Dinah said in her presence.

"I'm serious," Dinah said again, drawing his attention back from Stella. "You don't know what will happen if you do."

This woman who seemed so dangerous before was suddenly pleading with him. There were tears in her eyes and Tad thought she teetered on the edge of a breakdown. Had it been anyone else he might feel sorry for them.

He'd had full access to her memories. All he had to do was think about what he wanted to know and her mind helped him fill in the blanks. He had seen her life working for the Mossad, the joy that followed it with her husband, and more importantly, the nightmare that was the last eleven years.

Those eleven years would never make him feel sorry for this woman. He couldn't keep the sneer from his face.

"Please," she begged again. "It's almost over. If you tell anyone now, it'll have all been for nothing. Everything I did—"

"It's already all for nothing. What's wrong with you?"

"I had to. You don't know what he would do—"

Again he interrupted her. "I've just been in your head, I know the stakes."

She stared at him, struggling to speak as her mind dealt with the shock of what he'd done.

"You were the one in the alley that night, not your daughter."

The mention of Jen made Tad want to kill her and he was glad Stella was in the room. Without her to witness the act, he might have taken the opportunity.

"Of course it was me. She's just a little girl, you monster."

SECTION

"Not the first to do something unbelievable though."

"That doesn't make it any better."

"Anyone want to fill me in on what's happening here?" Stella was over her shock and her anger returned. She looked from Tad to Dinah, no longer wanting to throw him out but annoyed at being left out of the loop.

"Please," Dinah begged one last time. Tad just shook his head.

"This ends tonight. You're not taking anyone else to him."

"You can't stop him," she snapped angrily. "You must have seen that. Of all the Proxies I have taken over the years, he's beyond any of them. All those new powers you play with now, he was doing that back at the beginning of all this. He's beyond you. If you can't stop him, you might as well keep quiet and gift my family some safety. Otherwise no one wins."

"You call that winning, Dinah? All those people… those children. That's not winning." She flinched when he said children and it robbed her of her ability to respond.

"Dinah?" Stella asked in confusion.

Tad waited a few seconds while he stared at Dinah, then turned back to Stella. He didn't want to tell her anything. He'd had as much as he cared to take from her for one day. She was willing to kick him out of this investigation, why shouldn't he do the same to her?

Because I still need her, he thought. As much as it would be good to leave her high and dry after her treatment of him, what Dinah said was right. Her employer was beyond him. Even through Dinah's memories he felt this man's incredible power. Tad had never felt anything close.

If this nightmare was going to end, he needed the police on his side. That meant he needed Stella.

"D.I. Martin, meet Dinah Mizrahi. She used to work for the Mossad until about twenty years ago when she left Israel to come to the UK with her husband. Eleven years ago she started kidnapping people for money. She doesn't remember how many people she has kidnapped as there have been so many." Turning back to her he sneered again and said, "Amongst their number were over thirty children. They're all dead now."

"How do you know this?" Stella asked.

Tad didn't answer, just took a few steps closer to Dinah and leaned in close. "If I were you, I'd cooperate. The only protection left for your family is through the police. You'll need to tell her everything you know for that."

He was about to walk away when suddenly he stopped and looked back. "Who is he? I never got his name?"

She opened her mouth to speak but then just as quickly closed it. "I can't tell you. He'll kill them."

"He'll go after them anyway. From what I've seen, he won't risk them being alive."

"He's more likely to leave them alone if he thinks I haven't co-operated."

"How will he ever know?"

She snorted. "His ghosts tell him everything."

"There aren't any ghosts here now."

"Then his people would tell him the rest. You don't realise who this man is. He has people everywhere."

Tad just shook his head and turned away.

"All yours D.I. Martin," he said as he tried to push past Stella. She flinched away from his tone, then reached out to stop him.

"Tad I—"

He didn't let her finish. He wasn't interested. After what he had just seen he needed to be as far away from Dinah as he could get. He'd also had enough of Stella for one day.

"I thought you said I was done here," he snapped. With just a shake of the arm he pulled free of her grip and he ignored the hurt look in her eye as he stormed from the room.

Maggie was waiting for him outside. Wisely she said nothing, just followed him through the station and out to his car.

In spite of having a literal ghost in the car with him, it was his memories that haunted him. He had no idea what that man had been doing with Proxies, but Tad was sure it had something to do with his increased powers and the strange things going on recently.

More than that, he saw the faces of the Proxies themselves. There were far too many to remember them all and yet more than enough for him to never forget.

In his life he had dealt with ghosts that turned evil thanks to their acts in life and the lack of a Proxy in death. He had seen horrors that most people could not imagine whilst dealing with those ghosts. Yet he knew without a shadow of a doubt that this night he had met a bigger monster than all of them in Dinah Mizrahi.

What worried him was that his future held an even bigger one yet. Whether as his victim or as someone trying his best to stop him, Tad knew he would have to meet her employer at some point. Running was no good when he was facing someone that powerful. He'd always be looking over his shoulder for the rest of his life.

He didn't come out of his thoughts until he was home and saw Jen again.

She was the next on the list. Dinah's employer knew about her and wanted her by tomorrow night. What would happen when Dinah failed to show? Would he come after her himself?

The thought terrified him and he knew he needed to deal with the man first.

"Tad? Are you alright?" Jen asked, worried at the look on his face. He forced himself to smile. Whatever happened, she couldn't know about this. It was too much for a young girl.

"Of course I am. Just a rough day. What are you doing?"

"I was just about to watch a film."

"Sounds perfect. What are we watching?"

He didn't hear her answer. He was already slipping again, losing himself in his memories of what he had seen this night. How was he ever going to keep his girl safe?

He was still troubled by it when the movie ended. He had no answer by the time he went to bed. He remained lost when sleep finally claimed him in the early hours of the morning.

26

Saturday, 29th November 2015
08:15

Tad woke at eight, just four hours after falling asleep.

It was Saturday. He was running out of time, and he had lots to do. So long as Dinah's employer was out there looking for Jen, then he would never be free of the constant worry eating him up. If he ever wanted to rest properly again, he needed to get that dealt with.

First, he had to find out who he was dealing with, which meant getting more information. Dinah was now a dead end for that. He could try to enter her dreams again, but he got the impression she wouldn't be sleeping anytime soon.

If his recollection of her memories was correct, just the night before last she promised to have Jen delivered by Saturday. That meant that after today, this mystery employer might come looking for Jen himself. It gave Tad one day to do something about it.

There had to be something he could do. He swung his legs out of bed and paced around the room. He wouldn't leave this bedroom until he had a solution.

He started by going over everything he learnt the night before and tried to find a clue. That meant going through Dinah's memories again, which wasn't pleasant. He struggled to think back on everything he learnt from her, everything she had done.

It was useless.

He tried to come at it from a different angle. He was still thinking about her memories but this time he concentrated on everything she knew about her employer.

This strange man wanted Proxies. He was powerful enough to get information on Dinah that no one should know, and he had people everywhere. None of that information led Tad to anything helpful. He was growing frustrated. How could he save Jen before tonight if—

His train of thought stopped as abruptly as his pacing.

Her employer had been insistent that Dinah get Jen as soon as possible because he wanted her to find someone else. This other person wasn't a Proxy, but instead someone of interest.

It was thin, but if he could find this person, figure out what was so important and why this man wanted him, then maybe he could find out what to do next.

Suddenly excited, he rushed about his morning routine. After a shower, a shave, and a change of clothes, he felt like a new man. It was that man that greeted Jen and his ghosts in the kitchen.

The clock on the wall said it was ten o'clock, later than he normally slept in. That coupled with his behaviour the night before had all his ghosts looking at him funny and Jen asking if he was alright.

He was about to tell her he was fine and everything was okay, but with his new found clarity he realised he would be making the same mistakes again. He was fed up of this loop where he babied Jen and she acts out in return. It was time to change his behaviour, no matter how hard that might be.

"Not really. Let me get a coffee and we'll discuss it."

He made himself said coffee, and when he turned around, he found his ghosts waiting with Jen. He chuckled in spite of everything. He guessed it was time for a family meeting.

"What's going on Tad?" Miriam asked. "You were strange last

night. Is it Stella? Is she getting to you?"

Tad blinked at the question and shook his head. In the wake of everything he learnt last night, he hadn't had time to think of Stella.

"No. We've got bigger issues than D.I. Martin."

He started with his idea to go into Dinah's mind for answers, giving Jen full credit which pleased her immensely. Her pleasure didn't last.

By the time he was done telling his story, he faced a very pale Jen and sombre ghosts.

"So the way I figure it, we need to get moving on this, fast. I'll look for this Gideon Jordan and see where that leads us. Questions?"

At first there was silence, then everyone talked at once.

"One at a time."

Again there was silence, again everyone talked at once. Tad held up his hand to calm them, then pointed to Jen. "You first."

"What happens if you're too late? Am I—"

"I won't be," he answered, cutting her off and trying to sound confident. It wouldn't do any of them any good to dwell on that question. "Next?"

He pointed at Maggie who started to speak, but Jen butted in.

"Hang on. You didn't—"

"We'll figure this out, okay? I won't let anything happen to you."

For a moment she looked every bit as young and in need of protection as he always thought. Maybe he had made a mistake telling her this. After she took a deep breath and got hold of herself, she nodded to tell him she was fine, proof of how strong she could be.

No matter how he tried to make it otherwise, she did not live the life of a normal twelve-year-old. She had been exposed to things no child should face, and she had come out stronger on the other side. Maybe there was something to what she and Maggie had been telling him. Maybe he needed to start trusting her.

He stayed at the table for the next ten minutes answering questions before he said enough was enough. He needed to start looking. Jen said she wanted to help and for once he let her.

"I need you to look on the internet for anything you can find on this Gideon guy. Try to get creative with it, Jen. We need to find him."

She nodded very seriously. "Okay. What are you going to do?"

"I'm going to hit up Kate to see if she can help. Stella may no longer be on our side, but we still have one tame detective to rely on." He looked to Miriam and asked, "You coming?"

"No, I'll just be a distraction. I'll stay here and help Jen. Give Kate my love."

"I could do that for you," Tony offered and earned a slap around the head for his outburst.

Tad couldn't help but laugh. He had missed their bickering. It was their own version of normal and it had been too long since he had seen it.

"I'm not taking you anywhere near Kate when I need a favour from her," Tad said. Tony looked offended but didn't object. "Charles you coming?" Charles nodded. "I'm not even going to ask you," Tad said to Maggie who just grinned. She wanted to check in with Kate to see how things were going with her case. It was a good job she couldn't use a telephone or Kate wouldn't have been getting much sleep until Mark was finally behind bars.

"Come on then. Let's go. Jen, you okay with this?"

She looked sick but forced herself to nod. "I will be."

"I'm leaving you with just Miriam and Tony. If you have any problems, you let them deal with it and you run. You have your phone?" She nodded. "Is it charged?" She hesitated, then nodded again. Tad didn't trust that look. "Make sure it's charged and leave it switched on. If you have any problems at all, I want you to call me. I'm only a ten minute drive away. You got that?" Again she nodded.

He stepped around the table and kissed her on the forehead.

"I love you, Jen. I won't let anything happen, I promise."

She smiled and there were tears in her eyes, but she said nothing.

He turned away, nodded to Maggie and Charles, then he was out the door, ready to start yet another busy day.

***

Tad hovered over Kate's shoulder trying to look at her computer. She gave him the look she usually saved for Tony.

"You're not helping, Tad? Maybe you'd be more comfortable on the other side of the desk."

"But I can't see what you're doing over there."

Her response came from between clenched teeth.

"Exactly."

He was about to protest, but Kate was saved by a knock at the door. They both looked up from Kate's desk to see Stella standing at the office door looking sheepish. It was annoying that even wearing the same clothes as the day before and looking as though she hadn't slept all night, she still looked great.

"Any chance I could steal Tad for a few minutes?" she asked Kate. It was the perfect move to get under his skin. Speaking to Kate as though she was his keeper was almost as bad as Kate answering as though she actually was.

"Oh, God yes. Take him."

Tad sent one last annoyed glance Kate's way before he decided he had best go with the program and keep Kate happy.

"Keep an eye on her, Charles. If she finds something, I want to know as soon as possible."

Charles, invisible to everyone else in the room, nodded and took Tad's place. Confident he would know what Kate knew as soon as possible, Tad stepped out of the office and joined Stella in the hall.

Major police stations don't really close, but the few times Tad visited Kate on a weekend, it was much quieter. When he left Kate's office, he found himself alone with Stella who was waiting for him further down the corridor where they couldn't be overheard.

"What is it, Stella?"

She didn't answer immediately and he had no choice but to wait her out. The time he waited gave him chance to read her aura which was muted again, but slightly more readable this time. It was a mess of colours that he couldn't work out. She had mixed feelings and none of them were winning through.

"I need to apologise. Yesterday… I wasn't myself."

"No?"

"Look. I shouldn't have said those things to you. I was angry, and I took it out on you. I shouldn't have done that and I'm sorry."

The apology sounded sincere, but he felt it was only a half truth and there was more she wasn't saying. The question was whether he would let that slide or keep digging.

"That's fine. Apology accepted. Now I'm sorry, but I need to—"

"Tad, what are you working on?"

"Kate's case. She had something she wanted me to go over with her."

The flicker of purple annoyance was all too clear even if she managed to keep the look from reaching her face.

"You know, you've surprised me in a lot of ways since we've met. But the one constant with you is that I always know when you're lying. You're lying now. I know I was out of line yesterday, but please lets not go back to where you involve yourself in my investigation and lie about it. What are you working on?"

He sighed. "It could be nothing. It's just a hunch."

"Well it's more than what I've got. After you left, I confirmed what you said. She is Dinah Mizrahi, and she worked for the Israeli government, but that's it. She shut up as soon as you left and we've not been able to get a word out of her since."

He didn't think she would. Dinah thought she was keeping her family safe by not saying anything. If there was one thing he learnt about her, it was that her strength to do anything for her family was unending. If Dinah didn't want to talk, nothing Stella could do would make her.

"Fine. I'm getting Kate to see if she can find any information on a Gideon Jordan."

"Who's he?"

"The man Dinah works for asked her to find him. He said that first she was to get Jen and then this Gideon was the next target. But, he isn't a Proxy. I figured if I can track him down and find out why Jen's employer wants him then it might lead to something else. It's a long shot but—"

"It's more than what I've got." She sounded excited. "If you find him I want to go with you, Tad. You're not leaving me out of this."

It wasn't a request, and he knew better than to deny her. Besides, when Jen's life hung in the balance, having Stella, and by extension the police, on his side was only a plus.

"Fine. You can come. But no promises. We don't even know if we can find the guy."

Stella opened her mouth to answer but was cut short when Tad's phone rang. "Hang on, it's Jen." He connected the call. "Jen. Are you alright?"

"Yeah. I'm fine, don't worry. Tad, I've found him."

"You what?"

"Gideon Jordan. I've found him… or at least know who he is. He's fifteen, was raised in a place called Tenby, and there was a lot of fuss made about him on local websites, blogs and papers when he finished high school early and got admitted to Cambridge. He's in his second year there."

Tad was already getting an idea of what Dinah's employer might want from this kid. "What's he doing at Cambridge?"

"I'm not sure. The articles say different things."

"It doesn't matter. That's already good work. You say he's from Tenby. Do you think he still has family there?"

"Miriam thought you might ask that. She said to say there are a few families with the surname of Jordan within ten miles of Tenby. We've found the addresses of most of them and I've just emailed the last few names to Kate to see what she can find. Is there anything else you need?"

"No. You've been great. Thanks Jen."

He could hear her pride over the phone. She told him it was no problem and after a brief goodbye she hung up.

Stella had only heard one side of the conversation, but she could tell by looking at him that he had good news.

"What is it? Something in Tenby?"

He nodded and filled her in. She was less enthused when he finished. "It doesn't sound like much."

Tad shook his head. "I have a theory I'm working on. This new information on Gideon might tell us more than you'd think." He opened his mouth to explain, then shook his head. "I'm on a deadline. If you're coming, then you'll need to be ready to go in a few minutes. As soon as I see what Kate has found I'm heading out."

Stella nodded and was already moving away. "I'll be back here in five," she promised. He didn't get chance to answer before she disappeared around the corner at the end of the corridor.

Tad watched the space she had been standing for a second, trying to get his head around whether bringing her was a good idea. However, he didn't have time to waste thinking, and he forced the problem from his mind.

He returned to Kate's office to see what she had.

Five minutes later he and Stella were climbing into his car, and after a brief pit stop and a change of ghosts at his house, they headed west to find the Jordan family.

27

Saturday, 29th November 2015
15:55

The drive west was wet and long. Thanks to average speed checks, high traffic through Port Talbot and a crash near Carmarthen, the journey that should have taken only an hour and a half, took three.

Those three felt like nine to Stella. She had lost the easy conversation she once had with Tad. He still resented her treatment of him from yesterday, and she didn't blame him.

She overreacted to unfamiliar emotions that caught her by surprise. Stella remained confident that those feelings should be pushed aside as she couldn't trust them and didn't need them. However, she also felt like she was throwing something away.

She didn't know how to bridge the gap, so she said little on the way west.

Stella had been to Tenby before. The picturesque Pembrokeshire coastal town had been a popular holiday destination in her family. It was one of the few places where she actually made good childhood memories.

She remembered being impressed with the ancient walls that encircled the main part of the town and made the whole place seem like one big castle. Inside those walls was a nest of narrow, windy streets filled with old buildings, rich in character, and coloured in a mixture of vibrant, blues, pinks and yellows. The hodgepodge of unusual buildings, overly colourful facades and cobbled streets stood out in her memories, and she would be happy to see them again.

Once they parked in the town's multi-storey, she had no choice but to break the silence.

"What's the plan?" she asked. "Just knock on doors?"

Tad shook his head. "I don't have time for that. Between Jen and Kate they've narrowed the search to four addresses. That's what these two are here for."

He indicated Tony and Stella. Maggie had opted to stay at the police station to keep an eye on Kate, and Charles had been left with Jen.

"What will you do?" Stella asked. It was Miriam who answered.

"We'll take a look around the houses. We find any sign that we might be at the right location and we'll come find you."

Stella wasn't used to the casual way these ghosts had of ignoring the law. She understood there was no law governing whether a ghost could enter your property, she doubted she could enforce it if there was. However, she couldn't help but view them as people when Tad showed them to her, and it was hard to accept their ability to wander into other people's homes and snoop about.

"Okay. While they're doing that, what will we be doing?"

"Dinner," Tad said. The minute he said the word she realised she hadn't eaten all day. Suddenly she was starving.

"Now you mention it, that sounds good." An idea struck her and for the first time that day, a genuine smile came to her face. "Being as we're at the seaside, you fancy fish and chips?"

Tad shrugged and nodded.

Stella suggested a spot where they could meet up with the ghosts. Once decided, the ghosts vanished and Stella was left alone with Tad. The silence returned as she led them out of the car park and up to the town.

They entered the old town walls through one of the stone arch ways in the barbican gatehouse. They stopped off a few minutes later to buy their dinner and spoke only long enough for Stella to insist that they get takeout rather than eat in. With their paper wrapped parcels of food, Stella led them through the town and down the hill toward the sea.

Being a Saturday, there were plenty of people wandering about, moving from shop to shop and visiting the pubs. Above the sound of people talking there were the constant cries of seagulls. Stella found it relaxing and her contented feeling remained as they left the town square and followed the road down to the harbour and a grassy hill overlooking it. The winding path around the hill revealed several treasures including two lifeboat stations, a monument, and yet another medieval looking ruin. Most importantly to Stella, there was the view over the old island fort just off the coast.

By the time she found them a sheltered bench that was dry enough to sit on, she felt much more relaxed than she had in days.

"That's quite a view," Tad commented as he too stared at the old island fort, the beach surrounding it, Caldey Island off in the distance, and even the sea itself.

"It is. I used to love coming here in the summer," she said. "I haven't been in years."

They lapsed back to silence as they finished their food, but it was more comfortable than the last. Stella found it easier to break this silence when she was ready to talk.

"I really am sorry about yesterday. I took my frustrations out on you. I shouldn't have."

"What had you so frustrated?"

"It doesn't matter," she answered quickly, hoping he would move past the topic.

"It clearly does. Look. You say you took your frustrations out on me, but it's clear that those frustrations had at least something to do with me. What was wrong?"

She didn't know how to answer and Tad spoke up before she figured it out.

"Does it have something to do with me kissing Maggie?"

Again she didn't know how to answer and again he spoke before she could.

"I thought so." He sounded confident, as though he had somehow read her thoughts. Was she that obvious with her emotions? She had always thought she was good at masking what she was feeling. Not for the first time he surprised her with his ability to see through that mask. "I explained about the kiss—"

"I already said, it's none of my business."

"I don't buy that, Stella." He sighed. "I can't be bothered to tip toe past this. I'm no good at that sort of thing. Nothing will ever happen between me and Maggie. It never would have when she was alive and now she's dead it's still not going to. I had a crush on her for years but that was it. Those feelings are gone now, I promise."

"Tad, I don't need—"

"Do you know the one thing that hasn't sucked about the last few weeks? Spending time with you and getting to know you better. Back when we first met, I have to be honest, you were pretty scary. But since that night we were attacked, I've had more chance to see the real you and I like the Stella that I've got to know since. I may be taking a big leap in the wrong direction, but I thought you might like me as well.

"Maybe I'm wrong, but maybe that's why you had such a bad reaction when Maggie kissed me. Was I wrong? If so, just tell me because one way or the other we need to put this behind us."

The winter night was fast closing in, the darkness coming quickly even though it was not yet five o'clock. In spite of that darkness Stella knew Tad had no trouble seeing her expression. For the first time in memory, she had no idea what that expression might be.

He caught her off guard. There was something about such radical honesty that made it hard to respond and she struggled to even find an answer within her own mind let alone speak one aloud. The silence dragged between them and in panic she realised she needed to say something or things might go bad again.

"You might have been right. I've been… confused since that night we were attacked. I normally have a handle on things and—"

She didn't like how that sounded. She tried again.

"I'm not good with people. I've had a lot of bad relationships with both friends and family, and I find it's easier to be alone. Then this last week it's been so easy talking to you, it got me confused. I don't know what I was expecting, but when I saw Maggie kissing you it surprised me and I didn't know how to react."

She looked over to see his reaction and found him staring at her. There was a strange little smile growing on his face which made her forget what she had been about to say.

"What?" she asked.

"I knew you liked me."

Everything about the statement made her mind travel back to secondary school. From his tone of voice as he almost sang the words, to the actual statement itself, it all felt juvenile. She couldn't help but laugh.

"I never said that."

"Sure you did. You made me work for it and I had to read between the lines, but you definitely said it."

She laughed again. "I thought we were having a serious conversation."

"We are. I just like to know where I stand. It's all becoming clear now. I should have known. Women always get this way around me. They can't keep their heads on straight."

She tried to snort mockingly and laugh at the same time. The combination of the two had her choking. It must have been hilarious as suddenly Tad was roaring with laughter. He was laughing long after she had stopped choking, and his laughter only made her laugh as well.

It was one of those situations where each person's laughter was spurred on by the other. It kept the amusement alive longer was normal, and by the time they quieted there were tears in both their eyes.

When she finally calmed, she leaned back against the bench and turned to find him looking at her again. There was a big smile on his face and she wasn't surprised to find that his magic had returned. Once more his smile triggered her own. She didn't mind. If his magic power over her was to make her happy, then who was she to complain?

Now she had locked gazes with him she couldn't look away. Slowly his smile was fading, and he was leaning forward. The movement set off all kinds of alarms in Stella, but she leaned forward as well.

They were close enough that she could feel his breath upon her face and she was suddenly very aware of the smell of his cologne. She continued to lean closer, and she closed her eyes, waiting for his lips to touch hers.

After a few seconds she thought the hesitation would kill her. A few more seconds and she realised he wasn't going to kiss her.

A sudden panic washed through her.

Had she misread the moment? What did she look like to him right now? Leaning forward with her eyes closed... What was she even thinking? Hadn't she just spent the last two days telling herself that she didn't want to be in a relationship? She was married to her job. She didn't need this.

She opened her eyes to find he was no longer leaning in and had turned his head away. She was about to feel hurt by his rejection when suddenly she heard it too.

She only recognised one voice. It was a voice she had heard so many times when she worked with her that she could never forget it. It was too quiet to make out the words, but Miriam was coming towards them.

What surprised her was that the second voice didn't belong to Tony, and it sounded American. Another woman was talking to Miriam. That meant that whoever was coming could not only see Miriam but could interact with her. Another Proxy maybe? Stella didn't think so for some reason. Tad said they weren't here looking for a Proxy and she had the feeling they were unlikely to stumble across one.

Another ghost then.

She got her answer when Miriam, Tony and a third figure walked around the corner. She was suddenly glad that Tad had pulled back. If he hadn't, they would have walked around the corner just in time to see the two of them kiss. That would have caused yet more complications. Besides, she didn't even want anything to happen with Tad… did she? She was so confused right then that she was actually glad for this distraction.

"Finally, here you are," Tony said when he spotted them. "This place is a bit out of the way, Stella. If we hadn't had Emily to guide us, we never would have found it."

"Speak for yourself," Miriam said. "Some of us can read, so I'd have been fine."

Tony rolled his eyes and opened his mouth to speak when the third figure, Emily, beat him too it.

"You're Thaddeus Holcroft?" she asked. "The Proxy?"

Tad was turned away from her, so Stella only saw the edge of his frown when it appeared.

"I am. How do you know me?"

Emily was a small, black woman who looked like she was in her late seventies. She had a slight hunch and from the way she leaned over, Stella felt she should probably have a cane. Stella wondered whether ghosts would take such things with them into the afterlife. They seemed to take their clothes. She still knew too little about ghosts to guess at an answer and now wasn't the time to ask. She focused on the conversation.

"There aren't many Proxies left in Britain, so you've become famous in dead circles."

From what little Stella could see, Tad looked as confused as she was.

"Okay. I think I might be a little lost. Who are you?" Tad asked.

"We found her waiting for us at one of the addresses," Tony said. "You should have seen what was waiting at one of the other addresses though mate. There were these two chicks who were showing up Miriam and Kate if you know what I mean. They were gorgeous as well—"

"Tony!" Stella couldn't help herself and apparently neither could

Miriam and Tad. The admonishment came from all three at once and made the teenager blink in surprise.

"What?"

"Sorry about him," Tad said whilst ignoring Tony's question. "He said you were waiting for them?"

She nodded. "I was. In light of recent events, I had no choice but to come back here. I knew it was a long shot, but I thought someone might turn up."

Tad was shaking his head. "I'm sorry. I still don't understand what you're doing here."

"I'm Emily Jordan. Gideon is my grandson." She looked like she was about to say something else but then shook her head and changed the topic. "I think we should go somewhere we can talk. I have a lot to tell and you will have many questions, I promise."

"Okay," Tad said. "Before we go anywhere with you though, give me the short version."

Stella could tell by his tone that Tad didn't trust Emily. With all that had been happening lately she didn't blame him.

"Alright. As I said, Gideon is my grandson. He's in danger from the same man who has been seeking you. Now that his hunter has been taken into police custody, I knew it was only a matter of time before either you or one of his people would come for my Gideon. I came here to see what I could do to keep Gideon safe."

Tad was still frowning. "How do you know all this?"

"Because my Proxy is the man who hunts you. I know him better than anyone and if you want even a hope of stopping him, then you need to hear what I have to say."

Silence followed her statement. The news shocked them all, but it seemed to affect Tad and the ghosts more than it did Stella. She recovered quicker and asked the question she had wanted to know since she first started this case.

"The man behind it all. Who is he? What's his name?"

Emily hesitated and looked a little pained as though she didn't want to answer. Finally she took a deep breath, straightened herself out and spoke.

"He is without a doubt the most dangerous man you'll ever meet. You have no idea what the cost would be if he knew I was telling you this. But, I have no choice. Not when he's coming after Gideon."

She took another deep breath and said, "The man you're looking for, the man hunting you, is called Joshua King."

The name sounded familiar to Stella, but it stunned Tad. His ghosts also had a strong reaction, and she wondered if maybe it was a ghost thing.

"Who is that? His name sounds familiar."

Tad turned to her, his eyes wide, and said, "He's the man who's been paying off the corrupt police that Kate arrested the other day. He's the one that Kate thinks has been killing people and having the police cover up his crimes."

Suddenly his surprise made sense. Stella had been following Kate's case if only to see how her rival was getting on.

"Are you ready to talk now?" Emily asked.

Tad and Stella both nodded. It was time for answers.

28

Saturday, 25th December 1982
14:33

Poison.

It was the only explanation why everyone else was dead save for Emily and Joshua. Twelve people who had been breathing, eating, and laughing just five minutes earlier were now lifeless corpses scattered around the table.

So why was Joshua still eating?

Emily was shaking as she stared at the chubby, blonde boy. He was calmly cutting chunks of chocolate cake with his fork and putting them into his mouth. The look of rapture as he took every bite didn't belong amongst such carnage.

"If you're not going to eat yours, can you slide it down?"

They were the first words since it happened and they made Emily jump.

"What?"

"Your cake. I want it. Pass it down."

"But what if it's poisoned like the rest?"

"It's not. Please pass it down."

None of this made sense. Confusion had never been a feeling Emily enjoyed. People with minds like hers didn't get confused. Slowly the pieces fell into place.

"You did this?" she asked, knowing the answer before she finished speaking.

The boy laughed around a mouthful of cake as he scraped the residual fudge and cream from the plate.

"There's that big mind at work," he teased. "Took you long enough. Now Emily, please pass me your cake."

Emily still didn't move. He had killed them all, his entire family. He'd been teased and belittled all his life, but enough to prompt this?

His left arm was ruined when he was dropped as a baby. To people like the Kings, a cripple had no worth and they no longer cared about him. Emily cared though. She always thought he could be sweet when he wanted to be. She cared as that sweetness left him thanks to years of neglect. He had grown to be a loner, preferring his own company more often than not. She'd even seen him talking to himself.

She worried about him, but she never thought she'd have to worry about this.

"Emily. I'm losing my patience."

Emily recognised that it was best to do as he asked. She got up, taking her cake with her and stepping over the bodies of her old employers as she moved down the table.

Joshua smiled as he watched her approach and he pushed his own plate aside. He was graceful, almost reverential, as he took the plate from Emily's hand and laid it on the table before him.

Emily didn't know what to do. She wanted to leave, to go get help, but doubted he'd let her. Instead she turned and walked toward her seat.

"Don't be silly, Emily." The voice stopped her cold. "Don't go all the way back there. It's hard to talk to you from that far away. Sit here."

He nodded to the chair to his left. Emily hesitated. That chair was still occupied.

Talia King had been beautiful in life. She was slim, confident and loved by anyone who met her. She was his only sibling, and it was no secret that her parents considered her the future of the King family.

The figure that Emily had to manoeuvre from the chair was no longer beautiful. Her eyes were open and lined with red where they had bulged in her struggle to breathe. The strain on her face was still evident and her grimace was horrifying.

Emily tried not to look at that face as she half dragged the young woman from the chair, laying her next to her father.

"There, isn't that better?" Joshua asked between mouthfuls as Emily sat in the now vacant seat.

She didn't trust herself to answer.

"I suppose you're wondering why you're not dead with the rest of them?" he asked before scooping yet another fork full of cake into his mouth.

Yes, Emily wondered that. She was also wondering why the rest of them had to die.

"You might think it's because you're not like them," Joshua answered his own question. "But that's not the reason. I know you aren't family, but you might as well be. You've been living in this house longer than I've been alive."

It was true. Emily had been brought to England nearly twenty years earlier when she was fifty. She liked to tell herself it was her choice, and she had accepted a job offer, but the truth was that she was a prisoner.

In spite of being born in a time when those of African descent were not entitled to an education, Emily discovered she had a talent for numbers. She'd been taught to read secretly when she was younger, and a job working at a library at night had given her plenty of time to hone that skill. She used the time to further her education, and when she encountered mathematics she had discovered her true purpose in life.

She had no future academically. She was a black woman and no matter how much their world evolved she had doubted she would ever be accepted. She had tried to keep her talent a secret. It didn't last.

She had been discovered by a young man from Brooklyn. He was a small-time player in several illegal enterprises and he realised how someone with her talents could help make him a much larger player. He got leverage on her by threatening her husband and children, and she had no choice but to work for him.

She'd been twenty-one at the time and over the next twenty years her skills earned her the attention of five different men who each killed or paid a handsome price for them. Her final employer had been the one to set her current lifestyle. Samuel Delacross was so appreciative of her skills that he treated her like royalty, almost as though she was a member of his family.

She had helped grow his business at the expense of her family who had long since emigrated to the UK to be as far away from her as possible. She remained with him and grew comfortable until his youngest daughter married ten years later.

She married Francis King who spent a lot of time in England trying to grow Samuel's business interests across the ocean. Samuel gifted Emily to Francis as a wedding present and Emily's time in the United States was up.

In the nineteen years since that day, she helped grow a thriving empire, watched over the King children who became almost as close to her as son and daughter, and made no move to reconnect with her old family. She willingly gave up ties to her old life to keep her real family from harm. She threw everything she was into the King family. Now they were all dead.

"The real reason I left you alive is because you have something I want."

She started to feel a little more comfortable. She had spent her whole life dealing with people who wanted her for her skills. She knew how to deal with that.

"You want me to work for you like I worked for your father?" she guessed.

He laughed, spraying crumbs and pushing the second empty plate away. "Something like that."

His eyes moved around the large room, resting on places that held nothing of interest that Emily could see.

"I've been planning this for a long time. This isn't the only scene like this today. All over the country, there should be ten other Christmas dinners that have gone exactly the same way."

He chuckled, and the sound made Emily go cold.

"Today will be remembered in certain circles as proof that with patience, anything is possible."

"Why?"

"Why what? Why do this? Isn't that obvious?" Emily shook her head. "Because I can. I've spent my entire life being looked down on by these people. All because my stupid slut of a mother was too clumsy to keep me from falling to the floor. I've been overlooked because of a crippled arm. I think we can all agree that was a stupid thing to do."

"All of this is because you were overlooked?"

He laughed again. "You still don't get it. I didn't do this because I was overlooked. I did this because I could. Darwin was right, it's the strong who survive. Because of this," he motioned to his arm again. "I have always been thought of as weak. But there are different kinds of strength. You of all people should know that."

He tapped his head with his finger. He had always been clever, not on her level, but he was brighter than the other members of his family.

"They couldn't conceive that I was ever strong enough to do something like this, so they let their guard down. Tell me, when everyone around you is dead and you stand alone, who is really the strongest in the room?"

She didn't answer. He wasn't talking to her, he was just showing off.

"You said there were others massacres like this?"

He nodded eagerly. "Ten at least. The rest of the down trodden took little persuading. The girls who want to be taken as seriously as their brothers, the geeks, the infirm, and those otherwise deemed weak. Every family has someone who feels like they've been put down their entire lives. All it takes to show them the light is to prove to them how their supposed weakness can be their greatest strength.

"Them being invisible to their families is exactly what allowed this to happen." He leaned closer and said, "Right now they're sat at their own dinners and each of them are talking to one lucky dinner guest who is also not dead. They're making this same offer to those talented individuals on my behalf."

"What offer?"

"I want you to join me. I don't mean as my accountant. Look at you, you're so frail you might die any day now. Actually, no matter what comes of this conversation you will die today."

Emily's blood ran cold and she had to fight to keep herself from shaking.

"What do you mean? I thought you wanted me to work for you."

"I do, in a way. The truth is, I want you to work through me by proxy. This won't make much sense until you're dead. However, I need to talk to you now because I need you to stick around when you are dead. I can't have you moving on before we have chance to talk."

"What are you on about?"

"Like I said. That will soon become clear. What is important is that for now you know the stakes. When you're dead, I want you to know what will happen if you move on to the next life.

"I'm aware of your family, the one you thought we didn't know about anymore. I know they live in Pembrokeshire, how many of them there are, and even what they do for a living. I know that even though they haven't spoken to you for a long time, you'd still do anything for them. Isn't that right?"

Emily nodded, her mind racing as she tried to contemplate how he not only knew of her family but had found out where they lived. It had been so long since she had seen them that she thought no one knew of them anymore.

"The good news is that they'll be fine. However, how much longer they continue to survive is up to you. Now, I'm going to kill you in a minute. When I do, I need you to remember not to move on. You'll want to, trust me, but you need to remember what happens to your family if you do."

"Why are you doing this?"

"Like I said, because I can. I have learned that a common trait in those who succeed in life is that they take what they want, they don't wait for it to come to them. You have a talent I want. I intend to take that talent."

Emily opened her mouth to ask another question, but he spoke over her.

"I'm sorry Emily, but I'm in a rush. I have ten other places to be today, ten other souls to collect. The families that have died today make up the leadership of everything you and my father have built over here, so once I have collected my souls I have to act quick to take control of everything before it collapses."

He leaned back in his chair and reached under the table. Emily had to fight back a scream when his hand emerged with a black pistol nestled in his grip.

"Okay Emily, be brave. This will all be over soon."

She opened her mouth to speak, to beg for him to spare her life, but she never got the chance.

As calm as if he were doing the most normal thing in the world, Joshua raised the gun to her head and pulled the trigger.

Friday, 16th January 2004
23:29

All Emily sensed from him these days was pain. Nothing had ever pleased her more. Finally he was getting what was coming to him. He was dying a long and painful death. It would be a fitting end for Joshua

King.

Of course, it was too early to count him out yet.

She had seen too much to think anything was impossible for him. Once upon a time she was naïve enough to think she was smart, that she knew everything worth knowing in the world. Nothing prepared her for Joshua King's reality.

His was a reality of ghosts, nightmares and unlimited power for those with the stomach to take it. She hoped for different, but doubted even cancer could stop him. Since he learnt about it, his twisted mind had constantly been seeking answers. It was what brought them to Cardiff.

Joshua didn't bother picking the lock, he simply pressed his hand against the door and pushed. With more than a hundred ghosts in him at all times, the casual strength of Joshua King was staggering. The lock didn't even have chance to groan in protest before it snapped and the door swung inward.

Hopefully, he had left a fingerprint on the now broken door so the police could arrest him. It was unlikely, but it was one of a million fantasies about his downfall that played through her mind.

The reception beyond the door was dimly lit by the glow of an exit sign. King looked around with eyes that were more than sharp enough to peer through the gloom and was unimpressed. It was like the reception of any other office block with nothing special about it. Emily sensed his anger rise. It was not a good thing for his prisoner.

"Well, where is it?" he demanded.

The cringing woman who followed him in flinched as he looked her way. She had been proud when they first met her. She was young, pretty and had seven ghosts of her own. Emily had learnt that this was a lot for normal Proxies.

Joshua was not normal.

He barely broke a sweat as he annihilated her ghosts. One by one he destroyed them until she was begging him to stop. Once he was done, he turned his attention on her. By this point she was little more than a weeping a mess, no longer possessing any strength beyond that of a normal woman. It helped humble her which was always good in Joshua's presence.

"Well?" he asked again, his patience all but gone. "If you've brought me here for nothing, then so help me—"

"It's here," the woman blurted. "Surely you can feel it."

He was about to answer when suddenly he did feel something. Through him Emily felt it as well. It was a strange sensation. It felt like the chill of death that accompanies a mad ghost, only it was more widespread. It was a weak feeling, but in spite of that she knew it was massive. It was just a long way off.

"I do feel it," King whispered, his creepy smile back. "This is the place. I should never have doubted you."

"Then I can go?" the woman asked hopefully. The poor thing. She had no idea that the moment she laid eyes on Joshua King her life was over.

"Do you know why I needed to find this place?" he asked instead of answering. She hesitated before shaking her head, no. "It's the second part of a puzzle I've been trying to solve for a year."

The woman didn't care, but she played along. "What puzzle?"

"I've been looking for a way to fight off death. I mean, we Proxies are masters of death, aren't we? Surely if anyone can do it, it's us."

The expression on the woman's face changed to one of disbelief. "You want to become immortal?"

King laughed. "Who doesn't? However, my needs are more pressing than that. The only reason I'm still walking around is the healing power of my ghosts. But even with them there's only so much they can do. I need a better solution. As with most things, more power is the answer."

"And you think you'll find that here. You killed my ghosts for this?" Some of her strength returned with her incredulity. Emily wanted to warn her. He was not a man to take lightly. Try to overestimate him and you would still fall short.

"Yes. I did." King answered as though he didn't recognise the mocking tone behind her question. Emily was in his head, she knew different.

"You won't find that kind of power here. I don't know what you've been told but—"

Her words were cut off by his cold laugh. "It's typical. You stumble across this place and have felt its strength, yet you still don't know what you're in the presence of."

"A second ago you couldn't even feel it. That's how meagre the strength here is—"

"Not meagre. It's massive." He closed his eyes and extended his senses, feeling for the presence with his Proxy talent. "It's a long way distant but… Yes. That's the power I need."

He looked down again and this time it was his turn to be mocking. "How can you have felt this before and not learned what it is? It is ultimate power."

She shook her head. "I came here to deal with a ghost. That presence was stronger then because the ghost was here, and it gave me a boost in strength. But it didn't last. As soon as the ghost was gone, the strength left with it. It's just a freak occurrence. Nothing special."

King shook his head. "No, it's not a freak occurrence. This thing you connected with but failed to understand, is the source of our power. That presence is death itself."

The woman didn't know how to respond. Proxies had a way of knowing things instinctively, especially when it concerned death. He was telling the truth and she could sense that.

"I'd heard rumours about this type of place from other Proxies over the years. When I knew I didn't have power enough to save me, I figured this was the only place I might find it. This is a point in the living world where the barriers between life and death are weakest. Right here, on this spot, the two worlds make the slightest contact.

"It has taken a lot of research, but I understand what Proxies are now. We're somehow born of both worlds. Living creatures with power over death. The thing is, our power is only a fraction of what it could be because death doesn't have much of a presence in this world. I plan to change that."

"You're mad," the woman said. She was still afraid but she couldn't stop the words coming out.

King sighed.

"Why must people always insist on seeing me that way? Just because you don't understand my vision... Never mind. I'm getting bored with this. It's time to get to work. Time waits for no man, not even me."

"So I can go?"

King was shaking his head even as he took another step forward.

"Go? Of course not. You have a vital part to play in my plans, my dear. You're going to help me open the doorway. At the moment the hole in the wall between our worlds is little more than a pinprick. However..."

He moved. It was so much faster than any human that she didn't have chance to flinch before he was on top of her. With his bare hand he grabbed her by the throat and from there it was a simple matter of closing his fingers.

The poor woman's eyes widened, and she pulled at his hand. Her nails cut deep into his skin, but so strong was the healing factor from his ghosts that the wound closed almost instantly.

Emily felt his frustration. Seeing his wounds close before his eyes made him wonder why his ghosts couldn't heal his cancer. The answer was that some things couldn't be healed. The ghosts could accelerate his body's healing time, but they couldn't heal something that the body couldn't fix on its own if given enough time. They could only forestall the inevitable.

He pushed aside his frustration and continued talking as though he hadn't stopped.

"We are the means to open that doorway. When a person dies the barriers between life and death come down for a fraction of a second to claim that soul. A Proxy does the same thing every time they touch their power. When a Proxy dies, their power combined with the energy of a person dying creates a hole in the barrier between worlds that is not only bigger than a normal soul, but also permanent."

He motioned around himself at the room they were standing in. "That's the reason this place exists. A Proxy died here once upon a time and he left this path between worlds behind."

He'd long since let the woman fall to the floor in a heap. He was not paying attention to her motionless body, but instead looking at her ghost. She stood over her corpse, stunned. Evidently being a Proxy didn't prepare you for your own death.

"It got me thinking," King continued. "If one Proxy's death makes this kind of hole in the barrier, what might a second Proxy's death do."

Emily could already feel that presence grow stronger. It was still a long way off, but it was twice what it was before. King was grinning.

"As in most things, I was right. It worked."

"You're mad," the new ghost said one last time.

"Even dead you have no vision."

Once again he moved with impossible speed. Once again the woman was not ready for it.

"What are you doing?" she gasped as she struggled with his fingers about her throat.

"Now this I am sorry for," he said. He didn't sound sorry. "I don't need to do this for my plans to work, but I also can't risk letting you free. All I need is you warning another Proxy about me and things could get… difficult."

"I won't. I promise."

She realised what he was planning and was struggling twice as hard whilst begging at the same time. Emily had seen a lot over the last twenty-two years she would never forget. The look of horror on that woman's face was right there near the top.

The woman knew that he planned to do one of the worst things to her most people could think of. It was one thing to face your mortality with the fear that there was nothing after death, it was another thing to know it for a certainty.

She was fighting so hard because she was fighting oblivion.

"I can't take that risk. At least you get the pleasure of going with the knowledge that your death helped to change the world."

Emily had seen the sight before, but it had never quite bothered her as it did then. It was the foreknowledge that upset her. The fact that this woman was so aware of what was happening and was terrified of it.

The woman started to glow from within, her eyes going wide as King added enough power to her core that she started to overload and grow unstable. Once more she pleaded for mercy before her whole body stiffened and her mouth opened wide. Light was pouring from her mouth, her eyes, her ears, and soon from every pore.

Finally, the light exploded outward, and she was gone.

Emily knew it was a phantom feeling. She couldn't actually feel sick to her stomach. Yet she did feel sick. She felt sick and desperate. And she wasn't alone.

She shared her disgusting home with more than a hundred other souls who felt just as she did. Just like her, they were compelled to be his ghosts by threats against the people they loved most.

The only one who didn't feel sick was King himself. He had already moved on from the ghastly deed. It had been a theory that he could lower the barriers between worlds and it turned out he was right. Now his mind was racing as he planned what he would do next.

The barrier had opened wider, but not so wide that he could kill only a few Proxies and be done with it. He needed a lot of Proxies, more than he knew of. He needed help.

He was still thinking of it as he walked out of the office. He ignored the broken door and didn't look back. It didn't matter to him that the police would find the body. They would never get to him. Even if they did, Emily knew he was beyond them. Whether he did it through his many channels of influence or with his own supernatural powers, he would not spend a single day in prison for his crimes.

He walked away from that building with not a care in the world save one.

He needed Proxies. One way or another, he would get them.

29

Saturday, 29ᵗʰ November 2015
20:00

The pub they settled in grew busier as eight o'clock rolled around. Their privacy was disappearing.

They had walked back into town, finding an unobserved corner in a relatively quiet pub. Tad made sure the ghosts were visible so Stella could hear Emily's tale, but there was a worry that someone might look at their table on CCTV and be confused that there were three less people than could be seen with their own eyes.

Tad's worry was soon forgotten.

He was fascinated by Emily's story and it only added to what he already knew of Joshua King from Dinah's memories. If there was ever any doubt in his mind that he needed to fear Joshua King, it was long gone.

"One thing I don't get," he said when Emily finished. "Is what you're doing here now."

"I'm here for Gideon. Every now and again I slip away from Joshua to check on my family. I need to make sure he's holding up his end of the bargain."

"I'm surprised he lets you leave," Stella noted.

Emily shook her head and not for the first time looked jumpy.

"He doesn't. But he has so many ghosts he can't keep track of them all the time. Now and then we slip out and hope to be back before he thinks to check on us."

Once again Tad understood what she was saying but couldn't picture it in his head. The idea of not knowing if one of his own ghosts was not with him was preposterous. He was so close to all of them that they were always missed if they weren't around. But then he had nowhere near the number that Joshua King had. The thought made him shiver. It used to be hard enough keeping three ghosts in check when they were in his head.

"The last time I went back was the first time he caught me," she continued. "He forgave me, told me I was family, so he didn't mind. He just asked me to tell him before leaving next time."

She laughed bitterly. "I should have known better. He's not a reasonable man, and he's not forgiving. There was never any chance he would let the matter drop. For the first time in years, he explored my memories."

"And found out about Gideon," Miriam guessed. "He found out how intelligent your great-grandson was and wanted that mind for himself."

Emily nodded, and a tear rolled down her face. Even after thirty-three years she was not free of the human trapping of making tears when she was upset.

"It was the last straw," she said. "I've spent so long watching all the terrible things he's done because at least my family was safe. I can't say that any longer. He's crossed a line he said he would never cross, so I had to do something."

"Better late than never," Tony remarked bitterly. The comment was so uncharacteristically harsh that it drew all eyes at the table to him. "What?"

"It's not her fault, Tony," Miriam said. "She's been stuck—"

Tony's snort of disgust overrode her objections. "Really? I can understand wanting to protect a loved one, but I don't know how many people I could watch die before I found another way. I don't think it would have taken me thirty-three years."

He had a point. No matter the reasons, Emily had stood by and let hundreds of people die to keep her family safe. Just as he had after seeing Dinah's memories, Tad felt there must have been another route she could have taken. Of course, it was easy to say when he was looking at her situation from the outside.

"You don't know King. He's an absolute. There's either his way or oblivion for you and your family. Trust me, you don't get to walk away from him."

Tony didn't look convinced and seemed like he was about to say as much. Tad recognised this could get out of hand and there was still a lot he needed to know, so he spoke first.

"This mission he set for himself, to open a gateway to death, is it working?"

Like the woman in Emily's story, Tad knew what she said was the truth. As soon as she said he got his powers from that far off place, he knew it was right. He was born of both worlds and the knowledge of that second world was instinctual.

"What do you think? Surely your power has grown over the last few years. All of you." She looked at each of the ghosts so that only Stella felt left out. A lot of this conversation had probably gone over her head. Tad was impressed she hadn't interrupted to ask questions.

"We have been getting stronger," Tad admitted.

"And you've been saying for ages that you thought it was a sign that something is wrong with the world," Tony noted.

"Is it wrong though?" Miriam's question took him by surprise and he didn't know how to answer. "What I mean is, what's so bad about getting stronger? If we keep getting stronger, just think of where that could leave us. We might not need a Proxy to stay sane. We might be able to let normal people see us... touch us—"

"Are you willing to sacrifice the lives of other people just so you can be with Kate again?" Tad asked. He tried to keep the accusation from his voice but she flinched anyway. There was moisture in her eyes and his heart broke yet again for her. It would have been kinder had she and Kate never seen each other after her death.

"No. I suppose not. It's just… never mind." She turned to Emily and asked, "How many more Proxies does he need?"

"Not many. Each death doubles the size of the gateway. If he's close enough to send his hunter after my grandson, then I guess he thinks it will only take one more life."

Tad shuddered. If he was that close to the end then he would be desperate to finish. He had been working on that barrier for over ten years. He wouldn't let a little thing like Dinah being arrested stand between himself and victory.

Tad was suddenly eager to get home. He had been gone too long already.

"How do I stop him?" Tad asked, and the question drew the attention of everyone at the table.

"Tad. You aren't doing anything," Stella insisted. "This is a police matter. He's been killing people. If anyone is going to stop him, it will be us."

Emily was shaking her head yet again. "It's not that simple. He's beyond either of you. You go against him and he'll destroy you. If you bring this to your bosses, Stella, then you'll see just how far his reach goes."

"I know people who can be trusted," she insisted.

"Even then, how do you expect to get him? He is a single death away from having the kind of power you can't comprehend. If you somehow make it past that bunker he calls a tower—"

"King Tower?" Tad asked. "I always knew I hated that place. I always got a weird feeling when I passed it."

"You were right to. That place is a house of death. It's heavily fortified and guarded on the outside. On the inside it's pretty much a gateway to death. What you need to do is run and take my grandson with you."

Tad shook his head. "I can't do that. If he's going to be as powerful as you say, then he'll find us anyway. We need to face this before he gets all his power."

Emily looked at him in disgust, then stood up. "Then this was pointless. I came to you looking for help for my grandson. Instead you'll get yourself and your daughter killed. What part of him being beyond you don't you understand?"

"I understand it," Tad said. "But it doesn't matter. He's going to come after us anyway and I don't know enough about running to manage it. All he'd have to do is find someone like Dinah again and they'd find me for him. No, I need to end this before it's too late."

"We need to end it," Stella insisted. "This man has killed hundreds of people. With Emily's testimony and maybe some proof we'll be able to—"

"I want nothing to do with this," Emily said, making a gesture to show she was wiping her hands of them. "It was stupid to come here. I need to—"

"What other choice do you have?" Tony snapped. "Go back to him, watch him kill another hundred people. At what point is enough, enough?" He pointed to Tad. "We have a proxy. You can join with him, share your knowledge with him, and we can try to stop this before it's too late."

Emily was not the only one at the table surprised by his words. This was a much more focused and grown up Tony than Tad had seen before.

"Whatever happens, you can't let him get away with this anymore. He needs to be stopped. The real question is, are you willing to do the right thing for a change?"

Emily still wasn't convinced.

"Maybe you need to look at it this way," Stella tried. "You know that no matter what happens, King will come after your grandson. Would you rather him run and be caught later anyway, or would you rather we stop this now before it's too late?"

Emily sank back into her chair but she looked no less desperate.

"He's too much for you."

Tad was about to tell her she shouldn't be so sure when he was interrupted by his phone ringing. He apologised and pulled it out of his pocket. It was Kate.

"Hey Kate. Look, can I call—"

"Tad. Listen to me. This is important." She instantly had his attention. He'd heard that tone in Kate's voice only rarely and it was never followed by anything good.

"What is it?"

"There's been a major fuck up. We've had to turn Mark's friends loose, there wasn't enough to hold them. The trouble is, there's been a proper balls up with the paperwork and they weren't the only ones released." Ted felt as though his heart stopped beating as he waited the rest. "Tad, they've also released Mark and the woman you brought in yesterday."

"What? That's ridiculous. The cases aren't even related. Mark is one thing—"

"Tad, aren't you listening? When I say fuck up, I mean it with capital letters and exclamation marks. I'm not talking about a mistake, this was done on purpose."

Tad stood up so fast his chair went skidding backwards and toppled over.

"Shit. Jen. She's on her own with Charles. That won't be enough. You need to get over there, Kate."

"What? The munchkin. You think she's going after her again?"

"I know it. I don't have time to explain, but the man behind your case and Stella's case is the same guy, and he's desperate to get his hands on Jen. If they've been released, then he's pulled strings to send them after her. I'm leaving now, but even if I do eighty miles per hour the entire way and there's no traffic, I won't be there for at least an hour and a bit. Can you get to her—"

"Of course. I'm going now. I'll bring some people with me. Does Stella still have people on Jen? If not, she should do something her end to get that sorted as well."

"I'll talk to her. I'm hanging up now Kate. I'll be back as soon as I can."

He didn't wait for her response before he hung up. Everyone was staring at him, but his attention was focused solely on Emily.

"Time's up. You're either coming or you're not, but either way I'm leaving. It's not just your family in danger here and he's coming after mine first."

"What's going on Tad?" Stella asked. He shook his head and kept his attention on Emily.

"Decide. Keep burying your head in the sand or come help us stop him."

He didn't wait for her decision or let the others get the chance to ask questions. He pushed his way out of the pub, upsetting a few people as he went. Their irritation only lasted as long as it took for Miriam and Tony to catch up. All it took was Tony to put his hand through one guy's arm before there was a very wide path for all of them.

Tad was already out of the pub by this point and he had picked up his pace. Walking wasn't fast enough. He was sure that Jen was in trouble and no matter how he did the math in his head, he couldn't imagine getting home in time to help her.

Suddenly he was sprinting and still he wasn't going fast enough.

30

Saturday, 29th November 2015
21:14

Tad had been right.

She hadn't wanted to admit she wasn't ready for a ghost, but now Jen had no choice. In the wake of Kate's arrival and the news she brought, Jen was more frightened of Maggie than the woman coming to get her.

Since Mark was arrested, she had been almost easy to live with. She was still more inquisitive than Jen's parents, and constantly searched through memories she had no right to, but other than that she was okay. Now she was as close to a mad ghost as Jen had ever seen her.

"I can't believe you fucked up this bad," Maggie said on her way through the kitchen to the back door. She didn't need to look outside, Charles was watching for trouble. He would raise a warning if necessary.

"Any chance you can make her real so I can punch her?" Kate asked. Other than Tony, it was rare that anything got under Kate's skin. She'd only been there half an hour.

Jen didn't answer, didn't want to enrage Maggie any further. She had seen that look in Maggie's eye the night they went to Mark's house.

"What's going to happen, Kate?" Jen asked. "Are we sure they're coming here?"

Kate hesitated before lying. "No."

It was the first time Jen caught Kate lying to her and it hurt. Kate had always been on her side. Whenever Tad got on her nerves, Kate was there. Whenever she wanted to know the truth about something, she could rely on Kate.

Her lying only proved how bad things were.

"Are they coming here or not?" Maggie pressed. "If they are, then we need to be ready."

"We are ready. There are police outside, I'm here and Tad is on his way back. We're as ready as we can be."

Maggie didn't agree. "We can do more. We need a plan for when they get here."

"When they get here, let the police handle it. That's what they're here for."

"She's right—" Jen tried to say, recognising where this was heading.

"No. She's not. We both know there's more we can do. You can let me merge with you—"

"Out of the question," Kate interrupted. "If it comes to the point where Jen is in danger, we run, we don't make her fight."

"Why not? We know what Tad can do when merged with his ghosts. It makes sense for us to merge and fight them off. Think of what we could do, Jen. We could—"

"What was that?" Jen looked toward a sound she heard beyond the living room.

"What was what?" Maggie asked.

"A noise, like a crunch. It came from that way."

"I'll check it out," Maggie blurted. Before any of them to could stop her, she rushed toward the front of the house.

"Listen Jen." Kate's voice was insistent and Jen turned from the wall where Maggie disappeared. The large woman was grim, and it only added to the fear creeping through Jen's system.

"No matter what happens, don't let that woman merge with you. Tad told me enough to know it would be a bad idea."

"I won't." Jen's answer was sharp, she had no intention of ever letting Maggie in her head in her current state. She was still getting over the last time Maggie had came to her like this. She couldn't go through that nightmare again.

"Good—" Kate began, but was cut off when Maggie returned.

The ghost jumped through the wall with more excitement than when she left. There was a humourless grin on her face.

"They're here," she proclaimed. "The crunch you heard was them dealing with the police out front."

Kate jumped to her feet. "Are they okay?"

Maggie shook her head, but didn't look unhappy. "They're all dead. There are men surrounding the house." She turned to Jen. "We have no choice but to fight. There's no way out of this. You had better let me in."

"No," Kate answered for Jen. "How many of them are there?"

"Six, including Mark and someone else waiting in the van. I think it was that Dinah woman."

"Did you get the van's plates?"

Maggie looked disgusted. "Of course not. I'm more interested in the men who—"

"Go back and get them. I'm going to radio for help and pass along those details. If anything happens, then at least they have a way of finding us."

Maggie looked like she might argue, but finally did as asked. Jen felt a chill as she went, suddenly feeling alone and trapped. Kate was with her but she could use supernatural help right then. If those men were coming, what could Kate do?

Also, Dinah was there.

That woman scared her more than all the men combined. She had somehow taken hundreds of Proxies even with their ghosts watching out for them.

Jen's vision blurred. She didn't know what it was at first and turned to look at Kate. That movement caused the moisture in her eyes to spill and she realised she was crying.

Where had it all gone so wrong for her?

Over the past few weeks she got herself in danger three times. With the mad ghost, at Mark's house, and now here. Was this her fault? If she had just done as Tad asked and not taken a ghost of her own, could she have remained unnoticed?

Kate wasn't looking, instead staring out the window. Jen wiped away her tears. Kate had enough to worry about, she didn't need to see Jen acting like a baby. She wasn't quick enough to stop Charles seeing her though. He slid through the kitchen door making both Kate and Jen jump.

"Charles, where have you been?"

Jen had never felt such relief to see anyone. Charles had been her friend for years. He was an old fusspot, but he was kind, funny, and familiar. She felt a wave of relief to see him again, especially when he grinned at her. Who knew how much that grin cost him? He was a worrier, but was being strong for her sake. If he could do that, so could she.

"Sorry. I was going to come as soon as I saw them, but I thought I'd see what they're up to first. No point in not getting all the information, I say." Turning to Kate he said. "They've come in two vans. The first is parked out front with that awful woman in it and there's a second out back. The men out front have taken out the police and the three at the back are preparing to move in.

"They're dressed like those police on TV. You know, all in black with bullet proof vests and all the trimmings. God only knows what they think they'll find in here. They have battering rams, so we might want to think about moving."

Kate nodded. "You get the plates for the vans?"

Charles said he did and recited them to her. She was repeating them into the radio when Maggie returned. She was not impressed to see Charles.

"Great, you've finally turned up. Nice early warning."

"He brought us more useful information than you did," Jen snapped. She hated how Maggie treated her friend. Her resulting anger was a much hotter emotion than the cold fear. It actually felt good. "All you're doing is trying to get us to panic. At least Charles is helping."

Maggie scoffed. "Helping? This guy? He's too afraid of anything to help. Look at him, he—"

"That's enough," Kate snapped. "We don't have time for this. I've just called for backup and we have people on the way. But they won't be here for at least five minutes, so we need to hold them off."

"Then Jen needs to let me in. It's the only way." Maggie jumped on the opportunity.

"No. We need to fortify the house. Let's barricade the doors, then go upstairs, lock ourselves in a room and do the same thing there. It won't buy us long, but it might be enough."

"Oh, this is ridiculous." Maggie turned on Jen and took a step closer. "We can end this. You know you want it. Isn't this what it's all been about? To prove to Tad you're worth something."

Jen cringed and looked to Kate for support. The detective looked furious.

"This will not happen—"

Kate's words cut off when Maggie lunged for Jen. It was too quick for any of them to stop. Maggie dematerialised and though Jen flinched, she felt her ghost battering at her senses.

Jen didn't know what to do. No ghost had ever tried to invade her before, it should have been useless to try on a Proxy. However, she previously let Maggie in. Once accepted, it was harder to stop it happening again. She had to pit her will against Maggie, and as she knew from the countless times she had done it before, she was no match for the woman.

"Let me in," she heard in her mind. It was loud and Jen flinched. It was all the opportunity Maggie needed. Jen felt another shove against her senses and suddenly she wasn't in control anymore.

She could still see through her eyes, but they were no longer looking where she wanted. She was locked out and unable to control a single muscle. Her eyes were the worst. She didn't realise how often she moved her eyes. To have them not look where she wanted was making her feel sick.

Maggie waved Jen's hand in front of her face, twisting and turning it before curling it into a fist. Jen was helpless as she watched her own eyes turn to the breakfast bar. Maggie lifted Jen's fist and brought it down hard upon the counter top.

It was terrifying to realise that even locked out of control, she could still feel pain. The healing properties of merging with a ghost countered that pain, but Jen felt it as an ache in her hand. She hoped nothing was broken.

But something was broken. Maybe not bone, but there was a crack running through the granite worktop where Jen's fist impacted.

That sight was enough to forget her pain. Maybe Maggie was right. Maybe they could do this.

"Maggie. It's not too late—" Charles said. He was ignored.

Maggie turned Jen's head away from the portly ghost and looked toward the door.

Finally!

The word was clear in Jen's mind and it spoke with Maggie's voice. It thrummed with a tone of triumph and Jen was privy to the thought process that accompanied it. Maggie remembered the night of her death, how powerless she was, how her huge, ex-rugby player husband so easily overcame her defences.

The memory triggered a score more just like it and it fuelled her rage. Now he would see what it felt like to be powerless. Through Jen, she had the power to enact that revenge.

For the first time, Jen thought she might understand why they were called Proxies. She was not in charge, she was simply a conduit for Maggie's will. She was a bystander and had never been more afraid.

Please don't do this, she begged. It was no use. Maggie ignored her just as she ignored the others in the room. It was already too late. There was a shadow growing against the kitchen door. There was a bang, and finally Maggie got her chance for revenge.

The door didn't survive a single blow from the ram. The lock shot out like a rabbit leaping for safety, and the PVC and metal doorframe split.

Maggie wasted no time rushing forward.

It was like watching a video game. Jen had no control of her character, but she saw through its eyes. The world rushed by as they moved with boosted speed. The men grew bigger as they advanced and again Jen felt that icy touch of fear.

Maggie felt no such thing. She was consumed by fury. Maggie pounced on the first man, curling Jen's fingers into talons and striking with Jen's nails. The man had no time to react other than to raise an arm in defence. It wasn't enough.

With the added strength of Maggie's ghost, her nails sank into the arm, biting into the muscle and pulling it from his face. He wore a balaclava so Jen had only his eyes to gauge his reaction. Shock. Pain. Surprise. It was hard to tell, and she didn't have long to work with.

With her free arm, Maggie grabbed his forehead, throwing him back hard. He was wearing a tactical helmet, but the force of his collision with the wall guaranteed a concussion.

He dropped hard and didn't get up.

Jen felt sick. Maggie roared with primal satisfaction.

Maggie turned Jen toward the second presence and was just in time to see him recovering from the shock of their attack. She caught his hand, which held a baton, and squeezed it hard enough to make him yelp.

Even though she was not in control, Jen felt how little effort it was to overcome his strength. For the first time she felt excited.

Maggie was not in her right mind and didn't care about defending the body she was using. She focused only on hurting the man and paid no attention to the third shape that stepped through the doorway.

Jen felt her body moved aside, and it was neither Jen nor Maggie who had done it. Maggie snarled as she lost her grip on the man she was so intent on hurting and turned on Charles. Jen could see he helped her and wanted to thank him. Maggie saw only that he was in her way.

His back was too them as he sought where the next attack might come from, so he was unprepared for Maggie's response.

No!

Jen's cry was not enough to stop her. Maggie swiped at the side of Charles' head with contempt. Her strength against humans was incredible, but a Proxy always had the upper hand with ghosts and this was something else. It looked as though Charles' head had been struck by a train. It flew across the room, dragging a startled Charles behind it. He vanished through the wall and Jen lost sight of him.

She had no idea what would happen if you struck a ghost like that. She realised just how little she knew about being a Proxy. She should never have pushed Tad as hard as she did.

It's too late now, a cold voice whispered in her mind.

Maggie tried to surge forward yet again, to rain devastation on the men who were regaining momentum. This time it was Kate who stopped her by grabbing Jen around the waist from behind and lifting her from her feet. Maggie may be strong, but she had the body of a twelve-year-old girl, so she didn't weight much.

"Enough of this," Kate snarled in Jen's ear. "We need to—"

Her words cut off as Maggie grabbed Kate's hand and squeezed. Kate grunted and the grip around Jen's waist vanished. Maggie turned and pushed Kate hard, her hand striking between her breasts and knocking the wind from the large woman. Kate staggered back and tripped over a stool, landing on the floor.

Jen wanted to make sure she was alright. She was too late. While they had been struggling, more men had entered through the front door and even though their identities were hidden by their clothing, Maggie had no problem spotting Mark.

Again Maggie's memories flashed through Jen's mind. A blur of images that told the tale of Maggie's failed marriage and the events that led to her death. They added fuel to Maggie's rage.

She focused on Mark and with a scream so loud it made the men approaching pause, Maggie hurled Jen at her husband.

That was when she heard it. There was a sickening crack that sounded internal. Jen felt a flash of pain, but it didn't seem real.

The main thing she felt was confusion.

She couldn't understand why one moment she had been rushing at Mark, and the next the world blurred and the floor was coming up fast. She hit hard and felt that pain with more clarity than the first.

Maggie snarled, thinking she had tripped, and tried to push herself to her feet. Something was wrong. She was pushing up with her hands, but her legs weren't moving.

Now isn't the time to fight, Jen, she shouted internally. Jen didn't respond. She didn't need to. Maggie was a part of her mind and knew her thoughts.

Jen wasn't fighting for control. Her legs wouldn't respond.

A hand grab her arm. Maggie thrashed against the grip, her strength still enough to break the hold. But the hands returned. Their fingers were tight about Jen's flesh and it hurt.

Maggie was stronger than any man there, but she was not as strong as three without proper leverage or momentum. She struggled against them, but without her legs the strength had no grounding.

Jen was dragged from the spot where she landed and as Maggie thrashed to escape, Jen realised what happened.

Kate was down with one man standing over her while he secured her arms behind her back. Maggie had done that, made Kate vulnerable. Jen would never forgive her.

Maggie moved Jen's eyes from Kate to the men pinning Jen down. Mark wasn't one of them. They were the men who had come through the back door. The men Maggie ignored once she had seen her husband.

In confusion she looked from them to Jen's legs that were splayed out and unmoving. Jen knew what it meant. She would never see those legs move again.

The internal crack was the sound of a baton breaking her spine. Maggie's recklessness had broken her back.

The tears that filled her eyes should have been Jen's. Should have meant fear, pain and loss. Instead they were Maggie's, and they were from frustration. She cared only that she was losing her opportunity for revenge. Once again, Mark would get away with it.

Then suddenly there was another shape in the doorway.

He was tall, thin and familiar. Neither Maggie nor Jen recognised the look on his face. It made them cringe.

Everyone stilled in response to his presence. It was only a momentary stillness, but it was long enough for Tad to work out what was going on. His rage was terrifying.

Jen was staggered by what she felt from him. Considering how everyone in the room shrank back, she was not the only one to feel it. Something had changed in Tad. He was radiating a cold like a mad ghost, only this cold felt more focused, controlled.

It was terrifying.

Tad looked at Jen but something about his gaze told her he was staring at Maggie. There was hatred in his eyes.

"You were warned." His words were quiet and cold, and Jen's body shivered. The fear she felt wasn't hers, it was Maggie's.

Maggie opened her mouth to answer, but it was too late. Tad lifted his arm toward her and suddenly the only sound coming from Jen's mouth was an agonised scream.

It was not Jen's pain, but she felt it like it was. A white hot fire spread through her as Tad's power enveloped Maggie. It was cold as ice and hot at the same time, and it burned.

It consumed Maggie, and once in his power, Tad's hand clenched into a fist. Jen screamed again, and this time it was her screaming. Maggie was gone, ripped from her in a way Maggie was powerless to stop.

Suddenly Jen was in control again and she fully felt the pain of the men holding her arms, the numbness below her waist and the ache in her back.

Jen looked up in time to see Maggie hanging over her, surrounded by a nimbus of white light and eyes wide in shock. She looked from

Tad to Mark and then to Jen. There were tears in her eyes as she realised what she had done.

"I'm sorry," she whispered.

Tad shook his head. There was no forgiveness to be found there. "You were warned."

Suddenly Jen saw it, a surge of light along what looked like a spiderweb connecting Maggie to something a long way off. It was the connection to the next life, the call of death. The surge of light Jen saw in it was Tad increasing the strength of that call with his own power.

There was nothing Maggie could do.

The tears were still in her eyes, and she had a moment to look resolute and even nod in acceptance before she broke apart. Her edges blurred and features faded. She collapsed in on herself, condensing into a ball of white, spectral energy that hovered for a second before speeding along that spiderweb like a shooting star.

There was a sudden presence that everyone in the room felt. It was warmth, a gentle welcoming that Jen recognised. It had been stronger when her parents left, the warmth more profound and comforting. For whatever reason Maggie had not been welcomed as strongly, but the important thing was that she had been welcomed.

She was gone for good.

In spite of everything Jen let out a sigh of relief.

That sound broke the spell of stillness and the room exploded into action. Jen could do nothing but watch.

31

Saturday, 29th November 2015
21:28

Stella insisted on driving after seeing the state Tad was in. As soon as she made clear the trouble she could cause if he didn't do as asked, he relented. He needed to get home to Jen and didn't fancy doing that with police trying to pull him over every five miles.

She drove too slowly to suit him, though she was pushing eighty most of the way. It was constant effort from Stella and his ghosts to calm him down. All he could think of was Jen being in harms way and him not there to help. Even speaking to her on the phone and getting updates from Kate did little to calm him.

Stella was a bigger help than she knew. When she wasn't changing gear, she rested a hand on his leg, reminding him she was there for him. It was a different Stella than the day before and it was easy to forget his issues with her. Her touch was purely comfort, something he could draw strength from, and it was keeping him sane.

There was only so much sanity he could draw from a touch though. The minute he saw the empty police cars outside his house he knew something was wrong.

He climbed out of the car before Stella brought it to a stop. Any thoughts beyond his anger that anyone could think of hurting his daughter had no place in his mind. He only grew more worried when a shape flew through the wall of the house.

Charles' face was twisted in a grimace of agony, and his head was mangled as though he had been struck with a bat. Tad had no idea what could do that to a ghost, but he wasn't about to stop and ask. Charles needed healing, Tad needed information and the strength of a ghost. The solution to both problems was for Tad to merge with Charles.

He didn't even wait for Charles to land and neither did he slow his step as he rushed around the rear of the house. Using just his will, he pulled Charles into himself.

Charles was too stunned to resist, not that he would have, and he broke apart into mist that rushed towards Tad.

Tad breathed him in and slowed his step as he absorbed the knowledge Charles had for him. It took a fraction of a second to catch up, but the emotions that those events triggered in him were overwhelming. The primary one was anger.

How could Maggie do this? He had made the ramifications of hurting Jen all too clear.

Suddenly he'd had all he could take of his old friend. She had outstayed her welcome and violated every shred of trust he ever had in her.

He was about to continue on when a hand caught him and he was forced to turn.

"Tad. You can't just rush in there."

Stella held her phone in her other hand and Tad could see by the display that she had called for backup.

"Jen's in there. I need to go."

"There are too many. Think about—"

She was only thinking of him so he didn't get angry at her, but he wouldn't let her finish.

"I've got to save her," he said, then turned and ran around the side of the house toward his daughter.

Stella called something after him, but he ignored her. He could hear the sound of commotion inside and he wondered just how long Jen had left. Maggie thought she was invincible now she had control of Jen. She would soon learn how limited she was.

He got around the back of the house to find no one outside and the door open. He hadn't seen anyone around the front of the house which meant that Mark and his friends, along with whoever else King sent with them, were inside his house with his daughter.

That knowledge added fuel to the fire of his rage and the last few steps to the door were a blur.

Kate was struggling on the floor, held face down by the man straddling her as he tied cable ties around her wrists. Kate was strong, but the man had the weight advantage and the upper hand.

Jen was also down, held in place by two men who were gripping her so tightly her arms were immobile. Tad saw two distinct auras around her. One was the pale white of fear. The second, Maggie's, was the fiery red of anger. Tad knew his aura must be the same colour.

It didn't take him long to see that Jen was injured. Even though Maggie was thrashing, Jen's legs were motionless.

Three more men were also in the kitchen. One was unconscious by the door and two others were standing warily over Jen as though she were about to break free. Tad didn't pay them any attention. He was only looking at Maggie.

"You were warned."

The voice didn't sound like his. Other than his rage he was detached of emotion.

He raised his right hand, extending his Proxy senses toward Maggie until he could feel her. Then he tightened his grip. Once wrapped in his power, he made a fist and pulled harshly. Jen screamed in agony but Tad ignored it, his focus consumed by the woman he once loved.

Maggie burst free of Jen, a white light that coalesced into the shape of the dead woman. The men in the room jumped back in fright.

Maggie stared at him with hatred and fury. She had no idea what she had done wrong. That wasn't good enough. She needed to under-stand why he was about to end her time amongst the living.

As he did with mad ghosts, he forced her to see reality as it truly was, to recognise the extent of her actions and the ramifications of her decisions.

Her anger and hatred faded, and Maggie's eyes widened in horror. She looked from Tad, to Mark and then to Jen, her aura flickering through several colours before settling on the sickly, greenish brown of shame.

"I'm sorry," she said, and he knew she meant it. He could see by the look on her face that this was the Maggie he had once known and loved, a woman horrified by her actions.

"You were warned," he said again. No mercy, no remorse. He would do what he promised and would not look back.

There were tears in Maggie's eyes as she met his gaze. She smiled, showing him her dimples one last time as she accepted her fate. She nodded once to say she was ready and then Tad extended his will.

He reached for the thread that connected her to the next world, fed a trickle of power into that thread and let nature do the rest.

The call of the next life became too strong for Maggie even if she fought it. She didn't. Tad watched his friend move on and in the end he was himself enough to be gratified that he felt warmth as she slipped into the next life.

That touch of the next life had the same effect on him as it always did. He calmed. It was clear from the lack of movement within the kitchen that he was not the only one to feel that way.

Sadly, it was a peace that was not to last.

Jen let out a sigh, and that sound reminded everyone that their night was not over yet.

The two men holding Jen let her go and turned to face the new threat standing in the doorway. Kate was secured so her captor was happy to stand and face Tad. By the time Stella caught up there were five men ready and waiting for Tad to come to them.

He did not disappoint.

With just a thought he drew both Miriam and Tony into him, not bothering to leave anyone to guide his movements. He stepped into the kitchen.

The man who had secured Kate was closest. He swung his baton. Powered by three ghosts, to Tad it looked like he was moving through syrup. He had plenty of time to dodge or block the blow.

He did neither.

He dematerialised, letting the baton pass harmlessly through him. He materialised again a moment later, now standing behind the over-balanced man. It took little effort to help him to the floor and kick him brutally in the head once he landed. He heard a crack that very well may have killed him.

The next two men came at once, attacking from different directions simultaneously but with no more luck.

Tad vanished again, staying invisible this time as he moved a few paces forward. By the time he came back to the living the two men had staggered towards each other. A hand behind each of their heads drove them into each other with enough force to daze one and knock the other out.

Both landed in a heap.

Tad had already turned from the downed men as he readied himself for the next attack, but had to stop.

Recognising they could not stand against this supernatural foe, the two remaining men had returned to Jen. They stood behind her, one with their baton pressed against her throat and the other a few steps closer to the exit.

"Stay right there," the man with the baton said, his voice raised in panic. "Stay there or I'll break her neck."

Tad was about to answer when he heard a commotion at his back. He turned, afraid of someone coming up behind him. He was not in danger though, Stella was.

Dinah had appeared from somewhere, slipping into the room unnoticed and taking Stella from behind. She had Stella around the throat which forced the taller woman to bend her knees and lean back into her. It was a vulnerable position that she couldn't free herself from. There was a wicked blade pressed against Stella's flawless skin.

"No heroics Thaddeus, even you aren't that fast."

Dinah's voice was steady and calm. If she was affected by the action in the room and her own danger, she didn't show it. Tad was not surprised. He knew it took a lot to shake her.

"Let her go," Tad said. Then turning back to the men holding Jen he said, "You too. If any of you harm either of them, then there'll be nothing in the world that will protect you from me."

"Think about this, Tad. You can't act without at least one of these girls getting hurt. It's you who needs to see sense. You have lost. There's nothing left to do."

Tad wanted to tell her she was wrong, to act and prove he could save both of them. However, she was right. There was no way out of this. He thought he might be able to save one of them, but not both.

That left him with two options. He could either try to save one and risk sacrificing the other, or he could surrender and trust Dinah to let Stella and Jen go.

The trouble was, he knew who Dinah worked for. Joshua King could not be trusted. He would come after Jen and kill Stella just for being a witness.

There was no upside to him surrendering, which left only one choice; who should he save?

On the one hand Jen was the obvious choice, but she was in less danger. The man holding her was in shock and on the back foot. He was afraid. But Dinah was a trained killer and wouldn't hesitate to kill Stella.

However, he couldn't trust that logic. The man holding Jen was an unknown and he couldn't take the risk.

His eyes met Stella's. Those glistening blue eyes were wide and staring, and there were tears there. He could see she had come to the same conclusion.

He shouldn't speak lest he give the game away, but it was a compulsion he couldn't resist.

"I'm sorry."

The words had the result he expected. Dinah tensed her arm against Stella's neck and Stella flinched in terror. Tad forced himself to look away before it was too late. He turned his attention to Jen and the man holding her and he drew once more on his Proxy abilities and the power of his ghosts.

Ghosts were limited only by their perception. He knew this on an instinctual level, but there was a big difference between knowing and believing.

In that moment, Tad believed with his very core that with his Proxy power and his ghosts within him, he had just as few limitations. He chose to change his reality so he was no longer standing in the middle of the room, but was instead at Jen's side.

He believed so strongly that suddenly that was where he was. There was no blur to show him crossing the distance, barely even a flicker. One moment he had been in the middle of the room and next he was close enough to act.

The man holding Jen flinched, but before the flinch had even finished Tad had one hand on the baton and the other on the thug's head. He kept the baton in place no matter how the man might fight and with his other hand he pushed hard, slamming the skull against the wall behind him with enough force to put a crack in the stone. It was more than a crack to the skull though, as the rear of his head caved in.

He was dead before he slumped to the floor.

It was too much for the final conscious man in the house. By the size and shape of him Tad guessed it was Mark. He turned and ran away. Tad let him go. He had other things fighting for his attention.

He scooped Jen into his arms to stop her falling, and with her secure he turned back toward the door expecting to find Stella laying in a pool of blood.

But she wasn't there.

Both she and Dinah were gone. In the seconds it took Tad to overcome Jen's captor, Dinah had got Stella out of the house and was making her escape.

"I'll be right back," he said to a sobbing Jen. It broke his heart, but he had to free himself from her death grip to go after Stella.

He wanted to will himself out onto the street in front of his house as he had done just a few seconds earlier to save Jen. But the rage and purpose that had driven his focus had dispersed as soon as Jen was safe. He couldn't find the right frame of mind to believe that strongly again.

He was left with no option but to sprint out the back door and around the side of the house. With his ghosts in him he was faster than normal. He was not fast enough.

He reached the front of the house just in time to see a black Mercedes Sprinter live up to its name. For such a large van it was amazing that there was a half second of wheel spin before the tires found purchase and the van sped away.

Tad had no illusions about catching it. He could run fast with the ghosts in him, but there were limits. He thought about going for his car and chasing the van down, but what would he do? He couldn't force a vehicle that big from the road, and even if he could, he'd be leaving Jen and Kate alone.

He couldn't do that. There were unconscious and dazed men in that room who could still be a danger.

There was nothing he could do.

He was left standing in the middle of the road, staring after the taillights of the van as it disappeared around the corner up ahead. Dinah had Stella, and he had no illusions as to who would soon get his hand on her.

The thought made him shudder. Stella didn't deserve that, no one did.

A wave of depression threatened to buckle his knees. He couldn't help but feel as though it was his fault. He should have done something more, made a different decision. He had saved Jen at the cost of Stella and that decision felt as though it might kill him.

There was nothing he could do to help Stella though. What he needed was to go back inside and help Jen.

He expelled his ghosts as he walked, making them real enough that Miriam could help Kate get free as Tad went to Jen and once more took her in his arms.

She clung to him like she never had and she sobbed. He wanted to tell her it would be okay, that she was safe and he would let nothing hurt her again. But it would be a lie. He had already failed to keep her safe and he would never forgive himself for it.

All he could do was hug her and try to keep her safe until someone who was better equipped to look after her could take her from him. That was exactly what he did.

He held her close until finally Kate's backup arrived. They had been less than five minutes responding to Kate's call. They had all been too late. Tad had been too late.

Now Jen and Stella had to pay the price for his failure.

32

Saturday, 29th November 2015
22:46

"It's not your fault, Thaddeus. You know that," Charles said.

All Tad knew was that since he had taken Jen in, her life had been nothing but frustration and pain. Whether it was him forcing her parents to leave, ignoring what she wanted, or exposing her to the events that would break her back, he had been nothing but bad news.

He decided it was best not to answer. He remained seated in the waiting room, anxiously staring at his feet while he waited for news about Jen. The doctors had taken her for tests and they had been gone for more than an hour. The wait was killing him.

"What could you have done different, Tad?" Kate asked.

She sat on the opposite chair and he could feel her eyes on him. They were all watching him. He knew they were trying to break him from his depression, but all he could feel from their stares was judgement.

Tad was a Proxy, stronger than ever. He should have prevented this. Now Jen was hurt and Stella was missing. It could all be blamed on him.

Again he didn't answer until a new voice spoke up.

"Mr Holcroft?"

Tad looked up sharply at the doctor who was waiting a few feet away. He was a thin, balding man of Indian descent. What little hair he had left was grey and his beard was more white with black flecks than the other way around.

Tad didn't need to hear his words to know it was bad news. Tad stood and took a few anxious steps closer. His ghosts and Kate did the same, though the doctor only saw Kate. He glanced at her before turning his attention back to Tad.

"I'm afraid it isn't good. The attack on your daughter has done serious damage to her spine. We'll need to operate, but it's to limit future complications rather than to return the use of her legs. To be frank, I don't see her ever walking again."

Tad groaned as his last vestiges of hope slipped away.

"Does she know?" he asked.

The doctor shook his head. "In situations like these we tell the parents first. If you wish I could tell your daughter, but—"

"No. That's okay. I'll speak with her. Can I see her?"

He nodded. "I want to get her into the operating room soon, so you won't have long. She's just through there."

Tad thanked him and walked to the door the doctor pointed to, but stopped when his ghosts and Kate fell in behind him.

"Could you give me a minute? You'll get a chance to speak to her before she goes down, but I want a few minutes alone."

Kate nodded and backed off, but the others were much slower. Surprisingly it was Tony who was the most reluctant. He looked ready to fight Tad for the right to go to Jen first, but he nodded and went to sit by Charles.

Tad thanked them all, ignored the questioning stare from the doctor, and walked through the door.

He entered a large room that was sparsely furnished. There was a door to the left as he walked in, behind which was a small bathroom. Opposite he found a TV on the wall with a stock floral print in a cheap frame mounted beside it. There were two chairs in the room, one in the corner under the TV and the second, a larger wing backed chair, beside the single bed.

In that bed, looking smaller than ever, a scared little girl was watching him apprehensively. Her hazel eyes were wide and moist. She was not crying, but she had been. Jen was nervously chewing her bottom lip. Tad had to fight back tears.

How could he tell this girl that because of him, she would never walk again?

He pulled the seat beside her bed closer and sat down. He thought about holding her hand, but decided against it. As soon as he told her the news she would want nothing more to do with him. His touch would probably feel like poison.

"Jen. It's not... uh... I've got bad news."

Jen said nothing, but she breathed quicker and new tears rolled down her cheeks.

"I've spoken with the doctor and... I'm so sorry, but he said he doesn't think you'll be able to walk again."

She still said nothing. Just stared at him, tears flowing faster and her breathing becoming more laboured. He looked to her aura to see how she was handling it, but got no better read than before. Like with Stella, Jen was doing her best to suppress her emotions.

A lump formed in his throat, but he struggled to push past it. He needed to say a few more things. Even if they were the last thing she ever heard from him, he had to get it out.

"I'm so sorry about this. I know sorry is not nearly enough..." His words trailed off as that lump threatened to choke him. He shook his head and wiped away his tears. "I should have known better than to think I could give you a good home, or keep you safe. This is all my fault."

Again he wiped his eyes. "I wanted you to know you don't have to worry about it anymore. As soon as I leave, I'm going to see about getting someone more appropriate to look after you. I'll have a word with Kate's boss about getting you somewhere safe, somewhere you can disappear, and then you'll never have to see me again."

His words were growing faster with every sentence. It was all he could do to get them out and he couldn't help but rush. As soon as he finished he stood.

"I'm so sorry to have failed you. I..." He couldn't think of anything else to say, anything that would make it better. All he could see was her tears, the anguish on her face and the way her shoulders shook. The only thing his presence was doing was upsetting her more.

"I love you, Jen. I never meant for this... I'm sorry." He intended for those to be his last words and he started to leave. He stopped when Jen grabbed his hand.

She had almost thrown herself out of bed to grab him. He caught her and helped her back to her original position.

"Easy Jen. You're really hurt. You shouldn't be—"

"Please don't leave me, daddy," she interrupted.

It was her word choice more than the sudden panic in her voice that shocked Tad.

"Please don't go. I'm so sorry. I didn't mean for this to happen. I wanted to protect you, wanted to prove I was strong. Please don't send me away."

"What?" Tad asked, slowly sitting again. He thought to let go of her hand but she was gripping his so tightly there was no chance of that. "I thought... Jen. You're not happy with me and I can't keep you safe—"

"I am happy with you. I love living with you. I always have."

"No you don't. You're just confused. We argue all the time. Life isn't supposed to be that hard. Trust me. You'd be happier—"

"No." She almost shouted and Tad worried someone would come in to see what all the fuss was about. "Please. Don't leave me. I don't want you to go. I love living with you. You, Miriam, Charles and Tony are my family. Please don't send me away."

"But we argue all the time. I thought—"

"No. I just wanted you to show me how to be a Proxy. I wanted to be useful." She sniffed and wiped her nose with her free hand. "I wanted to be strong so I could protect you."

"Protect me from what?"

She didn't answer. She couldn't find the words and she blushed. Her aura was blazing again, and it was much easier to read. There was panic, fear and embarrassment all mixed in a glowing jumble.

Finally she said, "I didn't want to lose you too."

One thing Tad learnt from his time looking through other people's memories was how perception changed them. Memories aren't like movies. There is no final edit or finished cut. They change with perception, and it was something Tad found fascinating when he saw his ghost's memories change as they applied new knowledge to them.

Even amongst the living, perception was everything.

Tad felt that same phenomena happing then. With this new information he analysed his arguments with Jen over the past few years. He remembered how she got over the pain of losing her parents and started acting out. He thought she was rebelling against the man who made them leave.

Now he saw a girl trying desperately to never feel that loss again. Every time she pushed for him to teach her, she had always argued it was so she could protect herself.

She was trying to get strong.

Trying to protect him.

He was an idiot.

Suddenly he was squeezing her hand harder and forcing her to look at him.

"Jen. It's not your job to protect me. It's my job to protect you. You never needed to be stronger, you're already strong enough."

She sniffed and wiped her nose again.

"I didn't want to lose you. You kept going into all these dangerous places and—"

He leaned in close. "I'm so sorry. I never even thought about it. But you didn't need to worry. I've been dealing with this stuff since I was younger than you. I was never in any real danger."

"What about Proxies disappearing? What about Cleopatra?"

He sighed and shook his head. "We could argue about this all day, but I don't want to argue with you. We've got more important things going on. I can't believe… Look. From now on, some things need to change. We need to be more honest with each other. I've spent the last year thinking you hated me. You've spent it thinking you're not strong enough. Neither is true. That's down to bad communication. So, let's get this out in the open. Do you still want to live with me when this is over?"

Again she bit her lip nervously and she nodded. "Please don't send me away."

He smiled and shook his head. "I won't. I only said that because I thought it was what you wanted, what was best for you. It still might be safer—"

"No. I want to stay with you, dad."

There was that word again. He definitely hadn't imagined it. By the look on her face, it was the first time she noticed that she said it.

"Sorry. I didn't mean to call—"

"It's okay to call me that, Jen. If you want to that is."

"It's not… weird?"

Tad grinned. "Hell yeah. It's weird. It'll take some getting used to, but I could grow to like it."

Jen giggled, which turned into a wince as she aggravated her injuries. The look on her face sobered them both up and reminded them where they were.

"Right. It's sorted. What I need now is for you to get yourself better. They're going to take you for an operation soon. I don't want you to worry about it, okay? Whatever happens, we'll deal with it together."

"What about you? You're going after Stella, aren't you?"

For the first time he heard that note of accusation in her voice for what it really was, the fear of a daughter who didn't want to lose her father.

He was about to lie and tell her he would be right by her side, but he had just got done telling her they needed to be more honest with each other.

"I am. I need to get this sorted. I'm going to get Stella back and we're going to stop this once and for all."

He could see the look of panic on her face and he spoke over her. "I told you, I don't want you worrying about me. You need to concentrate on you. I'll be fine. Stella is a kidnapped detective, so I'm not going in alone after her. We know where she'll be and the police are sending everything they have for her. I'm just going as supernatural support."

Luckily Jen didn't know much about Joshua King. She hadn't heard what they found out in Tenby, and Tad kept the worst of what he had learnt from Dinah to himself. His words were enough to comfort her, and she relaxed.

"I don't want you to go," she said, softer this time as though she were more resigned to her fate.

"I'm not going anywhere yet. I'll be with you until you go down for your operation, and this will all be over by the time you're awake. I promise."

"Then what?"

"Then we get you better. That's the important thing. We need to get you better so you can come home."

She nodded and pulled on his hand to bring him close. He recognised that she was about to try to hug him so he moved in closer before she couldn't put any more stress on her back. She'd moved too much already.

After he released her, he called in the others. Jen put on a brave face for each of them and they tried to do the same for her. There were a lot of tears shed over the next few minutes, and it was almost a relief when the doctor came in to shoe them all out.

Tad remained as the doctor and anaesthetist did their work. Just before Jen went under, she got Tad's attention and said, "I love you, dad."

That directness was the kind of thing he always thought was cheesy when he'd seen it in movies. Now, when his daughter was about to face something so terrifying, he realised there was nothing cheesy about it. It was a powerful phrase that everyone needed to hear in the important moments of their lives.

"I love you too," he whispered.

The anaesthetist did her thing and had Jen counting backwards from ten. She never made it to seven before she was out cold.

Tad stayed behind as they wheeled her out of the room. He was terrified for her and still felt responsible for what happened, but he no longer felt down. Their conversation had breathed fresh life into him and as soon as he couldn't see her anymore he was ready to get to work. There was a lot to do and not much time to do it in.

He promised Jen he'd have it wrapped up by the time she woke up and he was determined to keep that promise. That meant he had until then to find Stella and confront Joshua King.

With renewed purpose he strode from the room and went looking for Kate. He was suddenly eager to get started.

33

Sunday, 30th November 2015
00:41

Kate slammed her hand on the roof of the car to get Tad's attention. Her glare was pure, white hot anger. Kate was a big woman… a valley's woman. Tad needed to tread carefully.

Her mood was not improved by the rain. It fell as though it was angry, bouncing from anything it hit and quickly soaking them. Her hair, worn loose during the day, was slicked back, her heavy coat was glistening, and the only thing about her that seemed warm was her fiery gaze.

Tad raised his hands in surrender, acknowledging that she had his attention.

"You need to think about this. There's no way this works out well for anyone."

"I made a—"

"Promise. Right. You told me on the way here. I understand, you don't want to disappoint Jen and you said you'd get this mess wrapped up by the time she woke up—"

"Which could be any time now. Who knows how long she has left in surgery?"

"I said I understand. But the thing is, Jen will get over you breaking this promise. She won't get over you getting yourself killed."

"I have no intention of getting myself—" he began to say, but was interrupted again. This time it was Charles, siding with Kate. Traitor.

"She has a point, Thaddeus. We don't know enough to go in there. You said yourself that King is beyond you. We could be walking into a trap."

"We could," Tad agreed. "But how would waiting be any different? King's got us beat on all fronts. He's stronger, better connected, and he's sitting on some kind of Proxy holy place. But those facts will never change. The one thing we have on our side is surprise."

"Tad, we don't even have police backup."

It was Miriam's turn to side with Kate, and Tad felt his temper slip. He didn't need this. So many things let him down tonight. First Maggie, then the police when they went to them for help, and now his ghosts. Maybe he should do this on his own.

"You have a point." All three ghosts and Kate let out sighs and wore the expressions of people who had finally breached the madness of a friend. "This will be dangerous and it might be best if you all wait here."

"Hang on a second. Don't be like that. If you're going in, then so am I." Surprisingly it was Tony who showed support. All eyes turned to the angry teen who took a step closer to Tad. "What? I don't like this any more than you, but I won't let Tad go in alone, that would be suicide."

"Without police backup, it's suicide anyway," Kate protested.

"Well we're not getting that, are we?" It was one of the few times Tony summoned the nerve to meet Kate's anger with his own. "Even you've got to admit they've let us down. One of their own is kidnapped and they refuse to act until they have proof."

"They're ready to act," Kate replied. "But they're the police, they can't just go barging into a place like King tower based on Tad's suspicions."

"Well is that going to change anytime soon?" Tad asked.

Tad could see Kate knew where his question was leading, but there was no way out of it. She shook her head reluctantly.

"Then what difference does it make? Here's the facts. There's a bastard in there who won't stop at anything until either Jen or me falls under his knife. On top of this he has Stella who was kidnapped trying to help me. However you look at it, there's nothing to gain by waiting."

"You're overlooking so many things. You can't just walk into that place and hope for the best…" Kate's words trailed off when Tad raised his hand.

"I'm not arguing anymore. I don't expect you to follow me, in fact it would be for the best if you don't. But I'm going in there. End of discussion."

"Shit. Well I suppose that means I'm going too."

Once Tad got over his surprise at Charles swearing, he offered his friend a grateful smile.

"I hate to say it love, but he has a point." Kate turned on her last supporter and there was hurt on her face. Miriam flinched from the look, but didn't back down. "He's right. Things have gone too far and they're only going to get worse. What choice do we have?"

"Go back. Investigate. Break those three idiots we got back at the station."

"We didn't have much luck with that last time." Miriam's words were gentle, and she took a step closer to Kate. "I'm going with him. But he's right, you should stay here. This isn't your fight."

"The hell it's not. That man's come after Jen, she's like my little sister. And where you go, I go. You know that."

Miriam's smile widened, but she shook her head. "Not this time. We both know it. I've been selfish these last few years. I should never have hung around and tortured you the way I have. You need to move on, be with someone else. You're still alive, Kate. You're still young…" her smile turned a touch evil, and she added, "…ish."

Kate snorted a laugh and tried to answer, but Miriam wasn't done.

"You've still got a life ahead of you. I haven't, none of us do. We all know Tad's a lost cause. We've got nothing to lose. You do."

The torrential downpour couldn't hide Kate's tears. She was a hard woman, and it was easy to think she couldn't cry. Tad had to look away and caught Tony and Charles doing the same.

"I can't lose you again," Kate protested.

"I'm not really here now. You can't lose what you don't have. Besides, there's one other person you're not thinking of. Jen. If everything goes wrong here, then someone needs to save her. If Tad can't come back then—"

"Then Tad shouldn't be going. I'll go with you guys and he can go back for Jen."

"You know it won't work that way. Without Tad we're as good as useless. There's a Proxy in there and Tad's the only counter we have to him. I'm sorry love, but this is the way it has to be."

After a moment of silence, Tad glanced back to see the two women locked in an embrace. Kate was sobbing and squeezing Miriam hard enough that she would suffocate if she needed to breathe. Eventually they separated, but Kate didn't let go.

"I'm not going to accept this. I'll stay behind for Jen, but this isn't the end for you and me. You got that? No matter what, you find a way to come back to me."

Miriam looked like she would argue, but she just smiled instead.

"Okay, I will."

Kate kissed her hard, and then before she could have second thoughts she spun to Tad.

"You get one hour. If you're not out by then, I'm calling for backup and coming in. You hear me?"

Tad nodded. Whatever happened, it would be over in an hour.

"Fair enough." He reached into his pocket and tossed her his keys. "Take these. I'll grab them off you when I'm back."

Kate looked at the keys in her hand and then at the car. For the first time that evening, she grinned.

"If you die, can I keep the car?"

Tad laughed. "You think I'd let Jen drive it? Of course you can."

Kate grinned all the wider and ran around to the driver side. "I suddenly feel much better about all this. Now hurry up, go. I want to get used to my new car."

Tad laughed again and on impulse hugged the woman. He had met her through Miriam and stayed in touch because of Miriam and Jen, but over the years he had grown fond of Kate. She was every bit a part of his little family as any of his ghosts.

She hugged him back almost as hard as she hugged Miriam, and then pushed him away.

With one last smile she climbed into his car and he turned away, looking at the King building and joined by his ghosts.

"Let's do this," he said, and before he could think better of it he walked toward the shadowy, King tower.

Tad was ashamed for not recognising this place in Dinah's memories.

Cardiff's tallest building, one of the tallest in Britain, King tower was the epitome of modern architectural design. It was sharp lines and bold angles. The top of the tower was a four sided pyramid that had been split into quarters and turned so the peaks were at the corners.

Tinted glass and polished, black stone made it a solid silhouette at any time of day. At night it looked like it had been carved from shadow. It was fitting considering what Tad expected to find within.

A tall wall made from the same black stone ringed the building. They approached it from the rear.

"What's your plan?" Charles asked. "I understand you're thinking of phasing through, but we have no idea what's waiting on the other side."

"He's right," Tony agreed. "Normally we'd scout ahead, but today..." he let his words trail off and he completed his sentence with a shrug.

"You can still scout ahead," Tad answered. "There's no ghosts on the other side of that wall... at least not immediately.."

Charles looked nervous. "How can you be sure?"

"I can't sense any dead on the other side."

All three ghosts shared a look, then turned to Tad.

"You can't sense any dead?" Miriam asked. "Tad, you wouldn't normally be so sure. You've been doing things all night that would've been impossible any other day. Not just that, you're acting as though it's no big deal. What's going on?"

"I'm getting stronger. I... I don't know how to explain it. I see a problem and the knowledge of how to solve it appears in my head. The new abilities are coming fast and I don't have time to question them. What does it matter if they're useful?"

"It matters because whatever's happening to you is happening to King. I don't want to be caught short by some new Proxy power I've never heard of."

"I don't know any more than you, and we don't have time to experiment. Is this going to be a deal breaker?" Three heads shook as one. "For now let's forget it. Tony, would you do the honours?"

Tony hesitated before turning to the wall. He took a deep breath, then stepped through... or tried to. Tony bounced off the wall as if it was made of stone... which of course it was. But it was stone for him as well.

It surprised him enough that he fell over, rubbing his nose where it had collided with the wall.

"What gives?"

The minute he spoke Tad understood. The wall was solid because it was imbued with the power of death. He could feel it, the will of the man who lived within. The strength of a Proxy ran through the walls and Tad was awestruck at the immense power of Joshua King.

"Shit. He know's we're here."

"What do you mean?" Charles almost squeaked.

"The walls are reinforced with his will. He will have felt Tony try to get through."

"My God. That's not good. Maybe Kate was right and we should come back another day."

Tad didn't answer, instead concentrating on the wall. Now he encountered it, he knew instinctively how he could create a barrier no

334 · GARETH OTTON

ghost could cross. The trouble was, he knew how taxing it would be, both on his endurance and his concentration. The Proxy power needed might come from the sheer number of ghosts King had, but even he had limits to his concentration, surely.

The more he thought on it, the more Tad realised there might be another explanation.

"We might be okay," he said to himself, though the others were listening.

"What do you mean?" Miriam asked.

"I was wrong. It isn't a barrier."

Tony, who had climbed to his feet, shook his head. "I beg to differ."

"No, it's not a barrier. I'm sure now. Rather than pouring his will into a barrier which would take a lot of concentration, he's made it so any ghost who steps foot within the boundaries of this building is real. It's like what I do with you guys when we're around other people, just on a larger scale. I doubt he's aware of our presence after all."

Charles and Tony relaxed, or at least as much as Charles could relax, but Miriam was still frowning. "That's not much better. Doesn't that mean that from here on out we might as well be normal people? If he makes us real, we lose our advantage."

"No. We just lose your invisibility and you can't walk through walls. But you can now interact with the living world. He's done us a favour."

"I don't think being seen and touched by normal people is a favour, Thaddeus," Charles remarked.

"No? Think about it. You're ghosts. You can still do amazing things even if you can't walk through walls and become invisible. If we run into any trouble, you'll be able to help rather than me having to do everything on my own."

They weren't convinced, but the more Tad thought about it, the more he realised this could work.

"So the new question is, how are we supposed to get in? Surely the only way left is the front gate. That's bound to be guarded," Miriam noted.

"We go over the wall."

As one, all three ghosts looked up at the top of the wall which was over twenty feet above them.

"Oh, good idea," Tony said. He then made a show of patting his pockets before sighing theatrically. "Wait, I forgot to bring my grappling hooks and climbing gear."

"Ha, very funny. I'm serious. If I merge with you, I can jump it."

"I don't think—" Charles objected, but Tad interrupted him.

"Look. We don't have time to argue. It's nearly one o'clock, and that means Jen's been in surgery for two hours. We need to do this. Are you willing or not? This is your last chance to back out."

One by one they nodded with Charles holding out the longest. That was to be expected. Tad was surprised the big ghost was even there. He had spent his whole afterlife running from situations like this. Now they faced their most dangerous moment and the chances of a final death were higher than ever, Charles seemed to have found his backbone.

Again Tad felt the rush of increased strength as they merged. It was intoxicating with just three. He could only imagine what hundreds must feel like.

He pushed the thought away and concentrated on the top of the wall. It was tall, and he had doubts. He was stronger with three ghosts, even stronger again since his powers increased, but twenty or thirty feet? It seemed too high.

There was no point waiting. He took a few deep breaths, looked around one last time to make sure no one was watching, then jumped as high as he could.

"Whoa... Shit!"

The wall rushed by in a blur then disappeared as Tad continued to rise. He drastically underestimated his new strength. He passed the top of the wall and kept going.

It was strange being up so high. Not only did it feel odd as the world fell away, but it was empowering. He didn't realise how much he was at the mercy of gravity until he was so blatantly defying it.

He rose nearly double the height of the wall before gravity put him in his place again. Suddenly he had a new reason to worry. That world that had been falling away was coming back at him much faster than he had left it.

The rush of power left him as that sudden twisting sensation in his stomach that accompanies a fall overcame him. He had to fight the urge to scream as he plummeted. When the top of the wall came into view, he reached for it and only just grabbed it with the tips of his fingers... big mistake.

The sudden agony that accompanied all of his weight being caught by his finger tips was enough to make him shout.

Increased strength or not, there was no way he could catch himself. He stopped his descent enough to swing his body against the wall, slamming him face first against the stone. He heard a crunch, felt an incredible pain in his nose, and his eyes watered.

It was overwhelming.

The falling, the agony in his fingers, and what he was sure was a broken nose, was enough to make him release his grip and fall again. A second later he landed hard, his knees buckling under the strain before he crumpled in a heap.

The lack of air in his lungs helped as rather than scream in agony, he only managed a simple, "Ouch."

He decided it was best not to move. Already he could feel his ghosts getting to work. Like everything else, this process had been improved, and he was healing much quicker than ever before.

It was a unique experience that was almost pleasurable until he felt another crunch at the front of his face as his nose shifted back into place. He had to fight back another scream as tears streamed from his eyes. Slowly that pain subsided and within a minute of his disastrous landing, he felt well once more.

He sucked in a few more lungfuls of air as he caught his breath before turning over and pushing himself to his feet. He found himself eye to eye with a man dressed like a security guard.

He was middle aged, losing his hair, and judging by the way his uniform bulged around his gut, had gained a lot of weight. His eyes were every bit as round as his belly and Tad guessed he had witnessed Tad's spectacular, if disastrous, entrance.

"Uh... hi."

Sanity returned to the guard and the shocked look vanished. His hand went for the radio clipped to his belt, but Tad was quicker. Powered by his ghosts, it was no effort to catch the man's hand before he reached his radio and hold it back. With his other hand, Tad grabbed the radio and crushed it.

For the second time in as many minutes he was surprised by his own strength. He expected it to buckle, he hadn't expected the extreme pressure on the metal and plastic handset would make it explode.

Shards of metal and plastic flew out from his fist, some of them striking Tad and the guard, others bouncing off the wall and the floor. There was no recovering the thing from such destruction. The guard looked stunned again.

"Probably best if you don't cry out," Tad said. "It won't go well for you. You understand?"

He nodded eagerly and Tad let him go.

"Don't," Tad snapped before the guard could think of running off. "I'll just have to catch you and that will make me mad."

"Okay, sorry."

His voice was high pitched but quiet. The fear Tad heard was disturbing. He had never thought of himself as scary.

"What's your name?"

"R... Randy."

"Really? You don't look like a Randy."

"Oh. Sorry. What do I look like?"

"Maybe a Harry, maybe an—" Tad caught himself and shook his head. He didn't have time for this. "Never mind. Randy, we need to get inside without anyone knowing we're coming. What's the best way to do that?" The man was about to answer when Tad spoke again. "And remember what I just did. I'm in no mood for games. Be honest and you'll live. If you lie then…"

He left the threat hanging but Randy understood. He swallowed hard.

"Just go in through the car park. If you take my key card, you'll be able to get in through the door easy enough and no alarms will go off."

"That's it. Just take your key card and go in through the door. There's no other security between here and there?"

Randy shook his head. "Mr King doesn't let us in the building unless it's an emergency. We just man the gate and patrol the perimeter."

Tad wasn't sure whether to believe him and that indecision must have shown on his face.

"Trust me. None of us want to go in there. Mr King is scary."

The fear in his voice was every bit as real as it had been a moment before, and Tad believed him.

"Alright Randy, I trust you. Hand it over."

Randy pulled his key card from one of those extendable key rings that act like a retractable dog leash. The minute his hand touched it he hesitated. "Mr King will fire me if he finds out I gave you this."

Tad thought he'd be lucky to be fired and not killed, but didn't say that.

"That's why I have to do this. Sorry Randy. But trust me, this is for the best."

"What is?" Randy asked as he handed over his card. Tad answered by punching him.

This time he was careful with his new strength and held back. Even so, he thought he might have killed the guy after his fist struck Randy's jaw and Randy's head whipped around as though he'd been shot. He crumpled and in a sudden panic Tad followed him, landing on his knees with his fingers against Randy's neck as he sought a pulse.

He didn't need to worry. The pulse was strong, and he was breathing. With any luck he'd be okay.

"That was badass, Tad. I didn't know you had it in you," Tony said when Tad expelled his ghosts.

Tony was grinning from ear to ear while the other two looked at the poor guard with concern.

"He's not dead," Tad told them.

"There had to be less brutal ways, Thaddeus," Charles said.

"I didn't mean to hit him so hard."

"Nor jump so high," Miriam noted. There was a smile curling her lips, and she was trying not to laugh.

"Okay, it wasn't my most dignified moment. Can we move on?"

For the first time Tony and Miriam saw eye to eye, and they laughed.

"Okay. Very funny. That's enough, we're still trying to go under the radar. Let's not make too much noise."

The laughing stopped, and they sobered up.

"So what next?" Tony asked. "Do we trust the guy about the car park? It seems too easy."

"Don't mock easy," Miriam said. "We don't want hard. That'll come later."

"Tony's right. I think we should find another way." Charles said.

From Dinah's memories, Tad remembered an entrance at the front of the building and one in the car park. He couldn't remember seeing any others, not even a fire door. That alone should have been reason enough to know this place was not what it seemed.

"I don't think he was lying. Let's just go along with it."

"I don't like it," Charles protested, but he fell in line as they walked toward the car park.

The only thing between the wall and the building was a single lane road that circled the building. His ghosts followed him, growing quiet as they remembered where they were. It must have been an odd experience for them, being as visible as any other person.

They reached the car park without incident. Though built from the same black stone as the rest of the building, it looked like any other car park. There were less cars, and the floors were cleaner, but it was still a series of painted white boxes and concrete ramps.

"I don't see any cameras," Tony said, breaking the silence and causing Tad to jump. He hadn't realised he had stopped walking. Tony must have thought he was looking for cameras.

He wasn't.

He hesitated because of the impossible to ignore presence. It was only as he stepped past the threshold of the carpark that he noticed it. It was the feeling that had driven him away from the building before. The presence had grown so subtly that he missed it until he was standing right on top of it.

It was vast beyond imagining and impossible to get his head around. It was the same feeling he felt when he reached for his power, but magnified a thousand... a million times over. There were no words for what he felt waiting within the building.

For the first time he thought about calling an end to their adventure. He wanted to get Jen and run.

He couldn't do that. He had to get this over with. He was also curious about what waited within. He was both afraid and attracted to that strange presence. As he took his first step into the carpark, he knew he had to see what it was with his own eyes.

As Randy said, there was no one to stop them. All three levels of the car park were deserted, and there weren't any cameras. Tad wondered whether it was arrogance or some other reason Joshua King didn't want digital security. It wasn't important, he just needed to be thankful.

Tad remembered the double doors from Dinah's memories. There was a black box beside them for keycard access. If things would ever go wrong, it was right then.

Tad held his breath and swiped Randy's keycard in the slot provided. The half a second gap before the beep of success stretched on forever.

There was no alarm. Just a beep, a green light, and a second later the sound of a heavy click as the locks unbolted.

Tad looked to his ghosts and they at him. Nothing needed to be said. They lived in each other's heads and didn't always need words to communicate. Tad knew they were thinking the same thing.

This was the point of no return.

Tad was the first through the doors, Charles the last. The poor ghost hesitated for what seemed like minutes before he summoned the courage to cross the threshold. The click as the door shut behind him made him wince as did the surprise of feeling Tad's hand on his shoulder.

"You alright?" Tad whispered.

"I will be. Let's go find your girl."

Tad had to fight not to laugh. "She's not my girl."

"Whatever you say. Lead on you lunatic."

Tad turned from his friend and faced the strange corridor with no doors. It had creeped out Dinah, but Tad was just intrigued about what waited deeper in the building. The presence had grown unbearably strong, and it felt like it was calling to him. He was afraid of what it might be, but at the same time was desperate to find out.

All too soon they reached the end of the corridor and stepped into the reception. On their right were glass doors that lead outside. To the left were double doors and answers. There was no keycard entry, no lock at all. There was just a handle waiting to be turned.

Tad took a breath, reached for it and opened the door. He stepped into the darkness beyond.

The moment he crossed the threshold that darkness became absolute. He knew the door was still open and there should be light coming through, but there wasn't. He had somehow stepped into a world of complete shadow.

If it was the world of Death, then he found that fitting.

His friends were just as surprised as he was. They each gasped as they stepped through the door and were silent afterwards. Tad winced as the door clicked closed behind him. It seemed abnormally loud in the silence.

"What is this place?" Tony asked, his voice hushed with awe. "I've never seen anything like it."

"Nor I," Charles admitted. His voice was not filled with fear as Tad expected, but wonder. "I have never seen colours so vivid. It's beautiful."

"What? Colours?"

Tad couldn't see them look at him, but he felt it. He had a sinking feeling that his worst nightmare was coming true. He saw nothing but darkness, but they could see him.

"Please don't joke, that's not funny," Miriam said. Her words a reprimand, but the worry clear.

She had reason to be worried. They were already on a fool's mission, they needed Tad to stand a chance.

With a sinking feeling, the last of his hope faded.

"I can't see," he said and was appalled by the panic in his voice. "I'm blind."

34

Sunday, 30th November 2015
01:12

"What do you mean you're blind?" Charles asked.

"It usually means he can't see anything, you idiot," Tony snapped. "What makes you think now would be different?"

"Shut up you two," Miriam said. Tad felt a soft touch on his arm but didn't flinch. He knew it was coming. He spoke before Miriam could.

"I'm okay," he said. "Just panicked for a second. It's not as bad as I thought."

"You're not blind?"

"I'm blind, but it's like when I'm asleep. I can't see, but I know what's going on."

"You'll be okay to keep going?" Tony asked.

"I'll have to be. The door seems to have vanished."

The silence was accompanied by his ghosts looking back the way they came. Each wore a frown and Charles was close to panic. Tad laid a hand on his shoulder before he went too far off the deep end.

"What is this?" Charles asked. "Where'd that door go? Where are we?"

"I'm not sure about the door, but I'd guess Emily was right. King has brought down the barriers between life and death."

"You mean we're dead?"

"No… well yes, you lot are. But I think we've stepped into the world of Death."

Tony was looking around.

"It's not what I expected Death to look like. I mean, maybe the red sky belongs here, but it doesn't look scary."

"Red? Are you colour blind? That's clearly purple."

Charles laughed. "You're both wrong. That sky is the most wonderful orange I've ever seen. It's like all the sunsets the world has ever known have been collected into one stunning vision."

Tony snorted. "How many times have we got to tell you, you're not *that* Charles Dickens? Stick to history and leave that poetic stuff to creative people."

Tad could sense an argument coming and interceded.

"I expect you're all right."

"How can we all be right?" Miriam asked.

"What's the first thing we teach new ghosts? Your reality is what you make it. It's only fitting that Death would be that concept on a larger scale."

"So you're saying the sky is red, purple and—"

"Filled with the light of a billion sunsets," Tony finished for Charles, earning himself a smack around the head from Miriam. "Ow. You know what. One of these days I'll do that to you and you'll see what it's like. Ow! Stop hitting me."

"Shut up, both of you." Tad felt like the only adult amongst children. "Have you forgotten where we are? This place may be weird and not what we expected, but we're still in King Tower. Or maybe where King tower used to be… uh… I don't know how this works. What's important is that this is still a dangerous place. We need to be on our guard and stop shouting."

Tony was looking around. They stood in a field of lush grass that rolled on to infinity, and they were definitely alone.

"It's not like anyone's in a position to overhear us, Tad."

Tad shook his head. They were alone, but he knew the rules were different here. Things could turn on them any second. He was about to say as much when everything changed.

He turned, facing away from his ghosts. The door was not there, but where there had been endless fields of grass, there was now an outcropping of rock. It grew silently behind them, taller than any mountain. At the base of that outcropping was a huge cave that was filled with impenetrable blackness.

"Holy shit," Tony gasped, staggering back a step. "That wasn't there before, was it?"

None of them had missed it, it was impossible to. It had simply appeared.

"Should we see what's inside?" Miriam asked.

"No need. It's coming to see us," Tad answered.

"What do you—"

Charles was only half way through his question when they saw it. Tad had felt it only seconds earlier and was suitably awed. It was massive.

"No way. That's awesome. Is that really a dragon?" Tony asked.

Tad shook his head. "No, it's a nightmare."

The creature he sensed was not a dragon, but a massive ghost. It was as featureless and spectral as any of the mad ghosts he had faced, but grown to an impossible scale.

Just as with the sky, he knew this creature was different for each of them. He didn't ask what the others saw. That thing before them was either their biggest nightmare or something they felt they couldn't overcome.

He had a feeling that if he wanted to find King, he would have to go through that.

"What do we do?" Charles asked. "Could we run?"

"Where?" Tad replied. "We're penned in."

Sure enough, when Charles turned he was facing a large stone wall. On further inspection they found themselves in the bottom of a huge canyon.

"That's just creepy. A place shouldn't be able to change like that without telling you."

"This is Death, Tony. Expect the unexpected." Tad took a step forward but stopped when Charles grabbed his hand.

"What are you doing?"

"I'm going to fight that thing."

"You can't fight that. It's huge."

Tad shook his head. "We all knew this wouldn't be easy. But I think I know how we can get through this."

"How?" Each ghost asked together.

"This place is based on perception. Everything is what you want it to be. Don't forget that. Down there I see a ghost. A fucking massive ghost, but it's still just a ghost. Banishing ghosts is what I do. I have to believe my gift can work even on something as large as that. So if you'll excuse me…"

He shook himself free of Charles' grip and ran towards the huge spectre that waited just outside the blackness of the cave. It remained where it was, guarding the entrance to its den and watching him approach. It was thirty feet tall and just as wide, a cloud of shadow in most places but the odd human feature appearing in white at random spots. There was no face that Tad could sense, but he knew it was looking at him.

With each step he concentrated on schooling his terror. This was all perception, he had to believe he could deal with it.

He reached for the power he had been born with. The moment he touched it he knew he could deal with this being. King was right. This place was the source of their power, so it only stood to reason that in this place, their power would be unimaginable.

However, even with that much power and belief, sensing something that big coming for you can shatter any confidence you might feel.

It exploded forward, trailing shadow in its wake. The ghost covered the distance between them in a heartbeat, but it was not as quick as Tad's thoughts. He called upon that vast reserve of power within him and, as he always did, used it to force sanity upon the deranged spirit… only, nothing happened.

He knew he had done it right, knew the power had connected, but the ghost shrugged it off as though it was nothing. Tad dove aside at the last moment to avoid being struck. He hit the ground and rolled, which hurt, but not so much as the ghost's passing did.

If strong enough, the ghosts in his world could chill with their presence. This one didn't just chill him, he felt the freezing burn of ice as it formed in his clothes. It was so strong that Tad felt as though he had just stepped onto an icy tundra. The feeling did nothing to help his confidence.

"Tad!" Miriam screamed from somewhere in the distance. He cast his senses out and knew they remained against the rock that penned them in, waiting to see what Tad could do.

They weren't in danger. Miriam was screaming for his attention as that ghost had turned and was coming back.

Tad felt a moment of despair. How could he defeat this creature if his power didn't work on it? It was a nightmare beyond…

The answer was in the question. It was a nightmare, not a true ghost. If it was a nightmare, then it had no human spirit to revert to, it was just a spectre and nothing else. He couldn't force sanity on something that had no sanity to begin with.

He rolled again as it struck, this time doing his best to ignore the icy feeling but knowing that on the next pass he would be dead. The temperature had dropped lower than he could survive. Already he was fighting uncontrollable shivers, and he felt numb everywhere.

He sensed the creature turn again for one last approach. Once more Tad reached into the ocean of power he felt all around him. This time he applied that power in a new direction, and this time it worked.

The creature froze as though it had been turned to ice by its own touch. The shadows stopped flickering, and all forward momentum stilled. It was trapped by Tad's will and it was starting to glow.

The familiar light grew from its core, banishing the surrounding shadows until all that remained was a glowing skeletal figure that was lit by an inner light. As always the glow grew so bright, Tad knew his ghosts would be looking away.

He felt the touch of that light like the first rays of the morning sun. It was warmth, and as it exploded outward from the destroyed creature, the icy feeling vanished from the world.

A moment later the four of them were alone again at the bottom of the canyon. His ghosts ran to his side.

"That was amazing. How did you do that?" Tony asked. What must that brief battle have looked like to him? Tad smiled as he imagined it from Tony's point of view, a battle with a dragon, and shook his head.

"I told you, it's all about perception. I just had to believe it was a ghost that could be affected by my power. The trick is to not let yourself doubt."

"Easier said than done," Charles noted. Tad had to agree. It was the first lesson all ghosts needed to learn, but one that no ghost ever truly managed, no matter how long they were dead. It was too hard to let go of the limitations that are hard-wired into people during life.

"Should we expect more things like that?" Miriam asked.

Tad nodded. "That's not what worries me though. I'm more troubled about getting lost here. I've got a feeling this place is every bit as big as our own world, if not infinitely bigger. We need to find a way to seek out Stella and get her out of here."

"How do we do that?" Charles asked. "I'm still trying to figure how *we* get out of here. Have you forgotten the door to this place has disappeared?"

"There must be a way out," Tony said. "Otherwise King wouldn't be able to come back to the real world. We just need to find that too."

"I think if we find King, the rest will come to us."

His ghosts shared a nervous look in response to Tad's words. In the following silence, Tad searched his mind for a way to find Stella and King. He thought about going into the cave the nightmare had been guarding, but had the suspicion it wouldn't work. That was the expected path, an entry into a maze that had been constructed just for them. It would lead nowhere.

King had done this. Tad knew that in his core. King had somehow mastered this world and had set this up to... what? Test them? Stop them reaching him?

Tad wasn't sure of his motives, but knew deep down that they couldn't find King and Stella by looking in the same way they did in the real world.

So he tried something different. He looked internally, seeking his connection to this place and the power he got from it. Through that connection, like with his dreams and his power in the living world, he gained instinctive knowledge. He dove into the ocean that was his power in this place and drew memories of Stella in his mind.

It wasn't hard. As crazy as the last few weeks had been, Stella had made an impact. She was the one positive surprise to emerge from the craziness. The hard and dangerous predator that Tad had first seen her as, had slowly morphed into a friend, maybe even more. He'd be lying if he said thoughts of Stella hadn't occupied his mind, and he wasn't surprised that the image of her came quickly.

He submerged himself in memories of her, both good and the bad, and slowly he felt it work. The more memories he recalled, the stronger he got a feel for her presence. He focused on the aspects of her that were uniquely hers. She was strong, determined, funny when she wanted to be, and smart. He remembered looking into her eyes as she told him of her past in that cafeteria. He'd seen the real her then, the vulnerability of an abused child and the strength of the woman who had put that past behind her.

Those vibrant blue eyes had reflected Stella's soul, and as soon as Tad realised that, he found the key to finding her. Suddenly he knew exactly where she was, and the secrets of this world revealed themselves to him.

Not only did he find her, he knew how easy it was to get to her. It was just a matter of thought.

A startled curse from Tony along with Miriam and Charles' sudden gasp brought him back from his recollections of Stella.

The world changed. They were no longer surrounded by walls of stone. Now they stood in the centre of an ancient garden. Flowers, unrecognisable but beautiful, were laid in wondrous beds that spiralled outward from their central location.

There was grass under their feet, trees interspersed amongst the flowers, and a stone pathway that weaved through it all. In front of Tad was a fountain that rivalled anything he might find in the living world. A large pool surrounded that fountain, both of which were formed of living rock. Men and women in various states of garb were carved into that rock, spitting water from their mouths. Though they were marble, they danced and moved with each other causing the water streams to dance with them.

It was stunning and distracted all of them from the person knelt in front of it.

For the first time since he had known her, Stella's beauty did not compare to the world around her. At her best she might have belonged in this garden, but she was no longer at her best.

She knelt on the floor, her hands chained to a link in the stone ring jutting from the wall of the pool. There were bruises on her lovely face, her lip had split and had scabbed over, and Tad could only imagine what other damage lay hidden beneath her dishevelled clothing. She had put up a fight.

Stella was looking at the floor when they arrived, but when she noticed them her eyes widened, a look of hope crossing her face.

Tad rushed to her, falling to his knees and reaching for her chains. The knowledge of how to free her was instinct. All he had to do was know they would open at his touch and open they did.

The chains slipped from her wrists and fell to the ground. Stella stared at her freed wrists, at the cuts and bruises on her hands where she had tried to free herself. Then she lunged forward and threw her arms around Tad's neck, drawing him closer so she could whisper in his ear.

"Thank you. I wasn't sure you'd come... thank you."

Tad was about to reply, but another voice beat him to it. It was deep, strong, and resonated with untold power. It was the first time Tad had heard it with his own ears, but he remembered it well from Dinah's memories. It was every bit as chilling as he remembered, and worse thanks to this place.

"How touching. You came for her after all. I owe Dinah an apology. When she said she had brought me the next best thing to either you or your daughter, I almost killed her on the spot."

Tad turned toward the sound of the voice. He didn't need to in order to sense him, but it was a habit from the living world that was hard to break. As his senses turned on King, he got a feel for the man. He felt any remaining hope fade. For the first time he realised just how stupid he had ever been to think he could do this. He knew right to his core that he was about to let Jen down.

The man stood before Tad was not human any longer. The skinny balding man with the crippled arm was gone and in his place stood a figure from Greek mythology, a God of Olympus.

He still wore King's face, but all weakness was gone. He had doubled in height and built a physique to make Arnold Schwarzenegger in his prime cry with envy. He still wore a suit, but it did nothing to diminish his impossible presence.

Beyond everything, Tad got a sense of power unlike anything he could have imagined before. With his senses he could see not just King, but the hundreds of trapped souls within him, each of them granting him impossible strength in this place.

Despair filled Tad's mind, and he knew all was lost. He was unable to find words so King continued to speak.

"I should have learned to trust Dinah by now. She always comes through for me in the end. I have to say, it was good of her to bring you all too me like this. Though, there seems to be one person missing."

"Jen's not coming," Tad snapped, finally able to find his voice. "She's beyond you now."

King laughed at his bluff. "Oh, I don't think so. I have sources everywhere. I know she's undergoing surgery to help with a broken back. I'm sure you'll be glad to know it's going well. She won't walk again, but she'll be well enough for me to claim her whenever I need to.

"No, I was talking about the person you left outside. The getaway driver. I thought it was rude that you didn't invite her to the party, so I sent Dinah out after her."

"What? Kate. No, you leave her alone." Miriam was frantic and lunged for King. Tad reacted quicker, stopping her with a thought. He knew how useless it would be for Miriam to go against King in the real world, in this one she would have even less chance.

"Yes, the detective. I couldn't have her going for backup, could I? Ah. Speak of the devil, here she is."

His eyes had gone distant as though he was seeing something a long way off. Tad sensed him call on his vast powers and then Kate was with them. Again Tad had to hold back Miriam to stop her from going to Kate's side.

Kate was on her knees, an agonised grimace on her face as the woman standing over her had Kate's hand in a lock. Dinah's eyes swept over the group in the garden before settling on King.

"Dinah my dear. I should never have doubted you," King said. Dinah didn't reply. "You keep bringing me such wonderful presents. The question now is, what are we going to do with them all?"

"You have me so why not let them go? You don't need them."

King laughed at Tad's words and shook his head. "No. I don't think so. It's not worth the risk. Your two detective bitches here will call in back-up the first chance they get."

"What good will that do here?" Tad asked.

"Nothing. But I can't stay here all the time." For the first time Tad detected discomfort in King's voice. He didn't like that he couldn't stay in this place. "It's not healthy to live here too long."

"Not healthy? What happens?"

King shook his head. "It doesn't matter. What matters is that you're here and with your death, we might remedy that." The smile slipped from his face and his eyes focused on Tad. "But I have to admit, you've caused me more than a little trouble getting you here. You've brought the attention of the police upon me and I'm not at all happy about that." He took a few steps closer so he was towering over Tad. "You need to be punished."

"Killing me isn't enough?"

"No. I think it would be more fitting if you get to watch all these friends of yours die first. Why don't we start with…" He paused and made a show of thinking about it for a second before he pointed to Kate. "Her."

"What? No!" Miriam screamed and once again fought against the restraints that Tad had placed upon her.

Tad didn't let her move. She would only get in his way. Keeping her in place, he threw himself at King, snarling as he did so and reaching for his own power. It was no good.

King simply looked at him and Tad was gripped by a force he couldn't overcome. Every muscle locked in place as though he was stuck in stone. Even breathing felt impossible, and it consumed all of Tad's will to do that much. He had no chance of saving Kate.

King smiled at Tad, then raised a hand toward Kate, and extended his will through the gesture.

Kate looked at Miriam one final time before suddenly her head spun around sharply and a loud crack sounded as her neck broke.

Dinah stepped back in shock and let Kate's body crumple to the ground. That was when Miriam screamed.

Tad couldn't believe what he had just witnessed. It left him numb. How had this just happened? Surely he could have done something? King's will was still holding him in place, but he felt he could have acted somehow. There must have been some way he could have stopped it.

The answer never came. He felt lost, powerless. Miriam's screaming didn't help. What really made him go cold was the other sound. It was a sound that made Tad feel weak and sick at the same time. There was no escaping this for any of them. That sound was the sound of their doom.

King was laughing.

35

Sunday, 30th November 2015
01:46

Miriam's scream was the worst sound Stella had ever heard. Her loss was unimaginable. Miriam had done what Stella never could, opened her life to another person, shared her most vulnerable moments, and loved completely. Stella could have told her it only ended one way, with pain.

Why then did she envy her so much?

Stella's attention was drawn to Tad. His back was to her and at first she thought he was frozen in shock, but it didn't take long to realise it was more. His veins stood out and his arms were shaking. Everything about him told her he was straining against something. But what?

She got her answer from that laughter. Such an evil sound and so filled with madness. King was everything she feared. Worse, he was so much more than Tad.

Tad had surprised her at every turn, shown her things she couldn't dream of, and exposed her to a new world. When she had heard Emily's tales of Joshua King, she could not imagine someone so far beyond Tad. She had been wrong. King was in a different league.

"You're looking angry, Thaddeus," he teased, taking a step closer to Tad.

"I'll kill you for that," Tad said from between clenched teeth.

King laughed again.

"Still defiant right to the end. I like that. It makes these final moments more interesting, don't you think?"

"Why'd you do it? Why not let them go? They're no threat to you, not really."

"One of the many lessons I learnt when I was young, was that no one will give you what you want in life, you have to take it. I have lived by that rule my whole life and it has served me well. But I'm not prepared to take any chances with what I have. After all, if someone else wants it, they might one day take it.

"Why take the risk? I leave your detective friend alive and who knows what trouble she could bring to my door. Either of them."

He looked pointedly past Tad to Stella who shivered under his gaze. She had never felt less comfortable and she turned away.

She was surprised to find a woman standing over Kate's body, a woman who looked like Kate. No. It was Kate. Somehow she was standing over her own body. For a second Stella's fragile mind couldn't wrap itself around the problem.

It was Kate's ghost.

"Oh thank God," Miriam said loud enough to catch everyone's attention. All eyes turned to her in time to see her break free of whatever restraints she had been under so she could run to Kate. The two hugged fiercely and Stella could see tears in their eyes.

It would have been touching had King not been there, had he not started laughing again.

"Ah. Welcome back. I see you're a glutton for punishment. You could have moved on and spared yourself oblivion."

Kate looked up from Miriam defiantly.

"I've come back to help them kill you."

King laughed again. "Keep thinking that, love. We'll see how far you get with it later."

He turned his attention back to Tad. "Only one more life to take before I start on your ghosts Thaddeus. Any last words to say to the lovely Stella before she dies?"

Stella's blood ran cold.

She found herself filled with a nervous energy fuelled by terror. The trouble was she didn't know what to do with that energy. She could run, but where would she go? She had seen enough of this place to know she couldn't escape it. Maybe she could fight him? No. That was ridiculous. If Tad couldn't fight him then what chance did she have?

She looked at Tad one last time, seeking a glimmer of hope. She found none.

There was something strange about his eyes. Normally they were sharp, a reflection of his intelligence. Now she saw nothing. It was as though he were...

A memory triggered from one of her many conversations with him. There had been a time before his ghosts when his eyes didn't work. Was he blind again?

The longer she looked the more sure she became. He was blind. With that blindness, any last scraps of hope fled.

Tears filled her eyes, and she struggled again to think of something to do. There had to be something. She had spent her whole adult life making sure she could protect herself. Why was she looking to Tad for protection now?

Suddenly something clicked in her mind. King might kill her for what she was about to do, but he would kill her anyway. She might as well try it.

She kept looking to Tad, not letting on to King what she was thinking, but preparing herself nonetheless.

Her fingers curled around the hated chains and manacles that had secured her to the fountain just minutes earlier. They were hard and heavy. They could be a weapon.

Her muscles bunched and her heart beat quicker. She'd only get once chance.

"Well, Thaddeus. I'm waiting. I don't have all night," King teased.

Stella jumped to her feet, dragging the chains behind her and swinging them in a long ark. Tad was only two paces ahead of her, King maybe two beyond that. Two steps and he'd be within reach. Surely even he couldn't react that quickly.

She had already taken the first step and was starting her swing. She knew she was on target. Once they completed their path, the chains would catch King in the side of the head. She didn't care how powerful he was, that would hurt.

The second step was nearly complete, and she saw the chains blur past as she competed her swing. Through it all King stood still, smiling at her with contempt written across his expression.

The manacles were within a fraction of an inch of his face when he moved.

It was like something from a TV show. He moved so quickly he blurred, his head moving back out of reach and then moving back into place again once the chains had passed.

Stella was stunned, worse she was over balanced. The chains were heavy, and they were dragging her with them. She took another step forward, unable to help herself as she stepped into King's waiting hand.

His fingers were as hard as the iron she held in her hands and they clamped around her throat. It was like running into a stone barrier. Her head stopped moving but her legs kept going.

The only thing that stopped her falling was King's unmoving grip that held her off the floor.

"Nice try," he said. "But foolish."

Stella was barely listening. She was fighting hard at the hand holding her throat, digging her nails into flesh and trying to pry him loose. It was no good. The hand might as well have been carved from stone.

"It's about time I put an end to you," King said. "You should have died in the alley that night. Nothing personal of course. It was all just—"

His words cut off as a hand wrapped around the wrist holding Stella. For the first time King looked shocked as he followed that hand to the person connected to it.

He opened his mouth to speak but was forced to let Stella go and defend himself as Tad came in swinging. Stella had time to see Tad attack King's surprised face before she fell to the floor.

She wanted to watch, but it was no use. She desperately needed air, and she coughed as her eyes watered and she struggled to catch her breath. She was so preoccupied with doing this that she had to fight back a scream when she felt a hand on her shoulder and another on her arm helping her up.

"Easy Stella, it's just me," Miriam said from her place at Stella's shoulder. Stella turned to the other arm and found one of Tad's ghosts, Charles, helping her to her feet. He wasn't looking at her though, he was staring forward with naked terror.

"Come on Tad," he whispered.

"What happened?" Stella asked as she turned her gaze to the direction he was looking. "How did Tad get free?"

"Because there's more fight in Tad than King knows," Tony answered. He was riveted by the fight. In spite of his words though, he looked terrified. Tad had lost the upper hand.

King had been surprised that Tad had broke free of whatever bonds had been holding him, but that surprise was quickly overcome. He was smiling again as he dodged Tad's clumsy punches. He actually laughed when he countered, landing a heavy blow to Tad's ribs which lifted him off his feet and sent him face first into a bed of unidentifiable flowers.

"I'm impressed," King roared. "I didn't think you had it in you. How did you break free like that? You shouldn't have the strength."

Tad didn't answer, just pushed himself back to his feet with a roar and came for King again. King was ready this time. He held up a hand and Tad froze mid-step... only to move again a fraction of a second later.

Once again this caught King by surprise and this time Tad landed his punch. It was a hell of a blow that caught King just below the chin and staggered him back a few steps.

Stella was as stunned as King.

Not only was that a great punch, much stronger than a normal man's, but Tad had somehow thrown it blind. She had no idea how he was moving so well without being able to see, but she could tell by the look on his face that he was still blind.

He tried to press his advantage, but King had already recovered.

He didn't use his Proxy powers to counter Tad this time, but instead used his hands. He caught Tad's fist in one hand and backhanded Tad with the other. The blow rocked Tad's head around so fast that Stella was surprised his neck didn't break. Something cracked though. Judging by the blood that flew from his mouth as he turned, Stella wondered if it had been his jaw.

"You continue to surprise me," King said. He was not smiling now. Instead he looked wary, a predator who realised that the prey he had caught had horns and knew how to use them. "We had best get this out of the way before you can surprise me anymore."

Stella would have swore that the giant stone table that looked all too much like an Aztec altar had not been there a moment before.

Tad was still stunned from the blow to his head, so he didn't put up much resistance as King casually dragged him toward that table and threw him down on top of it.

"No!" Charles cried, making all of them jump, including King. Charles' charge might have looked comical at any other time were he not so serious about it. The anger evident in his roar was enough to make Stella think he might actually be in with a chance.

There was no chance though.

King didn't even gesture to exert his will. He looked at the approaching ghost and Charles stopped dead.

"Please. You wouldn't even be an annoyance," King said to the fat ghost before he raised his free hand toward Charles. At once Charles' body went rigid and his eyes opened wide.

"Oh no, Charles. What have you done?" Miriam gasped.

"What?" Stella asked, not yet seeing the significance. She didn't get her answer. They all just watched in horror as a light started to grow within Charles.

"Charles," Tad gasped from underneath King's hand. Stella's heart broke at the expression on his damaged face. "Move on."

It didn't look like Charles had heard him. He remained stiff, growing ever brighter. Finally Stella saw an imperceptible shake of the head.

"It's better than this," Tony shouted from beside Stella. "Don't be stubborn Charles, move on."

Again the shake of the head.

"Don't be afraid Charles," Tad said. "I promise, you have long since made up for your sins… they weren't even that bad to begin with. If you ever trusted me, please, find that trust one last time. Move on, my friend. Please."

The conversation was going over Stella's head, but she could hear the anguish in all the voices around her and knew that whatever they were talking about was significant to them.

Charles didn't shake his head this time, but neither did he do as asked. He remained locked in King's power, looking terrified and undecided. He was clearly struggling against what was happening and the naked fear on his face was the kind that made Stella feel sick. The light within him was growing so bright it was no longer the red light that shined through flesh, but was turning white.

"The stubborn fool," Miriam groaned. "Why doesn't he move on? It can't be worse than this. Surely."

Stella was about to ask her what she meant, but never got the chance as Tad spoke up instead. His words were barely audible and he was struggling to speak as he fought back his own despairing tears.

"Charles, my oldest friend. Please forgive me for this."

Tad focused on his ghost as Stella tried to make sense of what happened next. The glowing figure of Charles collapsed in on itself, almost as though it was being destroyed. Stella would have thought that was exactly what was happening were it not for the look on King's face.

His was a look of astonishment and a touch of fear.

The shape continued to collapse until it was little more than a sphere of white mist. It hung in the air for a heartbeat before zipping away into the distance far quicker than the eye could follow.

Suddenly it vanished and when it did Stella felt a warmth like she had never felt before. It settled over all of them, gentle and loving. It sunk deep within Stella's body, easing the pain from her bruises and chafing wrists. The deep terror and hopelessness that had been overwhelming her since she had been brought to that place abruptly left, and she was at peace.

Stella could see that everyone felt the same, save one person. King. He did not look at peace, he looked terrified.

He turned and grabbed Tad's shirt. With a fist full of material he hauled Tad off the table to bring him to eye height.

"How did you do that?" he demanded. "That was impossible, you can't make ghosts move on. How did you do it?"

It was Tad's turn to laugh at his enemy. His face was bloodied and a big bruise was building over the side of his head. It made the laugh seem all the more sinister and mocking. In spite of that laugh, there were tears in his eyes that spoke of the pain he endured over what he had just been forced to do.

"Don't you know? I thought you were the all powerful Joshua King, a Proxy without equal. How do you not know how to do something so basic?"

The words landed on King as though they were physical blows and he took a startled step back, dropping Tad back to the stone altar. Tad landed with a heavy thud and Stella winced as his head bounced off the table.

"It's impossible," King muttered to himself. He continued to mumble for a few seconds before shaking his head. "Never mind. If you can do it, so can I. I just need to figure it out."

In control of himself again, King took that step back to the altar once more. Suddenly there was a knife in his hand. Stella had not seen him draw it. It was almost as though it had appeared from nowhere. King had simply dreamt it up.

"I'm done with you. You're too dangerous to leave alive." He took another step closer. "It's time to finish this."

Stella watched in horror as he positioned the knife over Tad's chest. She had just enough time to realise she should do something, try to help Tad as he had tried to help her. But it was too late.

King brought the knife up overhead and with startling speed and strength, the knife descended towards Tad's unprotected chest.

Stella heard a scream. She was surprised to find it was her own. It cut off abruptly as the knife stopped with a thud.

36

Sunday, 30th November 2015
01:58

Charles was gone. Tad couldn't believe it.

Since he was nine, Charles had been his constant companion. Now, he was not only gone, but Tad had forced him to face his biggest fear to save his soul. It didn't matter that it paid off. All that mattered was he was gone.

Between his swimming head, the pain in his jaw, and losing his oldest friend, Tad barely noticed King raise the knife.

He was suddenly exhausted.

He'd been feeling tired for a long time. Since he had first learnt of Proxies disappearing, it had been one long succession of losses, sleepless nights and perpetual worry.

He was ready for it to be over. Maybe he would welcome death. All he had to do was make sure he moved on before King could get him. Then he could be with Charles again.

A frown formed as King lined the knife up with his chest. Something about Tad's last train of thought didn't seem right.

Charles had moved on, but where to?

Weren't they in Death? Wasn't that the point of killing Proxies, to lower the barriers between life and death? If this was Death, then where had Charles gone. It wasn't part of this world, Tad knew that much. He sensed it when he added his power to the spiderweb that connected Charles to the next life.

No, there was something beyond this world. Tad was confident that King was partially wrong about this place. He wasn't wrong about it being the source of their strength, but it wasn't Death.

So, where were they?

The more he thought about it, the more he knew he was onto something. All the clues were there, and he just needed the time to put them together. Time was something he didn't have. He was aware of King's intense focus on him, of his hand moving closer to Tad's chest and the shining blade he held in his fist.

It was typical. Tad was seconds away from death and he felt he was finally on the verge of something important. He was tempted to stop thinking about it, to focus on the knife and the moment of his death. A part of him was screaming to keep thinking though, telling him he was close.

Suddenly it came to him.

It was obvious now he thought of it. The clues had been there all along and he was amazed he hadn't discovered it before. The best part was that if he was right, there still might be a chance.

He focused on the knife that was an inch away from his heart and forced a realisation on himself. Yet again it was about perception. This time, if he was right, it would change everything.

"I am dreaming," he stated out loud.

He not only stated it, he forced himself to believe it.

The knife stopped.

The tip was touching his chest and had actually drawn a droplet of blood. But it had stopped.

Tad turned his attention from the blade to King. He was frozen in time, a grimace of hatred on his face mixed with triumph. No doubt he thought his work was complete.

Tad's attention wandered to the figures behind King. Stella, Tony, Miriam and Kate were locked in place as well, each caught in mid stride as they ran towards King, coming to rescue Tad. The tableau moved him greatly. They were ready to risk their lives to save his. They would be late, but it was the thought that counted.

With just a thought he was standing beside King. Now he'd had his epiphany it was all so easy.

This world that King had been trying so hard to merge with their own was not Death, it was Dream. It was the realm that all people went to when they slept, it was a place where anything was possible.

The more Tad thought about it, the more it made sense. He should have realised the minute he stepped into the world and had gone blind. It was exactly like it was in his dreams. Then there was the nightmare that attacked them. It was like the world had been trying to tell him, but he was too dense to listen.

As was the way with memories, this new knowledge changed them. He looked back through his mind and see things from a new perspective.

His interactions with the ghosts all started with dreams. That was where they merged minds. Then there was the time he spent in the dream world with Jen, how Jen had reached him when he was unconscious, and how he had got through to Dinah's memories.

He shook his head and laughed. A sudden leap of intuition lead him to the obvious conclusion. Proxies were never conduits of death, but instead they channeled the power of dreams.

"But why ghosts?"

He asked the question aloud as though hoping for an answer. All around him were stuck in a frozen moment of time, held that way by his will until he was ready to continue. The answer instead came from the world itself, in the same way so much of his knowledge did.

Dream was the realm between worlds. It was a place where the spirit could exist without being either alive or dead. It was where the spirit went when the body shut down and recharged during sleep. It was where ghosts could stay by ignoring the call to the afterlife.

All this time Proxies had been wrong. They were never masters of death, they were the lords of dreams. They interacted with the dream-world even when awake, and their abilities were to bring the infinite possibilities of dreams into the world of the living.

In dreams, what you imagined was real. Perception was everything. When you know you're dreaming, you become the master of your dreams.

Poor King. He was so close to getting what he wanted and he had never understood it at all. He was powerful in this place because he was powerful in the living world. There, his ghosts gave him a stronger connection to Dream which made him more than Tad could ever be. Here everyone was equal as they were only limited by their imaginations and perception.

King had perceived himself strong and therefore he had been. But he also knew he had limitations. As Tad had proved by the fact that no one was moving, there were no limitations in this place.

With a thought Tad healed the injuries he had endured, making them vanish as though they had never been. It put a smile on his face and for the first time in a long time, it left him feeling confident.

Tad set time free.

The first sound he heard was the thud as the knife struck the stone of the altar followed by King's startled exclamation.

"What?" he demanded, then turned to find Tad standing behind him. "That's impossible."

Tad just smiled and shook his head.

"How little you know, Joshua. All this time you were so close, but you never understood."

King might not understand, but knew he was being mocked. His lip curled, and he moved to strike, turning the knife around and aiming for Tad's chest. Like before, he moved faster than was humanly possible, but nothing was faster than thought.

Tad let King strike where he had been, but once more Tad changed his position. Now he was standing behind the man and it was he who held the knife in his hands.

"Is this what you used to take all those innocent lives?" he asked.

King stumbled and almost fell, righting himself only through his supernatural talents and turning on his heel to face Tad. His eyes were wide with frustration but there was a hint of fear as well.

"How did you do that?"

Tad sighed. "If you don't know now, you never will. Not even with all your ghosts. Speaking of which…"

With a thought Tad expelled every soul from King's body that was not Joshua King's own. King shuddered as though his whole body had sneezed violently. All at once ghosts burst forth, hundreds of them in a crowd that filled the garden.

King looked at the startled faces in horror, and again perception was his undoing. As far as he knew these ghosts were the reason for his strength. His mind perceived his lack of them as losing his power and applied that reality to his body.

The popping and cracking sounds were his left arm as it broke and twisted, withering away as it had been in Dinah's memory. The rest of him deflated, the muscles wasting away and the skin losing its colour as it grew taut across his skeleton. Dark rings spread around his eyes until the onetime god looked like a frail old man.

"What did you do to me?" he gasped.

Tad didn't answer, instead turning to the assembled ghosts.

"None of you need fear him any longer. He has no hold over you and no power to control you. I have cut that from him."

At first no one believed him. They had been trapped by King for so long they had no reason to believe Tad now. King was their nightmare, what they feared more than death.

Slowly understanding spread. For the first time King was without ghosts. More than that, he had not yet exercised his will to draw them back. One by one, the ghosts realised that maybe Tad was right. Their confusion turned to anger.

They crowded in around a terrified King, blocking him from Tad's ghosts and Stella. But they could hear his screams as the ghosts started in.

Tad could sense what was happening and knew King was getting exactly as he deserved. It didn't last long enough for justice, but it was more than enough for Tad to stomach. King's screams were agonised and pitiful, and Tad had no stomach for that sort of thing. It was why he was glad when Dinah ended it.

Dinah, who'd remained silent since Kate died, somehow made it through the ghosts to get to King's side. With an expression close to ecstasy, Dinah slid a knife into King's back, directly into his heart.

The withered husk that was Joshua King gasped as the knife pierced his heart and then slumped, ripping the blade from Dinah's hand and falling to the floor in a heap.

Tad paid no more attention to the thing that had been Joshua King. Instead he turned his senses to the presence growing amongst the ghosts who had moved away from the corpse as though they couldn't stand to be near it.

That presence was a newly freed spirt trying to coalesce into the image of what it had been in life. A mist could be seen over King's corpse that took on the appearance of the dead man at its feet.

The surrounding ghosts moved in closer, ready to start in on the man once more. Tad had other plans.

He found every last spiderweb that connected the hundreds of souls to the next life and increased the energy of the pull to move on.

They had no chance to fight. As one they collapsed in on themselves, shrinking into balls of white mist until only King, Dinah, Tad, Stella, Miriam, Kate and Tony remained. Each ball sped away just as Charles' had, each seeking a different destination.

Tad felt the warmth of the next life, but also the cold. The souls were called to various locations and the collision of hot and cold caused great peals of thunder, the drumroll of the gods, welcoming the souls home.

The thunder echoed throughout the garden, deafening them until it rolled on by and they were alone.

"What now?" King asked, breaking the silence that followed.

"Won't you send me on my way too?"

Tad shook his head.

"No. I can't risk that. I have no idea what waits for us in the next life and can't risk that you might find your way back. You, I destroy."

King actually looked pleased.

"Better that than where I'd be headed," he said. Tad couldn't help but agree and he rethought his decision, but came to the same conclusion. As far as he knew no one had ever returned from the next world, but he couldn't take that chance. King had to go.

There were no gestures, nothing dramatic to tell others what he was doing. He simply looked to King and thought that he wanted him gone. The light that rose this time was more like the flash of an incredibly bright camera than a slow build up. One minute King had been there and the next he was gone forever.

Standing behind where King had been was Dinah. She was looking smaller than ever and there was a weary smile on her face and tears running down her cheeks. She looked to Tad and her smile widened.

"Finally," she said.

Tad could have stopped her if he wanted, but he didn't. Dinah took the knife from King's corpse and plunged it into her own neck. Stella and the ghosts gasped, but Tad wasn't surprised. He had been in her head. She had done horrific things, but she never taken that final step to becoming a monster. She had never enjoyed them.

Now the reason for her evil acts was gone she was free to leave this world. Her spirit didn't even try reforming before it moved onto the next world. Yet again Tad felt the chill of death as Dinah was taken to the next life. It was not as cold as he expected, but it was not warmth either.

With that done, only Tad and his friends remained. Each looked at the other, none prepared to break the awkward silence. Finally all eyes turned to Tad who was struggling to smile at them reassuringly. He should feel triumphant. They had won, it was over... but the cost was too great.

Charles.

His oldest friend, a brother, a father to him in some ways. He had been with Tad for so long and he was gone now, forever. Tad forced him to face his biggest fears and he could never see his friend again to ask for forgiveness.

Yes, he had won the battle, but he had lost so much more.

"How about we go home?" he said.

Before they could answer the world changed. The garden vanished, the grass turned to carpet, and walls grew around them. Everyone save Tad gaped at their new surroundings.

Miriam and Tony let out surprised little chuckles while Stella and Kate just looked confused. They had never been there before. This was their first time in Tad's round room of doors.

He motioned to the door behind him.

"Follow me," he said. Then without waiting for a response, he opened the door and led them back to the world of the living.

37

Sunday, 30th November 2015
08:10

Tad should have known better.

It was always the moments when he was most sure of himself when a new surprise came along to put him in his place. He stepped through the familiar door into the living world expecting to come out in King Tower. He expected everything would be quiet and it would still be night. He thought they'd be alone.

As Tad stepped out of the dreamworld and could see again, he had to blink and shield his eyes against the low hanging sun that had just risen over the horizon. Evidently, the passage of time was not the same in Dream.

Even with that blindness, he couldn't miss the crowd of people looking at him.

What was worrying was that some of those people had video cameras.

"What the hell is this?" Tony asked as he stepped into the sunlight. Tad turned to look at his ghost and found his teenage friend looking pleased with the reaction. "They here for us?"

"I don't know," Tad answered.

Stella stepped through the doorway and just as Tad had, she shielded her eyes. Also just like Tad, she didn't miss their audience.

"What's going on?" she asked.

"I have no idea." Tad was about to ask something when Miriam and Kate stepped into the world hand in hand.

Miriam's reaction was much like the rest of theirs, but Kate looked embarrassed.

"Shit, they came. I didn't think they would."

"What? Who came?" Miriam asked.

Kate blushed.

"The media. I was worried about you going in there without backup, so I thought I'd take matters into my own hands. I called a few reporters and told them that the police knew one of their own had been kidnapped and where she was, but weren't prepared to do anything about it. I also might have let slip a few key details about Joshua King... and... well... this is the result."

"Why do that?" Tad asked, struggling to get his head around the idea.

"To get this kind of reaction. This amount of media doesn't show up without police attention. I also hoped they might put pressure on the powers that be to send in backup." She grinned nervously. "I suppose my plan half worked."

"I'll say—" Tad began, but was interrupted.

"Tad," Stella's tone was insistent, and he got the impression she had been calling for his attention several times. She only got through when she took his hand and pulled hard on it.

He turned to face her and was about to ask what was wrong when he saw what caught her attention.

He had meant to exit the dreamworld inside the King compound, but had messed up. It turned out that was a good thing. When he looked back expecting to find King Tower, he found a pile of rubble and shattered glass. King tower was gone.

"What..." he began to ask before his mind put the clues together.

"Shit!"

"What happened?" Stella asked.

"Remember what Emily said, about King only needing one more sacrifice to complete his mad plan?"

"But he never got it. You didn't die, Tad."

"I'm aware of that. But he did, and he was a Proxy. What if he became the sacrifice?"

"But he wasn't on the stone table."

"I don't think that matters. That was just King showing off. All that mattered was that a Proxy died in that world. I think I accidentally finished what he started."

"And the building exploded?" Tony asked. "Was that always part of the plan?"

Tad shook his head. "I don't think it exploded. I think the portal, or whatever it is that King opened, expanded and took the building with it."

"Then where is it now?" Miriam asked. "I don't see that freaky place we've just come from."

Tad was shaking his head before she had even finished speaking. Now he was looking for it, he was surprised that he hadn't found it before.

"It's there, just not in the way you think."

"You'll need to make more sense than that Tad, because they're coming." Stella nodded toward the crowd of media over his shoulder and when he turned, he found them heading his way, microphones first.

"Oh crap. Alright. Uh, basically, King's plan worked, just not in the way he expected. The connection to that other world is stronger than we thought, you guys just can't see it."

"Still not making sense Tad, and we're almost out of time." Tony didn't sound upset by that comment. Already he was straitening himself out for the cameras and trying to look his best.

"Alright. It's hard to explain. King's plan worked. The two worlds have merged."

"Then where's all the crazy stuff?" Kate asked.

"All around us. It's everywhere. You guys just can't see it. King has made the two worlds one. They are both occupying the same space only... God this is hard to explain."

He looked at the crowd of reporters who were approaching fast. At first the sight made him panic and a good explanation became more elusive. However, when he spotted a camera, he had an epiphany.

"Think of the world like a TV. Until now there has only been one channel, let's call it the Living channel. King has created a second channel called Dream. You can only watch one channel at a time, but just because you're not watching it, doesn't mean its not there."

"Dream?" Miriam asked.

"Oh yeah, I forgot to mention. It turns out that place wasn't Death, it was Dream. That's what Proxies have been channelling all this time. I... look, I'll have to explain this later. There isn't time now."

"So what? You're saying the reason we can't see this... dream-world... is because we're not tuned into the right station? What do we need, some kind of remote?" Tony asked.

Tad grinned. "Not a remote, a Proxy."

As soon as he said it he knew it was true. Like with most things about his talent, the knowledge was just there for the taking. No matter where he was, he could step into Dream, tune into that other channel, whenever he wanted.

The hand he didn't realise he was still holding, tightened. He looked up to find Stella once more nodding behind him. He turned just in time to flinch away from the microphone shoved in his face.

"Who are you?"

"What happened here?"

"Where did you come from?"

The questions came thick and fast from every direction at once. Tad had no idea what to say. It was overwhelming, and he didn't want to be there. He gripped Stella's hand a little harder, drawing strength from her touch.

"Uh," he said, a nice eloquent start. "Well... I suppose that I should start by saying I didn't blow up this building."

"Actually, you kind of did, Tad." Tony said. "If you hadn't—"

"Not helping, Tony!" Tad blurted, talking over the teen, but not nearly quick enough.

"So you did blow up the building? Why did you do it?"

"Was it to rescue Stella Martin? Are you D.I. Martin?"

Again the questions came from everywhere at once, again Tad didn't know what to say.

"Look, this was an accident. It wasn't supposed to happen, it just… ah forget it. No comment."

The questions kept coming after that, but Tad was in no mood to answer. He held out his free hand to Kate and said, "Everyone join hands."

It was a testament to his ghosts that they didn't question, they just did as asked. As soon as Tony completed the loop Tad fell back into his power and in his mind, he changed the channel.

As quick as thought the questions stopped and the world around them changed. One moment they stood on the road outside the destroyed King tower, and the next they were standing in a round room that was no longer filled with doors. There was only one set of double doors that Tad knew would lead to the rest of Dream.

He didn't need this room anymore. Dream was his to command, and he didn't need the round room to find his way around. But it was comfortable and familiar.

"Oh my God, where are we?"

That voice wasn't familiar. Tad didn't need to turn to see who it was. Once again he was blind and could sense the world around him.

Behind him were three reporters and a camera man who must have been touching Tad when he changed the channel. He had accidentally brought them too.

"Oh, sorry. I didn't mean to bring you here."

"Where are we?" the one reporter to keep her wits asked again, thrusting the microphone into Tad's face as the camera pointed in his direction.

"Uh… I'll tell you what. You all get one peak outside and then you go right back. Tony, could you open the door?"

Tony did as asked. The reporters gasped.

Beyond that door was an alien reality. The wild garden and grasslands beyond was akin to a vision of the garden of eden, only with colours that could barely be imagined. They were vibrant and intense colours that had no place in the spectrum that humans can see.

Even the reporter who had kept her wits about her to that point was lost for words.

"Ladies and gentlemen," Tad said, drawing their attention. "Welcome to Dream."

He enjoyed their speechlessness for a couple of seconds, then touched the nearest reporter on the shoulder. Another channel change and they were back in the living world.

There were startled shouts as they appeared from nowhere, but Tad ignored them. The camera man hadn't been touching the reporters, so with another change of the channel he was back in the dreamworld.

"You too buddy," he said.

The man flinched, but wasn't quick enough, and the moment Tad made contact he was back in the living world eliciting more startled yelps.

The reporter who asked him the question in Dream had recovered quicker than anyone else yet again.

"Are you telling us you have discovered another world, sir?" she asked before he could disappear.

Tad hesitated. The young, blonde reporter looked like she was barely out of school. She kept her head when no one else had, and she kept asking questions. Tad felt that deserved at least something.

"What's your name?" he asked her.

"Lizzie."

"Well Lizzie, it's not another world. It's another reality. It's the dreamworld that we go to when we sleep." He knew this had only created more questions, but Tad was fine with that. He was about to leave again when a new thought struck him.

The world had changed, not just for him but for everyone. Even though only Proxies could hop between realities, the worlds were merged now and there was bound to be bleed over. That meant that the limitless possibilities of Dream would start infecting the world of the living. People had a right to know what to expect.

"You got a card?" he asked Lizzie.

She nodded and reached into her pocket to pull out a white card that was crumpled at the edges. Tad took it and put it into his jeans pocket, smiling once more at the reporter.

"Give me some time to get my head straight, and I'll call you. See you later Lizzie."

Before she had chance to say anything else he changed the channel again and returned to the round room where his friends waited.

The hospital room wasn't big enough for all of them, but that didn't put them off. Tad took the seat next to Jen's bed and held her hand. Stella leaned against the windowsill behind him and rested her hand on his shoulder. Tony sat on the other end of the windowsill and watched Jen with uncharacteristic solemness.

Kate and Miriam were whispering to one another on the other side of the room. Tad could tell it was serious, but he didn't eavesdrop. He was only interested in Jen.

They waited in the dreamworld only long enough for Tad to explain what happened. He told them, as calmly as he could, about his epiphany while on the sacrificial table. He had to ignore the rising guilt he felt about not figuring it out quick enough to save either Kate or Charles. He explained everything until they were overwhelmed by the information.

In the silence that followed, his own mind started working again, remembering how late it was in the real world and also remembering his promise to his daughter. He refused to take any more questions, there was only one thing on his mind. With just a thought he changed the channel again, this time letting his instinct guide him so he came into the real world in a new place.

To say the people sitting in the waiting room were surprised when Tad and his entourage appeared was an understatement. He ignored them. All he was interested in was finding and talking to Jen's doctors.

When he found them, the doctors said the operation was about as successful as it could be. Now Jen had a few months of recovery and a life time of acclimating to a reality where she couldn't walk. Tad wasn't looking forward to that and would give anything to change it. That being said, he had some ideas he would test as soon as Jen was ready.

He looked up as Miriam and Kate came to stand on the other side of the bed, Miriam reaching for Jen's other hand.

"She'll be alright Tad," she said. "You both will."

Something about the tone of her voice sparked a suspicion in his mind.

"Why does that sound like a goodbye?" he asked.

Kate grinned. "See, he's not as stupid as you thought."

"It's because it is, Tad," Miriam answered. "We're moving on."

"What? Why? You two have just had a reunion and the world has just had a major change. It's bound to mean big things for ghosts—"

"Exactly. Big things that might not be good. I don't know if it escaped your attention this morning, but everyone outside King Tower saw us. Were you doing your thing to make them see us?"

Tad shook his head.

"I thought not. That means the world is changing for ghosts too, it means that people can interact with us now. The more interaction others can have with us, the more likely it is we can be hurt, maybe even destroyed.

"I've spent three years separated from Kate. I don't want to risk an eternity without her. We've been talking and we've decided. We're moving on."

Tad was speechless.

"I thought you weren't staying behind just for Kate," Tony said. "You always said you stayed behind because you could help people."

"And I did, partially. But I'm realising that people can get by without me. I'm more at peace than I once was." To Tad she said, "We've made our decision. Once we've said our goodbyes to Jen, we're moving on."

"That soon?" Tad asked. He couldn't believe it. First Charles and now Miriam. Not to mention Kate. He hadn't merged with her yet, but he had already grown accustomed to the idea that she would be one of his ghosts.

"If we put it off too long then… well, who knows what might happen?" Kate said. "Besides. This was never for me. No offence, Tad, but it'll be a cold day in hell before you get inside my head."

He couldn't help himself, he laughed. They all did, and it cut the tension.

"What are you laughing at?" A small voice said from the bed. "They didn't shave my head, did they?"

Tad turned his attention to Jen who was blinking and looking around the room in confusion. When her eyes found Stella's they widened, and she quickly searched out Tad.

"Are you hurt?" she asked, taking in his dishevelled state and the blood he hadn't cleaned off his clothes. She was trying to sit up. Tad stopped her before she could hurt herself and tried to smile comfortingly.

"No, Jen. Nothing to worry about."

"It's over?" Jen asked. "I mean you obviously got Stella back, but—"

"Yeah. It's over. There's nothing to worry about."

Tony coughed suggestively.

"What?" Jen asked. "What's wrong?"

Tad shot a withering glare Tony's way, but he ignored him otherwise. "Nothing's wrong. I promise. There's just been some… uh… changes. Let's wait until you're a bit better before we talk about them okay?"

She frowned and her aura flared with the usual purple irritation before it faded again. She sighed and closed her eyes as she accepted his words. "Alright dad. I'm tired anyway."

Tad couldn't deny the tingle of warmth that ran through him when she called him dad, and he grinned.

Soon he would have a long conversation with her about what happened in Dream. He'd have to share the news about Charles with her. But for right now she was fragile, and he felt this news could wait, especially with the shock she was about to get.

"Okay Jen. Don't go back to sleep yet though. Kate and Miriam want to talk to you." He turned to the two ghosts and asked, "You want time alone with her?"

They nodded, and he stood up. "I'll be right outside, Jen." He leaned in and kissed her on the forehead, then stepped away. Stella took Jen's hand, smiling down on her before joining Tad.

Tony was next and like Tad he kissed Jen on the forehead. He whispered something to her that Tad couldn't hear. It made Jen blush and smile at the same time, and then he too joined Stella and Tad in leaving the room.

"What did you say to her?" Tad asked once the door closed.

"None of your business," Tony answered.

Tad felt a flicker of irritation. "For the love of God Tony, don't push me today or I'll send you packing as well."

Tony just grinned at him and shook his head. "No you won't. And like I said, it was none of your business. It was just between me and Jen."

Tad was about to say something else when he felt someone take his hand and he calmed down. He looked at the slim hand holding his own and followed it up to Stella who was smiling and shaking her head.

She was right. This wasn't the time or place for anger. For once he would let Tony's annoying behaviour slide.

When he looked back up, Tony was grinning at him knowingly and Tad felt himself blush.

"I think I'm going for a walk," Tony said.

"Tony wait. You're not going to do anything stupid like move on are you?" Tad asked in sudden panic.

"What? Are you kidding me? Things are just getting interesting. See you soon."

He turned and walked off leaving Tad and Stella alone in the corridor. Neither spoke for a few seconds, just standing in silence, holding each other's hand.

"She'll be fine," Stella whispered to break that silence.

"I know. I just wish… never mind. There's no use in wishing for things that can't happen."

Stella laughed. "Who knows around you? You seem to have a way of making the impossible happen. Like saving me last night. I can't believe you did that."

Tad felt himself blushing again and hated himself for it.

"Yeah, well… It was nothing really, it was—"

He was interrupted as she gripped his chin and turned his face towards her. Then those fingers were around the back of his head pulling him down as Stella rose onto her toes so she could kiss him.

For a few seconds Tad was stuck in a state of shock. His mind that had already had to deal with so much that night had finally taken all it could and overloaded. It meant he had to react instinctively.

His hand tightened around hers, his other arm finding its way around her waist and pulling her tight against him. Stella's lips curled into a smile as he returned her kiss and that smile remained as she came up for air.

It took another few seconds for Tad to catch his breath and his train of thought before he asked, "Was that a thank you kiss or…?"

Stella laughed. "Yes, it was a thank you kiss," she said. "There might be a few more coming your way soon if you play your cards right."

Tad couldn't help but grin. "Really? So you've finally admitted it to yourself then. I told you women get this way around me—"

"Shut up you idiot," Stella laughed as she spoke and there was no heat to her words.

"Okay. Shutting up. Seriously though, what gives? I thought—"

"When King took me, I thought for sure I was dead. Then you all came for me and… well, that meant a lot. The truth is though, it was Kate and Miriam who clinched it for me. If they died last night they would have lost each other, but at least they would have had something to lose. I realised that by never taking a chance I was still a loser in all this."

"You know, they say you shouldn't make decisions immediately after life or death situations," Tad said.

"Will you shut up, Tad? I'm trying to tell you something." He grinned again and nodded. "What I was trying to say is that I realised that if I died last night, I would have regretted never giving this a chance."

"So that means plenty of thank you kisses?" Tad asked.

She laughed. "My God, you're like a child."

"It's all the time I've spent with Tony in my head. Keeps me young."

She laughed again. "And you're weird. Maybe I should go find another guy instead."

"Hey. How many guys do you know who can literally take you to another world?"

"I suppose there is that."

"Exactly. Just remember that in the future. That and the price of admission to that other world."

Stella raised an eyebrow. "Oh? And what might that price be?"

"I'm sure we can work out something," he said, then leaned down for another kiss. This time his whole mind was engaged, and it went much more smoothly than the last.

A suggestive cough interrupted them and Tad turned guiltily to find Miriam and Kate standing in the doorway with big grins on their faces.

Stella and Tad parted, both of them blushing.

"Oh, don't stop on our account. We just thought we'd stop by and say goodbye is all," Miriam said. Tad chuckled and was still blushing when he stepped away from Stella and opened his arms for a hug. Miriam was quick to step into his embrace and hugged him hard enough to make him grunt.

"Are you sure I can't get you guys to change your mind?" Tad asked as they parted again. There were tears in Miriam's eyes as she shook her head.

"No. We're decided. Listen. I wanted to say thank you, Tad, for everything. The last three years have been some of the best of my life, in spite of everything. You made me part of your family, shared your life with me… I can't thank you enough."

He grinned at her and wiped away the tears in his own eyes. "Please. It was my pleasure." He turned to Kate and added, "Thanks for loaning her to me for the last few years."

Kate was grinning and crying as well as she too stepped in for a hug, one just as hard if not harder than Miriam's had been.

"I'll miss you, Tad," she said, "Look after the munchkin and keep Tony away from her until she's old enough to knock some sense into him."

"I heard that," Tony said, drawing attention to himself. He was trying to look angry but his own tears made the lie obvious. "Besides, Jen has always been old enough to knock sense into me. You made sure of that ages ago."

Kate grinned and poked Tony in the chest. "And don't you forget it."

Tony was about to say something in reply but Kate silenced him with a surprise hug. It was every bit as hard as the one she gave Tad and knocked the imaginary breath from him.

When they parted Miriam stepped in to do the same, but this time Tony was ready. He hugged her with one arm while his free hand reached around to grab a handful and a squeeze. Miriam yelped, released Tony from his hug and smacked him around the head.

She was grinning though and Tony was smiling right back at her. "Worth it," he said triumphantly.

"I should think so," Miriam said, and they both laughed together.

Finally Kate stepped up and took Miriam's hand.

Slowly the smiles faded. Miriam and Kate waved to them one final time, their eyes meeting Tad's last before they turned to each other and, looking into each other's eyes, they faded.

The process from there was familiar, followed by the welcoming warmth of the next world.

The three of them that remained stood in silence. Tony kept his eyes downcast and Stella took Tad's hand again, leaning her head against his arm.

Once again Tad's mind seemed to shut down as it dealt with yet another shock to the system. When it finally rebooted he had only one thought; Jen. She'd be every bit as devastated as he was by the departure of their friends.

Squeezing Stella's hand a little harder, he led her and Tony back into Jen's room so he and his daughter could grieve together.

Epilogue- Part 1

Thursday, 24th December 2015
15:50

Mark couldn't believe it.

It had been nearly a month and still it was the number one story they played around the clock. The fucking Merging. That's all anyone talked about. The day before Christmas and even then they couldn't take a break from it.

BBC 1 was showing the latest explorers who entered the Dream-world at the Cardiff King Gate. They'd named it after the tower that had fallen. It was the only place where anyone could cross into Dream, but it wasn't the only place affected by the Merging.

ITV was showing footage from Swansea. It was over forty miles from the King gate, but well within the Borderlands. Anything within a hundred miles of Cardiff had been classified as the Borderlands. These were the lands where the Merging had taken hold the strongest. This was where all the weird shit was happening. Mark got out as quick as he could. He wanted nothing to do with that place and the nightmares there.

Channel Four, Sky and bloody MTV news were all covering stories from within the Borderlands. Every day there was some new wonder to report. Miraculous healing, sightings of dragons, people flying. Anything you could imagine was happening in those lands and the world was lapping it up.

Not Mark. He wanted nothing to do with it. That was why he came this far north. He'd holed up in Edinburgh until one of his contacts came through with that fake passport. Once he had that, he was getting as far away from King Gate and the madness that poured from it as he could.

He turned off the TV in disgust and walked to the window. He was stashed away at an old friend's place. It wasn't a five-star establishment. The wallpaper was peeling in the corners, the floor was heavily stained, and there was only one spot on the sofa he was prepared to sit. The one thing going for it was the view over Edinburgh.

The flat was situated right at the heart of the city, and from where he stood he could enjoy the sun setting over the horizon behind the ancient buildings of the oldest part of the city.

It was beautiful, and helped take his mind off the madness in the world.

The sunset only lasted so long, and soon it was over and evening set in. It would be bloody cold again. It was always cold this far north. Cardiff had it's chilly months, but not like Scotland. He couldn't wait to be rid of this place either.

He walked to the kitchen to grab a beer. Now the sun was down he didn't mind getting started on his nightly ritual of getting blind drunk. He'd go sit in that same spot on the sofa, and try to find anything on the TV that had nothing to do with Cardiff. It was Christmas, surely there'd be a movie on.

He was taking his first sip from the can as he walked back into the living room, so he missed her at first. When he finally saw her, he spat the precious mouthful of beer over the carpet, adding to the myriad of stains.

The girl sat on that one clean spot, legs together, hands on knees, and calm as you could be. She was familiar, and he knew he should recognise her. His mind refused to let him remember as though trying to protect him from something.

She was dressed for the cold. Jeans, boots and heavy black coat done right up to the chin. She would be a damn sight warmer than he was, he suspected.

The girl brushed back an errant curl of copper hair that had fallen over her eye and tucked it behind her ear, smiling kindly at him as she did so.

"Hello Mark," she said. "We've never actually been introduced, but I figure you know me well enough. I would get up to shake your hand but that's a bit of a problem these days. I have you to thank for that."

As stubborn as his mind could be, even he was not drunk enough to ignore all those clues. Even though she was just a little girl, his legs shook. The worst weeks of his life surrounded events involving this little girl. He had lost all his friends the night he was sent to take her.

"What do you want? How did you find me?"

If she heard his questions she showed no sign. She kept talking as though she hadn't stopped.

"Don't worry about me, Mark. I'd rather be able to use my legs, but it turns out it's not as bad for me as it is for other people. You see, I have a very talented dad and he has shown me a few tricks.

"He can take me to Dream, and it turns out that because of what I am, when I'm there I can walk. I can also walk in the Borderlands with a bit of effort. So like I said, things aren't that bad. It's only when I come out of the Borderlands when I have a problem."

She waved a hand dismissively at him, then smiled. "Speaking of my dad, he said he wanted to give you a message. That's why we're here. Sorry it's taken so long to track you down."

Mark had the sudden terrifying feeling that someone was behind him. He slowly turned and sure enough, there was a man standing on the other side of the room. He had not been there when Mark had walked into the room, he was sure of that. He had somehow come in as the girl had been talking.

Mark jumped back almost all the way to the kitchen, not even trying to hide his fear.

He knew exactly who this man was. Had known him back when he first met Maggie and the man had just been some skinny geek that his wife had taken pity on when they were children. After all the events leading up to the Merging and all the time he spent on TV, it was hard to see him as just that anymore.

Those idiots on TV were calling him The Dream Walker.

It was a bloody stupid name, but it stuck. Now it was hard to think of him as anything else. It was hard to remember the wimpy guy called Tad he had once known.

"Hello Mark," the Dream Walker said. "It's been a while. I mean, I know you came to see me a few times last month, but we never really talked."

"What do you want?" Mark asked, almost tripping over the words in his effort to get them out.

"Oh, nothing much. I have a message I said I would deliver."

"A m…message. What Message?"

"It's one from Maggie. I'm paraphrasing, but I know she'd approve. I'm just sorry it's taken this long to deliver."

He took a step forward and Mark took a step back, slamming himself against the wall.

"Stay away from me you freak."

Tad sighed. "Come now. What's the old saying, don't shoot the messenger."

"Just get the fuck away from me and take your freak of a daughter with you."

Tad sighed again and shook his head. "I wish you hadn't said that. It wasn't very nice. But it doesn't matter. Like I said, we're just here to deliver a message."

He took another step closer and Mark had nowhere left to go. Tad, the Dream Walker, raised his hand in a wave. The moment he did Mark's whole body went slack, and he slipped down the wall.

By the time he landed, his body was limp, and he crumpled face first on the dirty carpet. He didn't care about that, didn't care about anything in the living world. He cared only about what he saw in front of him.

Mark took a deep breath, and the screaming began.

Epilogue- Part 2

Thursday, 24th December 2015
16:00

"What did you do?" Jen asked her dad, having to raise her voice above Mark's terrified screams. They creeped her out.

Tad turned his back on the screaming man and walked across the room to stand in front of Jen.

"I found a nightmare and locked him in it. His body will remain in this world but his mind will be stuck in that nightmare from here on out. He'll be a madman for the rest of his life."

Jen's jaw dropped. "We can do that?"

"Yes, but I'm not going to show you how. Not yet anyway. Maybe when you're older."

A month ago that would have made her want to strangle him. Now she just shrugged and accepted it. With all the cool things Tad had shown her recently, including their countless trips into Dream, she didn't care that he held a few things back. There was so much more for her to learn in the meantime and so much that Tad didn't mind showing her.

"I'm glad we got him back for what he did to Maggie. I felt bad for her in the end."

Tad nodded to her legs. "Even after all that's happened?"

His nod reminded her that there was actually something wrong with her. With all the time they spent in Dream and the Borderlands, she sometimes forgot.

The few times she was back in the mundane world and couldn't use her legs, was always a shock. It didn't hurt anymore, it was just a numbness and a surprise that they didn't respond when she wanted them to.

"Even after all this," she agreed. "The thing is, the same night they broke my back you were responsible for the Merging. I went straight from being able to walk to being able to do so much more." She grinned. "In a way it feels less like someone crippled me and more like someone set me free."

Her words made him smile. "I'm glad." He looked out the window, over that impressive view of Edinburgh. "I hope you don't mind not having your legs a little longer. While we're here, I figured I'd get your help choosing a gift for Stella. You know how bad I am at picking gifts for girls."

"I've always liked my birthday and Christmas gifts," Jen protested.

"I always had Miriam to help me then."

As always Jen felt a little sad when he mentioned his old ghost, but even that loss was getting easier to deal with. It helped that Jen knew that it was what Miriam wanted. She and Kate had been together as they had moved onto the next life. It was Charles that worried her. He was always so afraid of moving on.

"Please Jen, I really need your help on this one. It's our first Christmas together and I need it to be special."

Jen grinned. She was happy he finally had someone. He had been alone the entire time she had known him and even though he still mourned the loss of his ghosts, she knew Stella made him happy. And she liked Stella. She'd spent a lot of time with her over the last month and saw her as a friend.

"Alright. Let's go shopping. I hope you brought your credit card."

Tad winced. "Nothing too expensive."

"I thought you said it had to be nice."

Tad winced again and Jen giggled. He walked a little closer and with practiced ease slipped one hand under her legs and his other around her back. Jen wrapped her arms around his neck and when he stood, he lifted her from the sofa.

"Alright," he said. "You've got a bit of a budget. But remember, anything extra you spend on Stella, comes out of the money I was going to use for your Christmas presents."

Jen frowned and stared hard at her father. "You haven't got my Christmas presents yet?" she asked in a dangerous tone.

He grinned in that evil way he sometimes did, and then with just a thought, he did what he liked to call *changing the channel*.

They both vanished.

THE END

Afterword

I'd like to thank you for taking a chance on this book which is my debut novel... or at least the first novel that I have felt is worthy of publishing. I hope you liked it.

If you did, it would really help me out if you could leave a positive review on sites like goodreads.com and Amazon. Also, please be sure to recommend this book to anyone you think might be interested in reading it.

As a first time author with a limited budget, I committed the cardinal sin of publishing this novel without getting it professionally edited first. With that in mind, I would welcome any feedback you might have after reading this book. Both good and bad comments are welcome so long as the criticism is constructive.

You can get in touch with me by heading over to the contact page on my website: **http://www.gareth-otton.com**. Not only is that website the best place to get in touch with me, but it is also the best way to keep up to date with information about my future novels.

Talking of future novels, this isn't the end of the story for Tad, Stella, Tony and Jen. With the world completely changed after the events in Proxy and Tad being publicly seen at the centre of that change, there's big things coming his way soon. Not only will he have to deal with the loss of his ghosts, but he has new Dream related abilities to explore, and he somehow has to learn how to cope with his new found celebrity status. If that's not enough on his plate, then he also has to worry about other Proxies/Dream Walkers who have had their world turned upside down, and governments who struggle to adapt to their new reality of dreams, nightmares and Dream Walkers.

So to find out more about the next novel in this series and more, head on over to my website.

And once again, thanks for reading.

Gareth Otton